THE PATH KEEPER

N. J. SIMMONDS

Published by Accent Press – 2017

Print ISBN: 9781786155061
eBook ISBN: 9781786153883

*To Joan and Reg Simmonds ... until we meet
again. In memory of Peter Drake Snr.*

ACKNOWLEDGEMENTS

When I started writing this book I never imagined that one day it would be read by anyone, let alone see it in a book shop! Like anything special in life, it was only possible thanks to the constant help, support, advice and love from an amazing group of people.

The Accent YA team have been a pleasure to work with and I can't wait to see where the rest of the series takes us. So here's to my editor Alexandra Davies (never has so much red done so much good), the marketing team Bethan James and Emily Tutton, Joe Moore, Hazel Cushion and the amazing Sales and Distribution guys who have been behind me all the way.

A huge thank you goes to the Simmo Girls - my biggest cheerleaders since forever and the most formidable women on this planet. Thank you Mum and Jemma for listening to my ideas before I put pen to paper, Ana my marketing guru and Angela, Wendy and Emily for enjoying it and cheering me on every step of the way. In fact, thank you to my entire family (including the married-ins)...honestly, what would I do without you all?

When you write your first novel, letting someone read it for the first time feels like standing naked in the middle of Piccadilly Circus (ie: excruciatingly scary and embarrassing). So thank you to those that were there from the very beginning and read the first draft without laughing - even though it had a very different (quite terrible) ending. Thank you Linda Drake, Tanya Galizia, Kelly Monk and Abigail Rutter for all your great feedback and for talking about the characters like they were actual people (you don't know how much of a thrill that gave me).

A great big hug to the super talented Glass House Girls and wonderful friends Emma Wilson and Samantha Curtis, you always said I could do it and you were right (Sam, I'll be forever indebted to you).

I also wouldn't have got very far without the guidance of Lorraine Mace (aka Crime Thriller author Frances Di Plino), whose writing classes shaped my work and gave me the confidence to see it through to the end.

Elaine Kayes, thank you for being such an unwavering friend and making my life easier at every turn – from tracking me down to squeal down the phone when I got the book signed, to being my home from home every time I'm in London. You're amazing. And Renée Veldman-Tentori, thank you for all your support and friendship in a brand new country, The Netherlands would have been scarier and a lot less fun without you by my side.

And how could I forget my Loomies? Your humour, understanding and never ending support has kept me afloat more than you'll ever know - especially Emma Gibbard, Tina Yngvesson, Amanda Faithful, Sarah Norris and Fiona Masterson (the one that first threw me in the Loo and saved my sanity).

Lastly I wish to thank my own true love and little angels – Pete, Isabelle and Olivia. Thank you for giving me the space, time, encouragement and opportunity to write this and for always believing in me. I love you so much and will do so in every lifetime to come.

PART ONE

'In love, ther is but litel reste.'

Geoffrey Chaucer,
Troilus and Criseyde, IV

PART ONE

CHAPTER ONE

Mistakes didn't happen in his world. Miracles did.

He knew the girl was on her way, and he would wait as long as it took. He was good at that. He shifted on the bench and arched his back as the nineteenth bus in three hours pulled away in a cloud of choking smoke. London always suffocated him. As far back as he could remember, the city had wrapped her iron fingers around his throat and brought him to her, time and time again. If he stood still long enough for the world to stop just a little, he could hear the capital whispering her secrets. Even she had secrets.

The city had a rhythm, a drumbeat only her people could hear as they hurried from A to B. He pitied them. They didn't understand that every step left a footprint upon layers of history stacked beneath their city's pulsating pavements. Neither did they care that every one of their laboured breaths had been inhaled a million times before. There was nothing new here; there never would be.

He stretched his legs. A light fluttering in his stomach was followed by a dull ache. Nerves? The sensation was new and he didn't like it. It hadn't been like this with the others; he had done his job, his call of duty, and he had been satisfied. But this girl was different; she had always been special, and she was on her way.

1

He continued to watch people streaming by, fixated on their comings and goings. Didn't they realise the present didn't exist? That it was nothing but a monotonous treadmill pulling them along, tripping them up, and dragging them into a future they hadn't yet created? But the past was always there, waiting. It never hurried. It was a safe place, a private space where every story lay, holding all the clues and all their answers. But the people continued to file by – busy and forever moving towards the next life without a backward glance.

He squinted against the weak September sun at a bus trudging its way up the hill. This was it. The girl's appearance would have changed, that was normal, but would she be the same? Would he recognise her? Of course he would.

The soft hiss of the bus doors opening pulled him out of his reverie, and, with the measured actions of one who had done it a thousand times before, he stood and leant against the bus stop. A man in paint-splattered trousers stepped out and turned down the hill, followed by two schoolgirls laughing and pushing each other toward the Tube station. Nobody else followed; she wasn't there. He sighed and headed back to the bench. Then he heard her voice.

'Bollocks! *Esto es una mierda!*'

A young woman was marching to the front of the bus.

'How can you say it's the last stop when we are in Archway and the front of the bus says Highgate?'

She was younger than he had expected and wore her hair differently. It was still thick and brown, but this time in tousled waves that tumbled down her back. He

2

wondered what it would feel like to dip his finger into one of her curls, pull on the silky lock, and watch it bounce back into place. She pushed her fringe out of her eyes and peered into the bus driver's window.

'Oi!' she shouted, banging on the glass. 'I'm not getting off, you have to take me to the top of the hill. My bags are really heavy, for God's sake.'

She turned her back to the glass and sighed, blowing the hair out of her eyes. The driver twisted the dial to *Not In Service* and kissed his teeth.

'Look, lady, I don't make the rules. Get off the bus or I'll radio the police.'

She shot him a dark look, shrugged on her backpack, and grabbed a large bin bag in each hand. She half carried, half dragged them to the exit and stumbled down the steps as the closing doors folded shut. She kicked the heaviest bag down the last step and sent dozens of books tumbling in a flurry of pages to the pavement.

'*Hijo de puta*!' she shouted as he pulled away, leaving her squatting on the floor inspecting the torn plastic bag.

She looked up in the direction of the bus shelter.

'Excuse me. Yeah, you. Can you give me a hand?'

The girl was talking to him; he was the only one there. What was he going to say to her, after all this time? His stomach clenched again as he raised the hood of his grey hoodie and grasped the frayed cuffs in his fists. It felt good to hold on to something.

'Oh, it's you,' she said as he squatted beside her. She picked up two books and looked at him again. 'I know you, don't I?'

'Not yet.'

She turned her attention back to her ripped bag, her

olive skin failing to hide her blushes. Together they stacked the crumpled paperbacks into two neat columns on the side of the road.

'Thanks.' She stood up and wiped her hands on her jeans. 'There goes my good deed turned to shit. I'm Ella.'

So that was what she called herself. He let her name hang in the air, feeling it form behind his closed lips, his tongue flicking against the roof of his mouth. Ella. Ella. It was close.

She kicked the curb with the toe of her boot, waiting for him to respond, but he was there to listen.

'These aren't mine,' she said, pointing at the books with her foot. 'The librarian at uni … I'm at RCU. Royal City? Anyway, the librarian mentioned she had loads of books she didn't need and I offered to take them to my local charity shop because the bus stops right outside. Except for today, of course. Prick!'

She jerked her thumb at the stationary bus on the opposite side of the road, her hands flying up and flopping against her thighs with a smack. The flickering sign above their heads displayed the minutes until the next bus. She glanced at it and screwed up her face.

'Twenty minutes? What's the matter with this bullshit city?'

She kicked the torn bin bag and he watched it blow down the road. He envied its freedom.

'This is bollocks. I might as well leave these books here,' she said. 'I can't be arsed, the bags are all ripped. *Mierda*!'

While Ella moved the books out of the gutter with the tip of her shoe, he took the opportunity to look at her. Really look – at her thick lashes that framed her Bambi

4

eyes, the tiny freckle on her cheek, the curl of hair above her ear that kept coming loose no matter how many times she tucked it away. He wanted to remember every detail.

'I'm heading for Highgate too,' he said, nodding at a long, black hold-all under the bus stop bench. 'Put the books in my bag. It'll be quicker to walk.'

She shrugged a 'why not' and helped him fill the bag.

They walked side by side in silence, the bag slung over his shoulder which he shifted occasionally as the sharp book corners dug into his back. His neck strained with each step and small beads of perspiration ran down his temples. He pretended not to notice when she looked at him, although every one of her glances scorched his skin. Maybe she found him familiar. She would never remember who he was.

'Was that Spanish you were speaking?' he asked after they had been walking for a few minutes.

'Yeah, sorry, it just slips out when I'm a bit, um … stressed.' Ella rubbed her finger along her ragged thumbnail then filed it across her teeth. 'I'm Spanish,' she continued. 'Well, half. My dad's Spanish. Never met him, the waste of space. My mum's English.' She turned to him but he didn't respond. 'I've only lived in London a few months. I was brought up in Spain, in the south. We moved to England after she married Richard Fantz.' She slowed down. 'As in the hotel owner?'

He kept his pace and Ella quickened hers to catch up.

'You never heard of him? OK, well, he's beyond loaded and now she's turned into a real air head. Would have followed him to Mars if he'd asked her. I have no idea why I'm telling you this. Anyway, she's a selfish cow. I liked it in Spain. I could see the sea from my bedroom and it was always sunny. You can't be pissed off when it's sunny.'

'Why come to England then? Could you not have gone to university in Spain?' he asked.

A shadow passed over her face and he wished he hadn't said anything.

'I was going to. The plan was to stay with Juliana and study in Malaga. You know, keep my life as normal as possible.' She noted his look of incomprehension. 'Juliana was my grandmother, the closest thing I had to family. She raised my mum and came to Spain when I was born.' She rubbed her eye with the back of her sleeve. 'She died six months ago. I could hardly leave my mum, she was in bits.' Ella sniffed and cleared her throat. 'I wanted to go travelling, but me and my mum had a huge fight about it. She made this big deal about how she never got the chance to get a degree so I had to and that I could go abroad any time. As if I was going to be stupid enough to get knocked up on my first holiday like she did. So here I am.'

The landscape softened as Archway melted into Highgate. They passed a church with two green domes and a large stained glass window, and stopped to catch their breath outside the gated entrance to a park. Highgate Village was just visible at the crest of the hill. He dropped his bag and rolled his shoulders, looking at the cutesy shops with little signs swinging above their doorways.

'Posh,' he remarked, nodding at the row of town houses sporting glossy, wrought iron fences, flowers at the windows, and stone steps leading to pillar box red and racing green front doors. 'You got one?'

'Nah, mine's bigger.'

His grin made her giggle. He closed his eyes and let the sound wash over him. Her laugh hadn't changed. It gave him hope.

'The house isn't mine, of course,' Ella said. 'It's my stepdad's. It's nice though, right in the middle of Highgate Village, but hidden. It's like you're driving down a little side street, then there's a small turning – no one would know there was anything there – then there's these huge gates. It's like the TARDIS, you'd never think a big house like that would fit there, you know? Anyway, they sweetened me up and gave me a massive room. It's OK, I guess.'

He peered over her shoulder. 'Is that the shop?'

Across the road was a blue doorway crowded with over-stuffed bin bags seeping discarded clothes and shoes onto the pavement. She nodded and they walked over. The Closed sign was partly hidden by the mountain of debris. He crouched and placed the books one by one on the step. Ella picked up his bag and shook it, the books flying into the doorway and narrowly missing his head. She read each one aloud as they slithered to the floor.

'*Of Mice and Men, The Great Gatsby, Paradise Lost*. Gives you flashbacks of English Lit classes, eh?' she said.

'I don't know. I haven't read them.'

'What? Not even Dickens or Shakespeare? You're joking! Here.' She handed him a small paperback in shades of red and yellow. '*1984*, Orwell. It's about a guy who lives in a world where the people in control are complete dictators and he can't do anything about it. Story of my life. Keep it.' She gave him a wry smile and looked at her watch. 'Speaking of tyrants, I better go. My mum

7

flew back from Italy today and she'll be hounding me soon.'

He put the book in his empty bag. 'Where shall I meet you to return it?'

'Oh, don't worry about it. Just sling it in the doorway when you're finished.'

She took a breath as if to say something else, but was interrupted by her phone ringing. She glanced at it and pressed the red button.

'My mum,' she said.

'You don't like her, do you?'

'Not really.' She sighed, leant against the wall of the shop, and put her phone in her pocket. He stood back up. Her eyes were asking if she could trust him, but little did she know what he would have done for her. 'OK, it's like this ... What kind of woman decides to marry an old widower – who, by the way, already has a son and happens to be minted, then insists he adopts her daughter as part of the deal? No biggie but I was *sixteen years old,* for God's sake, and he has a son, so it's not like he needed another kid. So three years ago I was made to change everything – my birth certificate, my passport, they even had to rename me at school. She said his surname would make my life easier. Yeah, right!'

She waited, her eyebrows raised.

'His surname's Fantz.'

He didn't react. Her brow furrowed.

'Come on, wake up! My name is Ella. Ella Fantz. I spent the last three years being called Dumbo and hearing trumpeting noises every time I walked into a classroom. So yeah, that's the kind of mum I have.'

He didn't laugh. She picked at the pink skin of her

thumb, pulling at a hangnail until it bled.

'What's your real name, Ella? The one you were christened with?' he asked, though he already knew.

She blew out a puff of air.

'Right, like that's any better. My *real* name is Arabella Imaculada Santiago de los Rios. Honestly, what was my mum on when she came up with that? She reckons she hardly knew my dad, doesn't even have a photo of him, but she gives me his surname and a middle name after the Virgin Mary. Can you believe it? She's not even religious.' She pulled her coat tighter around her. 'Oh, and get this. She said she never even liked the name Arabella. Why name me Arabella in the first place? The woman's nuts.'

'I like Arabella.'

'Whatever.'

He laughed. It felt good to enjoy himself for once. She was a lot more fiery than he was expecting, it amused him but it didn't surprise him. After all, she was different every time. It was clear that he intrigued her, the way she looked at him through her outgrown fringe when she didn't think he was looking. Did he make her nervous? The thought thrilled him. Either way he wouldn't allow himself to get close to her – he could never do that. He was not going to stay.

'Your surname is Santiago de los Rios. Rios means Rivers, doesn't it? Restless, yet beautiful. It suits you.' He smiled. 'It was nice to meet you, Rivers.'

He nodded and turned to go.

'Wait!'

She reached for his arm, which flexed under her touch.

'Thanks for your help. Um ... I don't know your name.

Shit! I've been, like, half an hour telling you my life story and I don't even know your name.'

He liked the way she used her hands when she spoke, each word illustrated by a twist of a wrist or a flutter of fingers. He wanted to take her hand, feel her fingers intertwine with his.

'I'm so rude, sorry. What's your name?' she asked.

He dropped his empty bag on the pavement and lowered his hood. Running a hand through his damp hair, he scanned her face for a flicker of recognition, but there was none. She was already less guarded with him, but thankfully she had no idea who he was. She swallowed and he noticed her breathing had got shallower. He held out his hand and she shook it, flinching at his touch. He had felt it too, but it was too late. Maybe this time it could be different.

'Nice to meet you, Rivers,' he said. 'I'm Zac.'

CHAPTER TWO

Ella's arm hummed from Zac's touch. She rubbed it as she watched his retreating figure merge into the bustle of the high street.

What the hell just happened? She tied back her hair and blew her fringe out of her face.

He must have thought she was a complete idiot. Why did she blabber on so much about herself? She couldn't believe she didn't even ask his name. She'd been flustered, that's what it was. It was bad enough after the issues with the bus and the books and her mum calling, but when Zac had looked at her with those eyes, she lost it. Christ, those eyes!

She shuddered and smiled. Had he seen her looking at him? She'd kept checking to see if he was wearing contact lenses. His eyes were unreal, bright blue turning to lilac where the sun hit them. She had wanted to ask for his number, then her bloody phone had rung. Not that he would have been interested – nice guys that hot were never single. Well, that was that. Just her luck. The only bloke she'd met since she'd arrived in this shitty city and he'd disappeared as quickly as he'd appeared.

Her gilt-edged gates gave a ceremonious buzz as she placed her thumb on the security system. It hadn't sunk in yet that this palace was where she lived – she still got a thrill that she didn't need a key to enter.

Nothing about her new home was subtle. The landscape artist had made a miraculous job of shielding the house from view by importing tall cypress trees to surround the perimeter, creating privacy while still letting in the light. She loved those slender, pointy trees; they conjured up images of Tuscany, a place she had always felt a spiritual connection to even though she had never been to Italy. The Fantzes had two gardeners who ensured the lawns were green year round and not a leaf was out of place, yet most of the time Ella was the only person who got to admire their hard work.

The marble fountain at the front of the house was switched on, signalling somebody was home. It was the height of pretentiousness – not to mention a waste of water and money, as were the decorative white columns flanking the double wooden doors whose gold studs the poor cleaner had to polish every week. None of that occurred to her parents. As long as their house reflected their status, it was enough for them.

It was rare for Ella to enter via the front door – she only did it when she knew someone would be home to greet her, which wasn't very often. She normally entered through the back as it led directly to her bedroom, where she spent most of her evenings. She hated walking through the echoing hallways alone. Her mother had made the mistake of not carpeting the ground floor. It looked impressive, but the clip-clopping of heels against the shiny tiles put Ella on edge and made the place appear cold and impersonal. It felt like a grand hotel, although considering Richard's profession, that wasn't surprising.

Her mother's shrill cry bounced off the stark walls before Ella had time to shut the door behind her.

'Darling, you're home! I've been ringing you all afternoon!'

Felicity Fantz didn't walk, she glided, her golden mane swishing in time with her hips. Her feline eyes were always dark and smoky with heavy lashes that gave her a sleepy, satisfied expression.

'Richard, quick, I think Ella is actually smiling. Honestly, darling, are you feeling OK?'

She laughed at her own joke and gave her daughter a light kiss on each cheek, resting her manicured fingers on Ella's shoulders. Today she was wearing a black jacket over tight jeans and skyscraper heels. Had Ella looked anything like her mother, people would have thought they were sisters. When they entered a room together, nobody noticed the little, dark-haired girl.

'Seriously, sweetie, you are definitely flushed. If I didn't know better I'd say you met a nice young man. Oh, look! She's hiding a smile! Come on, tell Mummy.'

Ella shrugged off her jacket, draped it over the bannister, and kicked off her trainers. Ignoring her mother, she headed for the kitchen and threw her backpack on the counter.

Richard replaced the phone into the receiver and beamed at Ella, loosening his tie and giving her a hug. She'd liked her step-father from the moment she'd met him, even if he was old enough to be her grandfather. It was obvious how much he adored her mother and, most importantly, he always took Ella's side.

Since the death of his first wife, when his son Sebastian was just a toddler, Richard had been linked to countless models but had never re-married. Within two weeks of meeting Felicity, he'd proposed and announced to the world he'd found The One, a story her mother never got bored of telling and had dined out on for the last three years.

'So what's all the commotion?' he asked. 'Have you got yourself a beau, Ella?

'God, can't I just be in a good mood?' Ella bypassed him and walked to the kitchen. 'No boyfriend, don't get excited. I've just had an interesting journey home, that's all.'

Her mother was right, of course, she always was. She thought of Zac and the curl of his lip when he smiled, how soft but strong his hand had felt and how he'd stared at her until she'd teetered on the edge of discomfort. How could twenty minutes with a complete stranger affect her like that? He didn't feel like a stranger. She thought she'd recognised him at first, that maybe he was in one of her classes or she'd seen him on TV. She was glad she hadn't said anything else and embarrassed herself. Her heart was still racing at the thought of their encounter and she couldn't wipe the stupid grin off her face.

Felicity raised her eyebrows. 'If I'd known bus journeys could be *that* exciting, I would have ditched the chauffeur.'

Richard gave a deep, throaty laugh and wrapped his arms around his wife's waist, reducing her to a fit of giggles as he kissed her neck.

Ella looked away and groaned. 'Get a hotel room, for God's sake. It's not like you're short of them,' she said, making them laugh harder.

'Darling, guess what we're having for dinner?' Felicity sing-songed.

'You've cooked?'

'No silly, of course not. Richard's new sushi chef is over from Tokyo and has compiled an amazing menu for the New Year's Eve restaurant opening, so we are sampling it tonight. Scrummy! Oh, and talking of Asia, Sebastian called from Cambodia this afternoon. The hospital build is coming on wonderfully; he thinks he might get a mention in *Time* magazine. He sends his love, by the way; your brother always asks after you.'

'Stop calling him that! He is *not* my brother!'

Shit. She hadn't meant to shout. It had been over a year since she had last seen Sebastian, Richard's angelic son, the doctor. Mr Sexiest Millionaire of 2016 as voted by *Cosmo*. Mr Charming. Mr Complete and Utter Bastard. He was miles away and still managing to fuck up her day.

'There's no need for that tone, young lady. Sebastian welcomed you as a sister from the day we got married and all you have done ...' Felicity stopped and frowned. 'What are you doing?'

'Making a sandwich.'

'I just told you, we're having dinner, darling.' Felicity plucked the mayonnaise out of Ella's hand. 'Don't be a piggy.'

Ella snatched it back and squeezed it onto four slices of bread.

'No, you said we are having *sushi* in two hours.' It's hardly a banquet. Anyway, I'm hungry *now*, what's your problem?'

She knew exactly what her mother's problem was. Since Ella had arrived in England ten weeks ago, there had been a photographer outside her house every day. The media were intent on making her London's new It Girl, the smart, pretty girl that completed the perfect Fantz family, and her PR Director mother had assigned herself as her agent. Ella had already been coerced into an interview with *The Sunday Telegraph* and a shoot for *Elle* magazine. It was humiliating. Some days she wondered whether her mother paid those eager men in black to point their cameras at her every time she stepped out the door. With interest in the new addition to the Fantz dynasty mounting, there was no way Felicity was going to run the risk of any magazine blaring out a *Herd of Ella Fantz* headline about her daughter, so what she ate and when had become a constant source of contention between them.

Ella rolled her eyes and piled on an extra layer of gruyère cheese for good measure. She may not have inherited Felicity's long legs or blonde hair, but Ella was just as slim as her mother, although she was as averse to exercise as Felicity was to flat shoes.

'Do you have to put cheese on everything?' Felicity said. 'Honestly, darling, you have an obsession. It's full of fat.'

'Let her be, Flic,' Richard said. 'She's a young lady. What's a little sandwich in the big scheme of things?'

Richard smiled indulgently and Ella gave him a grateful look. She grabbed her towering creation and stomped across the kitchen flagstones.

'Don't leave that plate in your bedroom, darling,' her mother called after her. 'Ylva cleaned in there today and told me she found six bowls under your bed. Six! I was mortified! And please don't wear those jeans again. You have plenty of clothes; those make your bottom look *huge,* sweetie.'

Ella counted in her head, promising that if she could

get to her bedroom before she reached twenty, she wouldn't scream. It hadn't always been this bad. Before England, before Richard, her mum had been normal. On Ella's sixteenth birthday, it had all changed.

It had been one of Spain's hottest springs. The streets were empty in the day, the town coming to life once the sun had set and everyone could breathe again. Ella hadn't wanted a big fuss, but her mother had other ideas. She'd said there was no point living in the most fashionable place on the coast if they weren't going to enjoy the lifestyle.

Stepping into the white marble foyer of Marbella's newest and most prestigious hotel, La Estrella Blanca, Ella and mother attempted to blend in with the other guests that had been invited to the grand opening. Ella had never seen a hotel like it. Felicity smiled and nodded at a lady she knew from the press and a gaggle of snobby charity organisers. She accepted a glass of champagne from the waiter and they followed the rest of the guests to the back of the hotel. Outside was every bit as magnificent as in. The infinity pool appeared to cascade over the cliff edge and straight into the sea. Large marquees furnished with white sofas had been erected on the lawn. They sat beneath a chandelier that speckled their bodies with tiny diamonds.

Felicity fanned herself with her hotel brochure and smiled at Ella.

'Can you imagine staying here, sweet pea?'

Ella couldn't. 'Thanks for letting me come, Mum; my friends are going to be so jealous.'

Her mother worked for a local newspaper – part journalist, part ad sales. It was low paid and low interest and most of the stories she covered were about ex-pats or abandoned animals, but she got the occasional perk, like tonight's launch party.

'This place is magical!' Felicity said, staring at the ocean. 'Imagine what it would be like to be here with a man who adores you, walking hand in hand down that path. See the one that leads to those steps? He'd lead you down to the beach, holding your hand as you made your way to the bay. You'd lie on one of the big double beds and draw the curtains around you. I bet if you had enough money the hotel would let you have that beach to yourself all night. They would make you a romantic picnic with lobster and champagne and you could look at the stars and feel like you were the only people in the world.'

'Don't break out into song just yet, Cinderella,' Ella laughed. 'Honestly, Mum, after all the shit Dad gave you, I can't believe you still think one day your prince will come.'

Felicity drained her glass in one go but kept it clasped in her hand, staring out to sea.

'Ella, there are things in this world I will never understand, things beyond our control. What is meant to be is written in the stars and I have grown to accept it.'

Her mum liked to speak in riddles, but she never complained or spoke badly of others. It infuriated Ella. After Felicity was left pregnant at nineteen then disowned by her parents, Ella figured her mother had more than enough people to slag off. Felicity, though, remained tight-lipped about her past. The little Ella knew about her family had been garnered from a photo album she'd found under her mother's bed when she was ten years old. There had been one particular photograph, faded and creased, of an old man with a bushy moustache and a blonde girl on his lap. Behind them stood a slim woman with wispy hair and a far-off look in her eye. It had given Ella the creeps and she'd never looked for the album again.

They sat in the hotel marquee for over an hour, taking in the beauty and listening to the rustle of the waves lapping at the rocks below. Ella got up to look for the restroom and that's when everything changed.

How Ella wished that she'd made the most of that night. What would she have said to her mother had she known it was to be the last time she would have her to herself? What would have happened had her mother accompanied her to the bathroom, or they'd gone home early?

When journalists asked Felicity how she'd met Richard, she always replied that they were introduced that night by friends, although the truth was a lot less glamorous. Ella had got lost on her way back from the bathroom and mistaken Richard for a waiter. How different would her life be if she had turned right instead of left? Would they have met anyway?

One of the first things Ella noticed about Richard as he led her to the pool area was the way he moved. He reminded her of an animal keeper she'd seen at Fuengirola Zoo: slow and unthreatening. Every gesture was measured and deliberate. His first words to her were, 'Have you lost your mother? I'll find her.'

And find her he did. He also kept her.

Ella and her mother had no idea who Richard was at first. Estrella Blanca was only his second hotel in Spain and he wasn't as well-known there as in the UK.

'But I thought we were looking for your mother?'

Richard said, giving Felicity a wide smile. He had a kind but strong voice, dripping with wealth. 'Surely this is your sister?'

This was nothing new. The only reason the boys in Ella's class had ever wanted to come to her house had been to check out her mum. No one ever believed Felicity was old enough to be her mother. Richard introduced himself and shook their hands and Ella thanked him for his help. He then bid them a good night, joining a nearby couple that had beckoned him over.

'I think that's Richard Fantz!' Felicity mumbled, gazing at him across the lawn. She handed Ella her shoes and said, 'He owns this hotel. I have to speak to him. It makes sense now; I know what he meant.'

To this day, Ella couldn't understand her mother's reaction. She was mortified that Felicity was literally running after this stranger, jogging across newly watered grass with specks of green staining the soles of her feet. Ella cringed when her mother pulled Richard away from a plastic-faced blonde and her fat, cigar-smoking husband and ushered him to a corner.

Ella couldn't hear what they were saying but she watched them through her fingers. At first, Richard listened politely, and then Felicity stood on her tiptoes and whispered something in his ear which made his expression change. His eyes widened as if he'd awoken from a deep sleep and it had taken a moment to recognise the woman before him. He said something and Felicity agreed, making him grin broadly and shake his head in disbelief. Then he kissed her, a deep kiss that made Ella hide her face even further and Felicity raise her bare foot from the ground, pointing her green toes in a balletic pose of Happy Ever After.

Ella never discovered what it was that Felicity had whispered on her sixteenth birthday, but Ella soon learnt that it was that precise moment where she'd lost her mother for ever.

CHAPTER THREE

Ella had no friends. Of course, she'd had more than plenty in Spain, back before her new step-father changed her name, her school, and her very existence. They'd been frightened off by her new-found wealth and now remained distant Facebook friends who occasionally liked a photo on social media. They didn't have her telephone number, and even if they had, they wouldn't have called. Ella didn't care – the fewer people in her life the fewer chances of it being fucked up further.

She was sitting at the breakfast bar in the kitchen eating cereal when her mother breezed past, filling Ella's mouth with the acidic scent of her perfume. Ella put her spoon down.

'Ah, darling, I'm glad I caught you before you left for school,' Felicity said, removing Ella's sugar bowl off the counter and handing her an apple.

'It's university, Mum. You know, big girl school?'

Felicity waved the words away, wafting her thick perfume closer and making it catch in Ella's throat.

'I have tickets for a fashion show tonight, would you like to come?'

Ella shrugged.

'It's Chanel, sweetie, next year's spring/summer collection. Front row, no less!'

'What are you on about?' Ella sighed. 'I don't wear

anything designer, let alone Chanel. Anyway, I'm busy.'

'Really?'

'Yeah, I'm seeing friends,' she lied.

Felicity sat on the stool beside her and patted her hand.

'You made some friends, that's fantastic. You must invite them round for tea.'

Was this woman for real! The idea of inflicting her overzealous mother on any friend – imaginary or otherwise – was too much to bear. She mumbled a maybe and left, noting not to return that night until her mother had gone. Even if it meant sitting in a pub on her own until closing time.

Ella shuffled along the queue of the canteen and peered into the large metal containers. What was that crap? It was all either fried or turd-like and floating in its own congealed goo. Most days she brought a sandwich with her or went to the café. Sometimes she took the bus to Soho for noodles, but today it was raining, *again*, so she stayed inside and attempted to find something remotely edible. She settled on a carton of juice, a dry salad, and a ham sandwich – boring and tasteless but least likely to kill her. Finding an empty table by the window, she stared out at the grey, wet streets. God, this country was depressing.

'Excuse me.' A small, sparrow-like girl with a sharp black bob hovered beside Ella. 'Are you ...?'

Ella rolled her eyes and gave a smile.

'Yes, I am. I'm Ella. Hi.'

She recognised the girl from her Anthropology module – she never said much and was always the last to leave. The girl stared at her chunky trainers, the only thing that seemed to be stopping her from floating away, her head twitching from Ella, to the table, to the window. Her mouth opened for a second too long before she found her voice.

'Sorry, I know who you are. Everyone knows who *you* are. I was actually going to ask if you're using that chair. There's nowhere left to sit.'

'Right, yeah, of course,' Ella said, waving at the seats in front of her and taking a bite of her limp sandwich.

'I'm Mai Li.'

Ella swallowed and wiped mayonnaise from the side of her mouth with her sleeve.

'I'm Ella, but you already know that.'

Mai Li looked around the room, her Tupperware unopened. A flicker of a smile passed over her porcelain face and she gave a small headshake as a tall blonde girl ran over in small steps, her heels clicking against the wooden floor. Mai Li's slight frame and shiny hair made her a miniature china doll in comparison to the curvy Barbie now standing beside her. Mai Li gave Ella a smile then jumped at her friend's shriek.

'Oh. My. God!' The blonde spun round to face Ella. 'Mai Li, is Ella Fantz actually sitting at your table?' She scraped the spare chair back and sat down like a woman who had been on her feet all day. 'Oh my days, someone told me Ella Fantz was studying here, but I thought it was, like, a *rumour*!'

Ella looked up and cleared her throat.

'Why are you talking about me like I'm not here?'

The Barbie stared at her with her mouth open, a masticated ball of fluorescent gum ready to roll off her pierced tongue.

'Ella, this is my flatmate Kerry,' Mai Li said.

Kerry waved and blew a bubble, giggling as it popped and spread a sticky web around her lips.

'Do you study Anthropology then?' Ella asked Kerry. Why was she even engaging in conversation with the bimbo? The smell of synthetic strawberry was making her gag.

Kerry wrinkled her button nose. 'Shut up!' she said, making each word three syllables long. 'Nah, no way. That would be boring. I'm actually in my last year in Linguistics and Theology.'

Ella felt her cheeks prickle – that would teach her for being a snob.

'It's quite interesting,' Kerry continued. 'Of course, there's been a lot of Aramaic stuff, bore on, and blah-di-blah about the lost languages of the Incas. But what I'm really interested in is these different Hebrew dialects that existed before the birth of Christ and their influence on religious scriptures. That's probably what I'll write my PhD on.'

The three of them fell silent, save for the smacking of Kerry's chewing gum. Ella was wondering what excuse she could make to leave when Kerry grabbed her arm, her manicured nails digging through Ella's jacket.

'Oh my God, Ella, I need to know. Has it been, like, totally weird that your ex is here?'

'What? I don't have an ex. I don't even have a boyfriend.' Ella thought back to the guy at the bus stop. Zac. Where would she find a man like that around here?

'Joshua De Silva, the actor stroke model you were totally in love with?' Kerry made a chopping action with her hand when she said the word 'stroke'. 'You were mega cute together.'

'Newspapers are always making up crap about me. I've never heard of him.'

Kerry grabbed her other arm.

'Oh my God, how can you not know who he is? He's, like, a total sex god. His dad is that director Paolo De Silva. You know, the one that makes those Hollywood action movies. Josh is, like, the most gorgeous man ever and he's even modelled for Armani. Oh my God, you should see his abs.' Kerry's grip on her arms tightened the faster she spoke. 'I haven't actually seen him here, I thought it was made up, like you being here. But maybe, if *you're* real, then that means he's here too. Oh my God, that would be so friggin' *awesome*!'

Ella prised Kerry's fingers off her arm one by one.

'I might have heard his name somewhere,' she muttered, not wanting to appear out of touch with the real world. Whatever that was. Ella looked at her watch. Her next lecture wasn't for another forty minutes. She had to think up an excuse to leave.

'Well, you lived in Spain, right?' Kerry continued. 'I guess the hotties are different there. What was that like? Was it amazing? You know, I feel bad for you that your mum married Richard Fantz,' she said, her hand back on Ella's arm. Ella shook her off.

'What the hell do you know about my family?'

Kerry shrugged. 'Only what I've read, which is that you live a fairytale life. But now I've met you I don't believe you do. I'm guessing you probably preferred your life the way it was. I know I did.'

Ella frowned and looked at Mai Li.

'Kerry's mum moved to Australia to be with her new husband, so she's on her own now,' she whispered.

'Yep. My stepdad is, like, such a *nice* guy. You know what *that's* like? I want to hate him but I can't, so I've just got to accept that my mum chose him over me.'

Ella gave a small nod and blinked three times. Was she seriously going to cry in front of these strangers? Kerry perked up and a huge smile spread on her face.

'I wish I hadn't been wrong about you and Josh. You kinda match, you know? Should we hunt him down?'

Ella wanted to laugh. Maybe Kerry wasn't so bad. Maybe if she was to make any friends in this fucked-up city, she had to give people a chance.

'OK, whatever. Tell me more about this guy.'

'Josh? Oh, you'll love him, every woman does. He's perfect. I bet if you two met it would be true love, like the newspapers say it is. I read this morning he was going to Indigo for his birthday.' Kerry frowned. 'Wait, I thought he would have invited you. Obviously not. Shame. *We'll* never get entry to a place like that.'

Her petulant expression would have looked ridiculous on any other woman, but with her full, glossy lips and bouncy hair, she looked like a Playboy bunny. A student walked by, his jeans slung so low his hips stuck out at an angle in an attempt to keep them from falling. He flicked his earphones out and did a double take, slowing down to say something. Kerry gave him the finger then winked at him. He lost courage and left the canteen, attempting to pull his trousers up while simultaneously replacing his earphones.

'What's Indigo?' Ella asked, looking from the boy to Kerry to Mai Li, who shrugged. It was good to know she wasn't the only clueless person.

'Seriously?' Kerry screeched. 'Oh my God, Ella,

where have you been the last five years? Indigo is this, like, amazing club in Camden that's so exclusive it's got no website, no Twitter, no one's even seen photos of the inside. Its reputation is, like, *totally* word of mouth and it's impossible to get in. They have a mega strict member's policy.'

'Is it really expensive?' Ella asked.

'That's the weird thing, because it has nothing to do with money,' Kerry said. 'My friend had a friend whose neighbour went and he lived in a council flat in Tooting, but Madonna and Princess what's-her-name have been turned away. I mean, what is that about?'

'When's Josh's party?'

'Tomorrow night.'

Mai Li had lost the thread of the conversation a long time ago. Ella grinned at her and plucked her mobile phone from her back pocket, pressing three on her speed dial.

'Hi, Caroline. No, I don't want to speak to Mum, thanks,' she said. 'Can you get me entry to Indigo for tomorrow night? Yes, me and two others.'

She hung up and beamed at the girls, who were frozen in awe. Her phone beeped and she looked at the screen.

'It's all done. Where shall we meet?'

She knew it was pathetic to use her fame to make friends, but it felt bloody amazing. The week was shaping up to be rather interesting after all.

CHAPTER FOUR

Fuelled by excitement and champagne – one of Richard's vintage classics Ella had taken from her step-father's collection – the three girls chatted as they made their way to Indigo.

'I'm not lying, I swear,' Kerry said. 'Some girl was interviewed in *Cosmo* and said she thought Indigo pumped weed through the air con system because she left the bar feeling like she was floating, totally, like, super-chilled. Oh, and they have some cocktail called Indigo Sky which is meant to be amazing.'

A buzz of excitement was growing in the pit of Ella's stomach. It had been over three years since she'd gone out with a group of friends, and although they were a somewhat motley crew she was having fun. It was good to laugh and have a chance to wear some of the high heels her mother insisted on buying her.

'Do you think Josh will be there?' Kerry said. 'I think I'd *die* if we got to sit anywhere near him. This is seriously going to be the best night of my life.'

'Who's Josh?' Ella asked.

The blonde gave her an incredulous look. Oh yes, the actor *stroke* model.

Camden had a split personality. During the weekends, the suburb was a Mecca for every hippy and punk wannabe. Eager teenagers spent the day with ten pounds, looking for cheap silver jewellery or forbidden tattoos with enough change to get a kebab for their journey home. Its colourful market along the canal throbbed with tourists clutching falafels in one hand and shopping in the other, navigating the rabbit warren of tunnels and walkways that led to the converted horse stables where they would be over-charged for thirty-year-old clothes branded as 'retro'. But at night it was a different story.

Although the student flats were within walking distance from Camden High Street, in the not-so-cool district of Mornington Crescent, the girls rarely ventured into Camden after dark. Mai Li flinched as an elderly man with a can of Tenants in his hand stumbled into her and burped an apology, then turned and held out his hand just in case. The Tube entrance erupted with a group of young men in their uniform of tight jeans and T-shirts. In the shadow of the station wall leant a skinny boy with a beanie hat pulled over his eyes, the lads speaking to him in hushed tones as his thick-necked dog strained at its rope leash.

The girls crossed over the lock and turned a sharp left, gratefully exited the High Street, then walked down the long steps to the water's edge.

'Are you sure it's under the next bridge?' asked Mai Li to no one in particular.

They peered ahead into the gloomy tunnel. Tracks of green slime trickled down the walls, forming puddles in which they tiptoed, their footsteps echoing the drip-drip of the water.

'Now what?' Ella asked.

The canal was on their left and three moored barge boats bobbed up and down beside them, their garish

Romany decorations a cheerful distraction.

'Do you think anyone actually, like, lives in those things?' asked Kerry. 'Hey, maybe they know where Indigo is?'

Ella shrugged and looked around. A faint glow was visible through the undergrowth beside the lock. They walked down a rough path that had been beaten through the trees until they reached a carved wooden door flanked by torches. Two men stood outside. One was dark with a wide neck and broad shoulders, the other younger with floppy, bleach blond hair and tight jeans that cut into his hip bones. They both wore dark T-shirts bearing a faded logo on the front. It looked like a Greek symbol, but it could only be seen when the light caught it at a certain angle.

'Is this it?' asked Mai Li. 'It doesn't say Indigo anywhere.'

The thin man glanced at his iPad then at Ella. 'Miss Fantz and guests, please follow me.'

The girls looked at one another wide-eyed as the bouncer opened the large doors. They followed the doorman down a flight of stone steps dotted with tea-lights where silver lanterns flickered, projecting their shadows along the smooth walls. The sound of their footsteps was loud against the slate flagstones.

At the base of the stairs was a white room with an oval carved in the wall, behind which sat an exotic gypsy girl. Her thick, black hair, held back by a glittering silver scarf, shone a deep purple in the candlelight, and her large eyes were highlighted with eyeliner.

'Welcome to Indigo,' she said, her accent hard to place. 'Please leave all bags and possessions here.

No cameras, telephones, or money allowed on the premises.' She handed Ella a silver bracelet with a small chip hanging from it. 'The barman will scan you when you order drinks and you can settle the bill when you leave. Enjoy your evening, Ella, Mai Li, Kerry.'

The girls handed over their coats and bags, looking at each other in mild panic.

'I didn't know you gave them our names,' Mai Li whispered.

'I didn't,' Ella said.

The doorman scanned them with a handheld metal detector, then once satisfied, walked to another set of wooden doors and yanked them open.

The club wasn't as big as she had expected and she couldn't see any electric lighting. The central strip of ceiling was transparent, although fragments of starry sky could be seen through the canopy of leaves that dusted the glass ceiling. There were lanterns on every wall and surface, huge, church-like candles dripped over the bar. Candelabras stood in the corners, and above the tables hung hundreds of glass globes, each one with a tea-light in its centre. Some walls were draped in sheer white fabric and others painted in shades of lilac, mauve, and dark blue. All the tables were low and surrounded by plush, white cushions and sheepskin rugs. Small cavern-like spaces had been gauged out of the walls and filled with low white beds.

Kerry gave a low, long whistle and Mai Li giggled.

'OK, try and play it cool, yeah?' Ella whispered, her heart hammering against her chest. 'It's just a club. Nothing special.'

Who was she kidding? It was something from another world.

Most of the tables and beds were already occupied by couples and groups, sitting or lying on the cushions and talking softly.

'I can't see Josh. This doesn't look like a club to me. There's nowhere left to sit, either,' mouthed Kerry. 'And no music. What the hell *is* this place?'

There was a soothing noise emanating from the speakers but it was hard to distinguish. It sounded like nature sounds, but nothing like the irritating CDs Ella had been forced to listen to the last time her mother had booked her in for a facial. It was more than that – it was the sound of lying in the garden in spring time: the quiet rustle of leaves, a distant bird call, the wind blowing gently. A hushed reverence descended on them, like entering an ancient cathedral during mass. Ella could see why Indigo needed to remain protected, why it was so secret. She watched a couple open a glass door into a narrow hallway then go through another door to a space packed with writhing bodies. She pointed it out to Kerry, who visibly relaxed; there was music and dancing after all.

'Let's get a drink first,' Kerry said, looking around for an empty seat.

The doorman appeared beside them. 'Follow me, ladies.'

He led them to a wall draped with muslin and signalled to a waitress wearing the uniform dark T-shirt. She pulled a tasselled cord and revealed a small room hidden behind the curtain.

The space was piled high with more cushions and

silver lanterns hung from the ceiling. There were candelabras at each corner and on the low table in the centre stood a silver ice bucket with two bottles of champagne, along with a selection of canapés on silver trays.

The waitress poured their drinks into three glass flutes. 'Enjoy your evening, ladies.'

'This is totally amazing, Ella. I heard there was no VIP but oh my bloody God, this is it!' Kerry said running in and throwing herself on the cushions. 'You are, like, the bestest friend in the whole world. I mean, look at us!'

'Everyone *is* looking at us,' Ella said.

'Who cares? That's because we are officially the most Very Important People here. Like, wow, we even get free ...' Kerry picked up a canapé and popped it in her mouth. 'I haven't a clue what it is but it's delicious. Could this night *get* any better!'

'I think it could,' breathed Mai Li, easing herself down beside Kerry but looking in the direction of the entrance. The girls followed her gaze to another hidden alcove, where a sandy-haired man in a leather jacket sat surrounded by friends. They were all laughing and taking it in turns to knock back shots of a clear liquid.

'Holy crap, that's him, that's Josh!' whispered Kerry, elbowing Ella in the ribs. She plumped up her hair and leant forward, giving him a huge smile and a view of her copious cleavage. 'Ella, you need to talk to him,' Kerry hissed, even though he was too far away to hear them. She turned to the waitress. 'Hey, go tell Josh De Silva that Ella Fantz requests his company.'

Ella whacked Kerry on the arm. 'I can't believe you did that!' she exclaimed. 'God, he's looking over. Shit,

shit! Mai Li, stop laughing, you're making me look like such a ...'

'Hey, birthday boy, come join us!' Kerry shouted as Josh approached their table. 'Shuffle up, Ella, there's plenty of room. Do you want some bubbly?'

Josh looked at Ella, who shrugged, and he sat on the cushion beside her.

'Hi.' His voice was deep, which sat awkwardly with his boyish features. Kerry handed him a glass of champagne but he ignored her, his eyes trained on Ella. Now they were face to face, she recognised him from the kind of magazines they had in the hairdresser's. The girls weren't wrong; Josh was hot, in a perfect kind of way. What were the chances of Ella meeting two attractive guys in one week? She thought of Zac and her tummy flipped.

'Finally, I get to meet the illusive Ella Fantz. I'm surprised to see you here,' he said. 'I didn't think you did celeb hangouts.' He shuffled up and leaned in closer so only Ella could hear him. 'Did you know that according to *Extreme Magazine* we were an item last summer? It was very cruel of you to dump me for a football player when we were so madly in love.' He sat back and laughed, two dimples appearing in his cheeks. 'Nice to meet you at last.'

Ella shook his hand and smiled politely. It was easy to see what her friends were getting so excited about.

'Hi. This is Mai Li and Kerry.'

He nodded briefly and turned his attention back to Ella. He'd clearly spent a long time sculpting his hair into a tousled, windswept style, light strands falling into his almond-shaped eyes and over his perfectly arched brows.

His skin was flawless, his lips full and he had very straight, very white teeth, far too straight and white to be natural.

'This fame thing's tough, right?' he said. 'That's why I love this bar, it's so discreet.'

Ella smiled but kept quiet.

'So, how are you going to make my birthday special?'

Kerry sighed far too loudly and Mai Li poured herself another drink. They turned to Ella simultaneously, waiting for her answer. Josh's shoulder was pinning hers against the sofa and she twisted her body to the side to make room.

'I didn't realise I was the entertainment,' she said. She was probably the first girl not to have dropped to her knees for him.

'I've heard so much about you,' he said. 'Ever since I found out you'd moved to London I was hoping we would meet. Is there anywhere we could sit and talk? Just you and me?'

'Just a minute,' she said, clambering over him. 'I need the … you know … the loo.'

She grabbed her glass and headed around the corner to the bar and out of view. What the hell! Josh was on every other girl's Wish List but he was making her feel really claustrophobic. Perhaps she wasn't ready for dating again after all. He seemed nice enough, and she couldn't deny he was attractive, but he was so full of himself. No thanks. With any luck, Kerry would get her claws into him and Josh would forget about her. She'd just hide until he got bored. She should probably be angry at Kerry for inviting him over, but the club had made her too mellow to care. She understood now what the magazine had meant about the place making you feel stoned.

She signalled the barman over, pointed at the Indigo Sky cocktail the person beside her was drinking, and held up one finger. The barman smiled and scanned her bracelet. He was straight off the pages of *Vogue*, with caramel skin and cheekbones too sharp to waste on a bar job. Did this place only hire models or was she suddenly finding every guy she came across insanely attractive? He handed her a long drink and she felt herself flush. God, she should get out more.

The cocktail was in graduating shades of blues and lilacs, and she took a small sip then finished it in two gulps. It tasted of blueberries. Surely it wouldn't hurt to order a second before Kerry and Mai Li noticed she was missing? She leant over the bar and tried to catch the barman's eye again, forgetting her glass of champagne on the counter. As she signalled him over, she knocked the glass with her elbow, sending it smashing to the slate tiles. A shard of glass scratched her ankle. Ella stumbled and slipped on the wet floor.

'*Mierda*! For fuck's sake!' she shouted. But she was caught before she hit the floor.

'Whoa, Rivers, there you go falling at my feet again.'

Ella stood up quickly and adjusted her dress. 'Zac? Shit! What are you doing here? What are you … I mean, how … you remember me?'

He was on his knees, dabbing a paper napkin to her bleeding ankle.

'How could I forget the girl with a face of an angel and the mouth of a sailor?'

Ella crouched too. Face of an angel? She liked that.

'Thank you,' she said, taking the napkin from his hand. 'Déjà vu. You save me, I thank you, we end up squatting on a damp floor together.'

He laughed and helped her up, their eyes locking and sending her stomach into a familiar spasm. Maybe she *was* ready to date again?

'I'm with friends,' she said, checking if they could see her. 'Well, they aren't really my friends, they're in my class. What about you? You here with friends, or a girlfriend, or …' She was jabbering like an idiot again. 'I mean, do you come here often?'

For fuck's sake! Could she sound any more pathetic?

Zac laughed again then reached behind the bar and brought out a mop.

'Yep, I'm here every night.'

He worked there. Of course he did – he was wearing the same T-shirt as the rest of the staff. It was tight across his chest and arms then loosened around his toned waist. As he reached for the bucket, she glanced at his backside. Yep, small and tight. No surprise there.

'So you live near here?' she asked.

'No, in Highgate, near you. Not far from the park.'

Why hadn't he mentioned it before? Had she even asked? She thought back to when they met and how she had done most of the talking.

'You live near the park? Is your house one of the pretty ones with the sash windows?' She pictured an airy, open plan sitting room with abstract paintings and strategically placed carvings from his travels. She didn't know why she imagined it like that – he just struck her as someone who had seen the world.

He kept his eyes down and wrung out the mop.

'No, nowhere that nice. It's very small. I'm really not that interesting.'

'I wouldn't say that,' she said, far too quickly.

She handed him the broken champagne flute. His fingers brushed hers, sending sparks shooting down her arm and into her aching stomach. Unlike before, he was looking everywhere but at her, his eyes flickering in the direction of the bar. The colleague with the sharp cheekbones was mouthing something at him. Zac raised his palms up apologetically and turned back to Ella.

'I really should get back to work. Are you OK, Rivers?' Zac nodded at her scratched foot. 'You need help getting to your table?'

She'd forgotten about her injury – it didn't hurt any more.

'Nah, I'll live,' she said. 'But can I buy you a drink? Are you allowed to join us? We're back there.' She pointed to the far end of the club. 'In the VIP area.'

'No, no, you get back to your friends.'

'Please, Zac. You would be doing me a favour. They're trying to set me up and, well, I'd prefer to talk to you than this Josh guy. He really rates himself.'

'You should give him a chance.'

Zac was looking straight at her now, his eyes narrowing and his brows furrowed like he was trying to solve a complicated puzzle.

'What? No! Not now I've bumped into you. Come on, join us.'

He sighed. 'OK, I finish my shift in an hour. I'll come and say hi before I leave.'

Ella floated back to her friends, a huge grin plastered on her face. Bloody hell, she had been thinking about him all week and he only lived two roads away. At least she knew where to find him now.

'Where's your sex god got to, Kerry?' Ella asked.

'He left as soon as you did. He's *so* into you. He asked all these questions then said he had to get back to his friends. You took, like, for ever in there!' She folded her arms theatrically and crossed her legs.

Ella flopped down and spread out her arms. 'I *adore* this place,' she said, hugging a cushion to her chest. 'I don't care about Josh. Let's go and dance.'

The music was nothing any of them had heard before. Ella's body moved instinctively to its own beat. She was on a high. Everyone around her was smiling and letting go. When they returned to their exclusive VIP area they found three Indigo Sky cocktails waiting for them.

'This bar rocks,' squealed Kerry. 'Man, do they know how to look after you. You seen the bar staff? Hot hot hot!'

Mai Li sipped her cocktail and gave a small smile. 'I like those T-shirts the guys are wearing, they're very ...' She giggled and mouthed the word 'sexy'.

Ella grinned but Kerry didn't. 'Something's been really bugging me about the logo for this place, the one on their uniforms,' she said, frowning and running her finger along the rim of her glass.

'What are you on about?' Ella asked.

'Well, it looks like a letter "I" right? Like, Indigo, which I get, because it's all purple and dark blue inside the bar. But that squiggle is a really old sigil.'

Her friends stared at her.

'The word "sigil" comes from the Hebrew "segula",

which is a talisman meaning "remedy". I recognised the mark from one of my classes. It can be traced back to the Neolithic period, way, way back. I think it was used for, like, communicating with ...'

Kerry stopped dead, her gaze travelling over Ella's head to someone behind her.

'So, Rivers, this is where you've been hiding.'

Ella jumped and threw her arms around Zac's neck, burying her face into his hair and breathing in his peppery scent. What was she doing? She had to be drunker than she thought. She hardly knew the guy – why was she throwing herself at him? Oh well, the cocktails were strong and his body against hers was even stronger.

His breath tickled her neck as he laughed. 'I see you missed me.'

Mai Li and Kerry's mouths were two perfect Os. Ella noticed that even Josh was looking from his table.

'Zac, these are my mates, Mai Li and Kerry,' Ella swept her arm out. 'This is Zac. He's a friend of mine. Well, more like a sexy superhero. He's very good with damsels in distress.'

Kerry was silent for the first time since Ella had met her and Mai Li's mouth opened and closed like a dying fish. Ella realised what she had just said. Oh well, now he knew she fancied him. Big deal. He hadn't once flirted back so he clearly wasn't interested. He probably had a girlfriend or, knowing her luck, a boyfriend.

'I can't have a drink, I'm afraid,' Zac said. 'Company policy, no fraternising with clients.'

He winked at her friends and they giggled, knocking back the rest of their cocktails.

'Guys, do you mind if Zac and I have a quick dance

before he goes?' Ella asked. The girls' heads shook but their faces remained blank. She grabbed Zac's hand before he could protest and he followed her to the glass doors of the dance floor where it was quieter.

'Rivers, I'm really not a good dancer, and I ...'

'Hey, we could share a cab back to Highgate,' she said, putting on her huskiest voice. He looked uncomfortable.

'No, you stay here with your friends. I don't want to ruin your night.'

'Ruin it? But you're the highlight!' she protested, regretting it at once.

'Rivers, you don't know me, you don't know what you're saying.' He looked down at his trainers and ran his hands through his hair. 'I saw the way that guy looked at you, he likes you. Maybe you should be dancing with him.'

Why was he so eager for her to talk to Josh? His mouth was saying one thing but his eyes were saying the opposite.

'He's no one, Zac. I'm not interested in *him*. Just one dance? Please?' She opened the door to the dance floor, and their voices were drowned out by the music. 'One dance, I promise,' she shouted, draping her arms around his neck again.

The music slowed and Zac rested his hands on her hips, her body swaying and merging with his. After a few seconds, his body relaxed and he pulled her into him. His arms slid up her back and she rested her head on his shoulder.

'You don't understand. It's not me you should be dancing with,' he whispered, his lips brushing against her

44

ear. 'I'm breaking all the rules.'

She pretended she hadn't heard him and wrapped her arms tighter around him.

CHAPTER FIVE

Ella buttoned up her collar and adjusted the strap on her backpack. She had worn her light jacket and realised her mistake the moment she'd stepped outside. It was mid-October and the smell of soggy leaves and smoky embers was quickly being replaced by the crisp bite of winter. She was in a rush, her strides quickening as she hurried to the bus stop, hoping her half jog would warm her up. Her phone rang and she fumbled with it, her fingers numb from the cold.

'Morning, Mai Li,' she said, her voice coming out as sharp bursts as she hurried to the end of the road. 'I'm heading in now. Sodding alarm didn't go off.' Her mind hadn't been on her studies lately. In fact, there was only one thing, one person, she could think about.

'I haven't seen you since the club last week,' her friend said. 'How amazing was that place!'

'I've been meaning to ask you about that. Do you remember getting home?' Ella's memory was hazy; she recalled every detail about seeing Zac but nothing after their dance.

'Zac got us a cab, I think,' Mai Li said. 'To be honest, I felt so floaty I can't really remember. He was just looking at you all intense, like he was from another planet and you were the first woman he'd ever seen. I can't believe you didn't ask for his number, but if it's meant to be, God will find a way to bring you together again.'

Mai Li was sounding like her mother with her soulmate bullshit.

'He's just a guy, Mai Li,' she said. 'What were you calling about?'

Her friend's reply was staccato and robotic then she was cut off. Ella would call her when she got on the bus, although she had probably missed it. She broke into a run, then stopped when she saw the bus stop was empty. The owner of the nearby newspaper stand nodded at her in recognition, then looked at the main road and shook his head. Highgate Village was jammed with cars and cabs, much more than usual. The noise was like a swarm of flies and the intense smell of exhaust fumes was dizzying. Ella couldn't understand why she hadn't noticed it earlier.

'What's going on?' she asked the vendor.

He handed her a copy of the local paper and pointed at the headline.

'Bus strike,' said a voice beside her. 'Unions announced it last night. Complete chaos.'

Ella looked up from the newspaper and grinned.

'Zac! How do you do that?'

'Do what?'

'Appear out of nowhere every time I'm thinking of you.'

'Maybe that's because you're always thinking of me.'

His words remained suspended in the air-tight space between them. He wasn't smiling. His eyes rendering her to stone again.

'I said you buying that, love?' the newspaper vender said, holding out his gloved hand, his impatient breaths like tiny puffs of smoke snaking between them. Without taking his eyes off Ella, Zac reached into his pocket and placed a pile of coins onto the counter.

'I'm heading for the Tube, what are your plans?' Zac said.

She had been so surprised to see him that she hadn't thought of the implications of the strike. He was right; with the roads gridlocked there was only one way to get to class and it was by Tube. But there was no way she was going to travel on the Underground. No bloody way.

'I can't. I'll just have to ask someone for their notes. I can't go on the Tube.'

He nodded. He didn't ask her why or try and convince her, he just waited for her to continue. So she did.

'It's really weird and stupid,' she told him. 'I'm not claustrophobic or anything. God, I've been on the Paris, Madrid, *and* Barcelona Metros, I even went on the subway in New York once without any issues. But as soon as I go near the Tube, even just the entrance or the steps down, I freeze and can't breathe. I feel like the walls are closing in. I remember my mum getting angry with me a few years ago when she wanted me to go with her and Richard to the opera. You can't park easily in Covent Garden, I get that, so they tried to convince me to get the Underground with them. I got as far as the escalators then had a massive panic attack. It was so embarrassing, the train staff called an ambulance and they had to write it in their accident book. Everyone was staring and pointing at me. Some journalist even wrote about it in one of those crap gossip magazines – *Tube Not Fantzy Enough for Millionaire's Daughter*. Made out I was so posh and disgusted by it that I fainted. But I'm not going down there. No way.'

The newspaper vender had stepped closer, watching them intently. Ella glowered at him until he turned around and busied himself rearranging his magazines. She signalled to Zac to follow and they sat down on a bench in the square. The traffic was at a standstill. She watched a couple get out of a taxi and head down the hill to the train station. It looked as if everyone was getting the Tube.

'Where you going, Zac?'

'I need to pick up my wages, I'm not working tonight. I'm not in any rush.'

'Can't they just put it in your bank account?'

'I don't have one.'

She wanted to ask him how he'd got to his twenties without a bank account but he continued before she could.

'Are you heading home now?'

She screwed up her nose. She couldn't really ask anyone to take notes for her – Mai Li and Kerry were the only people she knew and neither of them were in her Psych class. She had two choices: fail or risk having a public meltdown, again. Or even worse, make a complete tit of herself in front of Zac. She took a deep breath. Perhaps with his help it would be different.

'No, let's do it,' she said. 'I'll try and get the Tube, but only if you come with me. Please?'

He stood up and held out his hand.

'Thought you'd never ask. Come on, the longer we take, the busier it's going to get.'

Taking a deep breath, she stood up and took her first step towards the station.

They walked down the hill in silence. Ella distracted herself by looking at the different shades of orange and yellow of the oak trees lining the road, watching a mother holding her excited son's hand on the way to the swings at Highgate Wood, his mittens on a string swinging in step with his Wellington boots.

The station was on the main road but hidden, although through the balding autumn trees she could just make out the red and blue Underground sign peeking through the branches. Her stomach lurched. The Archway Road, the main artery from north London into the centre of town, was rammed with cars and lorries on one side with the odd car zooming by on the empty lane up north. Her head pounded to the rhythm of car horns. Like most of them, she too wanted to do a U-turn and head back the way she'd come.

Zac stopped and placed his hand on her arm.

'Rivers?'

She stood, staring across the road.

'Come on,' he continued, 'let's see how you feel when we get there.'

The entrance was at the end of a dark, narrow road, sheltered by towering trees with steep stairs leading down to the ticket hall. There was no way she could make it on her own. Her legs were slowly dissolving and her high-heeled boots weren't helping. She hovered over the first step as commuters pushed past them, tutting as she wobbled on her heels.

'Zac, can you hold my hand, please?'

Her voice broke and the steps blurred as tears pooled in her eyes. Gently, he moved her to one side and let the crowd pass. Ella was expecting him to hold her hand like the mother had with her little mitten boy, but instead, Zac threaded his fingers through hers and clung on tightly like he was never letting go.

As they walked through the ticket barrier he lifted her arm so she didn't have to let go of his hand. Her eyes darted to the steep metal escalators clanking and whirring beside them and her shoulders tensed. The passengers on the right side of the steps looked straight ahead, like rows of tin soldiers heading into battle, while dozens of suited men and women dashed down their left. Zac manoeuvered Ella to the wall and held her trembling shoulders, urging her to look away from the swelling crowd at the base of the escalator and swarming into the tunnels.

'Hey, Rivers, look at me,' he whispered. 'Look at me. It's OK.'

She turned and focused on his blue eyes, gazing at the navy rings of his irises melting into deep aquamarine, then fading to a misty grey around his pupils. She felt her breath steady and his grip on her shoulders loosened. He smiled and gently stroked her cheek.

'Welcome back. Do you think you can make it to the tunnel?'

She nodded.

'This is how we'll do it,' he said. 'You get on the escalator and I will hold you steady, face me and don't look down if it helps. I promise I won't let go.'

Ella wasn't sure if it was his voice, his words, or simply the fact that he was with her, but she felt calmer. This was the furthest she had ever made it. She braced herself and led the way to the top of the escalators. Gingerly, she placed her foot on the first step and turned to Zac, her face level with his chest. True to his word – his hand still firmly in hers – he wrapped his other arm around her waist and held her to him. She rested her head against him, inhaling the warmth of his sweatshirt as they sank lower. He turned her around just as the escalator reached the bottom and walked her to the wall. A rush of people pushed past them and she closed her eyes, concentrating on keeping upright and the feel of him beside her.

When she opened her eyes, she was alone and the station was still and quiet. The escalators were stationary and scattered with limp bodies, their limbs so twisted and tangled it was difficult to see what belonged to whom. They lay slumped on every wooden step, some curled into tight balls and others perched precariously on the edge, their clothes tired and tattered. Three young men in collarless shirts crouched on the steep metal partition and stared into nothing, a veil of cigarette smoke forming halos above their cloth caps. A red-headed girl in a full skirt sat cross-legged at the base of the stairs, tears drying on her sooty cheeks, ignoring the infant at her naked breast.

Ella tried to move but couldn't. She managed to take a step back against the cold wall and felt its rough grime settle on her fingertips. She turned her head away from the terrifying vision, the stench of urine and dirty bodies making her wretch.

Suddenly, a low, deep rumble sounded above. The men on the stairs looked up as a few of the bodies on the steps began to stir, white dust snowing on them. Small fragments of plaster soon turned to large chunks of brick which rained down and crashed at Ella's feet. The ground shook, the lights went out, and a baby started to scream.

'Rivers, hey, it's OK.'

Zac was beside her and the screams were hers. The escalator was no longer wooden and commuters continued to stream past, no one bothering to look at the hysterical girl in the corner.

'Zac, did you see that? The ceiling caved in,' she cried. 'There were bodies everywhere. I don't know. Did you not see it? I can't breathe. We have to get out, it's dangerous, I'm going to die …'

He pulled her to his chest and held her shaking body as her tears subsided. She wanted to take a deep breath but the air was too thick and still dusty.

'I know, I know.' He stroked her hair. 'It's all right, I'm here and I won't leave you, I promise.'

She pulled away and looked at him, wiping her eyes with the back of her sleeve. When had she heard those words before? What did he mean, 'I know, I know'? His hand in hers, his bright eyes, that voice, the smell of the dirty station … it was all rushing back to her but she didn't know what it meant. This was a bad idea; she shouldn't have come here. No assignment, nothing, was worth the fear that was currently coursing through every cell in her body.

'I don't think I can carry on, Zac. Get me out of here, just get me out …'

'Shhhh, you're safe,' he said. 'I'm here. We don't have to do anything you don't want to do. I won't leave you.'

There were those words again. He wasn't going to leave her, and she believed him. Nothing made sense. She was acting like a freak and he seemed to totally accept it. She took another deep breath and nodded. With him

54

beside her, she felt like she could do anything.

'You won't let go?' she said, tightening her grasp on his hand.

'Never.'

She picked her bag off the floor and they turned right, to the Northern Line platform.

Six stops, she told herself. *All you have to do is get on the next train, stand still for six stops, and it's done.*

On the platform, the electronic sign announced that the next Bank train was four minutes away. She felt sick. Bank, the business district in the centre of London's square mile and the home of the Bank of England, was not anywhere Ella had ever visited nor had any intention to, yet the name always evoked such strong emotions in her. In her mind's eye, she saw a grand white building with tall pillars, a horse, and a piercing wail. She could sense that ominous feeling creeping up on her again. When she glanced at Zac, it melted away.

What was happening?

'Zac, those visions, they were so real it was like I was transported to another time,' she said. 'Am I going mad?'

He didn't reply, just stared straight ahead and squeezed her hand. Why hadn't he run a mile from her psycho blabbering? Surely he had better things to do than give up his morning to babysit her? She could only think of one reason why he was still with her, holding her hand, and it thrilled her. If only she could get those awful images out of her mind. She would just have to keep focused and do whatever Zac said – he was the only thing keeping her from passing out right now.

A stale, metallic breeze swept her hair across her eyes and into her mouth, signalling the arrival of the train.

Travellers on the edge of the platform stepped back en masse as the train slowed down, and surged forward again as the doors split open. Ella was pushed from behind as the entire platform of commuters focused on the three empty seats in the carriage. She knew not to stand by the doors, so she shuffled to the glass partition at the back and leant against it, relieved to have finally made it in one piece. More passengers joined their carriage and, with each new person, Zac inched closer until his face was directly above hers. With their chests pressed together, she felt him shuffle his feet to avoid her toes.

'You OK?' he asked. 'You're still in shock. Just look at me, pretend no one else is here. Just me.'

Ella kept her eyes on his and concentrated on the feel of his hips against hers.

'I can do that.'

The doors shut then sprang back open. On the third attempt, the driver announced that something was blocking the doors so the passengers sighed and shifted, attempting to contort their bodies into the smallest available space. Ella couldn't believe people did this every day – and to think her classmates laughed at her for getting the bus.

She glanced to her right at all the people crammed between her and the only exit and tried not to think about her mounting anxiety. Then she looked at Zac and her stomach performed another somersault. He was staring at her, that same look, like a tiger that's seen something moving in the long grass. She shivered and glanced down, realising he was still holding her clammy hand.

He squeezed tighter and lowered his head, 'I'm proud of you, Rivers.'

The Tube jolted and his light stubble brushed over her cheek. She leant into him like a purring cat, breathing in his spicy scent. They stayed like that, his cheek resting on the crown of her head and her face buried into his chest, their bodies swaying to the movement of the train, for the rest of the journey.

'Come on, we're at King's Cross.'

Zac nudged her and she glanced up. They were still pressed up against each other even though the carriage was no longer as crowded.

She smiled and looked around. 'That was quick! Let's get out of this bloody place.'

She raced through the tunnels and up the escalators, her hand cold and empty without his, zig-zagging past commuters and straight to the ticket hall. A strip of white sky was peeking over the last flight of stairs and she ran up two at a time, never having been so happy to see King's Cross in all its grey, gloomy glory.

Once outside, she bent forward, her hands on her knees, and fought to get her breath back. She grinned from ear to ear and didn't care who was staring. Zac arrived beside her and she straightened up, noticing he wasn't out of breath.

'I did it! I only bloody did it!' she shouted, jumping up and down. She ran at him and threw her arms around his neck. He hugged her and spun her around, laughing. They stopped and the smile faded on his lips. This was it; the moment she'd been thinking about since she had first seen him. He leant in close, his hands stroking her waist and her breath shuddered in her chest. She closed her eyes and parted her lips a little.

Then nothing.

When she opened her eyes, Zac was looking at her with a frown on his face.

'Sorry, Rivers, I have to go.'

She looked at her watch. The journey had taken less than fifteen minutes but to her it had been a lifetime.

'Oh, right, of course,' she said, feeling stupid.

'See you around. Look after yourself.' He walked backwards, his hand in the air.

'But what about my journey home?' she said. 'How will I make it back on my own?'

'You'll be fine now, you won't have those visions any more.'

What did he mean, how did he know? What the hell just happened? She watched him turn and walk back to the station, his hands buried deep in his grey tracksuit top. Then he stopped. She stepped forward, but he was just zipping up his jacket and raising the hood, his shoulders hunched against the wind.

What was she doing? Was she going to let him walk away for the third time and keep hoping they would accidentally bump into each other? London was a big place; she wasn't going to be that lucky again.

'Zac!'

Her desperate cry was louder than she had intended. He swung around, his eyes full of concern. She ran up to him.

'Zac, sorry, I …' She hadn't planned on what she was going to say. Shit! She was such an idiot sometimes. 'I … um … I wanted to say thanks again. You know, thanks.'

He nodded and tilted his head.

'Shall we exchange numbers?' she continued. 'You know, so we can meet up some time, maybe have a drink? I was a complete loon after seeing that weird stuff and, well, I think I would have died if you hadn't been there. I really need to talk about it. Please, let me make it up to you and say thanks properly.'

'Don't worry, Rivers, you'll be fine. And you've already said thank you.'

'Well, can I have your number anyway? What's your surname? I could look you up on Facebook? You know, keep in touch.'

'I don't have a mobile and I'm not on Facebook. It's complicated.'

Ella felt her face reddening. What had she said to upset him? It didn't make sense. One minute he was holding her and now he was backing off. She gave a resigned sigh.

'Fine, well, maybe you would like *my* number? I'm not asking for your hand in marriage, Zac, I just thought it would be nice to meet up one day. Whatever.'

She picked at the skin around her nails.

'What time does your class finish?'

Her head snapped up.

'In three hours. I have some books I need to get out of the library, but I could be quicker than that. Why?'

'I'll meet you here at five o'clock,' Zac nodded at the station entrance. 'I don't want you going through that on your own.'

'Really? That's great. I mean, cool, yeah.'

Ella buttoned up her coat and shrugged her backpack on.

'Oh and, Rivers,' he said, laying a hand on her shoulder, 'I genuinely don't have a mobile phone, otherwise I would have given you my number the day we met.'

She grinned and hugged her arms around herself as she made her way to class.

CHAPTER SIX

Zac stood beneath the arches of King's Cross station and watched the reflection of the traffic in the wet paving slabs. He had promised Ella he would meet her after class but he was early. It had stopped raining but the misty air left him damp and cold to the bone. It hadn't taken long to travel the three stops to Indigo in Camden and back, so he had spent the rest of the day wandering around King's Cross and Euston, intrigued by the area's recent gentrification. The introduction of the Eurostar had turned it from a run-down industrial inner-city district to an up-and-coming European hub, complete with modern architecture, gastro pubs, five star hotels, and now one of Europe's most sought-after universities. It never ceased to amaze him how much could be achieved in so little time.

He stood stock still, as he had done thousands of times before, his eyes trained on the Tube entrance. The street was busy with harried businessmen and happy couples wheeling their tiny cases to the Overground, excited about their long weekends in Paris or Bruges. He envied them. How liberating it would be to do whatever he wanted, whenever he wanted. When had he ever been able to fly away on a whim?

Zac squinted through the winter afternoon darkness at the busy high road. He knew she wouldn't be able to wait another hour; she would be impatient to finish her class and would have hurried through the library without properly looking at the books she was taking out. These were the days of mobile phones, of checking status updates every five minutes. Ella wouldn't have been able to contain herself with the 'what-ifs', desperate to know if he would show up.

Zac was a lot of things, but he wasn't a liar.

He folded his arms and stepped into a doorway, out of the biting wind. He'd nearly kissed her that morning. He'd been completely reckless! All those other times in the past he'd managed to control himself, keep away, and not get close. Why now? He pushed away the image of her lips and the touch of her hand. For all her bravado and cockiness, Ella was young and far too vulnerable. Worst of all, she already desired him. She had practically offered herself up on a plate and it was getting harder to resist. What was it about her this time? She was pushy, needy, and had a filthy mouth – so why could he only think about what that mouth tasted like?

These new feelings unnerved him and left him struggling to focus on his mission. Allowing things to go further would be unfair on her and deadly for him. He would allow himself to see her one more time, just the once, and then he could return home.

He thought back to the others. No one knew how many there were – he'd never counted and there had been far too many to start keeping track now. None had been as complicated as Ella, but she wasn't like the others – she never had been. He sighed. He could see she had recollections of him, but he took comfort in the knowledge that she would never really remember him, not properly. His secret would always be safe because he was the only one with the power to tell her.

Ella was in sight now, and he watched her bedraggled figure stride to the corner of the street, her umbrella turning inside out as the wind tugged at her hair and coat. Even from a distance she was beautiful. Instead of crossing the road to the station she stopped, checked her watch, and ducked inside a shop. Zac would wait as long as it took. It wouldn't be the first time.

Eventually, Ella exited and searched up and down the road, then stood at the exact spot he had left her that morning. She glanced at her watch and leant against a car. She was forty minutes early.

Zac stepped out of the shadow of the doorway. He was never wrong.

'Rivers.'

'Christ, you scared me!'

He smiled and lowered his hood. The relentless wind blew his hair into his face and he raised it again. Ella pulled up her coat collar and shivered, her broken umbrella still in her hand.

'I'm a bit early. I didn't know you would be here already,' she said. 'Look, I feel really bad, what with you going out of your way to be so helpful and everything, but I'm not getting the Tube home. What I saw down there, I'm not going through that again. Anyway,' she waved her mobile phone in the air, 'I looked it up, the roads are clear so I'm getting a cab. Plus, I'm freezing my arse off. You want a lift? My treat.'

He smiled and nodded. It wasn't what Zac had planned. He wanted to see how she handled the Underground again, but he didn't blame her. The taxi rank was outside the station entrance. She threw her broken umbrella in the gutter and they stepped into a black cab.

'All right, love, where to?' asked the driver, peering into his rearview mirror. ''Ere, you're that hotel bloke's girl, ain't you? Had him in the back of my cab once, nice fella, good tipper. Bet you get to stay in some swanky gaffs, right?'

Ella gave Zac a sideways glance and smiled politely at the cabby.

'Highgate, please.'

She slid the plastic screen across and pressed the privacy button, slumping against the warm leather seat.

'This always happens,' she whispered. 'Everyone talks to me like they know me. It's embarrassing.'

The roads were empty, as most people were still avoiding them after the morning's upheaval. Zac could feel Ella's eyes on him as she pulled a carrier bag out of her backpack and handed it to him.

'Got you this. It's not much, but I wanted to say thanks.'

He stared at his lap. She was buying him gifts now? Ella's flushed face looked both nervous and eager as he pulled out a white box.

'It's a phone,' she blurted. 'Obviously you can see that. It's just, you said you didn't have one and, well, I thought it might be useful. It's linked to my account, don't worry about the calls, and it's already charged a bit. As I said, it's only a little thing.'

'Thanks, Rivers, it's very thoughtful,' he said slowly. 'Bit of an elaborate way of getting a guy's telephone number, though.'

'No, no, it's not like that. I haven't even written the number down. You don't have to give it to me either. It's

64

just a present, you don't have to call, I just …'

He laughed as she shook her head. 'Hey,' he placed his hand on her knee, 'I'm kidding, you can call me any time.'

She placed her hand over his.

'I wasn't sure if I was stepping on any toes. I mean, won't your girlfriend be angry?'

'Haven't got one.'

'Boyfriend?'

'Haven't got one.'

'Wife and kids?'

His eyebrows shot up and he laughed.

'No way. Totally against my religion. What about you, Rivers? Is holding my hand going to make any man jealous?'

She moved her hand back on to her own lap. 'Oh, millions will be crying into their pillows tonight, but no one you have to worry about.'

He wished he hadn't said anything; it felt good to touch her again. Distancing himself was getting more and more difficult every time he saw her. Each time he stepped back, she ran forward. There was no harm in a bit of friendly banter, he reasoned, she was lonely and he wasn't going to make her feel worse. It would be over soon enough.

They spent the remainder of the journey going through Zac's phone, Ella adding her mobile number, landline, email address, and Skype name.

'Let's check out the camera,' she said, bouncing up and down on her seat. She held up the phone at arm's length and pointed it at them. 'Say Selfie!'

She turned the phone around and looked at the screen.

'Oh, you must have moved. I can't see your face. Let's try it again.'

He gently took the phone off her. 'Leave it; you'll never get a decent picture of me, anyway.'

Ella had been curious about where he lived, and she craned her neck over his shoulder to see where the cab was pulling into.

'Well, this is me,' he said to her as they stopped outside Waterlow Park. She recognised the gates as the ones they'd stopped outside the day they'd met.

'I have your number, Rivers. All of them, in fact, so no excuses, right?'

He opened the door and ducked out. Ella shuffled up the seat and followed him out of the car.

'You don't have to walk me to my door, I'll be fine,' he said over his shoulder as he pulled a screwed up twenty pound note from his pocket.

'No, Zac, let me pay. Do you fancy a drink? I know you have to drop your wages back home, but I thought maybe we could go to a bar or something? If you're not too busy.' She tapped her thumbnail against her teeth and glanced at the cab purring patiently beside them. 'It's just you don't have to work until late tomorrow and no one's at mine tonight so I'll only be bored.'

Zac closed his eyes and sighed. 'Come on then.'

She threw a fifty pound note at the driver. Zac had already walked ahead of her.

'Hey, wait up, what's the bloody hurry?'

She jogged beside him as he strode down the hill. There were no houses in the park and neither was it a short-cut to anywhere. All was silent save for the crunch of their feet on the stone path and the odd hoot of a duck. It was early evening but the park was empty.

'Zac, stop a minute.' She was out of breath. She rested her hands on her knees and wiped her hair from her eyes. They'd passed the tennis court and were turning right before the large pond toward a cluster of trees. Ella knew it didn't lead to anywhere. Zac stood outside a small wooden shed, the kind where park keepers keep their tools.

He turned to her, his eyes restless in his stony face.

'We're here.'

He took a miniature key out of his pocket and fiddled with the padlock, sending the slatted door swinging open with a loud creak. Dust motes danced in the semi-light that forced its way through the window. It was just as cold inside as out. He reached to the ground and switched on a children's battery-operated light, but there wasn't much to illuminate. A mattress in the corner had three thin blankets neatly folded on top of it and beside it stood an old gas heater. A camping stove and frying pan perched on a shelf alongside a chipped bowl and some shopping bags, and a blue plastic bucket sat in the corner by a towering stack of books. Ella recognised the novels as the ones Zac had helped her take to the charity shop.

She looked at the cobwebbed roof and blinked back tears. So this was why he'd been so distant with her? Was this the secret he'd been keeping? He was so ashamed of how he lived that he didn't want anything happening between them?

Zac lifted his mattress without meeting her eye and pulled a black canvas bag from a hole that had been smashed out of the concrete floor beneath. He took the envelope out of his jean pocket, pulled out a couple of notes, then placed it inside the bag along with the box containing his new mobile phone.

'Still want to go for a drink?' he asked with his back to her.

'No.'

Zac sat down on the mattress and hung his head, raking his fingers through his hair.

'I get it, Rivers. Now you know me, you don't want to know me. It's fine.'

Ella watched a couple of leaves dance around her feet and settle beside Zac's bed. She shut the door but the wind blew it back open. Turning a wooden peg on the frame, she secured it shut and joined him on the floor.

'That's not what I meant,' she replied. 'I don't want to go for a drink because I don't want to sit in a loud, crowded pub. I want to talk to you properly. I want to get to know you, Zac. More than I've ever wanted anything.'

She took his hand and he raised his head to look at her. In the weak glow of the plastic light his face looked pale and haunted; his eyes were hollow and tinged with red. He snatched his hand out of hers.

'Just go, Rivers. I don't want your pity.'

'But I can help,' she said. 'What happened?'

'I'm not a charity case. This is temporary.' He stared out of the window at the park. 'I figured I could save money if I stayed here for a week or two. I used to busk as well as work in the bar, which was great until the shed got broken into and my stuff was stolen. That's why I dug a hole under my bed, to hide my things, but by next pay day I'll have enough money to find a room share or something, if I'm even around by then. It's not a big deal.'

Ella pulled at a loose thread on one of the blankets.

'I didn't know you played the guitar.'

'There's a lot you don't know about me,' he said quietly.

'Don't you have family you can stay with?'

'No.'

'Friends?'

'Not really.'

She stood up, the smell of damp tinged with bleach making her nauseous. With a sickening thud, she realised how useless her gift was – he had no one to call and nowhere to charge it.

'What happened, Zac? How come you're all alone?' Her voice came out a high squeak. 'Talk to me. I can help. Did you fall out with your parents? What happened?'

Zac jumped up and stood facing her. His hands that had held hers so tenderly that morning were now tightly grasped around her arms. He lowered his face to hers and accentuated each word.

'I don't *have* a past, Rivers. Leave it. Go!'

Ella shrank further back with each syllable, her throat tightening and her eyes stinging. She pushed her tongue to the roof of her mouth to stop the tears. She had overstepped the mark and embarrassed him. She thought they had something, that she could make it work, but she was clearly fooling herself. This wasn't some fairytale where the pauper got his princess. This was real life. He was right, she didn't know him … he was a stranger, a troubled one at that, and she was alone with him in the middle of a deserted park and it would be even darker soon. She pushed him away and unlocked the thin, wooden door. The wind caught it and sent it crashing into her, a searing pain shooting through her shoulder, but she didn't let him see. She lowered her head against the gale and stepped outside.

What was she going to do? All common sense was telling her to go and never look back, but her body wouldn't move. How could you crave and fear the same person?

Zac was behind her. 'I'm sorry,' he said, his voice barely audible. His chest was inches from her back. She could feel his warmth radiating into her and a trickle of hot liquid pooled into the pit of her belly. She stayed facing away from him.

'*Mierda*, Zac. I was trying to help. Just forget it, you don't have to see me again.' She made to go but he stepped closer. She froze as he slid his arms around her.

'Rivers, I'm sorry I lost my temper. Just no more questions. Please.'

'I just wanted to …'

'No more questions. I don't want to lie to you, so please don't ask anything I can't answer, OK?'

She nodded. All she could think about was the touch of his hands on her waist. He lowered his mouth to her ear, making her breath quicken and her nipples ache.

'Let's get out of here,' he whispered.

She turned to face him; the tip of his nose was nearly touching hers.

'Mine?'

He gave her a crooked smile. 'Yes. It's a bad idea, but yes.'

CHAPTER SEVEN

The taxi was still outside the park entrance. They could hear the driver on his mobile phone.

'Yeah, love, the pretty one, that hotel bloke's daughter. Honest! Ever so nice, though. About an hour or so, just leave it in the oven, yeah?' He glanced up. 'Got to go, love. Hey, you two, you ain't walking in this weather, are you?'

They turned to him but didn't stop.

'Jump in, guys. Come on, I'll give you a lift up the hill, no charge. Going that way, anyways. Know just where your gaff is, love. Did I tell you I had your dad in the back of my cab once? Generous he was, just like you.'

Ella rolled her eyes and stepped in. The quicker she got to her house, the better.

Ella watched Zac's face as they pulled up outside the grand entrance to her house. What was he going to think of her parents' mansion? The gates seemed larger and more golden than ever. It was embarrassing, she hoped he wasn't comparing it to the damp shed he currently called home.

'Take us round the back, please,' she asked the driver.

'No riff raff through the front door, is that it?' Zac laughed, but his eyes weren't smiling.

'Shh, it's not like that,' she whispered.

The driver had talked non-stop since they had entered the cab, and she knew he would be itching to tell his friends about them. She wasn't going to give him any extra fodder.

'I always go through the back gate. It's closer to my room plus I'm not sure what the front door alarm code is; they keep changing it.'

She could see he didn't believe her, but the truth was that she recognised the black car behind them. It belonged to a photographer that had been hounding her since her arrival that summer and she wasn't ready for pictures in the press of her and Zac. She never went anywhere interesting, yet she had already been linked to actors and footballers she had never met. The tabloids would really get their kicks if they spotted her creeping into her empty house with a handsome stranger in tow, let alone if they discovered his situation. She could see the headlines now, '*Lady and the Tramp – Fantzy Pants Falls for Down and Out*'. That was all she needed.

A private narrow road ran up the side of the house. Ella got out first and fumbled in her backpack for the keys. Zac followed but the driver beckoned him over. She watched them out of the corner of her eye, the driver oblivious as to how loud his whisper was.

''Ere, mate.' He signalled for Zac to lean in closer. 'I see a lot of lovebirds in my cab, yeah. This rearview mirror's a window to the world. I get all sorts. But I'm telling ya, I ain't never seen what you two 'ave. That's love, that is. You know, the real deal. The way you twos look at one anuvver, not a lot of people get that. Don't let 'er go. Not ever.'

Ella held her breath.

'It's complicated,' Zac replied.

'That what's worth 'avin always is, mate,' the driver said. ''Ere, take my card. Night or day, just call if you need a ride.' He tapped his nose, 'Discreet, I am.'

Zac tucked it in his back pocket then turned and tripped over Ella, who was still kneeling on the pavement surrounded by bits of paper, sweets, and make up.

'Ha, found them.' She waved her keys at him.

There were two doors set into the tall brick wall surrounding her house. One was for tradesmen and staff and led straight to the kitchen they used for events. The little wooden door beside it was the gardener's access. They took the smaller door into the flood-lit gardens and made their way down a gravel path leading to the back of the house. To their right was a small lake with an ornamental bridge and water lilies floating on its surface. It reminded Ella of the Monet painting.

Her mother had had the lilies shipped over from Indonesia. Ella remembered how it had taken her months to find the exact shade of pink she wanted and it was all she talked about for ages. Felicity had a thing about lilies. At the far end of the lawn, past the cypress trees, was a white metal pavilion where her parents held garden parties, something Ella did her best to avoid. She pointed out her room to Zac. It was part of the converted stables and linked to the main house by a narrow extension. From the outside it looked like a ground floor apartment with its own terrace surrounded by a low wall, a couple of sun beds, and a mini jacuzzi. She'd never used any of it.

Zac raised his eyebrows. 'Nice place, Rivers. How come the lights are all out?'

'It's just me tonight,' she replied, trying to make her

voice as casual as possible. 'My parents are organising the launch of Richard's new hotel restaurant, so they're staying there tonight. And the staff – well, housekeeper mainly – they don't live here. My mum hates the idea of strangers in her home.'

Ella punched eight numbers into a security pad by the side of her patio door and they stepped into the warmth. She unbuttoned her jacket and let it drop to the floor, kicking her shoes beside it.

'This is more than just a bedroom,' said Zac, looking around.

When the Fantzes had renovated the old mansion house, Ella had been given free rein to not only design the structure of the conversion with the architect but decorate it, too. She hadn't known where to start and mumbled two words, 'simple' and 'pretty'. The room was white, very white. In retrospect, Ella had wondered whether it was a sensible colour considering how good she was at spilling things. The interior designer had described the furniture as 'French Vintage Shabby Chic', which still made no sense. Her queen-sized bed was scattered with cream and white throws with three lace cushions neatly arranged in a line along her pillows. Ella glanced under the bed and sighed with relief. Thank God the cleaner had been. It hadn't looked like this that morning.

Her room appeared larger than it was thanks to a bank of mirrored wardrobe doors running down one side. At the far side of her bedroom, down two long steps, was a seating area with an L-shaped sofa and a television screen covering the entire wall.

Zac looked down at his muddy trainers against the thick cream carpet and took them off, leaving them side by side by the door. His eyes followed a curling staircase leading to a mezzanine level.

'What's up there?' he asked.

'Oh nothing. That's where my desk is, kind of a study area. Books, music, computer, you know.' She waved at the sofa. 'Take a seat, I'll get us a drink.'

Zac sat down and she dropped a wad of takeaway menus beside him.

'Pick one,' she said. 'They know the number. Wine?'

He nodded but still looked unsure, his eyes flitting around the room. Maybe a glass of wine would calm her nerves, too? She ducked down, opening a small cupboard by the side of the sofa. She handed him two cut glass goblets, her trembling hand making them clink together. He took them and she tried not to flinch as his fingers brushed hers. She attempted to insert the corkscrew into a bottle of Rioja as Zac's hand closed over hers.

'Let me do that. I'm the barman, after all.'

'Right, yeah, thanks,' she said. 'If you don't mind, I'm just going to freshen up. Get changed. Been in these clothes all day and I'm a bit … anyway, why don't you order? They know me. Sorry, I already said. What I mean is we don't have to pay. They bill us at the end of the month.'

Ella opened one of her wardrobe doors and buried her head inside. *Get a grip*! She'd been fantasising about this moment since the day she'd laid eyes on Zac and now he was here, in her bedroom, she was being a jabbering prat. She rooted through her clothes but nothing seemed right. She could see his reflection in the mirror as he flicked through the menus. He looked up, caught her eye, and winked. *Shit*! Her stomach flipped as she stood with a pair of knickers in one hand an odd sock in the other. Double shit, he was walking up the steps behind her. She grabbed a clean pair of jeans and a T-shirt and swung around.

'Pizza OK?' he asked.

Ella hid the bundle of clothes behind her back and nodded.

'Meat, extra olives, please.' She scuttled to the bathroom, avoiding his eye. 'Remote control's on the table, choose a film if you want,' she called as she locked the door behind her.

She leant against it and let out a rush of air. Taking three deep breaths she braced herself and looked in the cabinet mirror. Oh dear God, there was no way he was going to fancy her looking like that. She stepped into the shower, keeping the pressure low so he wouldn't hear the effort she was making, and shaved her legs far too quickly. She ran her fingers through her hair and applied some anti-frizz serum, a swipe of bronzer, a bit of lip gloss, and a thick layer of mascara. That would have to do.

She peered out from behind the door but the room was silent and the patio door was open. There was no sign of Zac.

'*Mierda*!' she muttered.

She thought they were getting on so well. Had he changed his mind and left? She thought back to the shed and his bed on the floor, then ran to her dressing table and checked her jewellery. Maybe he was only interested in her for her money? It was all there. She ran upstairs. The landing was narrow and the mezzanine overlooked her bedroom; in one corner were two cream sofas and a wall of books, and on the other stood a white desk with a laptop and CD player on it. Nothing had been taken.

She sank down at the top of the stairs and nibbled her thumbnail. Being robbed would have been better than the humiliation of him sneaking out. Why couldn't she just play it cool for once?

She peered through the downstairs window at the blurred image through the glass. There was someone on the lawn. She padded down the stairs and stepped through the open door into the cold night air. It was Zac, kneeling beside the lake with his back to her, his arms outstretched and his forehead grazing the damp grass. He was talking but she couldn't understand what he was saying. It was like a long stream of consciousness and not in a language she knew. Was he praying? He sat up and she ducked into the lounge area before he could see her.

The two glasses of wine sat waiting on the coffee table. Ella downed them both in quick succession and filled them back up before the crunch of gravel signalled his return. She turned and smiled at him, her lips tattooed in tell-tale burgundy, hoping he couldn't see the uncertainty in her eyes.

'Hey, there you are. Thought you'd done a runner.'

'Just getting some fresh air in your lovely garden. It's been a long day.'

She handed him his glass, managing to keep her hand steady 'Too true. *Salud*!'

He clinked his glass against hers and took a small sip. 'We've learnt a lot about ourselves and one another today, Rivers. It's been a …' He cocked his head to one side and met her eye. 'A revelation. Here's to new beginnings.'

'New beginnings!' she chimed, taking a sip and wondering what he was referring to. Their Tube trip? His disgusting hovel? Or maybe it was more than that – was he talking about them? The thought of her and Zac being a *them* made her chest ache and she knocked back the last of her wine.

What on earth had he been doing outside? She would have to get used to the fact that Zac wasn't your average guy. She could handle that. Most girls would have worried about his background or been put off by his weird behaviour, but not Ella. He was the first person she had met in years that made her feel alive, as if perhaps there was a future worth living for. She hadn't been this excited about anything in a long time … although she was still finding it difficult to get the image of him curled up on the grass out of her mind.

'Zac? Can I ask you something?'

'Of course. Anything.' He moved closer to her. 'By the way, you smell amazing. What is it?'

He put his glass on the coffee table and brushed her hair away from her neck. His face hovered at her collarbone as he breathed in her perfume, her chest brushing against his arm. She stayed still, afraid he would hear how loudly her heart was beating. 'It's, um, it's a perfume I had made for me when I was in Paris – it's jasmine,' she said.

A small smile played on his lips but his eyes were far away, somewhere sad and distant.

'Of course, it grew everywhere in Fiesole. You look really pretty with your hair like that, it suits you.'

She had no idea what he was talking about. She'd never heard of Fiesole and she wasn't wearing her hair in any special way. She tried to remember what it was she was going to ask him, feeling silly that it was even an issue.

'Zac, I just wondered what …'

The doorbell rang, making her jump. Damn those pizza guys – they always took their time except the one night she wasn't in a rush to eat. Delivery men always came to the main gate, which meant Ella had to run through the entire building to open the front door. When she returned she was out of breath and half expecting Zac to be gone, or bowing to the lake again.

'So what film do you want to watch?' he asked, taking the steaming boxes off her. She smiled in relief and shrugged. There was no point bringing up his strange antics now – the moment was gone. It was probably nothing. The guy had been living in a shed, for goodness' sake – maybe he *was* just enjoying the fresh air, or the view, or thanking God for the nice evening they were about to have. Anyway, he seemed a lot more relaxed now and if she wasn't mistaken, the way he was staring at her, he was flirting a little. She walked to the book shelf and ran her finger over a row of DVDs.

'It's nearly Halloween, how about we watch a horror film? *The Exorcist*?'

'Never heard of it.'

'You serious? The scariest film ever made and you haven't heard of it? Honestly, Zac, have you been living in a bubble all your life?'

She tossed the case at him and he caught it mid-air, turning it over to read the back.

'Exorcism?' he said, wrinkling his nose. 'The Devil versus God? You believe in this?'

She sat down beside him and picked up a slice of pizza. Maybe it was a stupid choice. She didn't even like horror films, she was just looking for an excuse to cuddle up to him and hide her face in his chest during the head spinning scene.

'Well, I *was* brought up a good Catholic girl, so I would be lying if I said I didn't believe just a little.' She picked at her pepperoni. 'So yeah, I guess I believe in God most of the time. So there has to be a Devil too, right?'

'No, there's no God.'

'You can't prove that, Zac. No one can.'

He shrugged. 'It's a fact.'

Ella shifted in her seat. Why the sudden mood change?

'Well, I think that's sad,' she said. What made him so cynical? 'If you don't have faith, Zac, if you believe in nothing, then what *do* you have?'

'Time. You can always rely on time.' He stared down at his lap, looking young and lost. 'If you hang about long enough, every wrong in the world will eventually be righted.'

She thought back to him curled up in her garden, like a Muslim in a mosque.

'So you've never prayed?'

'Of course not,' he said. 'Although prayers *do* work, but not because there's an omnipotent being sat on a cloud, listening. I can promise you that.'

Ella didn't know why it was bothering her so much. What did she care what he believed in? But there was something about the finality of the conversation that irritated her.

'At school they taught us that man was made in God's image.'

Zac laughed. 'No, Rivers, *God* was made in *man's*

image. It's a myth. An extremely potent one.'

'So you don't believe He has a plan for us?' she asked, thinking to what Mai Li had said about God finding a way to bring her and Zac together.

'No!' He was getting agitated. Why did she have to push? If she didn't shut up, she was really going to blow her chances. 'We make our own decisions, Rivers, and it's up to individuals to control their own life.'

He looked at her intently, his eyes navy blue in the dim room. What did he want from her?

'Zac, do you believe in fate?' she asked. 'You know, destiny and karma? Things happening for a reason?'

He held her gaze. 'Absolutely.'

'Do you think there was a reason we met?' she said leaning into him, her knees touching his.

'I *know* there was.'

Ella stared at his mouth as the tip of his tongue ran along his lower lip. He leant in, his face inches from hers.

'Rivers?' he whispered. She held her breath. 'Why did you ask for extra olives when you've picked them all off your pizza?'

She looked at the soggy pizza box on her lap and exhaled. What the hell was he on about now?

'I like the flavour of olives but not the texture. Is that a problem?'

Zac laughed and ruffled her hair. She wasn't going to rise to it. If he wanted to tease her, then fine – two could play that game.

'So, Zac,' she said, 'you telling me when I die I'm not going to Heaven?'

'I know you're not,' he smiled.

'Good. I wouldn't know anyone there anyway.'

* * *

They watched the film in silence except for the occasional squeal from Ella or an impatient sigh from Zac. As the film got gorier, Ella shuffled closer to him until her head was on his chest and his arm was wrapped around her shoulder. He absent-mindedly ran his finger up and down her arm and she squirmed at his touch. By the time the credits were rolling, her eyelids were heavy. She didn't want to ask Zac to leave but she was exhausted and had an early class, but when she looked up he was already asleep. She smiled and closed her eyes. A moment later, she felt a kiss on the crown of her head. She snuggled in closer and sighed. She must have imagined it.

CHAPTER EIGHT

The humming and banging was relentless. Zac opened one eye, then the other, and groaned. How had he fallen asleep on her sofa? The sunlight streamed through the windows and his head ached from the wine – he rarely drank alcohol. He was sweating; Ella must have covered him with her duvet. He was used to waking up cold.

The humming noise got closer, then the door handle rattled. Zac searched the room for Ella or somewhere to hide, but the door remained closed. It was locked. He threw the covers off and stepped on a cold slice of pizza. Groaning again, he pulled off his sock and placed the box on the coffee table, knocking a folded piece of paper on to the floor. It had his name scribbled on it.

Zac,

Sorry I rushed off, I have an early lecture and didn't want to wake you. I locked the door so the cleaner wouldn't come in. Please stay as long as you want but leave around the back. Last night was fun, call me or come round any time.

I'll be back by mid-afternoon.

Love Ella x

PS. I've left you some things from one of my step-dad's hotels if you need them.

Beside the coffee table was a white paper bag with a gold logo emblazoned on the front. Inside was a hotel shaving kit, toiletries, a towel, and various packs of clothing branded with a spa logo. The Golden Star, it read. Zac rubbed his hands over his face. This was ridiculous! What was he doing playing house? Why was he letting her get close to him?

He knew, but he didn't want to entertain the thought. He had done it because it felt good, because he had stopped sticking to the rules, and was listening to his heart for a change. It was a relief to be alone with her. For too long he had imagined what her hand would feel like in his again, what her hair smelled like now, what his name would sound like on her lips. She had wanted more, and it had taken every ounce of strength left in him not to give in. It had to end. Today he would walk away and never see her again. There was no other choice.

But first he had to deal with more immediate issues, like his growling hunger and throbbing head. He found a new pair of sports socks in the hotel bag then he tidied up the pizza boxes and put the throw back on the bed. Her room was stuffy and he couldn't think straight. He turned the handle of the back door but that was locked too. A little red light blinked above his head and Zac sighed. She must have set the alarm without thinking when she left.

He pushed down the panic in his chest and glanced around. The clock on the bedside table told him it was just past midday. In her note she mentioned she wouldn't be back until mid-afternoon. That could be any time. He had no idea how long he would have to wait. He could hear voices outside the bedroom door and he pushed his ear closer. A young woman with a syrupy voice was asking the cleaner to spend the afternoon polishing the marble floors on the ground floor. He was trapped. He ran his fingers through his hair. For the first time ever, he didn't have a plan. He considered forcing the back door open but didn't want to risk setting off the alarm. He could chance it out the front, but the house was too big and he didn't know his way out, It wasn't worth the risk of being caught. He looked at the phone on the bedside table. He could call her but she had programmed her numbers into his new mobile – which he'd left in his bag in the shed. He would just have to sit it out.

He picked up the paper bag and a magazine that was lying on the floor and headed for her bathroom, the idea of a long, hot bath growing in appeal by the second.

Ella had sat in her class for two hours but hadn't listened to a word the lecturer said. All she could think about was Zac. She kept replaying the previous day in her head: the Tube ride, her strange hallucination, the way his body had pressed against hers on the train and how many times they had come close to kissing. She thought of their argument in the park. She hated the idea of him going back to that shed and sleeping on that disgusting mattress. She swallowed as she remembered the putrid, dank smell. He'd said he had no family, and she'd noticed he had no personal possessions in there – but everyone has friends or family of some sort. It wasn't normal. He'd looked so alone and scared when she mentioned his past. What was he keeping from her?

She stepped off the bus at Highgate Village, the sky already turning a pale shade of lilac. She thought about walking through the park and seeing if Zac was there, but decided to give him some space. He had her number and knew where to find her. Her stomach rumbled; she hadn't eaten anything since the pizza. Her mother liked to have Afternoon Tea on Fridays when she was home; she may as well indulge Felicity in her mother/daughter bonding time and keep her off her back for another week.

Ella entered the house via the back as usual but her door handle didn't budge. How had Zac managed to reset the house alarm? *Shit!* She must have done it in her rush this morning!

She quickly punched in the code and ran inside. There was a rustling sound from her upstairs study, where she found Zac sitting cross-legged beside the bookshelves and surrounded by piles of reference books.

'Zac, I am so sorry!' Ella ran to him as he stood up. 'Did I lock you in? I'm so sorry.' She was struggling to see his face in the dusky light. 'What are you doing in the dark?'

He switched off the small torch in his hand with his key hanging from it and gave her a lopsided smile.

'I was worried your mum or someone would see the light under the door.'

Ella turned the desk lamp on.

'I had a bath,' he added. 'Thanks for the clean clothes.'

He was wearing the spa tracksuit she had left him and smelt of fresh laundry and something lemony.

'I better get going,' he said. 'I have to be at work by eight.'

'I'm so, so sorry, let me make it up to you. Please stay a bit longer.' *You can't go back to that park and your cold, miserable shed*, she wanted to add. 'It's four o'clock, you have ages. Please don't go to work on an empty stomach. Are you hungry?'

He laughed. 'I am. Other than the cold, congealed pizza I scraped off my sock there wasn't that much to eat. Although I did find your secret stash of chocolate under the bed. Hope you don't mind.'

Ella gave him an apologetic look. 'If you can spare an hour, why don't you join me for Afternoon Tea?' She made a face. 'God that sounded really stuck up. I just mean that there's cake and sandwiches waiting downstairs and at least you won't have to go back out in the cold or spend any money. I can give you a lift to work if you like? I feel really bad.'

'You have a car?'

'Of course I do.'

'But you get the bus everywhere?'

'Yeah, well, there's no parking in King's Cross and I get impatient in traffic. I like to sit on the bus and look out the window. It's calming. So, you want to stay?'

Zac looked at the door.

'Won't your parents be there? I can't walk in wearing their hotel tracksuit.'

Ella beamed. Then she stopped smiling. Holy crap, he was going to meet Richard and her mum! Poor Zac, as if it wasn't bad enough that he'd been locked in all day, now he was being forced to meet her parents.

Zac placed the books he was reading back on the shelves. He looked nervous. *Well, of course he looks nervous*, she told herself, *you've just locked him in your house and now he has to meet your mum*! Oh well, what was the worst that could happen?

'Right,' Ella said. 'Let me get you something to

change into and you can walk to the front gates, wait a few minutes, then buzz. It'll look better that way. I don't want them thinking I'm hiding men in my bedroom.'

She ran back down the mezzanine stairs, out of her bedroom door, and returned with a crisp, white shirt on a hanger. Zac was on her bed, looking confused.

'Here.' She handed him the shirt. 'Put your jeans on with this, you'll look great. It's one of Richard's. It's brand new; he has hundreds. Come on, hurry up, I'm starving!'

There was a knock at the bedroom door.

'Sweetie, are you there? Are you joining us, darling? Ylva is bringing in a fresh pot of tea in a minute.'

Ella pointed at the back door and held up five fingers, hoping Zac would stick to their plan and not run off.

'Coming!' she shouted, running to her bedroom door and joining her mother in the hallway. 'I was just on the phone to my friend, Zac. I hope you don't mind but I invited him to join us.'

Felicity's eyes widened.

'*Him*? At last, you are bringing a boy home to meet Mummy and Daddy.' Her mother's heels clicked along the tiled floor as they entered the dining room and she tottered over to her husband. 'Richard, Richard, guess what Ella's told me!'

Ella ran after her.

'Mum, it's not like that. Please don't embarrass me; he's a mate from uni, just a *friend*.' She turned to her step-father. 'Richard, please tell her not to be over-excitable. He'll be here in a minute. He's only staying for a bit. I'm dropping him off at work later. Just be cool, please.'

Her parents laughed and Felicity put her hand on her daughter's shoulder.

'Calm down, honey, I was only pulling your leg. I will behave impeccably. Now tell me, is he gorgeous?'

This was a bad idea. She seated herself at the large table in front of her parents. In the centre were three cake stands stacked with thin sandwiches, tarts, and pastries along with a variety of teas and coffees. The doorbell chimed and Ella waved a warning finger at her mother.

Ylva knocked and showed Zac in.

'Mr and Mrs Fantz, Miss Ella, your guest is here.'

Zac smiled sheepishly at Ella. He'd tucked the shirt into his jeans and wiped his trainers clean. The shirt suited him; it made his hair darker and his eyes brighter. God, he was hot! Ella knew her mother was going to adore him, although that idea worried her too. He stepped forward and shook hands with Richard.

'A pleasure to meet you, Sir. Thank you for allowing me into your beautiful home. Mrs Fantz,' he took her small hand in his, 'a pleasure to meet you. Ella speaks of you often.'

Richard began to fill his plate, signalling for Zac to take the chair beside Ella.

'Please call me Richard, or Dick,' he said. 'Felicity and I are known in certain circles as Flic and Dick.' He laughed deeply, making his tea slop out of his teacup. 'Isn't that a riot?'

Felicity hadn't moved from the door. Her feline eyes were perfect round discs fixed on Zac.

'Sit down, darling,' Richard said, pulling on his wife's hand. 'Believe me, Zac, she is very rarely this demure. The women of this household are both beautiful *and* talkative. Maybe you should come for tea more often; I've never seen them so quiet.'

Zac's leg brushed against Ella's as he sat beside her. He jigged it up and down in jerky movements until Ella placed her hand on his knee. She didn't blame him for being nervous; her mother was still looking at him like a cornered cat would a dog, uncertainty thinly veiled as polite interest. Richard hadn't noticed, but clearly Zac had.

'Ella tells me you recently moved from Spain, Mrs Fantz. Is that where you and Richard met?'

Felicity didn't answer. Richard frowned at his wife and turned to Zac.

'That's right; we met at the opening night of my Marbella hotel. Felicity and Ella were celebrating something. What was it again, darling?'

Felicity shrugged.

'It was my sixteenth birthday,' Ella said. *The day my life turned to shit*, she wanted to add. *The day I lost my mother and she began to morph into a brainless idiot.*

Richard looked at his wife the same way he had on that night over three years ago.

'When I saw Felicity, I knew she was the one. She was the woman I had …'

'Seen in your dreams?' asked Zac. 'Like she was your destiny?'

Felicity gasped. Richard's smile faded and he narrowed his eyes.

'Yes, that's … exactly right. So, Zac, how did you and Ella meet?'

'Zac's at RCU, I told you,' Ella cut in. 'He studies, erm, music. He plays the guitar, you know.'

Felicity stared down at her plate, running her pendant along its gold chain around her neck.

'That's a very interesting necklace,' Zac said.

Felicity looked up, her eyes wide with fear.

'She never takes it off,' Ella said through a mouthful of strawberry tart. 'That necklace is older than me.'

'It's served me well,' Felicity said looking Zac straight in the eye, 'Potestatem Amethystus.'

He let out a soft laugh. 'That's right, Mrs Fantz.'

Richard frowned and Ella bit the inside of her lip, feeling the tips of her ears burning.

'So, Zac, you play music?' Richard bellowed. 'Give us a tune, boy. Run along, Ella, get the kid a guitar from the music room. Electric or classical?'

'I play acoustic, mainly Spanish,' he said, directing the answer at Felicity who flinched under his gaze.

Ella returned with a shiny acoustic guitar and Zac took it and checked it was tuned. 'You will have to excuse me, I haven't done this for a while.'

His hair fell over his face as he bent over the instrument and began to play, his hand tapping out a rhythm on its hollow body. A haunting flamenco melody filled the room, each note crying out about lost love, pain, and passion. Ella closed her eyes and lost herself in the Andalusian mountains, the place she had always called home. She could practically smell the oranges and wild lavender, feel the sun warming her back, and the dry earth on the soles of her feet. Through sleepy eyes, she gazed at Zac, mesmerized as he disappeared further into every note. His fingers glided over the strings and she imagined what they would feel like moving over her body, stroking and caressing her as gently as he strummed that guitar.

She looked at her mother, who was staring into the middle distance, her eyes still and glassy. Felicity blinked and a tear rolled down her cheek, splashing onto a solitary triangle of sandwich that lay dry and curled on her plate. Her chair screeched against the marble floor as she scraped it back and ran out of the room. Zac stopped playing.

'What the fuck was that about?' Ella cried, jumping to her feet and knocking over a jug of milk.

Richard held up his hand. 'Not now, Ella. That's enough dramatics for one afternoon. I don't know why your mother is acting so peculiar.'

Ella wasn't listening. She stormed out of the room, leaving Zac and Richard alone, staring at their empty plates.

Felicity sat at her dressing table mirror, black streaks running down her cheeks. She had lost it. What must Ella and Richard think? They would never understand why she had reacted the way she did. She'd told Richard some of the story, but only one person knew everything.

Ella had said his name was Zac and that she'd met him at school, which was plausible. He only looked a few years older than her daughter, after all. But it didn't make sense. It was him, it was definitely him. She would never have forgotten that beautiful face, his voice, and those eyes. But what was he doing with her daughter? She didn't know whether to throw the boy out of her house or throw herself at him and cry her years of pain into his strong shoulders.

Ella slammed her mother's bedroom door open, the door handle leaving a dent in the wall.

'Mama, what the *hell* was that about?' she screamed in Spanish. 'Do you know how embarrassing that was? The first friend I bring home and you do *this*!'

'Don't shout, they can hear you,' Felicity said, her tone low and flat.

'What's your problem? Was he not flirting enough with you? No one giving you enough attention?'

'Keep your voice down.'

'I don't care. Zac doesn't speak Spanish.'

'I wouldn't be too sure.'

'What are you on about? What is going on?'

Felicity dabbed a tissue to her eyes, watching her daughter in the mirror.

'I'm sorry, darling,' she said. 'Your friend reminded me of someone I knew, that's all. I got a tad emotional.'

'A tad? A *tad*!' Ella screamed. 'I get a *tad* emotional watching *Bambi*; I get a *tad* emotional at the end of *Romeo and Juliet*. That was not a *tad* anything. That was just crazy.'

Felicity rounded on her daughter.

'You don't know crazy. I've seen crazy. Don't you ever call me that!'

Ella gave her a look of disgust and walked out, slamming the door behind her.

The atmosphere in the dining room was tense; Richard had moved on to a second plate of sandwiches and Zac was tightening the guitar strings. Ella strode to the table.

'I'm sorry about that, Zac.'

'*No pasa nada, guapa*,' he replied with a wink.

Ella stopped. *Shit*! His accent was flawless. Her mother had been right. How did she know? She wondered how much Zac had heard and how much he'd understood.

'Oh what tangled webs we weave,' said Richard, wiping his mouth. 'That is more than enough excitement for one day, kids. Ella, did you mention you had to take this nice young man to work? Where do you work, Zac?'

'I work in a bar called Indigo, Sir.'

'You play guitar there?'

'No, I just pour drinks and clear glasses. Part time, nothing special.'

Richard patted him on the shoulder and smiled. 'Well, son, you have a promising career ahead of you. If that's the kind of reaction you get to your music, you'll have women around the country throwing themselves at your feet.'

CHAPTER NINE

Ella's car was a small, black two-seater that Richard had bought her and that she never used. Her dashboard showed it was five degrees outside and the streets shone with drizzle. Ella turned the heating dial to maximum but she still felt cold.

'You're very quiet, Rivers. What's the matter?' Zac said a few minutes into their journey. He smiled and squeezed her knee.

She took a large breath and looked straight ahead. Why did he do that? He was guarded and mysterious one minute, then friendly the next. More than friendly! Her throat ached and her eyes prickled with the onset of tears. God, she was as pathetic as her over-emotional mother. What was it about Zac that made her so extreme? She spotted a parking space on her left and pulled over. She had to get a grip; she couldn't even see clearly enough to drive. Her breath came in racking sobs and her shoulders shook.

Zac unclipped both of their seatbelts and turned to face her.

'Hey,' he said, rubbing her knee again. 'Don't be upset, everything's fine.'

Except everything *wasn't* fine. She hated that she already cared too much about him, that he was becoming an obsession. He wiped away her tears with his thumbs and she tried to turn away but he wouldn't let her.

'We're friends, right? Tell me what the problem is.'

She sniffed and tried to control her trembling lower lip.

'Why didn't you tell me you spoke Spanish?'

'Is it important?'

'Yes! Yes, it is. I'm so embarrassed. I just know when I drop you off I'll never see you again.'

'Why do you think that?'

'Because *look* at me! I'm a mess, you're always having to look after me. I fall over, have public meltdowns, say stupid things. My mum's a nut job and I've made a total idiot of myself.' He still had his hand on her cheek, and she placed her own over his. 'I really liked it when you stayed, Zac. I can't let you go back to sleeping in that shed. What kind of friend would I be? Let me help you. Stay at mine until you're back on your feet. If you still want to know me, that is.'

'Of course I want to know you,' he replied, taking his hand from her face. 'I just don't think staying at yours is a good idea. For a start, your mum doesn't like me, plus there's a lot you don't know about me and ...'

'Please,' she said, taking his hand again. 'They're never home. I don't want to be on my own any more.'

Zac closed his eyes and sighed.

'OK,' he said, reaching into his pocket and handing her a tiny key. 'I'll stay at yours. Could you please pick up my bag on your way home tonight?'

She fell into his arms with relief and he held her, stroking her hair until she was calm enough to drive again.

Ella couldn't sleep. She lay awake staring at the numbers on her bedside clock, guessing what time Zac would be back. He had told her the bar closed at 1 a.m. and that it took a while to cash up and tidy, so she had given him the key to the back gate and left her bedroom door unlocked. It was a reckless thing to do – her parents would kill her if they knew what risks she was putting herself and their home in. Luckily, she hadn't had to speak to them again that evening. Felicity and Richard spent Friday nights out with friends and would then stay at their suite in the London hotel. She didn't expect to see them until Sunday.

She flipped her pillow over to the cold side and plumped it up. The clock shone 2.26 a.m. Maybe he wouldn't show. Her heart was thundering.

He'd said all the right things in the car – how it pained him to see her upset, that he was glad to have her as a friend, that he didn't want to take advantage of her kindness and would only stay a couple of nights. He had emphasised the word 'friend' and she had received the message loud and clear. She was thankful to get that much after such a disastrous afternoon.

She threw the covers off and turned over for the hundredth time, her silk camisole top and shorts twisting around her body and riding up her legs. She wasn't expecting anything to happen, but it didn't mean he had to see her in her old flannel pyjamas. It was impossible to sleep; every time she closed her eyes she could see his face and kept reliving the last two days. Why hadn't he kissed her? He'd had so many opportunities, and she'd seen in his eyes that he wanted her, but something was stopping him. His stupid pride, probably. She thought of his laughter as he'd swung her around outside King's Cross station, what his hard chest felt like against her back and how he'd stroked her waist and whispered in her ear. Then this afternoon, how his fingers had skimmed over the strings of the guitar so smooth and effortlessly. Was that how he made love? Intense but gentle, losing himself in her the way he had with the music.

It was hot. Her mother had the heating on all day and it was taking a long time to cool down. Ella closed her eyes and stroked her inner thigh, thinking about Zac creeping into her room. Her hand went higher as she imagined him climbing into her bed as she slept, waking her with butterfly kisses on her neck, moving down her collarbone to her …

There were footsteps outside. She pulled the duvet back over herself and lay facing away from the door. Her thighs were damp and throbbed with anticipation.

She listened to Zac enter her room, close the door silently, and lock it behind him. Ella kept her eyes closed, peeking through her lashes as he walked around her bed and down to the sofa where she had placed a sheet, pillows, and blankets. She watched as he pulled off his trainers, leaving them side by side by the makeshift bed, and draped his jacket over a chair. He pulled his sweater off, his black T-shirt rising across the tight muscles of his chest, the ripples of his taut stomach highlighted by soft light flooding in through the window. She heard the jingle of his belt as he unbuttoned his jeans and let them fall to the floor, finally removing his socks and gathering his clothes into a neat pile beside his black canvas bag. She expected him to move to the sofa or the bathroom, but he didn't. Wearing just his T-shirt and boxer shorts, he turned and walked to her bed. Ella held her breath – she didn't want him to know she had been waiting for him. He was inches away from her and she could feel his breath on her neck as he leant over her curled body. His hand came close to her and she fought the urge to reach out for him. She continued to feign sleep as he brushed a loose curl off her face and stroked her cheek, gazing at her for what felt like for ever.

'*Te amabo in aeternum,*' he murmured before walking away.

Ella's pillow was vibrating. She reached beneath it and pulled out her mobile, which she had set to silent before going to bed. Mai Li's name was flashing onscreen. She'd forgotten to call her back the day of the Tube drama. Ella scrambled out of bed and glanced at Zac, his unruly hair just visible beneath the rise and fall of the duvet. Her stomach flipped.

'Hi, what's up?' Ella whispered. She stepped into the hallway that separated her room from the rest of the house.

'Hey. Where are you? You said you'd meet me and Kerry this morning.'

Since she'd met Zac everything else had ceased to matter. She was being a crap friend.

'Shit! I'm so sorry, I totally forgot we were meant to be going shopping. Something's come up.'

'Why are you whispering?'

'I ... don't want to wake Zac up.'

'What!'

Her friend's squeal was so loud Ella covered the mouthpiece with the palm of her hand.

'The sexy barman? Oh wow, Ella, is he in your bed right now?'

Before Ella could answer, she heard Kerry's unmistakable voice clamouring for the phone.

'What did she say? Here, give me the phone. Ella, you sly dog! Did you go back to Indigo without us? Have you just got it on with the hottest piece of ass in the city? Girl, you have to give us *all* the juicy goss. Mai Li, stop yanking the phone, put it on loudspeaker.'

Ella laughed.

'There's nothing to say. Don't get excited, nothing happened.'

'We saw the way that he looked at you at the bar, Ella, he likes you' Mai Li said. 'Don't you fancy him?'

'Of course I do.'

'You need to show him then, maybe you're being too subtle.'

'Right, Mai Li, hang on while I get a pen and paper. Maybe I could make a sign to hang around my neck that says *Shag Me Before I Explode?*'

Her friends laughed.

'What's he doing there then?' Mai Li asked.

'It's a long story. He came to uni with me on the Tube on Thursday …'

'But you hate the Tube,' interrupted Kerry.

'Exactly. Anyway, he had pizza at mine after and we fell asleep …'

'So he's been at yours two nights and he hasn't tried anything on? But you're beautiful! Have you stayed at his? Where does he live?'

'That's another story. I'll tell you when I see you next. Anyway, yesterday was a complete disaster when he met my mum and she –'

'He met your *parents*?' Mai Li shouted. 'You say nothing's happened and he's sleeping in your room and meeting your parents. That doesn't sound safe, Ella, not with you being …'

There was a sound like two cats fighting then Kerry came on the line

'Girl, you are hot, famous, and loaded. Who the hell is this guy? He could be an axe murderer, or worse, he could do a kiss and tell for the tabloids.'

Ella was on the verge of telling them that last night, as she'd feigned sleep, he'd stroked her cheek and whispered to her in Latin. But they wouldn't understand, it sounded too weird. Everything he'd done would sound strange when said out loud.

They were right – it was time to show Zac how much she cared about him. Regardless of what he'd told her about seeing her as just a friend, she knew it was bullshit. He had whispered to her and stroked her face as she'd slept. You don't do that if you don't like someone! Of course he liked her, but he was holding back. There was something he wasn't telling her.

'Oh yeah, listen,' Kerry continued. 'I've been meaning to tell you, you know I said the Indigo bar logo was freaking me out? Well, I looked into it and it's really strange, right, because not only is it a majorly old symbol for Jupiter, totally random, but it's also one of the signs used for …'

'Kerry, sorry, I have to go. I'll call you later I promise and you can tell me then. You girls are right; I need to tell him how I feel.'

Ella hung up to the sound of her friends' cheers and

tiptoed into the room. She felt bad letting them down but she wasn't going to let Zac slip away again.

He was still asleep, his tanned arms thrown above his head and one foot resting on the carpet. The duvet had fallen to the ground, leaving just his middle covered. She pulled the blind up halfway, filling the room with milky light. A pale smudge of sunshine was stamped on the white sky, its glow throwing shadows over Zac's bare chest. She wanted to rest her hand on it, feel his breath rise and fall beneath her palm and his heat rise through her.

'Enjoying the view?'

She jumped and he gave her a lazy smile through half-closed eyes.

'Sorry. Did I wake you?' she said.

'No. Unfortunately I can't hear your thoughts from here.'

His eyes travelled over her camisole top and shorts, his stare stroking her skin like a feather. Ella's cheeks prickled and her mouth was dry. Why had she worn so little to bed? She tucked her fringe behind her ear.

'It's still early. I'm sorry, I'll let you get back to sleep'

He sat up and pulled the duvet over himself. 'No thanks, I can think of more interesting things to do.'

She grabbed her bathrobe that hung on the back of her bedroom door and put it on, tying the chord tightly.

'Like?' she asked.

'Breakfast? I didn't get many of those Afternoon Tea sandwiches last night.'

Ella winced at the memory of her mother's behaviour. 'OK, good, I'm starving,' she said, not knowing if she felt relieved or disappointed at the lack of flirting. 'Stay right there, I'll bring some food. Oh, and I have a surprise.'

Ella had no idea what kind of food Zac liked – along with everything else she didn't know about him – but the fridge was always fully stocked. She loved to cook, but she rarely had the opportunity. She hummed as she fried bacon and added it to the other dishes then she picked up the heavy tray and made her way back to her room. She could hear Zac in the shower, so she bundled the blankets and pillows behind the sofa and out of view, and placed cutlery and glasses on her large coffee table. It was missing something.

She looked outside, at the white sky reflected in the lake. That's what she missed about Spain: colour. There was nothing in the garden but frosted grass and bare flowerbeds. She padded out onto the terrace, the cold burning her toes, and spotted a solitary lilac rose climbing the trellis of her bedroom wall. She snapped it off and added it to the table in a champagne flute, its heady scent reminding her of something.

The sound of running water stopped and Zac came out of the bathroom fully dressed and drying his hair with a hand towel. He looked at Ella through damp curls then noticed the breakfast table.

'You never cease to amaze me, Rivers. Angel Face, interesting. A late bloomer.' He took a chocolate croissant off the plate and took a bite. She must have looked as confused as she felt. 'The rose. That's its name, Angel Face. Did you know when you present a person with a rose that its colour has a certain meaning?'

Ella shook her head.

'Red for romance, yellow for friendship, white for sympathy.'

'And purple?' she muttered.

He licked a smear chocolate from the corner of his mouth.

'Love at first sight.'

'I didn't know that.'

'Evidently.'

Why did she have to go and pick that stupid flower? He was playing with her again and she wasn't sure if she liked it. She was always two steps behind him, as if he knew something she didn't and she was playing catch-up.

'Right, anyway,' she said, 'I didn't know what you liked so I made a bit of everything. I couldn't remember what you had on your pizza and no one ate much yesterday, so there are eggs, pancakes, bacon sandwiches,' she pointed at each dish, 'fruit salad, a few yoghurts, cereal, fresh pastries. Go on, sit down. I have some great news for you.'

She held one finger up, signalling she wouldn't be long, and ran out of the room, returning a minute later with a bulging bin bag spiky with metal hangers. She dropped it beside him and caught her breath. He was still standing where she had left him, wet towel in hand. He eyed the bag suspiciously.

'Look, Ella, you've done enough ...'

'It's a bit scrunched up but I made a few calls last night and picked these up from my mum's offices. It's all the designer samples and freebies she gets. Check this out.' She rummaged inside the bag and pulled out item after item, most still in their plastic jackets. 'Ralph Lauren, DKNY, Calvin Klein, McQueen, Armani, Nike. These brands just *give* their stuff away to her clients.'

'Who's it for?' Zac asked.

She nudged him playfully.

'You, silly. You can't wear the same hoodie and jeans for ever. I've only ever seen you in two outfits and those trainers are minging. I guessed your size but they look about right.' She rummaged deeper into the bag, avoiding Zac's stare. Her voice was muffled as she buried her face into the clothing. 'Oh, and the best part, Richard texted me last night saying he was really impressed with your guitar playing. He said he could get you a gig at his hotel bar, maybe even the restaurant opening on New Year's Eve, plus he'll recommend you to any guests looking for a musician for events. You know, weddings, Bar Mitzvahs, birthdays, whatever. You could be raking it in!'

Ella looked up to check Zac was still there as he hadn't made a sound, but her smile faded when she saw his face. What was that look? Pity? Regret? Resignation?

'What's the matter?'

'Rivers, you shouldn't have.'

'Don't be daft. It was the least I could do. I want to help.'

'No, I mean you shouldn't have done this,' he said, picking up a pack of boxer shorts and dropping them back into the bag. 'I've never asked for your help and I don't want it.'

His words were like fists, each one punching her harder in the stomach until she sat back on her knees.

'But that's what friends do, Zac.'

'No, Rivers, friends buy you a pint or lend you a T-shirt. We met three weeks ago and you're already housing me, feeding me, clothing me, and apparently employing me too.' He turned his back to her and stared out of her window at the bleak winter garden. 'I'm not your friend,

105

Rivers, I'm your project. I don't need this … this … attention.'

Her eyes stung but she blinked back her tears. She wasn't going to let him see her upset. This was ridiculous! She'd spent all evening yesterday rushing around. She wanted to show she cared and he was taking it the wrong way.

'What's your problem, Zac? I've been nothing but nice to you and you're throwing it in my face!'

He shrugged, walking to the sofa and putting on his trainers.

'Zac, don't go, I'll back off. I just worry about you out there. You can't keep sleeping rough.'

'I was fine before I met you and I'll be fine on my own. I don't need your charity.'

'Fine, fuck off!' she shouted, jumping to her feet. 'Fuck off back to your shed and your shitty bar job and your crap life. You aren't doing me any favours hanging around here.'

Zac bowed his head and reached for his black jumper.

'If I go now, you won't see me again,' he replied, his voice barely a whisper.

'I don't care. Just fuck off, *hijo de puta,* and stop fucking me about. I'm better off without you, anyway!'

He sighed again and nodded as he walked to the back door, his hand resting on the handle. Her room was silent but for the slow tick of a clock and her sobs. She was struggling to keep her chin from trembling so she jutted it out and cocked her head to one side, her hair falling over one eye. They stood staring at one another, but she wasn't going to be the first to look away, not any more.

Zac let go of the handle. Ella waited for him to say

something but instead he walked straight up to her. She stood her ground, rigid with anger and indignation.

'What are you doing?' she said.

'It's not what I'm doing that's the problem; it's what I'm not.' He placed a hand on either side of her face. 'There's one thing I need to do before I leave.' He tipped her face to meet his and kissed her. Their mouths moulded perfectly to one another's, his tongue parting her lips until she could taste the salt from her tears. She closed her eyes and melted into him, her arms hanging limply by her side. All too quickly, he stopped, but Ella remained still, her eyes half closed. She wanted to shout, say something, but she was rendered speechless.

'I didn't want it to end this way,' he said. 'But it should never have begun.'

Through her giddy fog, she watched him walk away and close the door behind him. He didn't look back.

So this was pain. Zac finally understood why he wasn't allowed to care and why he wasn't meant to feel. By the time he reached Ella's garden gate, she was screaming his name over and over again, each desperate cry like the call of an injured bird.

He pulled up his hood, shielding himself, and kept on walking. Of course he hadn't been insulted by her help – he was just waiting for an opportunity, an excuse, to leave behind the mess he had started. That was it, it was over. He'd finally walked away from her, his mission, and his unspeakable desire for the girl he couldn't have.

He'd done it for her – everything he had ever done had been for her. What a pity she would never know.

LONDON, 1940

We was always getting into scrapes, me and Dolly. We was like peas in a pod and closer than sisters. We lived near the docks opposite the Isle of Dogs. I ain't got a clue why they call it that, it weren't much of an island stuck there in the middle of the Thames and I never saw no dogs.

''Ere, take a gander at that one,' Dolly giggled as we walked through the docks on the way to Ma and Pa's shop. Oh, them saucy dockers! They had lovely strong arms what we'd take a peek at from under our brollies, I swear they would roll their sleeves up just so's they would press against their biceps like Popeye.

'What do you reckon that one has under his sleeve?' she asked. It was our favourite guessing game.

'A tin of baccy?' I said. 'A zipper lighter?'

'I reckon it's johnnies,' she shouted, loud enough so's he could hear. He looked up and we ran off laughing.

It was Dolly what got most of the whistles. She was a right looker – she'd had one or two callers but swore blind she never did nothing more than a peck on the cheek. Her real name was Dolores, which I thought was exotic. I really envied her for having a foreign name. Dolores Smith. My mum said Mrs Smith had ideas above her station and where did she get off calling her daughter such a fancy name what with her dad being just a builder and that. My chum hated it too, said it meant something horrible in Spanish or some such, so she called herself Dolly and oh, how she looked like one. I knew when we'd walk along the river, arm in arm, it weren't never me they was whistling at. 'He's looking at you, Evie,' she said, nudging me and opening her eyes wide. She had the biggest, roundest eyes I ever did see, like that Snow White *we went to the picture house to see once, but with bright blonde hair what she wore in the cutest bob.*

'Nice flower,' the docker shouted as we ran past. Dolly stopped, patted her hair, and dissolved into giggles.

I never knew how she did it but her hair swished when she walked, always nicely waved and never quite touching her shoulders. Every day she would pick a fresh flower to tuck into the ribbon on her hair or her lapel, like she was someone.

'Where you get them flowers from, Doll?' I asked her. She just shrugged and gave me one her smiles. I reckon it was easy to walk through life like everything was rosy when you looked like her.

'Look at that one over there,' she said, pointing at a sailing boat in the distance. 'That's the kind of boat my prince is gonna have. Sweep me off my feet, he will.' Dolly Daydream, I called her. Her head was always full of fanciful ideas. 'What was that song what Snow White sang?' she asked, skipping along the cobbles. 'One day my prince will come ...'

Off she went singing again, tiny like a delicate porcelain figurine what could shatter into tiny pieces if you hugged her too tight. She was a lot tougher than she looked.

'I'll be lucky if I end up marrying your prince's

servant boy,' I joked.

'Oh stop it. You're pretty as a picture with them big brown eyes of yours,' she said, whipping my hat off and fluffing up my hair. 'Stop hiding yourself away. Watcha have to be so shy about?'

I could feel my cheeks heating up. I hated my pale skin and red cheeks. They weren't rosy like Dolly's. She had that lovely blush going on where it looked like you had just told her a naughty joke. Mine were bright red and sore-looking from the cold wind, and there weren't nothing I could do about it.

'I just ain't as glam as you, Dolly. Look at my frizzy hair, it's the colour of dishwater.'

She shook her head and put her arm around my neck. 'What we gonna do with you, eh? You and your brother are the biggest lookers in our street.'

She had to love me to say such tripe. Although she was right about Ted, I'll give her that much.

Evie thought I was a right daft cow, but I'd always been a believer in love. Real true love. You know, the toe-curling, chest heaving kind what you get in books and them American films. I weren't naïve, I knew love could hurt, but I never knew it could kill.

Ted was Evie's brother and I'd known him all my life, although it felt a lot longer than that. He went to college and studied to be an accountant. His Pa was over the moon, thought he would take over the shop one day and make them rich, but Ted told us he was gonna work for a multi-national company. He had big plans, he did.

I don't know nothing about numbers or business and the like, but when Ted finished his studies and started as an apprentice in the local place up the high road, he wore a lovely suit and tie. He would look so dashing with brill cream in his hair and gold cufflinks you could practically feel a breeze from the sighs of the women he passed. Ted was an out and out gentleman. Even as a kid he weren't nothing like my three older brothers. They was brutes, used to pull my hair and call me names. Men's men they was, just like our old man. They had no time for women unless they was cooking for them. Evie was lucky having Ted as a brother. He was different.

Four years ago, on my fourteenth birthday, Mum bought me a new dress.

'You ain't a little girl no more, Dolores,' she said, looking me up and down. 'Time to get out of them short skirts and dress like a lady.'

I got a flowery yellow number with petticoats and a silky sash. Mum brushed my hair and scrubbed my face, showing me how to pinch my cheeks so I would look healthy.

'Stand up straight, and don't you be sticking your chest out or men will get the wrong idea.' I weren't quite sure what idea that was, but them girls what wore them bright colours and stood outside The Three Sailors at closing time, they made a big show of sticking out their knockers and I never wanted no one to think I was one of them.

I went straight round to Evie's that evening. Ted was there too, having his tea. I remember he was eighteen, 'cause me old man had been telling him it was high time he got his head out of them books and started courting some birds.

Ted smiled when he saw me then his face changed and

his eyes clouded over. It made me feel tingly, like he was thinking of a secret what he would only tell me. I was curious and excited and a little bit scared all at once.

'What we got here then? Give us a twirl, Señorita,' he said, and I did. I went round and round like one of them ballerinas, each time seeing his smile getting wider and Evie's face growing darker.

'Why do you always call me Señorita?' I asked him.

''Cause you got the face of a Dolly but the naughty sway of a Señorita.' He raised his eyebrows and I laughed. What a buzz that gave me when he spoke like that, like I was special.

'Oi, Ted. Leave her be. She's got enough brothers to tease her already,' Evie shouted.

He stopped because he knew his sister got jealous when we was friendly, but he gave me a big grin when she weren't looking.

Then suddenly Ted started having loads of girls around him. He must have been listening to me old man or something. He was no Jack the Lad, but he would have date after date for the local dinner and dance or to take to the flicks. Sometimes I would go round to Evie's house just to watch him get ready. He'd smooth down his dark hair and wink at me in the reflection of the mirror as he shaved. I could have stared at that face all day, I never knew whether it was the mirror what steamed up or my eyes going all dreamy.

I'd been working at Ma and Pa's shop since I was a kid. Well, it weren't real work 'cause I grew up among them shelves and counters. It was like I was skiving off school at first, but now I was eighteen it felt less fun. It was going

112

to be my job 'til I married.

'Ain't you glad you got out of them classrooms and come to work?' Ma used to say to me. 'Waste of time, sitting there all day filling your head with stuff you ain't never gonna use. About time you started earning your keep.'

Ma was nothing but sharp edges. She looked like she'd been made out of metal coat hangers. She always wore her hair pulled back tight at the neck, dark grey as a gun it was, and a halo of fuzz around the edges. She's where I got my frizzy hair from, and my thin lips. Not my eyes, though. Hers were small, dark and watery, like a couple of tiny fish in a milky pond.

'It's gonna be busy today, Evie,' she used to say when I first started working there. 'All this talk of war is making everyone panicky. Don't be too generous on your portions, eh, love.'

I'd nod and wrap the butter up in wax paper while Dolly would sit next to me. My parents was used to her always hanging about. The dairy counter was my favourite bit of the shop. I liked the smell of the cheese. I never said nothing to no one, that ain't something you say out loud, but I did. I liked the feel of cold butter too.

'Terence, them shelves are a bloody disgrace,' Ma shouted out, and went off looking for Pa. She was always harping on at my poor old man.

I loved my Pa. He looked just like a grocer should with his white hat and apron, round apple cheeks, and twinkling eyes. On quiet days he stood out front with his arms crossed, nodding at the neighbours and closing his eyes at the sunshine, smiling, always smiling. You couldn't tell when he was happy, mind you, because of his big moustache hiding his mouth, thick like a broom, and he was the only one I knew who could tickle your face with a kiss.

Pa was out the back having some soup out of a flask. I could see them from behind the counter.

'Terence! Will you stop slurping? What will the customers say!' Ma snapped, flicking him on the arm with a tea-towel. Ma always had something in her hand to hit you with; a wooden spoon, a newspaper, even a tin cup once. 'The pea soup is getting caught in your 'tache and making it green, it's disgusting.'

He looked up over the steaming cup and said, 'But my dear, how else am I meant to sieve the lumps out of it? I'd say I was the lucky one.'

Oh, how me and Dolly roared with laughter. We thought Ma was gonna wallop him again but she laughed too, then he put his arm around her skinny waist and she slapped him playfully. They was like that, squabbling like cat and dog but I saw him hold her hand under the counter sometimes and he would pat her bum when he thought no one was looking. I never knew nothing about love, not then, but I figured looking at them two that it must come in all sorts of shapes and sizes. You never know what you might get, and when it finally comes you ain't never ready for it.

It was 1940 when we was eighteen and I was working in the shop with Dolly and Ted. She had her job in the Post Office during the week and he had his office job, but Saturdays were our favourite because the shop was all ours while my old dears had a rest.

'Oh, you two don't 'alf make me laugh!' I said.

Dolly was singing that music hall song again, hummed it all blooming week she did. She was dusting shelves what didn't even need dusting and wiggling her bum when she got to the bit about dancing girls. Ted was throwing bits of broken biscuits in the air and catching them in his mouth, and when Dolly weren't looking he was aiming them at her arse. They had me in stitches.

When we was kids, my Ma used to make me and Ted pray every night. All I ever asked the angels for was to make Dolly my real sister. I knew it weren't never gonna happen, but looking at the way Ted and her were together, I started praying in my head that day. I started wishing for them to get together so she would be my real family. I knew that if she would only stop harping on about princes whisking her away, she could see just what a catch my brother was.

That afternoon I thought my wish was gonna come true. Ted started looking at her in a funny way. He weren't looking at her like you do when you look at someone, he was watching her like you do a stranger you think you recognise or like she was some rare and beautiful bird and he was too scared to move in case she flew away. She never had no clue. She was still too busy being Dolly Daydream, putting the wrong boxes on the shelf and wiggling her arse.

'You all right, Ted?' I asked. He looked surprised that I was still there.

'Yeah, sis. Right as rain.'

I had to think quick. 'I need to go and count the tins around the back. I may be some time,' I said this real loud so Dolly would hear me too. She never even looked up. I planned to sit on the back steps and count to a thousand, all the while listening. Not that I had any idea what falling in love would sound like.

'Where's that Evie got to?' I asked, looking about me. I loved helping out in the shop on my days off, it weren't nothing like working in the Post Office. For starters I got to stare at Ted as much as I liked. Not that he ever noticed. 'Skiving off again, is she?'

Ted shrugged. He was staring at me like I had something on my face. I ran my finger over my mouth.

'Quiet today, eh,' I carried on. 'Not much left to sell.'

We was all on rations. We managed all right at the beginning of the war, but now London was getting most of the stick. Fifty-seven nights in a bloody row them Germans threw bombs at us. We was living down our shelters most of the time, moaning about how hard it was to get decent eggs.

'I had another row with that old dear this morning,' I said, filling the silence. It was weird for Ted to be so quiet. 'She said the rations weren't big enough for her family. Funny how it's the fatter ones what make the biggest din. They never get no thinner though, eh!' He normally laughed at my jokes, but this time he just stood there. Staring. So I turned back around and carried on with my dusting.

Next thing I knew, he was right behind me. I wiggled my bum thinking he was going to chuck another biscuit at me, but when I looked up he was staring at me real funny still. I felt like all me brains had dropped to me belly, my head dizzy and me tongue all swollen.

'Dolores,' he said, which was weird 'cause he'd never called me by my full name before. His voice was

116

different, thick and eager.

'Yeah?' I knew that look. I weren't totally daft. I knew girls what used the start of the war as an excuse to drop their drawers for every sailor what so much as set foot on dry land, but not me. I believed in true love and I was saving that moment for the one man what would sweep me off my feet. 'Do you want something, Ted?'

But I could see what he wanted. His eyes were looking straight into mine. I couldn't explain it but I felt like I had found what I didn't know I'd been looking for.

He took my hand and I couldn't breathe. How silly was that! He'd held my hand hundreds of times as kids when we was playing, but when his fingers brushed mine I shivered. I know he noticed because he was smiling at me like he was a cat and I was a mouse. I thought he was gonna pounce on me on to them sacks of flour behind me, and I wouldn't have minded.

I always dreamed my true love would be a tall, dark stranger from some exotic land, but he weren't. He had known me all me life and was standing right in front of me.

'Mrs Green's waiting to pay, Ted. What you doing?'

We jumped and he let go of my hand as Evie walked back into the shop, like we'd been caught with our hands in the till. Ted mumbled something about getting to work and I avoided her looks. There was no way Evie would ever speak to me again if she thought I was sweet on her brother. I couldn't risk losing my best friend on a crush. Ted had plenty of girls to choose from. Surely he weren't thinking of me like *that*?

'It's time to shut up shop,' Ted said. It was only five o'clock but it was already pitch dark and bitterly cold outside.

'Ted, you should walk Dolly home. You've been in a funny mood all day,' Evie said, shoving him towards the door.

I was scared to look at him. I felt like the whole world would explode if he held my hand again. I followed him round the corner to Victoria Street. He didn't say a word and I didn't know what words to use neither. Everything seemed silly and unimportant all of a sudden.

We went round the back of the house – only sales people knocked on our front door, or posh visitors. Not that we ever had any of them. And of course, I never wanted me old dears to spot Ted neither, I wanted him to myself.

As soon as war had been declared my dad hadn't hung about. He'd had a rough time of it in the first war and said there was no way none of his near and dear was gonna suffer like his lot had. He had his own building company, so, along with my brothers, they dug out a shelter in the back garden and one in Evie and Ted's garden too.

Evie and I loved our shelters. We'd had to sleep down there most nights the last few months as they was dropping bombs left, right, and centre, though so far I never knew no one whose house got hit. But on Sundays when we weren't working, me and Evie, we'd take blankets and our rations of sweets down there and gossip for hours on them mattresses what my Pa had put down.

Ted and I stepped into the back garden and he looked at the bunker then at me, and I gave him a little nod, feeling for the key under the plant pot. He walked ahead down the stairs and it took every bit of strength in me not to reach forward and smell the back of his neck. I imagined it smelt of soap and Old Spice. I wanted to run my hands over his shoulders and kiss his smooth cheek. He'd only said one word to me in four hours, but already the ground was slipping away and he was the only one that could catch me.

I lit the gas lamp on the shelf and we sat down. He looked like he didn't know what to say; he was looking at me as if he we'd just met.

'Dolores,' he sighed, then he leant in and kissed me. It was the most sweetest kiss I've ever had. He was tender, his lips warm and soft, his hand holding mine while the other rested on my waist. I felt like an overripe strawberry what he was tasting for the first time. There was a low moan and I didn't know if it was mine or his. I wanted to lie back and feel those lips on every part of me. I wanted his hands to stroke across my belly and up under my blouse. I wanted to know what his fingers would feel like across my cold breasts that were already hard for him.

I had my eyes closed in that musty room and all I could smell was the warmth of the earth and the clean scent of his smooth neck, which I wrapped my arms tightly around. When he broke away his eyes were wide.

'Dolly, my beautiful Señorita, why did I never know this?'

Words were still failing me. His kiss had taken away my voice. I sat up, patted my hair, and straightened my ribbon. I had the man of my dreams next to me and all I could think of was my best friend Evie, sweet, trusting Evie, and how upset and angry she would be.

'We can't tell no one, Ted, especially not your sister.'

His hair had got messy and it made him look young and confused. He nodded and held my hand again.

'Dolores, I love you,' he said. 'I'll do anything to make you happy even if that means keeping us a secret. Please say you will step out with me, properly, let me take you out.'

I smiled and nodded, feeling silly around him like we was strangers all of a sudden.

That night I hugged my pillow tight and grinned from ear to ear. I was Teddy's girl and he loved me!

Everything changed after that strange afternoon and I blamed myself for meddling. Ted wasn't his usual fun self and Dolly was suddenly ever so busy with work and helping her Ma.

'Want to go to the flicks?' I asked her one day in the Post Office. I'd had to walk all the way to her work just to see her. We'd never spent so many days apart.

'Got to work til six,' she said, shuffling some papers and not looking at me.

So I thought I'd surprise her and waited outside the Post Office. Janey, that nosey girl she worked with, come out and I asked her:

'Where's Dolly got to?'

'Dolly left hours ago. She was all dolled up. You met her new fancy man?'

I couldn't believe my blooming ears. I could have gone to Doll's house myself and asked her what the bleeding hell was going on but I knew what she was like when there was a new fella on the scene and I figured she'd come running when she got bored.

'You've not seen a lot of Dolly, love,' Ma said as we prepared the carrots for Christmas lunch a few weeks later. 'You two had a falling out?'

'No, she's just busy. Her Ma's twisted her ankle so she's got to stay home and cook for the men.'

'But I just saw Mrs Smith in the butchers. There ain't nothing wrong with her. How peculiar.'

I sat round the dinner table Christmas Day and paid no thought as to how difficult it must have been for my Ma to give us such a feast with the rations she had been saving. Neither was I listening to Pa, who was going on at Ted about how he had done a deal with a farmer what supplies the veg for the shop and got us the best turkey on the street. I weren't paying attention at all. I was wondering why Dolly had lied to me and I was looking at my brother. Because he weren't listening neither, he was staring out the window and shovelling food down like there was no tomorrow.

'Ain't you gonna ask what I got you for Christmas?' I asked him.

He shrugged and carried on spooning peas into his mouth. He had hardly said two words to me all day.

'Got to go, sorry,' he said, running to the door.

'But I ain't brought the pud out yet,' Ma said. I felt bad for her – she'd made it months ago and was chuffed with it.

'I won't be long,' he said, his jacket not even done up as he shut the door behind him.

Pa shook his head. 'Only a pretty girl makes a man run away that fast when there's grub on the table!'

I sat on the mattress in the shelter waiting for Ted. When I heard his footsteps I was beside myself with excitement. I ran at him and took him by surprise. He lifted me, and as he lowered me down he stopped so we was face to face and he kissed me so hard I thought I was gonna faint.

Up until then we'd had a few kisses at the pictures, held hands, or he'd rested his hand on my knee when no one could see. But now, for the first time since our first kiss, we was all alone and my heart was racing.

'Happy Christmas,' he grinned into my neck, 'and how very, very happy it is indeed.'

My feet weren't yet touching the ground and I had my arms wrapped round his neck.

'I've only got fifteen minutes,' I said.

'I shouldn't be long either, my love. Evie has a right face on her. She misses you.' His words made my heart ache.

'We should tell her, Ted. It will be fine, I'm sure of it.'

'Let's just enjoy our alone time a bit longer, yeah? How about we tell her after New Year?'

I agreed with him. I always did. I would have walked over hot coals for him.

He liked the woolly socks I'd got him and a book about business stuff, thought they was very grown up presents and promised he would wear my gift on his first day back at the office.

'Them socks are just like us,' he said.

I wrinkled my nose up and said, 'What, stinky?' which made him laugh.

'No, a perfect pair. You and me, the only ones that fit together. Can't just have one sock can you? Without the other it would be useless.'

I thought that was about the most romantic thing anyone had ever said to me and I told him. He just rolled his eyes and said, 'Well, wait til you see your present then.'

I couldn't wait. I was wriggling about on that mattress like I had ants in me pants.

He reached inside his jacket pocket and pulled out a little box wrapped in red paper with a gold ribbon round it and handed it to me with a 'Ta da'. When I saw what was inside I nearly cried, honest, I had never seen anything so pretty. It was a white porcelain jewellery box painted with a gold pattern. I opened the clasp what looked like a tiny golden shell and lifted the lid and it played a lovely tune.

I kept winding it up over and over again, listening to it with my eyes closed, remembering how excited I'd been the first time Ted had taken me dancing. We'd danced cheek to cheek, his warm hand in mine. He had a way of holding my hand so's his thumb would stroke the inside of my wrist. I loved it, it gave me butterflies in my tummy and all sorts of other feelings in other places, I can tell you.

'She shall have music wherever she goes,' he said in a posh voice, then he took me in his arms and twirled me round and round, and we danced to my music box til I had no breath left.

When it was time to go he kissed me like that Rhett Butler had with his stroppy Scarlett in that picture *Gone With The Wind*, except I weren't fighting Ted off like that silly mare done. I knew then I didn't care what Evie or my family or his parents thought. I didn't care about exotic princes whisking me away or being the wife of a millionaire. I knew in that kiss on that magical day that I was going to be with this man for the rest of my life and we was going to get our own Happy Ever After.

New Year's Eve at the Three Sailors weren't no fun that year, not on me tod. Ted was there with his mates as usual and we tried our best not to look at each other. My old pair were with his Ma and Pa and they said Evie was feeling poorly so I sat with a small sherry and tried to pass the time with a few girls I recognised from our street.

I should have gone there and then to Evie's house and spoken to her. Maybe the whole thing might never have happened if I hadn't been such a coward. How I regretted afterwards choosing to sit in that smoky pub catching the odd glimpse of my Teddy over telling Evie the truth. I missed our chats and I missed her smile. I decided then enough was enough. I would take her out somewhere swanky the following week and tell her just how happy her brother made me.

New Year had been my worst yet. Dolly hadn't even popped by to see how I was feeling. It was business as usual a few days later. I went to open the shop and spotted a note tucked under the door. When I opened it and saw it was Dolly's handwriting my hands trembled. I was convinced she was already on a boat halfway to Timbuktu with her exotic lover. I read it out loud to myself.

Dearest Evie,
I know I have been acting ghastly the last month and you deserve an explanation. Please meet me Saturday night at 6 p.m. I would like to treat you to tea at the new

Montgomery-White Tea House in Cheapside. I will be waiting under the big statue of Wellington on his horse opposite Bank station. I've missed you so much.

I hope you can forgive me. D x

Well I never, I thought. She was up to something, that much I knew, but I never understood why she couldn't just pop in and tell me. I spent all day in the shop planning what to wear that weekend, how I'd press my best dress and nick Ma's only stockings and some lippy. It felt like I was stepping out with someone, which was silly as it was only Doll and I had never had so much as a kiss off no one, so what did I know about nights out? The Montgomery-White Tea House no less. Gawd blind me, that fancy man of hers must be rolling in it. It weren't cheap to eat out at such posh places and not in the middle of a blooming war neither. I knew that night was going to change everything.

Saturday night I set off early, which I knew was silly as Dolly weren't never on time, but it was going to take three buses and I didn't have a clue how she thought we was going to get home afterwards. What I should have done was leave at six so's that she would be the one waiting for me, but of course I never and I was there at half past five like a silly mare, freezing my arse off under that statue. The roads were busy and outside the Tube station there was a queue of people with overnight bags and blankets, waiting to get a space for the night.

Oh, how glad was I that we never had to do that because Dolly's Pa had been kind enough to build us a shelter. Not that I liked it much. That winter we'd all been down there more times than not, and each time it got worse and worse but Dolly loved it. She would make us take our books into that stinking hole and sneak biscuits out the shop. She said it was cosy and like a secret den. I hated it, the smell of the mud and knowing we was six feet under. Gawd, I felt like I was already blooming dead trapped under all that hot earth with them worms and maggots hiding in the muck, which made me laugh as the whole point of the shelter was to stop us dying in the first place.

I looked at them poor people standing in line waiting to shelter in the Tube station. Some had been there since the morning just to make sure they had a safe place to sleep away from Jerry's bombs. The queue was long and snaked all the way to the pillars of some fancy building behind me, the Foreign Exchange I think they called it, though I never knew what foreigners they was exchanging and what they was exchanging them for.

All sorts were in that line, mainly women and their snotty kids, some still in thin brown shorts, and in that weather! I can't say anyone looked too unhappy about spending the night in them tunnels, though I had regulars come to the shop and tell me they had had a right old giggle down in the stations during the air raids. Said there would be laughing, dancing, someone would play a tune on a tin whistle, and they would all have a sing song. Sounded just like New Year's Eve down at The Three Sailors. But I knew it couldn't have been that much fun; no one prefers to sleep in a stinking tunnel instead of their own comfy bed.

I'd been waiting for ages and was getting a bit scared. I'd never told me old pair or Ted where I was going as they would have me guts for garters. Two weeks before, a *load of bombs had gone and destroyed eight fancy churches and the Guildhall in the City and hundreds died. Course, four month ago was when all the bombs had really rained down. No one knew what to do with themselves and there weren't no one who didn't know someone what had been killed or hurt. Dolly's old man and mine talked about sending us away, keeping us safe, but the truth was there weren't nowhere we could have gone. We were grown ladies, not kiddy evacuees. So we done what Churchill told us to and toughed it out, acted like nothing was happening to our dear old London Town and just carried on as normal moaning about the cost of a loaf.*

Maybe that was where I went wrong. We should have been more scared, but you can't spend a year down a hole in your back garden eating out of tins. That's worse than dying.

It was a cold night and I was regretting having worn Ma's thin stockings so I wandered around a bit to keep warm.

'You joining us, dear?' an old lady asked, making room in the queue.

I smiled. 'Oh no, just waiting for a friend.'

I never knew how long was polite to wait for someone, but the war weren't a time for punctuality 'cause you never knew what kind of problems there might be on the road, so I tried to be as patient as I could. I was getting nervous about Dolly's news, and I was starving. I'd spent all day dreaming of the ten different teas they was meant to have in that tea house. Cakes and tarts too by my reckoning.

By half seven I was about ready to eat my own bloody

hat I was so hungry. I'd had a gander through the Tea Room window once at them toffs biting into the biggest cream tarts you ever did see, so much filling they'd be laughing on account of the cream getting stuck on their noses. Being in there would have been like there weren't no war at all, how I cursed Dolly for ruining it. I was starting to fret too 'cause I had to be home by nine o'clock weekend nights and was worried that maybe something had happened to her, or she'd run off with her Prince after all and I would never see her again. I suppose I was right in a way.

It was bitterly cold that Saturday and I was bored stiff at work.

It was only a Post Office and it was the same people what came in day after day. There ain't much fun to be had with rolls of brown paper and stamps. The delivery boys was cheeky and they always cracked a joke, made the day go quicker, but most of the time me and Janey would have a natter when Mr Pervy Percival weren't looking.

'Out again with your fancy man tonight?' she asked.

She was right nosey. She never had many suitors of her own, which I reckoned was on account of her thick glasses and two fat moles on her cheek, they was a bit hairy an' all, but she loved to hear the ins and outs of everyone else's love life, especially mine. I pretended I was being wined and dined by a French Count. I weren't gonna tell *her* the truth, she was right dim anyway and I could spin her any old yarn. Ted and I would always laugh about it afterwards.

'Where's he taking you this time, Doll?' she asked

again, but I just smiled and said nothing.

I'd told Evie to meet me at six o'clock as I wanted to get back home, change, and do my hair. I was nearly more excited than when I would get ready to see Ted. At least this time I wouldn't get a load of hassle off Ma about who I was seeing and telling me not to step out with too many men.

It was so dark now at night 'cause they never let you have any lights on. It always made me nervy. I had just rounded the corner of Victoria Street when I felt two strong arms wrap themselves round my waist from behind and spin me round. Blimey, I thought I was a goner. I went to scream but was stopped with a kiss.

'Bloody hell, Ted!' I shouted. 'You nearly gave me a bleeding heart attack; you scared the living daylights out of me.'

I couldn't stay angry at him for long, he was grinning like a Cheshire cat.

'Come on,' he said pulling at my arm, 'let's get down the shelter. I have something for you.'

'I can't, Ted, I have to meet Evie. I'm telling her about us, remember? I only have two hours and I want to get ready before I catch the bus.'

He held my hand and looked deep into my eyes. There was no way I was gonna say no to him. Whatever it was he had to say weren't going to wait.

'Oh, all right then,' I said, 'but you're gonna have to catch me first,' and I squealed as he ran behind me all the way to my back gate.

The lights were off in the house – the men were still at work and Ma went round to me Nan's on Saturday afternoons. I'd been looking forward to having a bath in peace and the hot water to myself, but at least this way I had some time with Ted without worrying that anyone would walk through the garden and catch us.

I could sense his eagerness. He was practically pushing me down them steps and his big smile was lighting up the dingy room. I locked the door and he pulled me down onto the big brass bed. My old man had had to do up an old house what got bombed and they let him keep two big beds which he had stuck down there. Ted had laughed when I first told him, said he was pretty sure Pa wouldn't have done that if he had known his little girl was gonna be down there with a fella.

'Go on then,' I begged, 'tell me.'

He took a deep breath. 'Alderman, Meyers & Sons have gone and employed me as an Accountant. I am going to be earning three hundred and twenty-six pounds ten shillings a year! They even gave me a bit in advance for the work I done for them last year.'

I weren't too smart with numbers like him but I knew that was more than six pounds a week. That was the most amount of money I'd ever heard of. I wrapped my arms around his neck and told him how happy I was for him.

'Wait up, there's something else,' he said, his lips twitching and his eyes dancing.

I didn't think I could take much more. He pulled a box out from inside his jacket and it felt like Christmas all over again. I was hoping it would be another music box, that would be just too much. This box weren't wrapped in paper though, it was black and velvet. I prised it open and inside was a gold ring with three light purple stones arranged in a higgledy-piggledy pattern.

'I didn't plan to do it like this, but I couldn't wait,' he

said, all breathless. 'Dolores, would you do me the honour of being my wife?'

I was shaking. I didn't know what to do. Handsome, wonderful Ted Brown, the rich accountant, wanted to make *me* his wife? I thought he had to be pulling my leg, then I saw he was looking at me funny 'cause I still hadn't said nothing.

'Of course,' I squeaked. As if I would have said anything else.

He kissed me long and hard and I melted in his arms, my fiancé's arms. That was going to be my new favourite word, fiancé. How posh did that sound! I planned to use it in every one of my sentences.

'It's amethyst,' he said, slipping it on my finger. 'I know it ain't traditional, but I got it in that antiques shop in Hatton Garden. They reckon it was once part of a set. This is the engagement ring then there was another one what fit next to it for marriage, and a necklace too. They showed me an old painting of some foreign lady wearing it hundreds of years ago, but they've no idea what happened to the rest of it. You've always loved lilac and it matches your eyes.'

'I love it,' I told him, and I meant it. 'Isn't it the most precious thing you've ever seen?'

'No,' he said. '*You* are. Dolores, I want to dedicate my life to making you happy. I am going to shower you with gifts every day, show you the world like the princess you are. You will want for nothing.'

'I already have everything,' I said.

The excitement was making me flushed. It was brass monkeys outside but deep underground with them gas lamps I was getting hot. I took off my coat and unbuttoned my collar. When I looked up, Ted's eyes was misting over like that time I twirled round for him when we was kids.

'You are so beautiful,' he said.

Well, his eyes might as well have been his hands 'cause every part of me shuddered. I was getting even hotter sitting next to him under his stare. Then I thought about it, this weren't Ted from down the road no more what was looking at me that way, he was my future husband. That handsome face was going to be the first thing what I saw every morning and last thing at night. His eyes would be the only ones that I would ever let look at me, and his hands the only ones I would ever let touch me.

'Dolly, let's get married straight away,' he said, shifting closer to me.

'A rushed winter wedding? Don't be daft, people will talk.'

'I don't care, I want you so much. I will buy us a big house and we will fill it with loads of beautiful kids, just like their mum. We are going to be so happy, Doll. I've waited all my life for you and I can't wait another day.'

Bleeding hell! I was so excited. We were going to have a lovely wedding, war or no war. I told him we should marry on Valentine's Day. I could see me standing outside the little church at the end of our road, him with his smart suit and me with a red rose in my hair.

Well, I thought, if we was just weeks away from being man and wife then I never had to hold back no more. I never had to worry about Ted thinking I was forward. I loved him and we was going to be together for ever. I weren't thinking about my tea with Evie, or when me old

132

man was coming home or even what people might think. All that existed was me, Ted, and these feelings of pure bliss.

I stood up, not taking my eyes off him, and unbuttoned the rest of my blouse slowly. He swallowed and didn't blink once as I let it slip down my arms and onto the floor. I wriggled out of my skirt and petticoat and kicked them under the bed. I couldn't believe I was being so brazen but I wanted him so much it hurt. I had done since he first said my name in that breathy way in the shop. He just sat there, too scared to say a word in case he broke the spell. I took everything off til I was totally starkers but for my girdle, panties, and stockings.

He stood up and kissed me, slowly at first then stronger until I was panting and aching.

'Dolores,' he breathed. He said my name over and over again as he kissed down my neck and collarbone, then stopped at my bare breasts that were reaching out to him. He licked and kissed one and then the other. I never knew men done that! My knees went weak like in the movies. I'd heard about having to lay down when you was married, do your wifely duties and all that, but the girls in the Post Office what laughed and joked about it made it sound like it was ever so boring. But this, this was like floating on a cloud, so I reckoned I must have been doing it wrong. Then I looked at Ted and realised that maybe they was the ones what had been doing it wrong all along. I was the lucky one.

He threw off his jacket, loosened his tie, and pulled his shirt off, throwing it to the dusty ground. For a minute I wondered what he was gonna say when he got back home covered in dry mud, but it was only a fleeting thought 'cause I looked at his hard chest and strong arms, which were better than any of them down on the docks, and I forgot about everything else.

'Are you sure you want to do this, darling?'

'Bit late to ask, ain't it,' I laughed. Me knees were shaking but it weren't that unpleasant. 'You've seen it all now, anyway.'

He gave me that smile of his and his hand started to stroke up my ankle, behind my knee, and past my garter belt.

'Not quite everything.'

I let my head fall back onto that big brass bed and told him to do whatever he wanted with me. I was his and I wanted every bit of him.

He was ever so gentle, kissing and stroking me, telling me he loved me over and over. When he finally put it inside me I was ready to burst! All that gossip I heard about it hurting and bleeding and stuff was just nonsense, it was the most glorious thing in the world. Ted and I were like one person and every move he made took me that bit further until he cried out my name and I clasped his damp hair and pulled his head into my neck.

We lay like that for ever, our sweaty chests sticking to one another, his breathing in time with mine. How I wished we was already man and wife and we could have just gone to sleep like that.

'Oh,' I suddenly cried. 'What's the time?'

I could have died. I had left Evie standing there in the bleeding cold for all that time after the way I had been treating her. I felt rotten.

'Why on earth did you say you'd meet her all the way out there?' Ted shouted when I told him where I was meant to be. 'You should have met at the shop and gone together,' he said.

He was right. What had I been thinking?

It weren't safe in the city and now she was on her own.

'Oh, Dolly. This is all my fault!' he cried. 'I'll get Pa's delivery van and drive you. I'll join you both, we can tell her our wonderful news together. She'll soon forgive us for keeping her waiting when we ask her to be Maid of Honour!'

We was grinning and laughing like fools as we stumbled up them wooden steps to the shelter door, thinking what a wonderful evening we was going to have, not knowing Hitler had other plans.

I'd had just about enough of standing there waiting for that Dolly Daydream. Who did she think she was, the Queen of bloody Sheba?

I was about to head back to the bus stop when I heard a humming noise getting closer and all the people in the queue looked up. There was no warning this time. Nothing. How I hated that noise. It went right through you like a hot knife through butter, dissolving your guts so's you'd feel them fall at your feet. Them planes haunted my dreams. Normally they was way off in the distance but this time we could see the numbers on the bottom of them.

The last of the people were making their way down the Tube steps.

'Come on, girl. Get down there,' one man shouted at me as he hurried down to the station steps. I was the only one left on the street, standing as still as the horse statue I was waiting beneath.

An old lady ran up to me and yanked my sleeve. 'Oi,

love, come with us,' she said. 'I have a spare blanket. Just wait it out til you know them bastards have gone. Ain't nothing going to happen to you down here. Safe as houses.'

I never wanted to go, really, I never. I avoided the Tube if I could, hated them closed in tunnels and that thick air. In the end I ran down with her to the ticket hall what was rammed with people, most trying to get to the platforms lower down. The old lady weren't having none of it and barged her way through, dragging me behind her by my sleeve, and we headed for the wooden escalators.

Blimey, what a sight. People was everywhere, not quite sleeping but lying down where there was space. Small kids dozing on their ma's coats on each step and dockers having a fag on the metal partitions. One of them winked at me, the cheek of him! I tiptoed over some of the sleeping bodies, giving them my best 'pardon me' voice, and when I got to the bottom I looked up and thought it was like something from them devilish paintings you see in Sunday school, a load of tumbling bodies falling into the pits of hell. That's what that was, a huge pile of people waiting to die, like rats scrambling on top of each other to find an inch of space to call their own.

And the stench! Gawd blimey, it was like what you got if you was unlucky enough to be passing the alley near the docks when the pubs turn out. The stink of piss and body odour was so bad I thought it was probably better to be shot by a bloody Nazi than die of suffocation down there.

Everyone was chatting and calling out to each other like they was all mates. There was even one woman with her rollers in, slapping Ponds cream on like it was her own private bedroom. No one looked all that happy though – I never saw no dancing or tin whistles.

Then it started. At first it was just a rumble and I thought it queer that we could hear anything at all. Then a dull thud. I don't know where the old lady got to, but I threw myself against them filthy grey walls and pushed my fingers against their grimy sooty tiles. Dust started to fall and I saw a woman wipe it off her little boy's face like it was the first snowflakes of winter. Then more fell.

I tried not to stare at them strange faces, keep myself to myself, but then there was an almighty explosion and I looked up and my breath stopped.

A young chap stood alone at the base of the escalators, staring at me. He didn't move an inch as white dust and debris rained down around him. I wondered what anyone that dashing was doing stuck down this stinking hole. As handsome as a film star he was, only better because he was in full colour and he was looking straight at me. He had the brightest blue eyes I ever did see.

I hardly noticed the commotion. His stare was pinning me to the wall, and me and him were the only ones what weren't screaming.

Then the ceiling started to fall in, great chunks of brick and plaster exploding at my feet, but I kept my eyes focused on his. I reckoned if the blue of his eyes was the colour of tropical seas maybe I would fall into them and be washed away to safety. A baby was crying, a high-pitched scream like a siren, and it went on and on and on, then it stopped. Everything stopped. Everything went black and there just weren't no noise any more. There was nothing.

I tried to open my eyes but they was all crusty and tight. I went to rub them with my hand but my face felt wet and my hand was sticky with the smell of metal, the smell of blood. I went to get up but my legs wouldn't move neither. Something heavy was lying on top of them. The dust was clearing and through a small gap in the rubble I could make out some shapes. Strange thing it is to see people lying face down, and even stranger to see legs when they ain't no longer at the end of a body. Everyone was the same colour, all dark grey and very still. A few faint moans was coming from the tunnels and I heard shouting and some man holler.

'There ain't no bloody emergency lights down here,' he was shouting. 'We can't help no one. Shout if you can hear us.'

Well, I ain't one for drawing attention to myself but I tried, truly I did, but nothing came out. I could only see out my right eye, the other one was glued shut and I never had the energy to try and move my hand again.

Then he appeared. A beautiful face without a speck of dust on it was looking at me through that hole in the rubble. He moved the pieces of plaster away, but it was useless 'cause it only made more fall. His bright blue eyes were bearing down on me and I remember thinking what a sight I must be. He looked so sorry, as if the carnage had been his fault.

He reached through the hole and held my hand tight like he was never letting go. I looked deep into them eyes knowing they was the last thing I was ever gonna see, but that was OK, they was lovely. Then it came to me, this was him. The one I had always loved, and oh how I loved him. I knew that the other stuff never mattered no more, and that it never really had.

He smiled at me, those cornflower eyes creasing at the

corners, then he spoke.

'It's all right, Evie, I'm here and I won't leave you. I promise.'

And you know what? He never did. He was there with me until the very end, and then he carried me Home.

PART TWO

'You pierce my soul. I am half agony, half hope.'

Jane Austen, *Persuasion*

CHAPTER TEN

Zac had kissed her. His words had killed her but his kiss had brought her back to life, she had felt his pain, his regret, but most of all, his need for her. It had been the closest she had got to discovering his truth and now he was gone.

Ella called out until her throat was sore and his name was unrecognisable. She ran after him, her socks soaked through on the dewy grass, but she was too late.

For weeks, she was thrown between anger and sorrow and eventually settled on common sense. She still had Zac's money, his clothes, and his mobile phone in the bag he had left in her bedroom, so surely he had to return eventually? She would see him again, she just had to wait.

Ella pulled down her woollen hat and checked her laces again. She had already been for a jog, but she was restless and wanted to kill some time until her parents left the house. Even the sight of them irritated her. Felicity had offered her daughter a weak apology for her behaviour during the disastrous tea with Zac, and Ella had done the same, although they had both done so to appease Richard. Ella was still angry but no longer had the energy to care.

'Darling, your water.' Her mother passed her a plastic bottle and applied her lipstick in the hall mirror. 'I have to say, sweetie, I am very impressed you've taken up exercise at last, although we have a perfectly lovely, and warmer, gym downstairs. Never mind, you've got to tighten up those bum cheeks somehow now you're back on the market.'

Ella snatched the water from her mother's hand.

'I was never *off* the market, Mum. I told you, Zac wasn't my boyfriend.'

'Darling, you have been mooning about with that face on you for two weeks. Honestly, he wasn't right for you. I told you there was something …' she waved her hand dismissively, 'I don't know, *unusual*, about him.'

Ella knew there was something different about Zac but it didn't scare her – it just made her want him more. And she hadn't been bloody sulking, she had actually been worried. How could he have lasted a fortnight with no change of clothes or money? The weather had turned for the worse and the thought of him huddled under those ratty blankets every night made her chest ache.

'Yeah, well, I'm fine. As I said, he was just a friend.'

'Was? Well, you know the best way to get over a man?' asked her mother.

'Get under another?'

'Oh don't be crude! No, a change of direction. Recreate yourself; come out of your dark cloud shining as fabulously as the sun.'

Her mother was so full of bullshit. Ella opened the front door and winced as the cold air hit her. She tightened her ponytail and sighed at her mother, who was stretching her arms up like a rainbow.

'Whatever,' Ella said, running into the wind.

144

Her daily route took her past Zac's park but she never went in, scared of finding herself face to face with him. But that morning, whether it was her mother's remarks or the realisation that he was probably never coming back, she changed her mind and headed through the large black gates, down the winding path toward the ponds. She planned what she would say to him. She would play it cool and stay calm – she didn't want him to know how upset she had been.

She sped up as the tennis courts came into view and pulled her scarf tighter. The park gates would be closing soon and she wondered how Zac got in and out when he worked so late. As she approached his tiny shed her heart missed a beat. The door was open. Zac must be in there. She slowed down and nudged the door wider with her foot.

'Zac? It's me, Ella.'

She hesitated then stepped inside. It was empty. There was nothing on the shelves, the mattress was torn and covered in cigarette burns, and the hole in the concrete beneath it was now full of beer cans and a screwed up box of condoms. The inside of the door had been scrawled with graffiti and the little window was smashed. Ella felt sick.

She backed out, as if the vandals who had destroyed his meagre home would be after her next, and ran back in the direction of her house. She had to find him. She glanced at her watch and calculated that she could be home, changed, and on her way to Indigo within half an hour.

* * *

Camden was no longer the chilled-out place it had first seemed. Ella walked along the lock and shivered at her reflection in its cold surface, its hundreds of years of debris lying hidden in its muddy depths.

She folded her arms and looked around. She shouldn't have come alone. There was no one standing outside the bar this time and she had to look closely at the strange symbol on the door to check she had the right place. What was it Kerry had said about that sign?

She knocked three times and waited, nibbling at the skin around her thumbnail. She knocked harder and stumbled forward as the door was opened by a tall woman wearing a thick silver necklace which shone against her mahogany skin. Her midnight-coloured uniform was tight across her braless chest and flat midriff. Ella felt like a pathetic schoolgirl beside her.

'Yes?' The woman's voice was as velvet as her skin.

'I would like to see the manager, please,' Ella said. 'I'm a member of Indigo and I am looking for my friend who works here.'

The woman stepped to one side and motioned her in with her eyes.

'I am the manager. Who are you looking for?'

'Zac. He works here, at least he does on Fridays.'

The manager blinked slowly and shook her head from side to side.

'He's about six foot,' Ella continued. 'His hair is dark with thick curls and comes to just above his jaw, and he has the bluest, most amazing eyes you've ever seen. Believe me, you would know who he was.'

'Girl, you have it bad,' the manager said without smiling. 'No one called Zac works here.'

The woman's face remained stony.

'He does! I was here a few weeks ago and he was working.'

'Was he behind the till?' the woman asked.

'No.'

'Was he serving drinks?'

'No.'

'Was he working the doors? The cloakroom? DJing, perhaps?'

Ella looked down at the floor, comparing her muddy boots with the manager's turquoise suede heels.

'No, he cleared up a glass I dropped. But I know he works here, he had on the same T-shirt as yours.'

She raised an eyebrow and walked them back to the entrance. Ella gave it one last shot.

'He picked up his wages, I think it was on the twenty-ninth of October.'

'Were you with him? Did you see him speak to me?'

Ella shook her head. It was aching and the hard ball in her throat was making it hard for her to swallow. She muttered a quick thanks and left. Zac was gone, properly this time. He had warned her that if he left he wasn't coming back and he had been telling the truth.

As soon as Ella got back home she took out Zac's grey hoodie, the only evidence he had ever existed, and held it to her face as she cried.

Zac watched Ella every day. The invisible ties between them were keeping him anchored, and it was impossible to do anything but stay. Perhaps if he could see she was all right without him he would finally be able to leave for good.

Each morning he sat in the same café in Pond Square opposite the entrance to Ella's road. Wearing a baseball cap and nursing a strong black coffee he would wait until he saw her familiar silhouette jog to the corner of her road. There, she'd bend down, as she did every morning, and retie the laces on her trainers. She would stretch, put her headphones in, and adjust her black woollen hat so it came down low over her eyebrows. He noticed that the grey sweatshirt she wore was too large, and she rolled up the sleeves, occasionally bringing the faded fabric up to her nose to take a deep breath, her gaze settling on the doorway of the blue charity shop across the road. She would then run as if her life depended on it, past the shops, down the hill, and past the park. If the weather was dry her run would take between thirty-four and thirty-nine minutes. She didn't like the rain, so on a bad day she would take a shorter route and be back in the square after twenty.

The two women that ran the café had a nickname for Zac, they called him Mister E. The first time he had entered, they had jostled each other out of the way, eager to serve the handsome man with the piercing eyes. He had greeted them with a warm smile and they had given him a complementary plate of homemade mini muffins. Their disappointment was obvious when he had taken his plate to the window seat and spent an hour staring out on to the awakening high road before leaving, his coffee and cakes untouched.

The following day he had done the same: ordered a black coffee, sat at the window for an hour, and left without taking a sip. The café was normally busy at that time, but when it wasn't, the girls would speculate as to who he was and what he was looking at. They decided that he was a secret agent who was working under surveillance on one of the town houses across the square.

They would never understand that he was simply waiting for the day Ella stopped wearing his baggy grey sweatshirt, as that would be the day she could survive without him and he could go home.

CHAPTER ELEVEN

Felicity called a family meeting. She never referred to them as such, she would simply declare 'Let's all have dinner together' which meant she had something important to announce.

Ella, Richard, and his wife sat at the same table where they had taken afternoon tea at with Zac nearly a month ago. In her mind, Ella could hear the melancholic strums of his guitar playing and she swallowed down the ache in her throat.

'Oh, isn't this lovely, darling. All of us round the table together. We haven't seen a lot of you lately.'

Ella shrugged. 'You haven't been around much.'

Her mother passed her a plate of smoked salmon blinis.

'What are your plans for Christmas, Ella? A beautiful, single girl in London this time of year must have lots of exciting things in her diary.'

Ella popped two blinis in her mouth and chewed quickly.

'I'm sure she must, Mum. I, on the other hand, will keep going to uni until we break up next week then doss about the house in my pyjamas watching films. I'm such a disappointment, I know.'

Richard hid a smile behind his napkin.

'And Christmas Day?' she asked.

'I don't know, you tell me,' Ella said. 'By the way, is this a starter or our whole dinner because I'm bloody starving? Most mums make casseroles and pies in the winter, not crappy fish on a biscuit.' She knew she was being a bitch but she still blamed her mother for scaring Zac away.

Felicity sighed and walked to the kitchen. How come her mum was serving dinner and not Ylva? This must be serious if she had let the housekeeper go home early. Felicity was saying something in the kitchen, something about America, but Ella couldn't hear her. She returned with a dish of homemade lasagne, which was obviously not homemade by her, and a large bowl of chunky chips. It was Ella's favourite childhood meal, so whatever her mum wanted to tell her she wasn't going to like it.

Felicity sat in front of her, her elbows on the table and her hands clasped together as if in prayer.

'As I was saying, Christmas in New York will be great fun.' Felicity's voice was injected with forced enthusiasm. 'Although we'll be back by the end of the month. Not going to miss Cloud Ninety-Nine's New Year's Eve launch, of course.'

Of course, how could Ella forget? It was all anyone had spoken about in her house since the last New Year. Cloud Ninety-Nine was going to be the tallest restaurant in the world on the top of the world's tallest hotel. Richard's hotel. Whatever. It was hard to get excited about anything any more. Ella served herself a large slice of lasagne, took a handful of chips, and went to the kitchen for mayonnaise.

'You're leaving me? At Christmas?' she shouted.

'No, no, of course not,' Richard said. 'I would – I

mean, *we* would love to have you there. We can have the Penthouse at the Manhattan hotel and skate outside the Rockefeller Center, like they do in films?'

Ella returned to the table and saw the look that passed between her mother and Richard. So going to New York had been Felicity's idea? Ella couldn't think of anything worse than being stuck in a hotel with two people that wanted to be alone. She did her best impression of looking disappointed.

'Oh, it sounds magical, but my friend Mai Li invited me to go skiing and I said I wasn't sure as I didn't want to ruin any plans you had. But you will have a much more romantic time without me.'

'Not at all, pumpkin,' spluttered Richard. 'We would love for us to be together as a family.'

Felicity smiled and touched Richard's hand.

'Come now, darling. Ella isn't a child any more and she wants to be with friends. She'll have a better time on the slopes than with us. Anyway, Sebastian won't be there either so it wouldn't strictly be a family gathering. Hopefully he will be back by the New Year and we can celebrate together then.'

Ella's flesh crawled at the mention of her step-brother. At least if her parents were away and he thought she was too, there would be no chance of him returning home early. Felicity clapped her hands and began to clear away the dishes while Richard and Ella were still eating.

'I'm glad that's done and dusted,' she said. 'It's worked out perfectly for everyone. Perhaps Richard and I will leave for the States earlier now you aren't coming, Ella.'

Felicity returned, holding a tray of Belgian chocolates

which she put in front of her husband.

'They aren't for you, Ella. Oh, go on then, you can have one but don't go crazy. They are full of calories and this is a very difficult time of year to stick to diets.' She sat beside her husband then jumped up again. 'Oh, I nearly forgot, we didn't tell her about the party, Richard!'

Ella grabbed three chocolates and hid them under her serviette, waiting for her mother to get on with it. Her favourite soap was starting in ten minutes and she had hoped this ordeal would have been over by now.

'Richard and I have been invited to the wrap party for the movie they've been filming at one of the hotels. They're having a huge do at a private house in Mayfair. You must come, darling. In fact, I think you may know one of the actors – he goes to your school. His father is the director.'

She didn't know any actors and she hated the fake small talk she had to do at these events. Not to mention the embarrassment of posing for photos and reading the crap they would write about her afterwards.

'*Uni* is a big place, Mum, I hardly know anyone,' she replied.

'Please come. It'll be such fun. It's fancy dress!'

Ella rolled her eyes. Fancy dress was embarrassing enough, let alone with her parents in tow,

'What's the theme?'

'Historical Greats. I'm going as Cleopatra and Richard as Anthony, won't that be a scream!'

Felicity was jumping on the spot. It was times like these that Ella remembered just how young her mother actually was. Maybe it *would* be fun, even just to see her mother's face when she realised she was one of fifty

Cleopatras. More hysterical than historical. She smiled at her own joke, and her mother took that as a yes.

As much as Ella fought against it, she was actually a bit excited about the wrap party. She had invited Mai Li, but her parent's restaurant was fully booked the last Friday before Christmas so she hadn't been allowed the time off work. She would have asked Kerry too, her friend would have killed for the chance to meet the rich and famous, but she had gone to visit her mum in Australia for Christmas. Ella had to face the music alone – or with her parents, which was essentially the same thing.

'You have to be joking, Mum. I can't wear this.'

Ella stared at her reflection. She hardly recognised herself. She was being fitted for her costume but it was not what she had expected.

'Helen of Troy had the face that launched a thousand ships, sweetie,' her mother said, looking at their reflection over her daughter's shoulder. 'She wouldn't have worn a toga like a bed sheet, would she!'

Ella pulled the silky white folds of fabric that cascaded over her chest and adjusted her elaborate golden headdress. She would have to take safety pins in her handbag – lots of them.

'Fine, but she wouldn't have looked like something out of a Kylie music video either. Honestly, Mum, what if I stumble and my boob falls out?' Ella pulled the fabric at her chest. 'Seriously, it needs adjusting. And the wig is itchy, I'm not wearing it. I'll just have my hair a bit posher. Since when were women from Ancient Greece blonde, anyway?'

Ella was getting far too worked up over a party she

didn't want to go to, but it was her first night out in the 'public eye', as her mother called it, since she moved to London and it was making her jittery.

She climbed out of her golden stiletto sandals and thanked the dressmaker, who looked relieved to be leaving. The party would do Ella good. Maybe she would have some fun for once and stop feeling sorry for herself. There was life after Zac. He hadn't exactly livened things up, anyway.

Ella blinked away the flashes from dozens of cameras crowding the entrance to the party and looked up the red carpeted stairs. There weren't as many people as she feared, and most were only a little older than her. The music was loud and everyone had a full glass of wine in their hand. The night was looking promising.

'There are two Cleopatras in there!' her mother hissed as she came out of the bathroom. 'We haven't got to the main hall yet and I've already seen two. Oh Lord, there's another. Richard said my idea was ingenious, but I'm not as original as I thought, am I, darling?'

Ella felt sorry for her. She should have warned her this would happen.

'But you are definitely the sexiest Cleopatra here, Mum. Look at that one, she's huge and her wig isn't on straight. Actually, I think she might be a man.'

The women laughed and linked arms, and for a moment Ella forgot that she wasn't meant to like her mother. Richard handed them each a glass of wine.

'Happy early Christmas to my two favourite girls,' he said, and they clinked glasses. 'Ah, there's the man himself, the director no less. Paolo, meet my beautiful wife and daughter.'

A short dark man sauntered over dressed in a simple suit with a cigar in his hand.

'Lovely to see you again, Richard. Or should I call you Emperor Fantz?' he chuckled, and turned to Felicity, kissing her hand. 'And here is the captivating Cleopatra and, let me guess, a young beauty with a striking air of indifference. This must be Ella of Troy?'

The three of them laughed and Ella wondered how long the fancy dress jokes would last.

'What have you come as?' Ella asked the director.

'Why, Hitchcock of course. The greatest of historical greats.'

'And where is your American beauty this evening, Paolo?' asked Richard, scanning the crowd.

'Serena couldn't come, she is a little under the weather. I came with my son, Josh, he plays a small part in my film. He's been looking forward to seeing you again, Ella.'

She looked in the direction the film director was pointing in and saw the back of a young man talking to a group of girls, all looking at him adoringly. She recognised him immediately – Joshua De Silva, the 'Actor Slash Model'. Ella felt a little guilty at her lack of excitement knowing her friends would have done anything to be in her shoes right now.

'Yes, we met briefly at Indigo,' she said. *But I was too busy falling at the feet of the mysterious bar man*, she wanted to add. She hadn't said goodbye to Josh that night, Zac was all that had mattered then. Perhaps now was time to let Zac go? Josh was cute and he obviously liked her.

Paolo and her parents talked about film locations and

PR opportunities while Ella zoned out and looked around. It was like a game of Where's Wally. She counted three Marylin Monroes, four Elvises (or should that be Elvi?), and at least ten Queen Elizabeth the Firsts. One woman had even come as Margaret Thatcher, which was brave, unless the middle-aged woman always wore lacquered hair and pussy bows.

'Ella? Ella!' Her mother was jabbing her arm with her sharp red talons. 'She's always away with the fairies. Darling, there's someone I'd like you to meet.'

Richard and the director had disappeared, and in their place stood a tall, Roman soldier. His costume made Ella feel uneasy, although his face was partially hidden.

'You are like Helen herself staring out to sea – a sea of celebrities in this case,' the soldier said. 'You look mesmerizing, Ella. I shall call you Helen of Joy.' He bowed to her, his helmet wobbling to the side.

'Darling, this is Rupert. His father is one of our biggest investors,' Felicity said. 'He was very interested to hear that you study psychology. He's a doctor, you see.'

Ella shook his clammy hand.

'Your mother is too kind,' he said. 'I'm not actually a doctor, but I do have a doctorate in Neuroscience.'

'You're a scientist?' Ella asked.

'No, I'm still a student, but I may become a lecturer one day. At the moment I am happy to spend my time lapping at the waters of the fountain of knowledge. In fact, I stick my swimming cap on and dive straight into it every day, let every drop wash over me!'

He laughed like a donkey with laryngitis. Ella's mother smiled and nodded her head encouragingly.

'I can see you two will get on famously. Please excuse

me, I have just seen an old friend.'

Ella's shoulders sagged. Her mother didn't have any friends, especially not old ones.

Rupert was trying to catch her eye.

'The enigmatic Ella. I have followed your rise to stardom avidly,' he said. 'You really are a beguiling creature, beautiful and untouchable yet not at all intimidating. You are, in fact, totally conventional in your simplicity. You must get that a lot, people finding you so very normal?'·

'Not really,' she answered, taking another glass from a passing waiter.

Beads of sweat started to form on the soldier's top lip and his sideburns were damp. He took off his helmet, revealing a receding, wispy blond hairline and a double chin that until then had been held in place by the thick leather strap of his helmet.

'Tell me, what made you choose Helen of Troy and this titillating costume?' He gestured at her cleavage. 'Was it an ironic statement against the sexualisation of young women and the way the press has the ability to make anyone – yourself included – into inviolable goddesses?'

No,' she answered. 'My boyfriend chose it.'

Ella gulped down the rest of her wine and glanced over Rupert's shoulder at the lone figure of Josh De Silva leaning against the bar.

'In fact, there he is. Do excuse me.'

She walked away as quickly as she could in her tall sandals and threw her arms around the startled actor.

'There you are, gorgeous. Been looking for you,' she said loudly.

She leant in and whispered in his ear, 'Sorry, the bald soldier is really freaking me out and I said you were my boyfriend. Go with it. Please?'

'My pleasure,' he laughed. 'He's still looking, shall we get rid of him? Nothing like an attentive audience.'

His hands slid down her silk dress and settled on her hips. It felt good to be touched – it had been a long time since a man had held her. In fact, the last contact she'd had with anyone had been Zac, when she had fallen asleep in his arms. She shook away the memory. A hint of a smile was playing at Josh's lips, and he looked even more attractive than when they had first met. She heard someone take a photo and thought how excited the press were going to get resurrecting their imaginary summer fling story. Oh well, in for a penny …

Josh moved her hair to one side so Rupert the soldier could see him and kissed her neck lightly.

'You think he's got the message?' Josh whispered.

Ella thought of Zac again and wondered what it would have felt like to have him hold her like this, what would have happened had his kiss gone further. Not that it mattered – Zac hadn't wanted her and now he was never coming back. Anyway, wasn't it him who told her to give Josh a chance?

'No, he's still looking,' she answered. 'I think we need to crank it up a notch.'

Josh laughed again and swung her into a theatrical dip, his lips meeting hers. She closed her eyes and let herself fall, her arms instinctively wrapping themselves around his neck. She kissed him. She hadn't meant to but it felt good. Natural, like it was meant to be. His kiss was soft but confident, not passionate like Zac's but nice. Very nice, in fact. She ran her fingers through his soft hair, shorter than Zac's, and kissed him harder. Josh was a celebrity, a minor one like her, maybe it *would* be fun for them to date. It would be nice to be known as more than just the hotelier's step-daughter. Instead of the shy girl with the stupid name she'd be the girl who'd won Josh De Silva's heart. Her tummy fluttered and she opened her eyes as he straightened her up.

'The creep's gone,' Josh said.

'We certainly gave everyone a bit of a show,' Ella said, smoothing down her dress and pulling her hair back into place. 'Think we'll make the paper tomorrow?'

'With a leading lady as gorgeous as you, definitely.'

'I can see why everyone says you're a great actor. That was a convincing performance.'

'I wasn't acting,' he said. 'I've wanted to kiss you for a long time.'

She clicked her false nails together, desperate to bite them. He obviously liked her – what was she going to do about it? He seemed like a nice guy and he was attractive. Really attractive. What the hell was there to think about? She bit the inside of her lip and closed her eyes, an image of Zac instantly appearing in her mind. Her stomach ached. She wasn't ready. She thought she was but what if Zac *did* come back? It wasn't worth the risk.

'Sorry, I'm not being fair on you. I'm still not over an ex,' she said.

'That guy from the club?' he asked. 'That's cool. Whatever.'

She had embarrassed him. For Christ's sake, maybe one day she would be able to talk to a man without offending him! She touched his arm.

'How about you give me your number?' she said. 'Maybe we could go for a drink when things calm down a bit? Probably best to wait, or before you know it the gossip columns will be marrying us off.'

Josh reached into his tuxedo and gave her a card.

'So who have you come as?' she asked. 'Bogart? Brando?'

He nodded at a full glass of martini beside him.

'Well, Bond,' she said. 'Let me buy you a drink for your services this evening.'

'Thank you. I'll have a bottle of beer, thanks, those martinis taste like shit.'

She liked him. Maybe she would give him a call.

CHAPTER TWELVE

Ella swayed as the bus turned the corner and climbed Highgate Hill. She stared out the front window, the streets a blurred canvas of oranges, reds, and yellows. Condensation streamed down the inside panes and she ran her finger on the glass, watching the drops race each other.

Her head was pounding and she felt sick. As was always the case on London buses, the heating was on full blast, filling the confined space with the smell of burning chewing gum and old dust.

Her woollen hat was low over her eyes, her hair tied loosely to the side, and she wore a long scarf and thick gloves. She thought about taking them off but didn't have the energy – she was just two stops away from home and would have to put them back on again anyway. It had turned bitterly cold. They were forecasting a white Christmas but she thought it was too damp to snow.

Oxford Street had been crazy with last-minute shoppers. She had no idea why she thought going on Christmas Eve was a good idea – she wasn't going to see any of her friends or family until the New Year so she could have waited. So much had been said about London at Christmas but Ella had never seen it, and she was relieved that it had exceeded her expectations. There was a buzz about this town, people pushing and shoving their way along the pavement, shoppers spilling into the stationary traffic, and pools of dark coats cramming their way into Tube stations. Just the thought of joining them made her panic – she hadn't ventured on the Underground since her first time with Zac. Perhaps he hadn't cured her after all.

It had only been two months since she last saw him, but it felt like another lifetime. She thought of him alone on the icy streets amidst the happy day trippers and groups of drunk office workers, and felt her chest constrict. It was crazy how much she missed him. The fancy dress party had been fun, and for one night she had nearly forgotten about him. She had actually enjoyed herself, but as soon as she'd got back to her bedroom he was everywhere she looked. She had Josh's telephone number but she hadn't called him yet. She'd told him she'd call in the New Year, but maybe she would call him sooner. Maybe it was time to throw away Zac's belongings.

The smell of roasted chestnuts and hotdogs clung to her scarf and the carol singers fought to be heard against the din of blaring car horns and scurrying footsteps. She smiled as she compared her afternoon in London with December in Marbella. She thought of old Spanish ladies wrapped in their furs in fifteen degree heat, complaining about the wind, tying headscarves over their perms and tutting at holiday-makers eating ice creams and letting their children paddle in the sea. To think she had thought winters there were cold.

This was her first Christmas in the UK and she was alone. To be fair, Ella had lied to her mother about going skiing with Mai Li, so she hadn't technically been abandoned. Although if Felicity had given it any thought she might have realised her daughter didn't own a pair of skis and hated the cold, but Ella knew her mother was glad for the excuse to go to New York alone with Richard. They had left the night after the party. They hadn't even waited for Ella to return from class to say goodbye. Felicity could only ever be one person at a time; now she was Richard's wife she was everything she thought he wanted and she'd forgotten what it was to be Ella's mother too. It still took some getting used to.

The dark windows and artificial heat were making Ella sleepy. She could tell by the bus's movements that it was approaching her stop and was thankful she knew the route so well as it was impossible to see out of the streaming windows. She descended the steep stairs to the lower level that was busier and a lot louder. A young mum stood by the exit door with her screaming toddler, her pushchair barely visible beneath a mountain of shopping bags hanging off the handles. Two elderly ladies at the front chattered and a group of guys in beanie hats and dark hoods laughed at the back, passing a bottle of cider between them. Ella's head was swimming as she joined the mother at the doors, eager for a hit of cold air to wake her up.

'Hey! Ella.'

Josh was standing beside her, grinning.

'Fancy seeing you here. Not got your toga on tonight?' he said.

What was *he* doing on a bus? She instantly felt guilty about not having called him, but the last two weeks had been busy. Anyway, she didn't owe him anything. She took a deep breath. She was feeling faint and wasn't in the mood for conversation. She gave him a tight smile.

'Hi.'

'Looks like we got away with our kiss the other day,' he continued. 'We might have to try again sometime.'

'Maybe,' she mumbled, turning back around. She felt too ill to flirt – she just wanted to go home. Ella's cheeks were filling up with saliva and her vision was getting fuzzy. She prayed the bus would stop before she threw up.

'Been shopping?' he asked, looking at the two large carrier bags in her hand.

Ella gave a small nod. She had been to Fortnum and Mason, and after staring at their magnificent window display for ten minutes, had ventured inside and spent a fortune on stuff she didn't recognise, but liked the fancy tins and jars they came in.

The bus had been static in traffic for a couple of minutes and her stop was just visible through the front window. The harassed mother was begging the driver to let them out, her son now scarlet with the ferocity of his screams and struggling against his tight pushchair straps. Ella knew how he felt.

'Look lady, I don't make the rules, I can't open the doors until I'm at the bus stop!' the bus driver yelled back. Ella, recognising the voice as that of the arsehole driver that had also been rude to her, sighed and smiled sympathetically at the exhausted woman.

Josh was still beside her. The bus wasn't crowded but he stood so close his shoulder touched hers. His friends were laughing and calling him back.

'She's not interested, mate, let Nellie get back to the circus!' shouted a small, dark-haired boy, clinking his bottle against his friend's.

Josh made an apologetic face.

'Don't worry about it,' Ella muttered, staring straight ahead and attempting to swallow down her nausea. 'What you doing on a bus, anyway? It's not your style.'

'You're right, it's not,' he said. 'We were in town and I saw you get on. It was going our way so I thought, why not? I wanted to talk to you, thought maybe you'd lost my number.'

Ella closed her eyes and concentrated on her breathing. The bus was moving slower than walking pace up the hill. Josh kicked at an empty juice carton at his feet in response to her silence.

'We're off to a mate's Christmas party in Hampstead, want to come? You can go as you are, it's not fancy dress this time.'

He laughed but Ella didn't join him.

'No thanks,' she said, resting her head against the cool metal handrail by the door.

'What's up, Ella, I thought we had something? You back together with that ex?'

She shook her head.

'What's your problem then?'

His friends had moved on to singing a song from *Dumbo*.

'You're making me look like a twat in front of my mates,' Josh said. 'I told them we were, you know, kind of seeing each other.'

Ella rolled her eyes, willing the bus to speed up.

'Why would you say that? I told you I might call you. Actually, I planned to, but you're acting weird now.'

He leant closer and whispered, 'Are you fucking with me? Do you want me to try a little harder? Is it a thrill having Josh De Silva begging you to talk to him?'

He gave her a hundred watt smile, a dimple forming in his right cheek. She knew his kind – beautiful, spoilt, not used to getting no for an answer. The bus changed gear and lurched closer to the bus stop. Ella thanked the heavens. To think she had once considered calling him. Stupid brat.

One of Josh's friends made a trumpeting sound and the other three howled with laughter. Ella had heard it all before yet it still amazed her that the joke was just as funny to a twenty-year-old as it was to a twelve-year-old. Someone stood up at the back of the bus and the boys fell silent. The dark figure walked towards the doors as the bus approached her stop.

Ella went to pick up her shopping but Josh grabbed her arm, hissing through gritted teeth.

'I've got *loads* of girls gagging for a piece of me. I don't need some stuck-up cow like you making me look stupid.' He smelled of beer and expensive aftershave. His grip tightened. 'Come on, one kiss. It's Christmas, for fuck's sake Just one little kiss and I'll let you go.'

The doors snapped open, sending a gush of icy air into Ella's face. She gulped it down in three long breaths, feeling her head clear at once. The driver looked at the harassed mother struggling down the steps with her screaming son then turned to Ella and Josh.

'Oi, lovebirds. You getting off or what?' he shouted.

'Nah, we're staying. Keep going,' Josh replied.

'Wrong answer,' said a voice behind them.

Josh cried out as he fell forward, landing on the pavement at Ella's feet. It was the man from the back of the bus, but his hood was obscuring his face. They

168

stepped off the bus together. Josh brushed himself off and scowled at the stranger. The street was dimly lit and their faces were in shadow.

'What's your problem, mate?' Josh's voice wavered. His eyes darted back to the bus where his friends hovered at the doors, looking at each other but not moving. The doors flapped shut but the bus remained stationary at the red light.

'I tell you what my problem is, *mate,*' the hooded man replied. His voice was low and Ella strained to hear it. He was face to face with Josh, at least three inches taller and a lot broader. 'My problem is that I've just spent half an hour listening to you and your friends talking complete filth, then just as I look forward to getting off the bus and away from you I see you harassing this nice girl, who looked like she was *far* from interested in you. Apologise to her.'

Ella stared at the stranger. It couldn't be.

Josh pushed past him and walked back to the waiting bus.

'Fuck you!'

He didn't get far before a sharp kick to the small of his back sent him skidding across the pavement. He landed on the edge of the curb, leaving a deep graze across his cheek. His hand to his bloody face, Josh scrambled back up and watched as the traffic lights turned green and the bus slowly began to pull away. He banged at the doors but the driver ignored him.

Josh jogged alongside the bus, hitting the side. 'Stop, my coat's in there. Stop!'

The dark figure turned to Ella and lowered his hood.

'Zac!' she cried, dropping her bags.

169

She buried her face into his chest and felt his hands in her hair. She had forgotten the warmth of his body, his solidness, how safe and calm she felt in his arms. Her legs were weak and she leaned into him to steady herself.

'You OK, Rivers?' he whispered.

She nodded.

'She said she didn't have a boyfriend,' Josh said by way of apology, dabbing at his bloody cheek.

He was standing in the road staring at them. Zac had overreacted, Josh wasn't so bad, really. Perhaps he wouldn't have acted that way if his friends hadn't been watching. She'd actually quite liked him at the party, but now, beside Zac he looked like the insecure little boy he was. It was drizzling and Josh wrapped his arms around himself, his thin shirt doing little to keep him warm.

'Looks like you have a long walk home. Catch.' Zac threw him a two pound coin. 'Get a bus, at least you won't get your pretty hair wet.' Zac put his arm around Ella's shaking shoulders and kissed the top of her head. 'Come on, let's get you home.'

CHAPTER THIRTEEN

The rain was falling so hard that it pooled in the collar of Ella's coat and trickled down her back. She rested her head against Zac and he pulled her closer to him as they turned into her road and stopped in front of the gates.

'You all right?' he asked. Raindrops clung to his lashes and his hair was flat to his head. She hadn't spoken to him yet.

'Will you be OK? Is someone home?'

'Not really' she answered. 'I'm on my own for Christmas.'

She kept her eyes on the steps as they approached the front door. The last time she had seen him he had told her their friendship was over and then kissed her. What had it meant? She'd been so long trying to get over him, yet here he was bringing all her feelings back to the surface.

'Where have you been?' she asked. He stroked her face, his finger collecting a tear as it rolled down her cheek. 'I looked everywhere for you,' she said. 'The shed was vandalised and some cow at Indigo was really cagey saying she'd never heard of you. Every day I looked for you, Zac. At every bus stop. Every day for *six weeks*.'

Her chest shuddered with sobs and she struggled to take a breath.

'Hey, hey, come on,' he said, holding her and stroking her hair. 'It's OK, I've been fine. I should never have walked out on you, I'm sorry. Let's get you inside.'

Ella was relieved at how warm the house was and shrugged off her parka, letting it fall to the floor. Zac remained in the doorway looking at his trainers.

'Come in, you must be freezing in that bloody jumper. Don't you have anything warmer?'

Why was it everything she said to him sounded like an insult? 'Sorry, that was rude. Look, I'm not being pushy but why don't you stay for a bit? You can have a shower. I've still got your bag of clothes, you can get changed. It's the least I can do to thank you for helping me … again. Please?'

He hesitated before shutting the front door. He took off his sweatshirt which was soaked through, his wet black T-shirt beneath clinging to his chest. They walked through the vast hallway, their trainers squeaking against the tiled floor.

'You haven't seen this part of the house yet, have you?' she said, watching him gaze at the sweeping staircase, beyond which stood a set of mirrored doors leading to a function hall. Inside was a small stage and a white grand piano along with sound and lighting equipment. A large Christmas tree stood in the centre, decorated in silver and white but there were no presents beneath it. Zac walked through the doors and smiled at the tree.

'Completely ridiculous, isn't it, having our own ballroom,' she laughed. 'One of my mother's many indulgences. *"We can't possibly host important soirées in any old room, especially when the press are here, daaaarling!"*'

'Why is there a doll at the top?' Zac asked. 'She

doesn't seem to be wearing underwear.'

'It's a Christmas Angel,' Ella replied. 'They don't need knickers; apparently angels are sexless.'

Zac laughed. She'd never heard him laugh with such abandonment, she couldn't help but join in.

'Come on,' she lay her hand on his shoulder, 'let's get ourselves dry, I can give you a proper tour later. This place is huge; it took me ages to find my way around.'

They turned down a long hallway and headed to the back of the house. To their right was an orangery and beyond that, an impressive herb garden just visible through the steamed panes of glass. She opened a door and they were in yet another hall that led to her bedroom.

'This is how you reach my room from the main house,' she said. 'You can really notice it's an add-on from this angle. I like being apart from them, it feels like my own little space.'

'Nothing little about it, Rivers, your room is bigger than most people's houses,' he said.

Ella's cheeks stung, remembering the shed he had called home. They stood in the doorway to her room, looking at where he had said his last goodbye. The tick-tock of the clock was deafening.

'Right, I can run you a bath in the upstairs guest room if you want? Just leave your clothes outside and I'll dry them, OK?'

'You have another bedroom upstairs?' He was smirking and she realised what she had said. Shit! 'So how come you had me sleep on the sofa?'

Ella looked down at her nails, noticing how short and flaky they were. What was she going to say? *Because I liked falling asleep to the sound of your breathing?*

Because knowing you were in the same room made me feel safe? Because I lay awake waiting for you, hoping you would read my mind and slip under the covers beside me?

'Don't know, I didn't think,' she mumbled, climbing the stairs. She opened the door to the spare room and beckoned him in. 'The bath is bigger in here,' she said pointing at a round sunken bath in the corner. The ceilings were original oak beams, preserved from when her room was the stables, and three long windows overlooked the garden. 'Take your time, I'll sort your clothes out.'

She ducked out quickly, avoiding his eye, and headed back downstairs. Holy crap, how had she managed to get Zac into her bedroom again?

How had he ended up in her house again?

Zac lay in the bath, bubbles up to his chin, and stared at the vaulted ceiling. Once again he had let it go too far! Why was it so difficult to say no to her?

Zac had been working that afternoon. He rarely rode on buses but today he'd wanted to avoid the Christmas crush on the Tube. He'd already been on the bus when she'd clambered on with her shopping bags, but thankfully she hadn't seen him and had headed straight upstairs. Zac hadn't planned their chance meeting this time – perhaps fate had changed direction and taken control away from him? He was going to get off at the next stop until that Josh had started talking about her. Ella and Josh were meant to meet – that was the plan. And Zac wasn't meant to be there, just like he wasn't meant to be with her now. But when that little weasel had put his hands on her, Zac hadn't been able to control himself. For the first time ever he hadn't been able to leave it to chance, fate, or destiny … he had stepped in, and now look where he was. Back to square one.

Every day he had watched her in secret, noticing her growing stronger, convincing himself she would be fine without him. Wouldn't she? He sighed and closed his eyes.

He couldn't walk out on her again. How could he leave her alone in this huge, creepy house over Christmas? He had never lied to her but he still wasn't prepared to tell her the truth. Whatever happened, that would remain hidden.

He peered outside the bathroom door and saw that while his damp clothes were gone, Ella hadn't left any clean ones. He wrapped a towel around his waist and came downstairs.

Ella was kneeling in front of her mirrored wardrobe doors in her bathrobe, brushing her hair. She watched his reflection as he walked down the steps behind her. She was so used to seeing him in his signature hoodie and jeans, and now he was in her room wearing nothing but a towel. His arms were strong and tanned despite the lack of sunshine in months. His hair was longer than usual when wet and reached to his jaw. A drop of water worked its way down his collarbone, across his taught chest, and down the ripples of his stomach. Ella's eyes followed it until it reached the towel tied above his jutting hip bones and disappeared.

'Nice bath?' she asked, keeping her eyes averted from his torso. He nodded. 'Your clothes are dry,' she said standing and pointing to the chair beside her.

He reached over her shoulder for his jeans, his face inches from hers.

He hesitated for a moment and she slowly reached up and stroked the back of his neck. He let out a soft sigh and she closed her eyes as her lips brushed against his. As she leant in further, he broke away.

'I can't. I'm sorry.' His eyes pleaded with hers. 'I'm not the right man for you, Rivers. Please, believe me. It won't work.'

Pulling her robe tighter around her waist, she nodded but couldn't look at him. Why did she always act so bloody desperate? For fuck's sake, what was her problem? Zac was in her house and there was a chance they could be friends, and now she'd scared him off again. His goodbye kiss had obviously meant just that.

'Right, of course. Sorry. I got the wrong end of the stick.'

She didn't know where to look. His eyes were drawing her in again and his body ... She stared at the wall behind him and addressed that.

'I thought you liked me. You know, *liked* me. I guess I was wrong.' She cleared her throat. 'Can we forget this happened and go back to being friends? Please? I've really missed you.'

Zac's jaw clenched and twitched beneath the surface of his skin. Had she made him angry? He stepped closer and lifted her chin with his finger, forcing her to look him in the eye.

'No. We can't go back to being friends. You're right, I don't *like* you.'

He was blurring around the edges. She hated herself for not being able to control her tears. Why was he making this harder for her? She swallowed as he lowered his face to hers.

'Ella.'

He had never called her that before. It was the first time she'd heard him say her name, seen his tongue flicker over the letters. Her stomach lurched.

'I can't do this any more,' he said. 'I don't just *like* you. I have literally, completely and utterly fallen for you. I *love* you. I've loved you longer than you can imagine. My heart doesn't beat if you aren't beside me. I can't breathe if I can't speak your name. I feel nothing without your touch and to look at you, well, that is my very reason for being.'

She held her breath, not daring to move. His body was flush against hers, moving her against her wardrobe door, its cold surface a relief against her burning skin.

'From the moment you spoke to me I've tried to resist you,' he said. 'I have tried to do the right thing, but I'm not sure what that is any more. How can anything that feels this right be wrong?' He brushed her hair from her face, gently pulling on one of her curls and watching it bounce back. 'Ella, there has only ever been you. Day, night, before, now, the future … it has always been you.'

His lips met hers and she leant into his kiss, moaning softly into his mouth. She ran her hand over his back and clung to his damp neck with one hand, the other moving towards his thigh that clenched at her touch. He was straining against the towel at his waist and she hooked her finger beneath the fold, letting it fall to the ground. He lifted her up effortlessly, his lips never leaving hers, and turned so the backs of her knees touched her bed. She fell back and he leaned over her, pulling at her dressing gown cord until it fell away, revealing her bare breasts which he took into his warm mouth. Ella struggled out of his embrace.

'Zac, do you have anything on you?'

He frowned.

'You know? Protection?'

He shook his head, 'I didn't exactly plan this. Do you want me to stop?'

'No! Don't you dare. You aren't going anywhere this time.' She put her gown back on and ran to the door. 'Maybe my step-brother has some in his room. Give me five minutes. Don't move!'

She ran as fast as she could, grinning like a madwoman. She hadn't in her wildest dreams imagined Zac would feel this way about her. He *loved* her. He actually said the word 'love'. No man had ever said that to her. She'd had the odd boyfriend and a few encounters she'd buried in her mind, but nobody had ever made her feel the way Zac did.

She stopped outside Sebastian's bedroom, her chest stinging with the exertion of racing up three flights of stairs. She wished she didn't have to go into his part of the house. He had his own apartment in Chelsea for the rare occasions he was in England, but Richard insisted his precious son still had his own room too. It was three times the size of Ella's, designed like a hotel suite, and took up the entire top floor.

She hurried through the lounge area to the master bedroom, looking over her shoulder the entire time though she knew she and Zac were the only ones in the house. She opened the top drawer of the bedside table, throwing aside a couple of magazines with girls in school uniforms on the cover and a roll of toilet paper. She wrinkled her nose and looked in the second drawer. Bingo! A wooden box. She peeked inside and found Rizlas and two boxes of condoms. She grabbed one and turned to go, then saw it only held three. She returned it and picked up the pack of twelve. She would replace them in a couple of days. Sebastian wasn't due back until next month so he would never know.

Leaving the room exactly as she had found it, she raced downstairs as fast as she could, stopping to compose herself outside her bedroom door. The lights had been turned off and the curtains drawn. As her eyes adjusted to the dim light, she saw Zac by her chest of drawers, lighting the last of dozens of candles.

'Where did you get these?' she gasped.

'I had a bit of rummage through your kitchen.'

He slipped his arms around her waist, drawing her to him.

'I figured if we're going to do this, we should do it properly.'

He took the box from her, took out a sheath, and dropped the rest on the floor, pushing her on the bed and climbing on top of her. She pulled him down and kissed him fiercely, their teeth clashing, his tongue deep inside her.

'I didn't know anyone could be this beautiful or anything feel this right,' he whispered.

His mouth and fingers mirrored every one of her thoughts and brought her to the edge and back, over and over again, her senses tumbling into a fuzzy abyss. Just as she didn't think she could take any more he entered her slow and hard and it came into sharp focus, clearer than ever before.

Not until then did she know the meaning of complete.

CHAPTER FOURTEEN

'You are the best present I've ever woken up to on Christmas Day,' Ella whispered in Zac's ear.

His eyes were closed but he was smiling. His cheek was crumpled against the pillow and tiny dots of stubble were beginning to form on his chin and jaw. She kissed his Cupid's bow lips, resisting the urge to bite them. He clasped the back of her head and she squealed as he rolled her over, landing on top of her.

'You want a present, young lady?' he said, pinning her hands to her sides and nuzzling her neck. Ella was laughing too much to reply. 'What do you want me to do? I'll do anything for you,' he said.

He kissed her on the mouth and she struggled to move, feeling him getting hard against her. He was a machine! They had hardly slept all night, the smallest movement from her had made him stir with pleasure.

'I don't think you need telling,' she said. 'How do you always know what I'm thinking?'

'Because I love you. You and I are one.'

Coming from anyone else that would have sounded cheesy, downright creepy, even, but that was Zac. His intensity was overwhelming but it made her feel cherished and alive.

'You know what I really want?'

He let go of her hands and kissed her neck, his hand

stroking the inside of her thighs that parted instinctively. It was exactly what she wanted without realising.

'No … I mean, yeah, but that wasn't what I was going to say. I was going to suggest some coffee, do you … I can …'

She gave up, and gave in. When he touched her, there was nothing she could do but hand herself over to him, body and soul.

They lay on the floor of the living room watching the crackling fire. Ella had never seen it lit but Zac had found enough dry wood outside to create a roaring blaze, which was burning her cheeks and making her sleepy.

She was stuffed – they had worked their way through the contents of her Fortnum and Mason goodies plus half a microwaveable Christmas pudding. She lay with her head in his lap as he popped another chocolate in her mouth followed by a kiss. Dean Martin crooned about letting it snow, and the dripping window panes were turning a deep blue as the evening approached. She had never been happier.

'You want to watch a film?' she asked him, so relaxed it was a struggle to talk.

He was staring into the flames, amber lights flickering and dancing in his navy eyes.

'I would prefer to gaze at you instead of a TV screen,' he said.

'I'm sure you'd get bored. Here, you choose.' She handed him the television guide but he didn't take it. 'Fine. How about *It's a Wonderful Life*? What a tear-jerker, you seen it? It's about a guy who –'

'Ella, I have to go.'

Zac stood up quickly. Her head bounced off his lap and landed with a thump on the rug. She watched him put on his battered trainers in the hallway as if it were still yesterday and he had just walked her home, as if he hadn't spent the last twenty-four hours proclaiming his love for her. She ran and threw herself at the front door, barring his exit.

'I don't fucking think so! What is the *matter* with you? Are you seriously walking out on me again?'

He rubbed his face and sighed. 'Ella, let me go.'

'Bollocks! You don't do this to a girl, Zac. You don't give her the best day of her life then shit on it. What's your problem?'

He cupped her face in his hands and she thought he was going to kiss her. Instead, he gazed deep into her eyes.

'Words, Zac, use words. I can't read your mind. You're freaking me out, just tell me. I thought we were happy.'

'I am, that's the problem.'

'How is being happy a problem?'

'I don't want to hurt you.'

'You're hurting me now. What's going on?'

'Let me go, Ella, and I promise I will explain when I come back. I promise. I won't be long.'

Ella believed him. She didn't know why but she did. What choice did she have? She stepped aside and watched him disappear into the darkness. She would give him until the morning and after that … What would she do after that? Forget about him and move on? Not likely.

It was nearing midnight. Ella had left the remnants of

their Christmas picnic on the rug and had climbed into bed to wait. She'd sat through two films without following either of them, eaten two entire chocolate oranges, and then changed into her pyjamas.

He wasn't coming back. He hadn't last time and he wouldn't this time. There was no point crying – she'd done enough of that over the last two months.

She locked the doors, turned out the light, and watched the silver shadows dance along her wall. It was a full moon and she hadn't drawn the curtains. She was scared that if she stared into pitch dark nothingness she would only see him. She touched the indentation on the pillow beside her where his head had been that morning and buried her nose in it. It didn't smell of anything.

'Ella, *te amabo in aeternum*,' he said, stroking her cheek. 'I will love your for ever.'

She didn't feign sleep this time. She sat up and switched her bedside light on, blinking at the glare.

'Zac? How did you get in?'

'I have something to tell you.'

Ella brought the covers up to her neck.

'About time. What?' She hoped she didn't look as worried as she felt.

Zac rubbed his face and took a deep breath. When he took his hands away, the look in his eyes scared her.

'I'm not who you think I am.'

'So what? It doesn't matter.' She wanted him to hold her, to stop talking and go back to how it had been. 'I've never known who you are, just that you're Zac who lived in a shed and may or may not have worked in a really cool bar. But that's OK. I don't care that I don't know your surname.'

'I don't have one.'

Ella threw her hands up.

'Spit it out, Zac! Do you have a girlfriend or something? Is this what this is about?'

He shook his head. 'I've only ever loved you.'

His jaw tensed and he didn't move. He fixed his eyes on Ella but she refused to look at him – she was scared of what he was going to say.

'Are you in trouble or something? *Just tell me, please!*'

'I'm not like you.'

'You can say that again. Look, if this is about me having money and you –'

'Ella, I'm not human.'

She brought her knees up to her chest and wrapped her arms around them. She trusted him, she trusted him, she had to keep telling herself that.

'What have you done, Zac? You might think you're a monster but I know you aren't. I know the *real* you. Maybe not your proper identity or past but I *know* you. You're a good person. Whatever you did, we can work through it. Just sit down and tell –'

'Shut up. For once, just shut up.' Zac accentuated each word slowly, his eyes bearing down on hers and his breathing slow and laboured. He swallowed and took a deep breath. 'I'm an angel.'

A small laugh escaped from the back of Ella's throat, sounding more like a yelp. She had studied a module about this disorder on her Psychology course. So he had mental health problems. That would explain a lot: his exclusion from his family and friends, his violent outbursts, his erratic behaviour. They could make it work – many couples did. There were pills he could take and she would pay for the best psychiatrists.

She threw off her covers and crouched at his feet, rifling through the bottom drawer of her bedside table. She was sure she had her notes there somewhere. She would ask him to explain his thoughts and see if they matched the list of symptoms.

'Don't worry, there's nothing to be ashamed of,' she said, pulling out sheets of paper and squinting at the writing. 'Have you been taking medication? I think they call it the Messiah Complex. Grandiose delusions can form part of multiple personality disorders or schizophrenia. People with bipolar can have a God complex. Or is it drugs? They can give you all sorts of hallucinations. I can help you get clean. I think I have some notes in here about –'

'Ella, look at me!'

His voice boomed and reverberated across the room. She dropped her papers and looked up. A whimper was trapped in her throat and she slid against the edge of her bed. The bulb of her bedside lamp burnt brighter and brighter until it burst and the room was plunged into darkness.

It was true.

Zac wasn't human.

He towered over her wearing nothing but jeans that hung loosely around his sharp hip bones, his shoes and jumper a crumpled heap at his bare feet. Her eyes were adjusting to the darkness and worked their way up his now-familiar body until they reached his shoulders. A faint rustle grew louder until the room was bathed in a crisp white light. Ella blinked and shaded her eyes with her hand. Brighter than the sun, the light shone behind him and through a pair of magnificent wings that were stretching across the width of her bedroom. Each feather was longer than her arm and as white and bright as freshly fallen snow. They filled her vision and blinded her. Zac's eyes burnt like lilac flames, daring her to speak. His hair lifted in an imaginary breeze but the air was silent and still. As silent and still as her heart. He stood, arms stretched out, like da Vinci's Vitruvian Man.

'I am Zadkiel, angel of mercy, chief ruler of the Hashmallim, and son of the Seventh Ray.'

Ella howled and buried her face in her duvet. She had to shield her eyes from the light. It was too beautiful and too sad. She understood now. He had never been hers. Zac kneeled beside her and she crawled onto his lap, allowing him to take her in his arms and wrap her in his wings. She'd finally discovered his secret.

LONDON, 1941

I opened the shelter door and the icy wind slapped me hard across the face. It weren't nothing less than I deserved – I'd left Evie waiting for me for hours while I was getting up to no good with her brother, and she weren't never gonna speak to me again. I was waiting for Ted to duck out the tin door so's I could lock it when I saw Ma come running out the kitchen door with something under her arm like she'd just robbed the place. Her scarf was round her head, her curlers bobbing about underneath like they was trying to escape.

'Dolly, thank Gawd you're here. It's all over the news, more planes and they're heading our way. Come on, girl. Get in the shelter'

Right on cue, the siren sounded. She pushed past us and fell to her knees, searching through the flower pots for the key. Her hand went from one pot to another, not caring about all them insects what she couldn't see in the dark until it landed on a pair of tanned brogues. Her eyes travelled up the crumpled slacks and stopped when they reached Ted's pale face. Ma was good at keeping a straight face.

'Oh, hello love, what you doing here?' she said. 'Evie gone home already, has she?'

I doubt she expected an answer – she was used to talking to men. She leant forward and steadied herself against the door as she carried on scrabbling among them pots, then the door creaked and she frowned, noticing it weren't shut properly. Finally she saw what I had been thinking about the whole time, that the key was already sticking out the lock. It took less than ten seconds but Ted and me, we was rooted to the spot like we was in a silent movie, except instead of a tinkly piano tune accompanying us it was the wailing of them sirens that had become the soundtrack to our winter.

Ma never said nothing as she headed down them steps, scuttling in that way of hers where her little legs moved double as quick as what they ought to without getting nowhere. My chin trembled and I reached out to Ted.

What about Evie? my face was asking.

His eyes were white in the moonlight and darting between the shelter and the back gate. All them bloody planes, what had we done! Ted took my elbow and pulled me towards the steep steps, but I shook my head and broke free, running as fast as I could to the gate. His long legs got to me in two strides and he grabbed me real hard.

'Don't be stupid, Dolly. It's too dangerous. We just need to get the all clear then we can go look for her.'

Ma was sitting on the bed with the gas masks ready and had picked up her bag of knitting what she already had down there to pass the time, except she hadn't taken the needles out, she was staring at something on the floor like she was scared that if she took her eyes off it, it might escape.

Ted and me followed her gaze. Oh, how I wanted a bomb to fall on us there and then! Like two sinful serpents, my bright red hair ribbon and Ted's belt lay guiltily entwined on the sandy floor, inches from Ma's slippers. She looked at my head, then at the floor, then at Ted's waist, then at the floor. She never had to say nothing.

She sniffed once then fiddled with the dials on the radio, which must have been the little box she had been carrying from the house, until after a time a whiny voice cut through the crackles. It told us a plane had just dropped bombs on the city and they was waiting for more news.

We sat down and Ted moved closer to me, taking my hand in his. It was fresh of him to do that in front of Ma but we never cared. None of us were looking nowhere but at the wireless, our eyes trained on its walnut finish, willing it to tell us more, but the newsreader just went on about Poland then Russia. I was too scared to move, thinking if I kept still that plummy voice would say it was all a mistake. Ma's eyes wandered from the wireless, to her knitting needles, then to mine and Ted's hands what looked like one large pink knobbly rock on account of our fingers clasped together so tightly. She'd spotted my ring. I'd forgotten it was on my finger. As soon as Ted had slid it on, it was as if it had been there for ever and I never thought for a moment to hide it.

'So, what you doing here, Ted love?' she asked sweetly, though she weren't smiling. He let go of my hand and straightened his tie.

'I met Dolly in the street, Mrs Smith. She was running late to meet my sister down by the river so I was going see about giving her a lift. In my Pa's van, you see. Bank ain't 'alf a long way for her to go so late.'

I was impressed he had thought of a story so quick.

'In the street, you say? But you was in our garden, Ted.'

He never had time to answer 'cause the man on the wireless came on again and said the words Foreign Exchange and Bank and Ted ran and turned up the volume. We sat as close as we could to the wooden box, our ears grazing its smooth sides and listened to how at one minute to eight a bomb had dropped on the station. They was telling us there was a flaming huge hole in the road and that the street had collapsed on top of the ticket hall. Some survivors had made it out but it had been so rammed with people sleeping down there they was going to have a job identifying the bodies. I looked up at Ted and screamed. I couldn't stop. My voice went all croaky but I kept screaming and screaming til he took me in his arms.

'She'll be fine, she'll be fine,' he kept whispering as he rocked me like a babe, though I reckon he was saying it as much to himself as to me.

Ma was the colour of marble and just as still. She had worked it all out, her head making little shakes from side to side in disbelief. Ted noticed too and lightly touched her shoulder, but she brushed him off.

'Don't worry, Mrs Smith. Our Evie will be just fine,' he told her. 'She won't have gone down the Tube, she hates it, see. Bet you she's in that tea house cellar right now having a nice cup of Earl Grey and telling everyone what a pain in the arse her mate Dolly is.'

I gave him a smile but I never believed a word of it, neither did Ma. I knew in my heart of hearts that my best friend was buried under a ton of London road and it was all my fault.

God died for me that day. That was His punishment to me and Ted for what we done that afternoon, then He disappeared and we never heard from Him again. Ted must have felt it too, that if he hadn't got me down the shelter and stopped me from meeting Evie it might never have happened. Or maybe he was thanking that bastard God for giving him the opportunity to save me from being blown to bits along with his sister. I'll never know.

The three of us sat like lumps of lead in our metal rabbit hole, listening to the terrible things what Hitler was doing to our city. When we finally got the all clear, Ted ran up them steps like lightning without even saying goodbye. I didn't know if he was off to the river to see it with his own eyes or straight home, either way I knew it was him what would have to explain the whole thing to his old pair and I was pleased it weren't me who had to come up with a story.

Ma was fretting too. She didn't know where to begin. She was mumbling about where the boys might have got to, and poor Mrs Brown, and that she should have kept the key to the shelter better hidden. She kicked Ted's belt under the bed as she shuffled to the stairs and slammed the door in my face as I followed behind her.

No one slept that night and as soon as it was light enough, Ted's Pa went and bought a paper and spoke to the police. He come round to our house and showed us the photo of the hole as big as a house in the middle of the road. I could see the statue of Wellington's horse and the columns in the background and they never had a scratch on them.

How I prayed to that useless God what I knew was no longer listening to me that Evie had sat right there by that horse and not gone to the Tube. It was a bloody waste of time – what was the use in imagining all sorts of happy endings? She would have been back by now if she was all right. It was the waiting what was killing us, but we never had to wait much longer.

Two o'clock that afternoon, Ted came round. A bobby had come knocking and said that Evie's hat and bag had been found by the station escalators. All her details were inside so they was able to find her house easy enough, Evie was organised like that. They said no one made it out alive and that Mr Brown would be asked to identify bodies as and when they was brought up. As soon as Ted told me the bit about bodies I was sick all over my back doorstep and some of it splattered onto his shiny brown shoes. He never noticed. He was looking past me into a different yesterday, one where me, Evie, and him were sat in that warm tea house cooing over my pretty ring and talking wedding flowers.

His face was like a scared mask that I wanted to rip off. I needed to see the calm, happy face of the Ted I loved what always knew what to do, but this man was helpless and it scared the hell out of me.

'We killed Evie,' I said, pushing him as hard as I could. 'I shouldn't have been with you. What have we done?'

I opened my mouth but no noise came out. The pain inside me was too big for my body to contain and it paralysed me as it struggled to break free. Ted picked up a rock from our path and threw it, making a loud clanking as it bounced off the roof of our shelter. He picked up more and did it again and again, roaring like an animal, his eyes wide and rolling in his head. I knew all about men, and he weren't never gonna stop til he got it all out, so I left him to it and went indoors.

In my bedroom I took off my ring, put it inside my music box, and hid them in my undies drawer. I couldn't face looking at them – there had only been one person I wanted to tell our happy news to and she was dead.

Three-and-a-half weeks later we had a funeral for Evie. It was more of a service, really, as the police never found much more of her stuff save a hanky with her initials on, which was black with soot and could have been anyone's. They stopped looking after two days, said there weren't nothing there but London's biggest grave. Poor Evie never got a proper coffin but the whole street turned out and filled up the church.

I couldn't look at Ted's Ma and Pa during the service. It was too much to bear knowing I had done that to them. Mr Brown had shaved off his moustache and at last you could see what his lips was doing but I knew they weren't never gonna smile again. Mrs Brown had her arm through his and it was all that was holding up her skinny frame. She was like a pack of cards and I held my breath in case the slightest puff of air sent her tumbling down. She never cried, she just stared at the church's statue of the crucified Jesus like she wanted to climb up and join him in his perpetual agony.

As for Ted, he got up and said a few words, did his job of talking to everyone and shaking hands, stayed strong like what men are supposed to do: stiff upper lip and all that. I wanted to run into his arms and take away that pain he was doing his best to ignore.

He only looked at me once during the whole service. His eyes was saying, 'This is the church we was gonna marry in but now there's no room left for our happiness because we don't deserve it.' And of course, like always, he was right.

They had a nice spread at The Three Sailors pub and the neighbours told us how lovely Evie was and what a sad loss it were, like we didn't already know. My guts had been hollowed out. I was empty inside. All day I looked for her pretty face in the crowd and at the bar wondering what she wanted to drink before it hit me as to why we was really there, and every time it hurt like new.

By the end of the day I felt quite queer, the sight of them pies and meat paste sarnies mixed with the pipe smoke of the old men in the corner was turning my stomach. I gulped some water and tried to breath proper.

'Dolores, we need to talk.'

Ted was beside me, the first time he had spoken to me since I was sick on his shoes and my heart skipped. He looked so dashing in his navy-blue suit, but I couldn't bring myself to think that way about him any more.

I followed him out to the waterlogged garden where a light drizzle was covering everything in tears, and looked at the pub windows, noticing for the first time the red paper hearts stuck to the inside. It was nearly Valentine's Day, our wedding day. Oh well, I smiled to myself. The weather would have been dreadful anyway.

'Dolly, I have something to tell you,' he said.

His voice was low and tight. I thought I had seen him at his saddest but this was much worse.

'I'm leaving.'

'What do you mean? Where are you going?'

'My darling,' he said, holding my hand in his own icy hands. 'I'm so sorry.'

I didn't know what I had done, what he was apologising for. My chin started to wobble.

'I've been called up to fight.'

I tried to say something. A million things were trying to tumble out of my mouth as he kissed my trembling lips.

'I love you with all my heart, Dolly. When I return we will tell our parents everything. We will get married and be together for ever, I promise.' He looked down and bit his own shaky lip.

I swallowed. Even that hurt.

'Can't you say no? I thought your boss said he could get you out of it if you ever …'

'I *want* to go,' he said, shaking his head. 'I'm joining the Navy and I'm going to find that bastard Hitler and kill him with my bare hands for what he did to Evie. It's my duty. She never did nothing to no one. He ripped my family apart, Dolly, and he took away our dream, our future. I ain't never going to forget that.'

I said nothing. I thought the longer I kept quiet, the longer he would have to stay with me. That he might change his mind.

'I'm leaving tomorrow for Portsmouth for training, then I'll come and see you before they ship me off. Hey.' He tried to smile and lifted my chin. 'This war will be over by the summer, just you wait. We'll have a lovely sunny wedding with your hair full of flowers, ain't that something nice to think about while I'm gone, my little Señorita.'

I knew what he wanted to hear, so I said it. I told him

that England was lucky to have such a valiant soldier fighting for us and that he was doing his country and family proud. I told him I would of course wait for him, til I was old and grey if that's what it took, and that he would return a hero.

'I'll be back before you know it,' he said.

I weren't so sure about that. I wanted to shout, '*Please don't leave me too. You said we was like socks, that we was useless on our own,*' but that would have sounded daft. I weren't good with words.

He kissed me again, my tears mixing with the rain, then he gave me a salute, a wink, and walked back into the pub. And that was the last I ever saw of him.

By May I had a few things to be happy about.

For a start, them sodding Nazis had decided London weren't worth bombing the hell out of no more, probably 'cause there was nothing left to bomb, so we could finally sleep safely in our own beds. I refused to go down that shelter again. When the air raids sounded I just got my mask out from my bedside table, grabbed my blankets, and slept under my bed

At first my Pa went spare, told me he hadn't made that bunker for me to end up hiding under the bed like some scared little 'un, especially after what happened to Evie and all. But Ma gave him one of her looks and for once he shut up and never said nothing after that.

It was a sunny spring too, how lovely it was to feel warmth on your face after such a long winter. You'd have thought the war was over the way people was carrying on, but it weren't, it was just Russia's turn to get all the stick now and England had a chance to get its breath back while that bloody Kraut found someone else to pick on.

Best of all, I was beginning to feel better. Three months had passed since I said goodbye to my best friend and fiancé on the same day, and that night I'd collapsed as soon as we'd stepped through the door. Pa had to carry me upstairs as I was all limp. I hadn't fainted like that since Sunday school when those incense and gas heaters would make me woozy. My Pa was used to carrying piles of bricks so I weren't no trouble, he held me in his arms like I was tissue paper what would tear if he weren't careful. I could hear him chatting to Ma as I drifted in and out, telling my brothers to keep the noise down. The world was black enough, but now it was closing in around me like the smoke from a blocked chimney and I was choking on my own grief.

'It's been a hard day for her, love,' he said to my Ma. 'Little Evie was like her shadow, we're all gonna miss that girl.'

Ma tucked me in like back when I was little. Before the war, and before money had got harder to come by, we'd borrow Uncle Ron's car to go see our Aunty Mildred in Southend. We'd make a day of it and have our sandy sandwiches on the beach, walk along the seafront, then all four of us kids would fall asleep in the back of the car, our faces pink and hair whipped by the salty wind. Pa would take us up to our rooms one by one, me first being the youngest, and Ma would run up ahead to draw the curtains and tuck us in. The night of the funeral felt like that, like I'd had the longest day and was now safe in me own bed. Except I never had thoughts of ice cream and seagulls to lull me off to sleep, I just saw black. An endless sea of black.

'She never ate nothing off that nice spread Mrs Brown did,' Ma whispered over my head. 'Not even a corn beef sarnie, and she never says no to a corn beef sarnie.' She went quiet like she weren't sure if to continue. 'Ted's off to war. I heard him telling his friends, he's leaving tomorrow.'

Did they know I could hear them? That I weren't that sleepy five-year-old again?

'Well, I got to say he's done the right thing, love,' Pa replied. 'Strapping lad like that? He'll show them Jerries a thing or two. Dare say he's broke a few ladies' hearts upon leaving.' He chuckled as he left the room.

Ma straightened the covers and stroked my cheek.

'You ain't wrong there, love, you ain't wrong there.'

Every day after that was like wading through treacle. Ma would sit by my bed and try to get me to eat a teaspoon of carrot soup to keep me strength up, but the smell would have me heaving, not that there were anything to bring up.

For weeks I felt like I'd had one too many shandies. I was so tired, even getting up for a pee in the night was hard work. My boss was understanding for a few days, then after that he told me I weren't the only one who'd lost friends and that I was lucky to have me house and old dears still standing. So each day I'd manage a few dry biscuits, or a slice of toast, but it was all I could stomach. If I weren't thinking about Evie or worrying about Ted, I was dreaming about crawling into me bed as soon as I got home.

Course, me old man had seen it before with the first war, he said it was normal with the nerves and grief and that everyone deals with it different. Ma would nod without really listening and glance at my waist from time to time, probably to see how much weight I was losing.

Then one sunny day in May, it went. I woke up and I never felt sick no more. In fact, I felt full of energy and bloody starving. Ma was tickled pink when I come down stairs and asked for extra eggs, and even the smell of them frying didn't bother me. Pa had got hold of a Morrison shelter what had been left behind in an old house – it couldn't be used no more on account of one side missing so we had it in the garden and kept chickens in it. I never much liked animals but I did enjoy going out in the morning with my basket and feeling about for them warm eggs.

I always complained about working in the Post Office but there were perks, and one of them was that you could collect your post before it got to your house. Worked a treat for me 'cause I never wanted Ma and Pa asking as to why I was getting so many letters 'cause they was all from Ted. If it weren't for them letters I dare say I'd never have left the house during them dark days.

Ted always sounded so jolly in his notes, telling me what hard work training was and how he hated being so far from home, but he couldn't wait to get out on them ships for real and show them Nazis what was what. Most of the letters were about his love for me, like he was drawing my portrait with his words. I know he did that for himself more than me as I never got to give him a photograph to put in his wallet. To him, them letters were a window between his world and back home, where he could hold out his hand and touch mine for a brief moment. I never saw it like that, to me them letters only meant one thing, and that was that he weren't there with me no more.

I went to work that sunny day in May and even Janey noticed the change in me.

'Dolly, you're looking very healthy, your cheeks are all peachy. You ain't got another man on the go, have you?'

I smiled mysteriously, but it weren't as much fun pulling her leg without Ted to laugh about it with afterwards.

'Oh, you ain't gonna believe this!' she cackled. It was a good job that Post Office weren't busy 'cause that girl never stopped jawing. 'Did I ever tell you about that tart Trixie from up our street? Remember a few weeks back I was chatting with her, I told you she leant over my fence as we was hanging out the washing?'

I rarely listened to Janey. I would stare out of the front window instead, watching people walking by and trying to remember what Evie's laugh sounded like or the exact shade of Ted's brown eyes. This time though, maybe on account of feeling a bit chirpier, I paid attention and I was pleased I did.

'Well, anyway,' she continued, pushing up her glasses and glancing about at no one in particular, 'she's been weeks going on about how she's been having the best "how's your father" with one of them darkies what come off the boats at the dock. Said he was a sailor from some island or other, but spoke good English.'

I could always tell when she was enjoying herself 'cause she would lean in real close.

'Well, this brownie had been filling her head with pictures of swaying palm trees and white sandy beaches. You should have heard her. She spoke about it like she'd been out there on her holidays when she's never gone as far as Bournemouth. Apparently he said he had a big house out wherever and she could go join him, 'cause with the little savings she had she could live like a queen. So, yesterday she was out in the garden again squeezing her clothes through the mangle and I look over 'cause I can hear sniffing and that, so I says 'Here, Trixie love, you got a cold?' and she looks up all red-eyed and I think 'Oh Gawd, why did I have to go and open me big trap'. She comes over and tells me everything. Apparently her foreign fella told her he was already married and had a family back home, then he just up and left on the next boat out. Well, he'd got his jollies, hadn't he, probably had one in every port. Silly cow.'

Janey was so close to me now I could smell the cheese and onion sandwiches she'd had for lunch.

'She was in a right state, so I knew it was more than that 'cause it definitely weren't the first time she'd got dumped. So I ask her why the waterworks, and she says she hadn't had her monthlies, two in a row, but couldn't go see her doctor on account of her not being married and all.'

Janey raised her eyebrows. I did it too but weren't sure why.

'Anyway, she saw old Mrs Potts from Mud Chute way and she sorted her out. Trixie said it was the scariest thing she ever done and that it was the last time she let some blooming sailor chat her up.'

I sat watching Janey's mouth open and close and her arms fold self-righteously. Gawd, she could be right stuck-up sometimes. She was probably jealous 'cause the lads in the docks never whistled at her.

Then I got to thinking about *my* monthlies and how I didn't remember having had any since Christmas. Janey had stopped rabbiting and was waiting for me to say something, probably along the lines of that poor cow getting all she deserved.

'So what did it mean then, her not getting her monthlies?' I asked.

She frowned.

'She was knocked up, of course. She thought it was her nerves, all that dizziness and not being hungry, but believe me she ain't someone who goes without a pie or two. She said she was sick as a dog for a while and thought it was 'cause of her bloke mucking her around. Luckily by the time she twigged she still had time to get it sorted.' Janey leant in again. 'Mrs Potts is good like that. She's been pretty busy I dare say since the war started. Probably the only one who's made money out of the unfortunate happenings lately. Dolly, you all right, love?'

I was swaying a bit on my stool and had to hold on to my desk 'til my head stopped spinning. Bloody hell. Bloody shitting hell!

'So who's this Mrs Potts?' I asked.

Janey was enjoying herself, it was the most attention I'd ever given her and she was so excited she never thought to stop and wonder why I was asking. She leant in closer so that I could see all them dark, tough hairs on her chin, and lowered her voice.

'Mrs Potts is a bit famous down our way, at least among the younger girls and all. She lives next door to the Oak and Anchor by the river, where the Quay is. She's had nine kiddies and never had no help from no one giving birth to them.' She stopped to get her breath, looking up to check no one had come in. 'She was a nurse in the first war, so she knows a thing or two, says she never liked hospitals 'cause she don't trust doctors. She can tell how far you're gone and she can get rid of it. No questions asked. She even helped one girl get her baby boy taken in by another family, I heard, and no one was none the wiser. She's a saint or a sinner depending on who you talk to, but in most cases it don't really matter what she is 'cause there ain't no other choice.'

I ran home that afternoon. I didn't need no Mrs Potts to tell me, I knew I had Ted's baby growing inside of me and she was going to be a beautiful little girl what looked just like her Aunty Evie. I should have been scared, or at least nervous, but all I could feel was that this little seed growing inside of me was a sign of hope. I had to tell Ted straight away, he would be over the moon. He'd said in his last letter he would be home soon, in a month or two, so maybe we could get married then and it would work out perfectly.

I must have written that letter to him a thousand times, week after week. I weren't smart like him, I couldn't find the right words. Of course he would be excited but I never wanted to make him sad that he weren't with us.

July was blooming hot. My bust was heavy and achy but I'd managed to strap myself down quite tight, and 'cause of all that weight I had lost to begin with I weren't really all that big. My tummy, what was normally flat as a pancake, stuck out a bit but not so's you'd notice. I loved it. I felt like a proper woman, like I had the most precious thing inside me what no one knew anything about. It was just me and my baby, and I swear she could read my mind – every time I thought about her I would feel a load of flutters like I was full of beautiful butterflies. I told Ted everything in that letter, every movement she made and every dream I had. I told him we was going to be a husband and a wife and a mummy and a daddy all at once. I knew reading them words would send him home running.

It was a Friday morning when I stuck the letter in an envelope. It was the hottest summer I could remember and I'd been sweating every night under layers of blankets in case Ma popped her head round my bedroom door and saw my bump. That morning I wanted to get to work early and hand the letter over to the sorting office before Janey could have a nose and start asking questions.

I was halfway down my stairs. I couldn't skip down them no more so I was holding on to the rail when there was this frantic knocking on the front door. Like I said, no one came by the front less they was selling something, but no one sells you nothing that early nor that urgently. Ma flew out the front room where she'd been dusting. I figured she'd had a peek through the curtains, and I stood there like I was watching a show. I nearly sat down on the step. Wish I had now.

At that point Pa came out the bathroom too, his face covered in shaving foam, moaning about the racket, and we both stood watching as Mrs Brown threw herself into Ma's arms.

That's when I knew. Ted's Ma hadn't said nothing but it was all over her face, like her very soul had up and left. Pa kept well out of it and went back to the bathroom, leaving me slap bang in the middle of them stairs with my sweaty head leaning against the bannister. I knew my Ted weren't never coming back, and I couldn't even make it to the bottom of the stairs.

From the middle step I could make out the top of Mrs Brown's frizzy grey head through the crack of the kitchen door, odd words and phrases floating toward me like inky black bubbles. His ship was on a training mission off the coast of Dorset, lost at sea. Never got to fight, unable to retrieve the bodies. He was five days from heading home. Then through the racking sobs Mrs Brown spoke about leaving. Ma had made her a cup of tea which Ted's mum weren't drinking but using to warm up her hands, even though it was bloody hot outside.

'We can't take no more, we're leaving for York in the morning to stay with my sister,' she said. 'Her husband's just inherited his mum's place up there so we're shutting the shop.'

Ma was making all the right noises. I wondered whether she was going to mention me but she didn't.

'We've lost everything,' Mrs Brown kept saying. 'Everything! Our babies! Both our beautiful babies are gone.'

Not all of them, I thought, but what was the point? It was too late. My letter to Ted, now scrunched so tightly in my clammy fist that it had left a dark pink line across my palm, rolled to the bottom of the stairs. There weren't going to be no Happy Ever After for Ted and me. Not no more.

I don't remember the rest of the day. No one came to tell me the news, as if by not telling me it stopped being real.

I imagine I went to work. I can't remember. I couldn't think about anything. There is only so much pain you can allow yourself to feel. I wanted to die, of course I did, but I had something to live for. I had a part of Ted growing inside me and I had to make a decision. The Browns were leaving London and they would never know. Pa would never allow it even if Ma was all right about it – which I doubted. There weren't no other choice. I got through the day and that night I had made up my mind.

I left the house as soon as I woke. I reasoned with nine kiddies Mrs Potts weren't going to grumble about someone calling for her before eight o'clock on a Saturday. I never even thought about my job or what my boss would say. I just got that bus to Mud Chute, then stood looking at these roads without a clue where to go next.

A lad was leaning up against a wall but I couldn't see his face proper on account of his dark wavy hair. He was handsome and, foreign-looking, I thought perhaps my Arabian Prince had come after all. Then I laughed to myself, stroking my swollen belly, because his timing was right off. The streets were silent. The lad had one leg bent behind him against the wall and he was whistling softly, his boot tapping out a rhythm. He looked up at me with piercing blue eyes what made me gasp, but I couldn't look away.

'I'm sorry,' I mumbled.

He stood up straight and walked toward me.

'You have nothing to apologise for,' he said. 'They forgive you.'

I should have been worried, he was obviously a complete fruitcake, but he didn't scare me. In fact, I felt calmer than I had since before Evie died.

He reached out and laid a hand on my arm. 'You will see them again, both of them, they will wait for you. The house you are searching for is over there.'

I turned to the street he was pointing at, a curved road what looked like an upside down smile. Some houses stood proud and white and tall, others had disappeared altogether, making it look like a mouth what had been punched so hard it'd lost half its teeth. Mrs Pott's house was there, the only one next to the pub. The other was a pile of bricks.

I went to thank the boy but he was gone.

Her house had three prams out front and they was all full. One little 'un looked big enough to run around on his own but had been stuck in there to keep him out of mischief. The other two babies were asleep.

I knocked and a large lady came to the door, her frayed apron covered in flour, and a snotty blonde girl clinging by her spindly legs to the woman's waist. I asked if she was Mrs Potts but she never said a word, just ushered me in and showed me to her front room.

Oh blimey, I'd never seen such a load of stuff everywhere, and there were more than nine kiddies in that house judging by the din what was coming through the kitchen door. Three little boys was hiding beneath the table playing at cowboys and Indians. It was already laid for tea, whether from the night before or it just stayed like that to save time. The big lady came back, shooed the kids out the room, and shut the door.

'So, my dear, tell me your story.'

Oh my Gawd, she was posh! I weren't expecting that and I felt dreadful for thinking badly of her. I couldn't see no sign of a man living there so maybe she was managing all them kids and her job on her own. It made me like her a bit more when I thought of her in that way, like she was fighting her own private war.

'I, err ...' I didn't know where to start. How could I tell her without sounding brassy? 'Me and my fiancé did it on the eleventh of January and I think I may be expecting.'

She smiled, which I reckoned was a bit insensitive all things considered.

'I take it that was your first time?'

'That's right, my only time. I know the date 'cause my best friend was killed by a bomb that night. It was his sister who we was meant to be meeting, you see, then he went to war and we never got to marry. He's dead now.'

I bit the inside of my lip as hard as I could til I tasted metal. I had never said them words out loud to anyone and now I wanted to tell this lady everything, I wanted to sit on her lap and cry into her pillowy chest. She was probably used to it 'cause she handed me a hanky what looked a bit grubby but I took it anyway. Them kids outside were making a right old din but she never so much as turned around, she just smiled kindly and I wondered whether them stories about her having been a nurse in the war were real.

She was talking about gestation periods or some such but I was doing the maths and I reckoned she had to be in her forties or even fifties for the nurse story to be true. She never looked it, though, fat girls never do on account of their plump faces ironing out all them wrinkles. I wanted to ask her where the little kiddies come from and if they was all hers or grandchildren or what.

'By my calculations, my love, you are about twenty-seven weeks. It will be here mid-October, I imagine.'

It was like she was talking in French.

'I don't understand, Mrs Potts. Who's coming in October?'

She looked at me all sad like and I swear she was going to hug me. Instead, she took my hand. Hers were like warm dough but dry as sandpaper.

'The baby, darling. You are having a baby in three months' time.'

I shook my head. 'But I can't have her, Mrs Potts. I can't have a baby, that's why I'm here. My pal Janey said you can make babies disappear.' She was my only chance, I squeezed her fingers. 'No one knows. Don't get me wrong, I want my baby girl with all my heart, but you have to help me, Mrs Potts. I can't have no baby, I just can't.'

But she weren't having none of it.

'I'm sorry but the baby is too big, darling, it's coming whether you want it to or not.'

'It's a girl.'

She never asked how I knew, it never made no difference anyway.

'Well, she will be here before you know it so we need to prepare.'

I weren't expecting that. I thought I was just lucky to have had the last six months with Ted's daughter squirming around inside me then I thought she would just go, that Mrs Potts would do whatever she done for Janey's neighbour and that would be that. But here she was, telling me I would have to have her, I would see her pretty little face and Ted's eyes staring back at me. I would get to hold her and feed her and bathe her. I would hear her cries and feel her heart beat against mine as she slept in my arms.

How that scared me. How was I ever going to be able to walk away from that?

Mrs Potts told me what had to be done. That I would move in with her at the end of September and that she would look after me and help me have the baby.

'Then I will find your daughter a good home, my love. I know a lovely Spanish lady who has been pining to be a mother for years. She would be overjoyed. Then everything will go back to normal again.'

But it never would.

That night I lay in me bed with a hand on me belly talking to Ted.

I said to him, 'Here, my love, did you feel that?' and put my other hand over me stretched bump, his hand on top of mine, and I smiled as our little girl kicked and rolled. I told him how lucky we was that something so beautiful had come out of this mess. I explained that he had lived after all. He understood I weren't gonna to be able to look after her, not properly, but I trusted Mrs Potts and I knew there would be a way I would find my way back to my little girl.

'You got two little señoritas now, Ted, what do you think of that?' I told him, and in my head I could see him smiling. I knew that wherever he was, he was happy because he loved us and that couldn't be taken away, not by war, not by death, not by nothing.

Since the Browns had left, Ma had hardly said two words to me. Maybe she thought death was spreading like a plague and that if she talked about it then one of us would be next. She'd given me the odd queer look, part pity and part disappointment, or maybe that was just how I saw it. That thick, sticky summer got cooler and every orange leaf on the trees reminded me that there weren't no getting out of it. This little lady was coming and would just as quickly be going again.

It was a horrible misty day when I finally got the courage to tell Ma I was off. She was out the back bringing in the washing, fussing 'cause she said it was gonna rain and the clothes weren't proper dry and she hated having them hung about the house. She went on and on, as if her millions of words were enough to keep mine away. I stood there holding the washing basket while she chucked the damp clothes in. My arms could hardly reach round it, what with my belly getting in the way but neither of us mentioned it. She weren't daft, she would shout at my brothers when they pushed me out the way and she'd tell Pa to carry the heavy bags when I helped with the shopping. They thought Ma was fussing over me, what with everyone dying an' all. Them daft men wouldn't have noticed if I had walked in holding the bloody baby.

'Ma, I'm off on a holiday,' I said.

She watched the leaves blowing under the back gate, and our old neighbour walking past with his scarf wrapped tight round his scrawny neck, and gave me a look. She never had to say it, her looks were legendary and one was as strong as a whole conversation. I knew she was thinking, '*Who the hell goes on holiday at this time of year?*'

'Janey invited me down to Devon. She has an aunt who lives by the sea, said we could spend a bit of time down there and get away from it all. It's quiet, see. I need a bit of quiet.'

Ma nodded and looked at the washing in my arms, blinking as the wind made her eyes water.

'That's probably for the best,' she said, and that was it. It was as easy, and as difficult, as that.

I took my bag on the bus to Mud Chute the next morning. Mrs Potts was waiting for me and she chattered on about how healthy I looked and that a nice young girl like me weren't gonna have no problems at all.

'You have your youth and you're strong, dear, nothing to worry about,' she said.

Thought she could read my mind, she did. It weren't the having my baby girl what was the issue, it was the not keeping her afterwards. We had talked about payment and she said she understood that young girls in trouble never had a lot of money. She said before the war, before things got complicated, it was the men that had got them into trouble what paid for it. But now it was different and she just wanted to do her bit and help where she could.

All I had was my engagement ring so that's what she got. It looked like it pained her to take it but if she was going to help me, the least I could do was help her.

So there we was, two women and a million children all crammed into three bedrooms. I had a little camp bed in her room so's she could be nearby if it started at night. The babes slept in cots and makeshift drawers with blankets, the little 'uns in the big bed with her and the rest of them top and tailed in the other two rooms. Not a lot of sleeping happened in that house.

There were days when the door went and I answered it

to a young girl crying on the doorstep or some tired old brass what looked like she'd been there before. I helped out around the house and when she had another girl to look after I would set up the parlour – the good room at the front of the house what had thick curtains – and there she would do whatever it was she did to help.

The baby came on a Monday. Monday's child is fair of face, that's what the poem says, and it was spot on. Her tiny puckered lips was ruby red, her hair dark, and her fingers was smaller than a farthing. Bright pink and wrinkled but so strong, she grasped at me and I couldn't stop staring at her tiny nails. They was so small you could hardly see them, but perfect, everything about her was perfect. I thought then that maybe God weren't such a bastard after all, maybe He had returned and was giving me one last perfect day.

I asked Mrs Potts if I could leave the baby a little present and a letter when I left, just a note so she had something to remember me by. She said it was a nice thought. It was early afternoon and I was told to rest, it had been a long day and Mrs Potts had stuff to get on with. I don't know if she meant go and speak to my daughter's new Ma, but either way she was going to leave us be. Just me and my baby girl.

'I'm going to call her Julia, Mrs Potts,' I told her. 'That was my best friend Evie's middle name. My baby's aunty; Evie Julia Brown. She has Ted's dark hair. Maybe she's more of a Juliana. She's a little Señorita, see.'

Mrs Potts closed her eyes slowly and pursed her lips into a straight line.

'Don't give her a name, dear. It will make it all the

harder to say goodbye.'

I weren't listening though, all my ears wanted to hear was the sweet snuffling my Juliana was making against my chest what ached with all that milk. Mrs Potts told me I had to give her a bottle, said it would make the milk go sooner, but I never done that neither. I fed her like a proper mum 'cause I knew that that was the least I could do and we both felt a lot better for it. We fell asleep like that, her nuzzling against my chest and me wondering what I could do to keep her. That maybe Ma would understand once she saw her, that she wouldn't turn us out.

By the evening, Juliana was ready for another feed and cried her little lungs out, but I was no use to her no more – I never woke up again.

Death's a funny old thing. You spend your whole life trying to avoid it, then when it comes you think, '*Oh, was that it then?*'

All them little trifles in life what keep you awake at night – the rows with your mum, the funny look your boss gave you what made you think you was out on your ear, the tests at school what you failed, even illness, faith, and loss – it turns out they never really mattered. At least not in the way you think they did at the time.

Apparently I died of internal bleeding. I was too happy to feel any pain or know something was wrong and Mrs Potts, the poor soul, never saw it coming neither. A ruptured uterus, to be specific, not that it mattered in the end.

That handsome boy with the blue eyes was right, they *was* waiting for me – Evie and Ted were there on the other side happy as could be 'cause we was finally together again. Not that it was really us, of course, we were what used to be us, although I would recognise them a mile off. Light and love, that's what they were now, that's what we all are in the end.

I looked back at my life and saw what a complete mess the three of us had made of it. What a pity, what a great pity that whole sad story was. We decided we'd try again, and Evie and Ted agreed that next time I'd be with my baby girl, and we wouldn't make the same mistakes again. You have to learn from your mistakes, otherwise what's the point?

PART THREE

'This too shall pass'
Anon

CHAPTER FIFTEEN

Hazy sunlight streamed in through the bay window onto Ella's forehead. Why were the curtains open, and why was it so bloody hot? Her mouth was dry and stale. She reached for the bottle of water on the side of the bed and took three loud gulps. The radiators hummed a reminder that they had been on all night, which explained her tight face and puffy eyes.

She pulled her covers off and tried to recall the previous day. Her body was aching pleasantly so she hadn't imagined the amazing sex. They had definitely eaten the Christmas treats as her tongue was still furry with orangey chocolate, but there was something else. Zac's arm was wrapped around her waist and she threw it back, waking him with a start. Clambering over him she ran her hands over his bare back.

'What are you doing?' He laughed and tickled her but she didn't laugh back.

'I had a strange dream or another hallucination or something. Let me touch your shoulder blades.'

He lay on his front obligingly as she straddled his lower half, running her fingers over his back and below his arms. She wasn't sure what she was looking for, a sharp nub, perhaps, or a loose feather.

He sighed and tried to twist around again.

'You didn't imagine it, Ella.'

She jumped off him, put on her T-shirt, and backed up against the wardrobe, the feel of its cool mirrors reminding her of how it had all begun. He smiled and propped himself up on his side, his wavy hair falling over one eye and his lips parted. He had a glow about him. How had she never noticed?

'You must have questions,' he said.

The bedroom walls vibrated with apprehension. Why was he with her? She wanted to cry or run away or throw herself into his arms. Instead she stayed where she was, her hands pressed flat against the glass.

'How many women have you slept with?'

Zac raised one eyebrow.

'I am an angel, Ella, a being from another realm. You can ask me anything about the past, the future, about God, and the answer to life, but your first question is how many women I've had sex with?'

'Yes.'

'OK. The answer is one, just you. Next question.'

'I don't believe you.'

Zac sighed again.

'I told you last night I've only ever loved you, and I'm not allowed to lie. Neither am I particularly permitted to fall from grace for a pretty face, but you are clearly irresistible and a bad influence.'

She could see the truth in his eyes, his unearthly eyes that were a different shade of blue every time she looked at them. He wasn't lying.

'Come and sit down, Ella. Nothing has changed.'

'Are you crazy! Of course it has, *everything* has changed! Yesterday I thought you were my boyfriend and now I discover you aren't even human. I thought we were

222

a couple. We even had *sex,* God knows *how* many times yesterday!'

'Four. Seven if you include the night before. Is that a problem?'

'Yes! Maybe, oh, I don't know. I'm confused, Zac, what's going on?'

She slid down the doors to the thick carpet, her knees drawn up and her head bent forward. She wrapped her arms over her head and remained like that until she felt Zac's hand on hers. He had pulled on a pair of loose grey sweatpants which hung low at his waist. She peeked over her arm and into his face full of concern.

'I thought I was imagining it the first time I saw you but we've met before, haven't we?' she said.

He sat down beside her and entwined his fingers through hers. It reminded her of their journey on the Tube. Did the strange vision have anything to do with this?

'Yes, Ella. We met a long time ago.'

'When I was a child?'

'Long before then.'

She unravelled herself and sat cross-legged beside him, feeling like a schoolchild waiting for story time. She needed to understand.

'It's hard to know where to start,' he said. 'This is the first time I've had to explain everything to a person. I'm an angel, they call me Zadkiel, and my role is to watch over people and assist them should they call upon guidance. I keep them true to their life's plan. A Path Keeper, if you will.'

'A what? A Path Keeper? It makes you sound like a gardener,' she said. 'I never prayed for your guidance, by the way. I didn't even believe in angels until last night.

223

What the hell are you doing here?'

'You're right, you didn't call me. But that's because you're different. An exception.' He brushed the hair from her face. 'I was there in your first life, which happened to be my own beginning. We met in an Italian town called Fiesole near Florence, over two thousand years ago. I've been in every one of your lives. Every birth and every death you've ever experienced I have been by your side. I fell in love with you the moment I saw you and I have been falling in love with you over and over in every lifetime you've had. Until a few months ago, I'd kept my distance and watched from afar or helped your transition from death to Home easier. But this time, this time you spoke to me. This time you noticed me and you wanted me too. It's impossible to walk away.'

Ella wanted to reach out to him, to stroke his cheek or brush her lips against his, but she didn't. He wasn't who – or even what – she thought he was. She tried to take her hand out of his but he clung tighter.

'Wait, my *other* lives? So we are, what, reincarnated or something? You've known me in different forms before this one?'

'Yes. Nearly one-hundred lifetimes. Each version of you has been female, and each one as wonderful as the last.'

'Why do I never come back as a man?'

Zac shrugged. 'Because your soul is still looking for me.'

Ella didn't understand. She had no recollection of any other lifetime or of him, not really, unless that vision …

'Who was I in my last life?'

'You were Evie Brown. Shy and beautiful Evie Brown

from number 2 Victoria Street, East London. You were best friends with Dolores Smith until she fell for your brother, Ted. Neither of them were the same after you died.'

'How did I die?' Ella asked, but she already knew. She could smell the cloying soot and hear the rumbling above her. It was closing in on her again, the grey people and their piercing screams.

'You've already seen it, Ella. A World War Two German bomb fell on Bank station on the eleventh of January 1941. You were at the foot of the escalators but the blast ripped through the entire station. You were one of the lucky ones, you didn't suffer.'

Ella nodded slowly, rubbing her nose with the cuff of her sleeve. Faint images were beginning to appear, like fragments of a dream or wisps of smoke, evaporating as soon as she tried to touch them.

'My mother let me down, didn't she? I wouldn't have been there if my mum had kept her word.'

'Mrs Brown was at home, Ella, she didn't know where you were.'

'You know what I'm talking about. Dolores Smith returned in this life as my mother, didn't she? It's all coming back. Mum and Dolores even look alike.'

Zac nodded.

'You've shared many lives with Felicity. Many people in this life have played a large part in other existences. It's all part of the game, the circle of life.'

'How very Disney,' Ella said. She had no idea what was real any more. 'So what was your role in that, Zac? Why didn't you save my life and spare me the pain of hundreds of tons of pavement falling on my head? I know you were there.'

'I'm not allowed to alter anyone's life path. Before someone is born they decide what their life's lesson will be, the direction their life will take, and the people that will feature in it. Of course, everyone has free will which can affect the course they take, and that's where angels step in. We nudge people along, influence them a little so they stick to their original plan. We give them comfort in their hour of need but we aren't allowed to save lives. We just come and go like any other person does. The eleventh of January 1941 was when you were meant to die and I was there for you. There wasn't much more I could do.'

Ella got up and threw open the patio doors. It was a bitterly cold but bright day and she breathed in the crisp air until it filled her lungs. Zac snaked his arms around her waist and she elbowed him, harder than she intended to.

'Don't touch me, Zac. I'm not ready to go back to normal, whatever the hell that is. I wish you'd never told me.'

'Ella, I warned you. I tried to walk away but you wouldn't let me.'

'How was I supposed to know you weren't human? I thought you were some poor confused guy. I could have coped with that. Why didn't you just stay quiet? Things were finally … perfect. It was all so bloody perfect.'

Zac was silent. She glanced over her shoulder at him leaning against the door frame. He was far from a majestic or heroic being. He looked like a little boy.

'I'm not meant to be here, Ella. I only came to see you again like I have done in every one of your lives. I just didn't expect you to *notice* me, let alone feel the same way about me as I have always felt about you. Angels can only stay on earth the time it takes to help the person we're meant to help, so I expected to be called back after a few days because you weren't someone that needed me. But somehow I've been here for months and I'm struggling to get Home. I'm going to get in trouble, I need to go back.' He took her hand. She tried to pull away but he increased his grip. 'Ella, I love you and I know you love me because everything you feel I feel ten times stronger. The problem is. I'm keeping you away from your life's True Path, one that isn't meant to include me, and you're keeping me here when I should be with my own. That's why I never wanted us to happen, because we were never meant to be together. I'm not meant to be with you.'

'How long do we have?' she asked.

Zac shrugged. 'A week, maybe. I'm surprised I haven't been forced back sooner. Our love is frowned upon in my realm, although angels and humans have been together before. The difference is that I revealed myself to you and you loved me back. If I stay longer. I'll be punished for standing in the way of you and your fate. I need to go so you can go back to the Path you chose to follow before you were born. As Evie, you chose to die when you did. In this life, you chose who you would marry before you were even born.'

'What? Who? Have I already met this dream man of mine?'

'Yes.'

'And it's not you?'

'It can never be me. I'm an angel, I have never featured in your life Paths.'

Ella's face was numb. She wasn't sure if it was from

the cold or destiny's slap in the face.

'And you got in the way of me and this guy?'

'Yes. I hit him.'

'Josh? Josh and I are meant to be a *couple*?'

'Yes, that's why I made sure you were both at Indigo. The bar belongs to us, the angelic realm. It's where our powers are strongest.'

Ella thought back to the strange symbol on his shirt that night and the excitement in Kerry's voice when she tried to tell her what it meant. So it was an angelic sign. It all made sense. How easy it was to get them in, the calm of the bar, and the gorgeous staff.

'So everyone that works there is an angel? Even that manager?'

'Yes, that was Selaphiel ... she's an Archangel.'

'She's a bitch.'

Zac suppressed a smile.

'Anyway,' Ella continued. 'What you said about me and Josh being together is bullshit. I don't fancy him. OK, maybe I did a bit at the beginning ... before you and I ... you know. But after the way he acted I don't want to even speak to him again. It's you that has been on my mind since we met. What am I meant to do, just forget about you and go out with that vain idiot?'

Zac looked at his feet and Ella felt the earth shift. What a load of crap! So fate had made sure that she and Josh had every opportunity to get together but Zac had got in the way? But it was Zac she wanted, and now he was saying he was going to leave anyway? What the hell was she meant to do with *that* information?

Minuscule flecks floated before her eyes. She thought back to the flashbacks of her last death and the plaster falling. Except she was alive now, getting another chance, and it was snowing. It was going to be a white Christmas, after all, just like she had hoped. Yesterday with their fireside picnic and festive songs was the closest Ella had got to the magic of a perfect Christmas and now Zac had ripped it away from her.

'Come inside, Ella, your feet are getting wet,' he said.

The flurry of snowflakes was swirling faster and thicker now, as if God was having a big pillow fight and covering her world in tiny fluffy feathers. She stared at the white sky.

'What's Heaven like?' she asked. 'Tell me about God.'

Zac steered her inside, his hands scalding her frozen arms. He wrapped her dressing gown around her shoulders and closed the door.

'That won't take long. Neither exists.'

She followed him inside.

'What? You said you are there in death to make the transition easier, so where do we go when we die? You called it Home.'

'That's right, we go back where we belong. We return to our original form. Light and love, that's what everyone is made from, that's all there is. Pure love.'

'So it's a different realm where we all float about like balls of light somehow communicating and plotting our next life? With no God, just a bunch of angels?'

She sat on the bed heavily.

'How can I describe a place you'll never see while alive when no human word has been invented to explain what it is? Just see living as a temporary state, like going to work, then we return to our constant state where we find peace. Which is why we call it Home.'

'So if there's no God, who's in charge?'

'The seven Archangels. Mikhael is their leader.'

'And us? Who's in charge of human lives?'

'You all are, individually and collectively.'

'But you are an angel. God is meant to be your boss.'

'No.'

'I need a drink.'

Ella walked to her sofa and thought back to the night they had fallen asleep together there. She thought he had been praying that evening – perhaps he had been talking to the angels. She ducked down to the cabinet and pulled out a dusty bottle of port. She had been thinking about it the previous day after having discovered it in Richard's wine cellar. She had planned to share it with Zac; they would open up the crumbly stilton she had been saving and watch a Christmas movie or play a board game. Instead he had repainted her world in colours she couldn't see.

She filled a glass, then a second, drinking them as fast as she could, the thick liquid warming her throat and settling in her belly like a pool of hot blood. She'd had chocolate for dinner the night before and was on her third glass of port for breakfast. As a child she had been told only God could judge, so maybe it was a good job he didn't exist.

She offered Zac a sip but he shook his head.

'This is ridiculous. I don't want to lose you, Zac. Isn't there anything we can do?' she asked, blinking back tears. He gently took the glass and set it on the coffee table. He knew what she needed, of course he did. She stepped into his strong arms and he held her tight, her bones turning to liquid along with her resolve, and she cried heaving sobs into the crook of his neck.

'There's only one thing we can do, Ella,' he said softly. 'We make the most of our time together.'

CHAPTER SIXTEEN

Ella sat up in bed eating what was left of the Christmas pudding straight out of the packet and drained her fourth glass of port. Zac lay beside her, bare-chested and in his tracksuit bottoms, an amused expression on his face.

'No, Ella, vampires and werewolves don't exist.'

'Don't laugh at me!' she said, spraying black crumbs over her sheets. 'After your wing-flapping trick last night you could tell me Father Christmas was downstairs banging the Tooth Fairy and I'd believe you.'

Ella took another bite of her congealed breakfast and coughed, washing it down with what remained of the wine.

'Have some water, you'll make yourself ill.'

'You don't get to tell me what to do, Zac,' she said, raising her glass at him in salute. 'I don't care who or what you are. I haven't forgiven you yet.'

He was right, she felt sick. The taste of cinnamon and orange peel from the Christmas pudding was burning the back of her throat. She wanted some water but wasn't going to give him the satisfaction.

'OK, another question,' she said. 'You're in the Bible, right? I've seen your name mentioned with Rafael and Gabriel and all those others. So, is that all lies too, everything in the Holy Book? How come some guys wrote about God and Jesus and millions have worshipped

233

it for two-thousand years if it's a load of bollocks?'

Zac laughed. She loved the way he threw his head back with complete abandonment. She wanted to jump astride him, run her hands over his tight chest, and kiss him hard.

'That's the most common question I'm asked,' he said, 'but no one has ever put it like that.'

'What? So other people know you're an angel?'

'Not recently,' he replied. 'I'm talking way back, hundreds of years ago, when people met angels on their pilgrimage through mountains and learnt the errors of their ways. It was easier back then, you could appear and they would fall at your feet, do as they were told. People are a lot more cynical now; you prefer coincidences to miracles, not that there is any difference. So I work in my human form, it's more effective.' He got up and crossed the room to her small fridge, taking out a bottle of water. 'Here, before your headache gets worse.'

She snatched it out of his hand and drank it gratefully.

'Jesus of Nazareth,' he continued. 'He was a good friend of mine.'

Ella coughed and wiped her face with the back of her hand. 'He existed?'

'Of course he did, he was the last and greatest Nephilim.'

'Nephi-what?' Ella shouldn't have drunk so much; her head was spinning and she couldn't keep up with this surreal conversation.

'Nephilim – angel-born. The Book was right about Joseph not being his father, but Jesus wasn't the son of God – he was Archangel Gabriel's child.'

'The angel?'

234

'That's right, you met him, actually. He served you at Indigo.'

'Gabriel, father of Jesus, made me a fucking cocktail? Are you kidding? You mean that black guy with the sexy jade eyes? Ha! So the angel was giving more than just messages to the Virgin Mary? I can see why, he's hot.'

Zac smiled. 'You really are quite vulgar, Ella, but yes. The virgin bit was added hundreds of years later. Mary was very much in love with Gabriel but never knew the truth about him; he appeared in and out of her life sporadically until he succumbed. She was quite a persistent woman. Back then, angels were curious about women – they watched human emotions and relationships unfold every day and wanted to experience it for themselves. They didn't realise how powerful love combined with a physical body was. Something I've only just learnt myself.'

'So Jesus was black?'

'Mixed race. Half Arabic, half angel, although his skin was dark.'

'Bet that wouldn't go down well with Bible bashers nowadays.'

'Yes, I have to say, Gabriel was somewhat put out when Jesus was depicted as a white man with a beard. People believe in things that make them comfortable. Unfortunately, Jesus didn't have a beard. In fact, he looked just like his father but with darker eyes and his mother's grace.'

'Shit. Wish I could go back to my convent school and tell the nuns that. They would have had a fit! Was that why Jesus had special powers, because he was a Nephithingy?'

'That's right. Gabriel had to leave Mary – he gave no explanation but promised her a gift. When she found out she was pregnant and that her true love wasn't coming back she panicked and confided in Joseph. He was a kind man, a poor but wise carpenter. He and Mary had been friends since childhood and he loved her, promising to stand by her and raise the child as his own. They had to leave their village, of course, people wouldn't have been fooled, so they headed for Bethlehem and ... well, you know the rest.'

'Did Gabriel tell her the truth about Jesus?'

'Of course. She had to know. A baby fathered by an angel is unique; there would have been no hiding it.'

'So how come the whole Son of God thing was invented? Why did they base a whole book on a lie?'

Zac plumped up the pillows behind him and sat up.

'Angels were powerful then, not part of myth or folklore like they are now. Everyone knew about us and feared us. Paintings from prehistoric times – the Egyptians, the Greeks – they all depict winged humans. We were no secret. The problem was that those in power before Jesus' time, kings and emperors and the like, were not as strong as angels and their people listened to us more than them. So gods and religions were invented. You see, if there was someone bigger and stronger than us, someone that controlled the human world *and* angelic realm, then that made us and humans kind of equal. And their representatives on earth, the kings and priests, they got to call the shots. They did terrible things in His name, they still do ... but it was so effective that eventually this all-knowing, powerful God that no one had actually seen *did* rule the world. Any messages we then attempted to impart were presumed to come directly from God so you humans stayed in power. It was very clever. Angels by their very nature are peace-loving beings; we just let you get on with it and carried out our work in a more subtle fashion.'

Ella was dizzy. She closed her eyes and concentrated on her breathing. He was tearing down the foundations of everything she knew. She thought back to the school masses she had sat through, how she had worshipped a fictitious God and stared at a dying Jesus. She'd always hated the way he'd hung from that cross, staring blankly at her through his bloody crown of thorns. Now she understood, now she could see his dark eyes hadn't been looking out at the congregation in peace and love – his stare had been accusatory, hating them for being so stupid and gullible. He wasn't a martyr for any cause, he was a good man persecuted for the sins of his father.

'What happened to Jesus after he died as a … Nephilim? Do they reincarnate like humans or turn into angels?'

A flicker of pain passed over Zac's face.

'Angels are angels and humans are humans, but Nephilims are special. They live the life of a human but have nearly all of our powers except the wings and teleportation. When they die they can choose to continue their angelic work as humans on earth in a constant cycle of re-birth, slowly shaping your world into a better and more enlightened one. There were hundreds of Nephilims before Jesus. Some have returned over thousands of years and been exceptional scientists, painters, philosophers, humans with a gift, talents that get diluted with every life but exceptional none the less. They've changed this world. They had an aura that made people worship them in their own way. Many died because of it, many of your great leaders and creative geniuses have suffered for their desire to make the world better. Not a lot has changed in the last two millennia.' He sighed. 'Humans have a problem with great people making a difference. Change propels the world forward, but most people prefer to stay still and retain their power. Jesus didn't come back – the human world wasn't one he wanted to revisit. Instead, He became an angel, like I did.'

'You? So you were born to a woman?'

'Of course, only the original seven Archangels are clean bloods. The rest of us came through the union of angels and women on earth. No angel has become a father by accident, and angels that choose to appear as women have never attempted to carry a baby because they wouldn't be able stay on earth long enough. Jesus was the last Nephilim. After we saw what the humans did to him to punish Gabriel and our kind, we couldn't let that happen again.'

'So you could have returned to earth in your human form? Does that mean we could have been together in all my past lives?

Zac shook his head. 'We first met in 5BC, during my first life on earth and yours, in the Tuscan hills of Italy. You were Arabella, I was a shepherd boy, born to the local whore and taken in by a farmer. After I was murdered I was banned from returning to earth. Archangel Mikhael took me back and forbade me from returning. I don't know why.'

She sat up. 'What do you mean murdered? By who?'

He got up and headed for the bathroom. 'I'll tell you in

a moment, but first I have a very real human call of nature.'

Ella smiled and closed her eyes. She was in love with an angel. A sodding angel! She was spending Boxing Day in bed with a half-naked ethereal being discussing their past lives. It was beyond surreal.

There was a light tapping at her bedroom door. Why would Zac go to the toilet and return via the bedroom door? She adjusted her pyjama top and opened the door. Her step-brother was leaning against the door frame, his snake-like torso void of any structural support.

'Sebastian! What the fuck are *you* doing here?'

'Charming as ever, sis. I've missed you too,' he whispered, cocking his head to one side and looking her up and down. 'A little birdie told me you've been moping about all winter.' He traced the seam of her collar with his finger, stopping at her chest. 'Did a boy break your heart, baby girl?'

She swiped his hand away and tried to shut the door but he jammed his foot in the way.

'Why are you here, Sebastian?'

'I've been away all year and this is how you welcome me home?' He gave an exaggerated pout. 'Don't be angry, little one, big bro didn't want you to have a lonely Christmas, that's all. Your precious mumsy called to wish me a merry Christmas and mentioned you went skiing, which was strange as my friend said he saw you two days ago heading to town …'

'You have people spying on me?'

'… and I thought, "Why is my sneaky little sis lying? Is she that sad that she'd prefer to be alone than in New York with Mummy and Daddy?" So I've come to the rescue. We are going to have a lovely time together, you and me.'

He glanced at her crumpled sheets and the single wine glass beside the empty bottle of port.

'Party for one? How naughty.'

'Fuck off.'

He stepped over the threshold. She tried to bar his entrance by stretching out her arm but missed the wall and stumbled into him.

'Bit tipsy? Last time you had a few too many you fell into my arms then too, funny that.'

'Why do you have to be such a creep, Sebastian?'

'I don't *have* to be, my little minx.' He leant in closer. 'I *choose* to be, and you love it.'

This was the game he played, she should have known from last time. The ruder she got, the more it spurred him on. He was smiling now, revealing his tiny teeth. He hooked his finger into her pyjama top and popped open the top button. She slapped his hand as hard as she could but he just laughed and undid the next one.

'Come on, Ella, don't you want a big, strong man to keep you company?'

'She has one,' said a low voice.

Zac stood beside Ella and wrapped his arm around her waist. She was thankful for the support. Her head felt heavy and the acid from the wine was rising in her throat. She swallowed and flinched as it burnt its way down, a throbbing pain building in the centre of her head. She watched her step-brother through heavy eyelids. Other than two faint lines creasing on his forehead, he remained unruffled. He held out his hand.

'Why, hello. I'm Ella's brother, Seb.'

Zac ignored his proffered hand and stared at him.

'No, you're not. You're Richard's son.'

'Yes, that's right,' her step-brother replied. 'And you are?'

'I'm Ella's,' said Zac.

'Ella's what, exactly?'

'Ella's everything.'

Zac dug his fingers into her waist and pulled her towards him, kissing her hard. What was he doing? Didn't he just say he was leaving again? Her body responded before she had time to decide what she wanted. She looked over at Sebastian, who was struggling to conceal his shock and it gave Ella a thrill of pleasure. Good, she thought, and leant further into Zac's kiss. She was falling into him, deeper than before. She knew what he was now, but instead of scaring her, it magnified her need for him. Zac loosened his grip on Ella, leant over, and slammed the door hard, forcing Sebastian to move his fingers away from the frame just in time.

CHAPTER SEVENTEEN

Ella broke away from Zac's kiss, rubbing her fingers over her swollen lips as if creating a barrier between them.

'I'm sorry, this is going too fast. What we had ... how could we ever go back there after ... you're ... you're not who I thought you were.'

Zac nodded and moved to her dressing table, where his T-shirt and jumper lay. He put them on and rooted through his black bag, taking out a ball of socks.

'I can't take it,' she continued, desperate to fill the awkward silence. He wasn't the same as her any more; he was more powerful and stronger and it excited and intimidated her in equal measure. And now Sebastian was back and had expected her to be alone. The thought sent icy shivers through every part of her. 'What was that about, Zac? You said you didn't have long here, so why are we carrying on where we left off? Are you out to hurt me more?'

Zac had his socks and trainers on now and walked to her. He cupped her face in his hands and ran his thumb over her lips that still had the imprint of his kiss on them. She fought the urge to take his thumb in her mouth, caress it with her tongue, taste him and feel him inside her again.

'See, Ella, you need this as much as I do. But you're right. We don't get a happy ending. In the next week or two I'll have to leave you and I can't say when, if ever,

I'll be back.' He let his hands fall to her shoulders. 'I shouldn't have kissed you then, it was impulsive of me, but I couldn't stand the way Sebastian was looking at you. I love you and I always feel your fear, don't forget that.' He smiled, 'and I feel what you're feeling now.'

Ella tried to ignore her cheeks heating up.

'He won't have liked it, you know. He will be even angrier now. He's relentless when he gets something in his head.'

'What's the story between you two?'

'You don't know? I thought you knew everything about me?'

'No, Ella,' Zac said, concern etched on his face. 'I haven't been watching you like some celestial stalker.'

'You don't sit on a cloud every day gazing down on me while you polish your halo?'

'Is that a euphemism?'

'You have a fucking dirty mind for an angel,' she said, smiling.

'And you have a filthy mouth for such a beautiful woman. No, I don't know anything about your past, not from this life at least. Do I need to worry about him?'

Ella didn't want to talk about it – she had spent years trying to block Sebastian from her mind and now he had arrived slap bang in the middle of her personal drama.

'He gets jealous, you know what big brothers are like.' Zac looked unconvinced. 'He's always been possessive over me, territorial, even. I don't know why.'

'I know why. This happened before, in our first life together in 5BC.' He looked at the bedside clock behind her and rushed to the back door. 'Look, I have to go now, it's urgent. I won't be long. I'll explain everything later.

Lock your bedroom door. I'll go out the back so Sebastian won't know I've left. I don't want you talking to him on your own, I don't trust him. I'll be back very soon, just wait for me.'

Ella nodded and did as she was told, locking the back door then turning the key in the bedroom door and putting it on her bedside table. Her and Sebastian in a past life? She already knew he was bad news, but she'd been able to handle him on her own so far. She was glad to have a few hours to herself – it would give her the chance to digest everything Zac had said and try to figure out how she felt about him. She loved him, of course she did, but what was the point of carrying on?

She went to the bathroom and splashed her face with cold water. She couldn't stand the idea of Sebastian having touched her pyjamas, so changed into one of Zac's T-shirts and a pair of knickers and got into bed. The effects of the port were wearing off; her head was throbbing and her eyes felt heavy. It was midday and her stomach was grumbling but she was too tired and confused to eat. She pulled the cool covers over herself and fell into a light, fitful sleep.

The click of her bedroom door unlocking woke her with a start. She sat up and blinked, struggling to focus as tiny specs of colour faded from her eyes.

'Zac?'

'Much better than that, little sis'

Ella ran to the door but was too late, Sebastian was already in her room.

'Get out!' she shouted.

Her step-brother shut the door behind him but stayed

in the shadows. She had forgotten how little she was wearing until Sebastian ran his eyes slowly up her body, his lascivious gaze like ice cubes dragged up her legs and across her braless chest. She pulled her top down to her knees but it instantly sprang back up.

Her step-brother remained slumped against the door frame and gave her a half smile, his blond fringe falling into his snakey eyes.

'How did you get in?' she asked.

'I have a key to every room in this house. I was here when they renovated, remember? What's the matter … you hiding something from your brother, baby girl?'

She hated everything about him. His tiny teeth, the way his voice squeaked like a teenager, the fact that he never stood up straight, always leaning against walls or draping himself over furniture.

'Just tell me what you want, Sebastian.'

He stepped forward and turned the key in the lock, placing it back in his pocket.

'What I always want. You.'

She lunged at the door handle and he pushed her back.

'Not so fast, missy.'

She struggled against him. He was slim, but he was strong. He pushed her back and laughed like a cat toying with a mouse as she reached for the handle again. Grabbing her wrists, he pinned her arms above her head and pushed her against the wall.

'Keep your hair on, firecracker,' he said, standing to her side as she kicked out and thrashed her head against him.

'This isn't funny, you moron. Get off me or

I'll scream. Zac's here.'

Sebastian laughed even louder. His breath smelt of cigarettes and something bitter. Whisky. She recoiled. He must have been in the pub while she had been sleeping.

'Scream as much as you want, no one is here. Not even your ickle boyfwend.'

The baby voice he used when he spoke to her made her want to punch him.

'I'm not your sister, I never have been,' she spat. She twisted against his tight grip, chafing her wrists and making them sting. She stopped struggling and kept very still. *Think, Ella.* He leant in closer and she turned her head from the rancid fumes on his breath.

'You like him, don't you? Are you in luuuuurve?' he whispered, spittle collecting in the corners of his thick lips. His laughter was forced and his mouth curled in a snarl. 'I heard what he said to you before he left.' He put on a whiny voice. '*We don't get a happy ending. I'm leaving you, eventually. We can't last.* I had to have a drink, thought I was going to puke. So lover boy doesn't want you any more but you're still getting your damp knickers in a twist. That is very, very *pathetic*.' He emphasised the last word loudly in her ear, his hot breath burning her wet cheek. 'Hats off to the boy. Fucks you and chucks you and you're still running after him with your panties around your ankles.' He tightened his grip, manoeuvering both wrists into one hand. 'Did you not think I would find out that you went into *my* room, flicked through *my* porn mags, and stole *my* johnnies so you could ride that pitiful kid's prick? Does his pretty face make you hot and wet or is it your big brother you've been thinking about while he's had his cock inside you?'

He pushed himself against her hip and she felt him twitch and stiffen. 'Hey, relax. It's just you and me, and we have all the time in the world.'

'He hasn't dumped me, you fucking arsehole,' she cried, blinking back tears of fear and frustration. 'You don't know what you're talking about. He's going to be back any minute so let … me … go!'

She was using all her strength but couldn't move. Sebastian tutted, shaking his head slowly.

'Baby girl, you are deluding yourself. I just saw him getting a bus into town with some blonde bird. See, you weren't that hard to replace. And even if he does come back, what is he going to do? The doors are all bolted. Like I said, it's you and me. Just like the old days.'

He wiped a tear off her cheek with his finger and licked it.

'Zac!' she screamed.

Sebastian leaned forward heavily, muffling her cries with his spare hand.

'Shhh, he doesn't want you, little one. Why are you wasting your time with a boy when you could have a *real* man? Don't you remember the first time we met?' He ran his finger down her raised arm and across her ribcage. 'Remember how upset you were that Mummy-kins was getting married, how you jumped into my arms and said how pleased you were to finally meet your big brother after being alone for so long?' His tongue flickered at the corner of his mouth. 'You practically *begged* me to take you there and then. It wasn't as if your mum gave a toss where you were, anyway – not when all eyes were on her at last.'

Ella had spent three years trying to erase all memories

of her mother and Richard's wedding day. It had been in all the magazines as 'Wedding of the Year', but all she could recall was Sebastian's face looming over hers, the weight of his body, her concentration at counting the cracks in the hotel ceiling and wondering when it would be over. She had always wanted an older brother and Sebastian had been so nice to her. She thought he would look out for her, be on her side, them against their new mum and dad.

'You told me you wanted to talk and led me to your hotel room. What a naughty slut you were. You kept saying how much you needed a hug, you were gagging for it.' He pushed harder against her hip. 'Dad told me that morning he'd officially adopted you, and there you were, my brand new baby sister, throwing herself at me. You don't know how much it turned me on. That bridesmaid's dress was too tight over your chest, but you didn't have these a few years ago.' He cupped her breast with his hand, running his thumb over it, his breath getting faster as her nipple stiffened beneath his fingertips. 'They were tiny little pink buds back then, just how I like them. You sat on my bed, babbling on about your sixteenth birthday, about being lonely and how you'd never had a proper boyfriend. Sixteen, I couldn't believe my luck!'

That's not how Ella remembered it. She'd been alone in the hotel lobby that dreadful afternoon and drank three glasses of champagne in quick succession. There were photographers everywhere and strangers were swarming around saying how lucky she was. She hadn't spoken to her mother all day, none of her friends had been invited, and she didn't know what was expected of her. The seating plan showed that the Head Table was just for

249

Felicity and Richard. They wouldn't even notice if she didn't go to the dinner. She'd stumbled to her hotel room intent on spending the rest of the evening watching television, then in the narrow hallway of the penthouse floor she'd seen Sebastian leaning against the wall and smiling at her. He had a kind face and she was so eager to get to know her brother at last, finally someone in the same boat as her. He'd hugged her and told her how much he'd been looking forward to meeting her. Ella had read about Sebastian being the UK's Most Eligible Bachelor and about his charity work in Asia. Richard had spent every possible moment telling her what an amazing son he had and how her new brother would take her under his wing, how she would no longer be an only child and could face the new world with confidence with her big, strong brother by her side.

'You were shy back then, still a baby, but your pussy was so tight.' He moved his pelvis in a circular motion against her stomach, his breath wet on her cheek. 'It's making me hard remembering how you whimpered. You loved it, couldn't get enough of me and you've wanted me ever since.'

Ella screwed her eyes shut and turned her head away, muttering Zac's name like a mantra over and over and over. Sebastian's fingers dug into her thighs and she suppressed her cries scared of turning him on further, wincing at the sharp sting as his nails clawed higher up her legs.

She clenched them together tighter.

'That's the last time you make a fool out of me, you tramp. You can shag all the boys in the world for all I care, but you will *not* say no to me again.'

His knee pushed between her legs, prying them further apart, and his mouth clamped on to hers, leaving her lip and chin slimy. He pushed his tongue into her mouth, making her wretch against the stale taste of nicotine and alcohol.

Then there was nothing.

Ella opened her eyes and rubbed her bruised wrists. Zac was beside her and Sebastian was a crumpled heap on the floor. His eyes darted from Zac to the locked door and back again. She ran into Zac's arms, her breaths ragged as he held her head to his chest. He stroked her hair and planted a kiss on her crown. Sebastian attempted to stand.

'How did you …' Sebastian stuttered.

Zac didn't let him finish. He had Sebastian by the throat and lifted him clear off the ground. Her step-brother peddled his legs and stretched his feet in an attempt to touch the cream carpet with the toe of his boots.

Zac spoke calmly and slowly. 'What kind of man gets off watching a woman suffer? Fun, was it?'

Sebastian shook his head wildly.

The muscles in Zac's jaw tensed and twitched beneath his skin. His shoulders were raised and his eyes burnt an electric blue. He didn't move for a long time, his left arm shaking at the strain of the dead weight. The room was silent save for the scraping of Sebastian's heels against the wall and his rasping breath as he struggled. Zac's grasp grew tighter.

A dull thud made Ella jump. Zac's punch to Sebastian's face had split open the skin around his left eye. Ella flinched again as Zac drove his fist straight into her step-brother's nose, this time making a splintering sound and sending streaks of blood splattering against her wall. She stepped forward and took the angel's hand. She wasn't going to defend her step-brother.

Zac turned to Ella and kissed her fiercely. The touch of Zac's lips on hers meant she was safe, she always would be. She felt the warm stickiness of her step-brother's blood on the back of her neck as Zac's fingers pulled her close, his kisses deep and urgent. She opened her eyes at the sound of something hitting the ground and looked over Zac's shoulder at her dressing table, where the two halves of a white iPhone lay like a cracked egg. Zac was still kissing Ella's neck, his left arm raised above his head.

'Zac,' she whispered.

He looked up. He no longer had his hand around her step-brother's throat. Sebastian was now suspended in the air by sheer magic, or whatever it was angels did. Her step-brother hung limply, his head bent as the back of his neck was pushed up against the ceiling. Her bedroom, once a lofty stable building, had walls over ten feet high. Blood slowly dripped from Sebastian's eye socket and nose, leaving tiny crimson spots on the cream carpet. He was staring down at them in pure horror.

Zac looked up at his victim, his arm still outstretched but his fist empty, and sighed.

'That wasn't meant to happen,' he muttered under his breath.

Sebastian tried to speak but his tears and mucus mixed with blood and his pleas were lost in the gurgling bubbles at his mouth. Zac let his arm fall and Sebastian dropped to the ground. He screamed as he fell, landing in a heap.

'What the hell are you?' he cried, his face distorted in agony as he clutched his ankle. He wiped his eyes with his arm, leaving red streaks across his white shirt. 'You've broken my bloody leg! Ella, please, darling, call me an ambulance. Call the police, he's crazy.'

Zac walked up to him and kicked him in the ankle, sending him writhing on the ground again. The angel crouched down and quietly spoke in his ear.

'Firstly, you are never to look at, speak to, or go anywhere near my girl again, do you understand?' Sebastian nodded, desperately gulping in air. 'Neither will you breathe a word of this to anyone. See your iPhone on the floor? Something tells me the police will be very interested to see what holiday snaps you took during your time in Asia. I'll be holding on to it for safe keeping. Do you understand me?'

Sebastian's body collapsed and he sobbed into his hands.

'You will leave this house and not come back,' Zac told him. 'If you bother Ella again I will get *really* angry. This is nothing compared to the hell I can wreak on your life. Now get up, you snivelling shit bag, you only have a twisted ankle. Unfortunately, you'll live.'

Sebastian limped to the back door, staggering as he inched his way across the mirrored wall of wardrobes, his fingers leaving a smeared bloody trail along its surface. Zac watched him stumble across the manicured lawn and out of the gate.

'Now I'm in real trouble,' the angel sighed.

CHAPTER EIGHTEEN

'Has he gone? Did you lock all the doors?'

Ella stood at the bathroom sink dabbing her inner thigh with cotton wool. The shower was running and the mirrors misting up. She opened the window a crack to let out the steam.

'He won't be back,' Zac said. 'But you need to get a proper lock. I hid his phone under your sofa.'

'What photos were you threatening him with? How did you know about them?'

'I didn't, I just felt his anxiety when his phone fell. When I mentioned it he panicked, so I think it's safe to presume that whatever he's been up to in Asia he wants to keep hidden.'

She wasn't going to look for herself. She dabbed at her leg again and winced.

'Here, let me take a look,' Zac said, washing his hands then taking the cotton wool from her.

Crouching down at Ella's feet, he brushed his fingertips across the backs of her legs, his face expressionless. Blood trickled down her thighs from four deep scratches, and red welts were forming from her knees to her pelvis. She flinched at Zac's touch.

'Bastard!' he spat. It was the first time she had heard him swear.

'I might need to get checked out at the hospital. The

scratches are quite deep, who knows where his hands have been.' She shuddered. 'I might need to get a jab.'

Zac's jaw tensed. Was he going to go after her stepbrother?

'Do you trust me?' he asked.

'With my life.'

He leant against the double sink and pulled her toward him so her back was resting on his chest. The T-shirt she was wearing was smeared in Sebastian's blood and her lace underwear was ripped on one side. He lifted up her top and slowly ran his hands down her legs.

'Just close your eyes and breathe,' he whispered in her ear. 'It won't hurt, I promise.'

She let her head fall against his shoulder and concentrated on clearing her mind. She was safe now. His hands moved deeper between her legs and she parted them as he placed his palms over her wounds. They stung under the heat of his touch and she hissed as she breathed in through gritted teeth. She stayed as still as she could, attempting to ignore the pressure of his thumbs against her underwear, inching their way under the elastic. If he was trying to take her mind off the pain he was doing a good job of it.

'Don't move,' he whispered, 'or it won't work.'

She closed her eyes and thought of the anger in Zac's eyes when he'd punched Sebastian and the kiss they'd shared. Something had shifted in him. He'd called her 'his girl'. Wherever he'd been, he'd heard her and come running. He would never let anything happen to her.

The cuts on her legs no longer stung. She raised her arm behind Zac's head and pulled his face into the crook of her neck.

'Zac, I know this is highly inappropriate, but you're really turning me on. Are you teasing me?'

He laughed and moved his hands away.

'Take a look.'

There was nothing on her leg but a few faint streaks of dried blood.

'How did you …?'

'Shhh.' He kissed the back of her neck. 'The less you know, the better. You've already seen that my talents stretch to more than a few feathers.'

She pushed her body against him and moaned as he planted tiny kisses along the back of her neck.

'Sometimes I swear you can read my mind. Can you?'

Zac grinned and moved his hand back between her legs.

'You tell me.'

He stroked the hem of her underwear, making her breath quicken, his other hand travelling to her waist, beneath her T-shirt, and to her breasts. His thumb pressed hard against the fabric of her underwear then he slipped his fingers inside her.

'Am I on the right track?' he murmured. With both of his arms around her, she couldn't move and she didn't want to. A delicious ripple began to unfurl in her centre, its waves spreading throughout her body until her legs trembled. As she began to climax he found her mouth, kissing her urgently.

The first night they spent together, he had been a slow and gentle lover, taking his time with her body as if he would never see it again; now he wanted her with a hunger and intensity that made her want to surrender herself at his feet. Zac was right – she was his girl and he was her everything.

He spun her round and sat her on the bathroom sink, her legs either side of him.

'Zac,' she breathed. 'What's changed? You're different.'

'You, Ella. You've changed me. You've released two-thousand years' worth of emotion. I'm struggling to control myself.'

'I'm not complaining.'

He picked her up again, kicked his trainers off, and stepped into the running shower, his jeans turning as indigo as his eyes under the jets of water. She yelped as her T-shirt was soaked flat to her body. He peeled it off and what was left of her panties disintegrated at his touch. The water cascaded over their heads with the same ferocity as his kisses.

'I want you, I want you so much,' he moaned.

Rusty water pooled at their feet, Sebastian's blood disappearing down the plug hole along with her thoughts of that morning. Zac lifted her against the shower wall and leant his body against hers as he unbuttoned his flies. He held her up by her waist as if she weighed nothing and she wrapped her slippery legs around his waist, groaning with ecstasy as he entered her.

'I love you, Zac,' she whispered, water streaming down her face.

How could she ever have been scared of him? She knew him, she always had. He was, and always would be, her one true love.

'Who was the blonde?' Ella asked as Zac stepped out of the shower and wrapped a towel around his waist.

'What blonde?'

She turned the water down while she massaged shampoo into her hair.

'Something Sebastian mentioned, he said he saw you getting on a bus with some woman.'

'Oh, she was work. Her name is Alice, she's a mother of four. She found out last week that her husband has gambled away all their money, lost his job, their home, and their car. I had to be there to help.'

'That's awful, what did you do?'

'Not much. Just asked her if she'd dropped something and handed her a newspaper folded to the To Let section.'

'Is that it?'

'Yep, sometimes that's all that's needed. On that page she's going to find her next home and attempt to re-build her marriage. Her kids will create new friendships that will help them get through it and her neighbour will end up offering her husband a job. She will tell all her friends for years to come what a coincidence it was that a stranger on a bus handed her a newspaper that changed her life. That's how it works.'

'So there's no such thing as coincidence?'

'Not really. Life offers every miracle you need, you just have to open your eyes. It's so sad how there are millions of people around the world praying right now; to their Gods, angels, loved ones on the other side, yet they never notice their prayers are being answered. So depressing how they get to the end of their life and think no one was listening.'

'But you listened to me, didn't you?'

Ella turned the shower off and Zac wrapped a fluffy white towel around her shoulders and patted her dry.

'I don't just listen to you, Ella, I *feel* you. Like I told you, everything you feel, I feel. Your voice is the only one I hear. So you can imagine what was going through my mind when I realised what Sebastian was doing.'

'I'll never be able to thank you for everything you've done, Zac. You're the only one in my life that's always been there for me.'

'That's not true. And I really shouldn't have done that.'

He helped her into her dressing gown and wrapped his arms around her waist, kissing her neck. She squirmed and giggled as he manoeuvered them to the cream and silver chaise longue in the corner of the bathroom, pulling her onto his lap.

'Honestly, Ella, who has a sofa in their bathroom?'

She curled her knees up and cuddled into him. He made her feel like a small child and a sexy woman all at once, protected and powerful. The bathroom was warm and steamy. She snuggled into the crook of his neck and felt her eyelids get heavy.

'What did you say?'

'That I don't understand who wants to lie on a sofa in their bathroom when their bedroom is next door.'

'Not about the chaise longue, what you said earlier that you shouldn't have done that. What did you mean?'

He let go of her waist and sat up.

'I don't know how to explain this without sounding cruel and heartless. I'm not sure you will understand.'

'Don't patronise me, Zac. Tell me.'

'I was on the other side of the door as soon as Sebastian locked it. I felt your fear and came straight away. I heard everything he said and as soon as he pushed you against the wall I wanted to break the door down and throttle him but I couldn't. I had to wait.'

Ella felt the earth lurch away from her, like she had missed a step and stumbled forward. How had he been able to stand there for so long and do nothing?

'What the *fuck*! I thought he was going to rape me, Zac. Why did you wait?'

'Ella, if it wasn't for the fact I'm madly in love with you I would have stood aside and let him continue. It isn't part of what I'm here to do.' Clearly her face said it all because he hesitated before continuing. 'Let me start from the beginning. Before anyone is born they've already picked their life path: their parents, the challenges they will face, the lessons they'll learn. That's the whole point; life's not meant to be easy.'

'You're telling me people *choose* to be sexually abused, or to die horrible deaths? You're telling me people that are injured in wars *ask* for it? What is wrong with you?' She stood up and poked his chest with her finger. 'I thought you were meant to be pure love and light? That sounds like a cop-out!'

'I knew you wouldn't understand. Look, I was with you when you chose this life and I know your path and the route it's meant to take. You don't, but I do. Humans are on this planet for a reason, each life is about struggling to remember the life they chose for themselves before they were even born … and eventually evolve to be better beings. The problem is that your path has changed, mainly because of me. By now you should be with your chosen love, Josh. You chose *him* as your love for this life which is why life keeps presenting him to you. Your relationship with him would have taken you to different places and

261

given you new experiences. Before you were born you chose Sebastian as your brother – not the exact details and depraved things he does – but the experience of that kind of relationship, in order to test your resolve. If I had stayed away from the beginning then today may never have happened – he may not have come back from his travels so early, he may not have been jealous, who knows? You may still end up with Josh, maybe not. One tiny change to your path can create countless forks in the road. The variables are infinite.'

'This is too much, Zac. I don't want Josh. And now you're telling me you stand by and let bad things happen? All those terrible things going in the world that you could stop, you don't?'

'That's right.'

'But that's cruel!'

'Ella, it's not cruel, it's life. Life is trying to get you on your chosen path and I keep interfering with your destiny. You weren't meant to see me at Indigo. You were sent there to meet the man you were destined to be with. I wasn't meant to be on the bus when Josh was chatting you up either, and you weren't meant to fall in love with me. It was meant to be him. My relationship with you is frowned upon as it is, but now I've revealed myself to two people and altered your life path it means there are going to be consequences, Ella. It's happened too many times.'

'So why did you do it if our time together was so futile?'

'Because I adore you. I've loved you for thousands of years, but it wasn't until now, after so long in this body, a shell made up of not just flesh and bones but millions of nerve cells and emotions, that I truly understood the way I felt about you. You are mine. I don't want any other man to so much as look at you. What Sebastian was saying to you, it took all my resolve not to kill him there and then.'

'You should have, he deserves it.'

'No, Ella, no one has the right to take the life of another. Not ever. An angel who kills loses his own life. I lost control this afternoon and gave myself away, it was unforgivable of me to have used such strength. Sebastian knows I'm not human which means I've put us both in a very dangerous position.' Zac closed his eyes. 'I'm being summoned.'

He got up and adjusted the towel around his waist. It reminded her of two days ago when he had stood just like that and told her, for the first time, how much he loved her.

'Who by?' she asked.

'My Master, Archangel –'

Zac cried out and grasped his stomach. Ella jumped back and a flash of panic passed between them. His back twitched and jerked and he rolled his shoulders.

'No!' he shouted. 'I'm not ready, she still needs me!'

Two dark marks appeared on his back. Slowly they split open like an invisible knife slashing at his shoulders, then something white and sharp pushed its way through. Like a slow-motion film of a plant rising out of the soil, the corners of his wings began to tear at his flesh and work their way out of his body. Zac arched his back, twisting at the waist then doubling over in raw agony.

'He's angry. He's taking me away.'

She looked on in horror as Zac threw himself to the floor and crawled to the toilet, heaving into the bowl. His wings were nearly fully grown and folded into themselves.

'Ella,' he gasped. 'I can't fight Him, He's angry. I need to go back. Please forgive me.'

He staggered to his feet and faced her, his wings rising over his head, magnified double in the mirror behind him. She couldn't lose him now – how would she survive without him?

'When will I see you again?' she cried. 'You can't just leave me on my own. Not again. Please.'

'I've caused you nothing but pain, Ella.' He took her hand and she laced her fingers through his. 'Don't wait for me, get back on your Path and live the right life. Don't call for me again, I can't come. He is forbidding my return.'

'Zac, don't go!'

His legs buckled underneath him. He let go of Ella's hand and fell to his knees, head bent, lying in the same position she'd witnessed in her garden all those months back. His wings were splayed on either side of him, pushing her away. He looked up, his teary eyes locking with hers.

'I'm sorry. I love you.'

She lunged forward and threw her arms around his neck but her head slammed hard against the cold, tiled floor. He was gone.

CHAPTER NINETEEN

'I have something that will cheer you up, darling,' Felicity purred, gliding into Ella's room on a cloud of Chanel No5 and carrying a large silver box wrapped in a cream ribbon. 'Your Christmas present! We got it in New York. Oh, you will just *die* when you see it. I thought it would look stunning with your olive skin.'

Ella sat on her bed in her pyjamas and slippers. She pulled her dressing gown tightly around her neck, burying her nose into it. She must have done that a thousand times since Zac had disappeared, but the scent of him was slowly disappearing. She hadn't moved from her bedroom since Boxing Day – it was now three in the afternoon on New Year's Eve and her mother was a-flutter with excitement.

'Come on, darling, you've been in a mope ever since we got back,' she said. 'Did something happen on your skiing trip with your friend? It's not another broken heart, is it? You were like this with that strange Jack boy.'

'Zac.'

'It's him again, isn't it? Oh darling, no man is worth looking this awful for.' She peered closer at her daughter. 'Oh dear, when was the last time you waxed your eyebrows?' She held her daughter's face in her hands. 'Right, you are coming tonight and that's final. The salon might be able to fit you in, get you a lovely facial and do your hair. Oh what a treat, some girly time!'

Felicity hugged her, turning to the side so her daughter's greasy hair didn't touch her face, but Ella remained limp and lifeless. She had hardly said two words since her parents' return – nobody had asked about her Christmas. Ella had moved her bedroom furniture around in order to cover up her step-brother's blood on the carpet, but her mother didn't remark on that either. As far as Richard and Felicity were concerned, Sebastian was still in Asia and everyone had had a super duper Christmas.

'Open the pressie, darling. It took me *ages* to choose it.'

Ella shuffled over to the package and untied the bow. She was curious even though she had no intention of leaving her room tonight, or ever, for that matter. She peeled back the transparent tissue paper and carefully lifted up the dark blue fabric, which rippled through her fingers like water.

It was the colour of his eyes. Was she ever going to get away from him? Could he still feel her? The thought was strangely satisfying and gave her enough strength to stand up and look at the gift properly. It was an utterly exquisite evening dress. Encrusted with dark blue crystals it had tiny straps and hung low at the back, falling into indigo pools around her feet.

Ella looked at her mother, who gestured she try it on. She stripped off and stood in nothing but her knickers in front of the mirror. Her mother was right, she looked like crap. Her hair was limp and un-brushed, her nails short and flaky, and her face harrowed with dark smudges circling her dull eyes. She slipped the dress over her head and shivered as it slid down her body, sending her mind racing to Zac's fingers and his caress.

She took a deep breath and looked up. Wow. Standing on tiptoes she could see what everyone else could see – a slim, confident, and beautiful woman. She pulled her hair up onto her head and stood to the side. The dress clung around her chest without needing any support, gathering in silky folds at the small of her back. As she walked it trailed behind her, swishing like the ocean at night.

She gave her mother her first genuine smile in months.

'Thank you, it's gorgeous.'

'Oh sweetie, you look radiant.' Felicity gave a little clap. 'You will be the belle of the ball. *Vogue* is going to be there tonight. Can you believe it! Not to mention some very important people, and their gorgeous sons. Here, try these on, they're Louboutin!'

The shoes were barely there, just thin silver straps with towering heels. Ella disagreed with her mother on most things but when it came to fashion, Felicity rarely got it wrong.

'Right, get yourself together; we're leaving for the salon in half an hour.'

'I didn't say I was coming,' Ella muttered, but it was no use.

Five hours later, Ella stood by her front door feeling nervous. Why did it feel like a betrayal? She had started to speak to Zac in her head.

It's like you've died and I'm talking to your ghost. You promised that as long as I needed you, you wouldn't leave my side. Well, I need you tonight, Zac. Please get me through this.

'Your new haircut is so on trend, darling.' Felicity

handed Ella a thick cream fur coat. She had no idea what animal skin it was made from, the thought repulsed her, but she didn't have the energy to argue.

Ella was still getting used to her new look. Her hair had been chopped to her shoulders, highlighted in golden caramel tones with a blunt fringe. She stared at her reflection in the glass panel of the front door. She looked like a totally different person, and it had nothing to do with her makeover. Because of Zac she knew too much now. Life had lost its mystery – Zac had taken it with him, along with her reason for living.

Felicity placed a hand on her daughter's cheek and Ella saw a flash of emotion in her eyes.

'You aren't my little Spanish *niña* any more, look at you, a proper London girl-about-town. Your father would have been so proud.'

It was the first time in years her mother had mentioned Ella's father, but Richard joined them before she had the chance to ask further.

'Wow Ella, very snazzy!' Richard lent forward and gave her a kiss on the cheek, then took his wife's hand and kissed it too. 'Felicity, my love, you look utterly ravishing as always. I am the luckiest man on the planet. Here, sweetheart, it can't compete with your sparkling eyes but it's a close second.'

He pulled a black leather box out of his inside pocket and handed it to his wife. A diamond necklace lay on a velvet cushion, each stone getting larger with the centre one surrounded by tiny lilac stones.

'I know you never take your necklace off but I thought you may make an exception for tonight.'

Felicity hesitated, then unhooked the thin chain around

her neck and placed it in the white porcelain musical box on the mantelpiece as Richard clasped the diamond necklace in its place. She moved her head from side to side, the light from the fire reflected off the stones, sending millions of stars racing across the ceiling.

'Thank you, Richard, it's perfect.' She kissed him then giggled as he helped her into her coat.

Ella watched them and wondered if she would ever be as happy. Whether there was a man out there that would make her feel the centre of his universe, someone she would drop everything and anyone for to make happy. She doubted it, not any more.

Their chauffeured Bentley sped through the North London streets with ease. New Year's Eve was the busiest time for the capital but no one was stupid enough to drive into town. Ella was simply relieved she didn't have to go anywhere near a Tube for a while.

'Right, darling, let me brief you about tonight,' Felicity said, slipping into PR mode. 'As you know Richard's newest hotel is the London Golden Star. You are familiar enough with it should anyone ask you any questions, right?'

Ella nodded.

'Good, just remember tonight is all about Cloud Ninety Nine. You don't know how lucky we are, honestly, sweetie, our marketing guys saw tickets for tonight's opening selling on eBay for six thousand pounds! Can you imagine? It's the tallest restaurant in Europe! You can practically see the sea! Anyone who's anyone is going to be there: magazines, newspapers, celebrities, and of course, *us*. And it's us that everyone is going to want to talk to, so make sure you *smile,* please.'

Ella felt sick. She went to rub her eyes then remembered the fake lashes. It was only a few hours, she assured herself. If she just posed for a couple of pictures and stuck with Richard and her mother all night it wouldn't be that bad.

'Darling, don't sulk. I remember the first time I was dumped, but you'll get over Jack.'

'Zac! His name is Zac, for God's sake!'

'Well, imagine *Zac's* face tomorrow when he sees you all over the papers looking so lovely. Won't he feel silly.'

'Doubt it.'

'Anyway, I told you before he wasn't right for you. There was something about him I didn't trust.'

Ella stared straight ahead.

'I didn't like the way he looked at you,' her mother continued.

'You mean he's the first man that hasn't tried it on with you?' Ella whispered, so Richard wouldn't hear.

Her mother narrowed her eyes and jabbed a taloned nail into Ella's arm.

'I don't need any of your melodrama tonight. This is a very important occasion for me and Richard. You will keep your mouth shut and your nasty little tongue still, do you understand?'

Ella understood all too well. They continued the rest of their journey in silence.

The Bentley stopped outside the glass-fronted hotel, and as soon as her door was opened Ella was hit by the roar of photographers lining the red carpet. She stood blinking at the onslaught of flashbulbs then followed her parents up the stairs, past security, and into the building. A huge Christmas tree stood in the centre of the large foyer, bedecked in silver and white. Three glass chandeliers hung from the ceiling, and the white marble walls and stairs shone. It was like standing inside a diamond and the glare was giving Ella a headache. She wanted to leave already.

'Please follow me, sir.'

A tall gentleman in a black dinner jacket led them to the lifts. Two women in long dresses were also being escorted, but made way for the Fantz family. Ella had visited the hotel a couple of times for lunch with her mother but had never been to the top floor, neither had she remembered that the lift was a transparent bubble suspended on the side of the building. She held on to the rail and closed her eyes.

'Keep your legs together, sweetie. We don't want any photos of your knickers,' giggled her mother, much to Richard's amusement.

It took three minutes to reach the penthouse restaurant and roof gardens. Ella gingerly stepped out of the lift, and once her feet were firmly back on the ground she summoned up the courage to look at the view. It was magical. London glittered below like a map of multi-coloured stars. The Thames snaked its way through the sparkles, and bridges criss-crossed the city, creating angular patterns over its surface, although they were so high up it was impossible to make out any landmarks except for the huge yellow wheel on the water's edge.

Swirls of fine mist began to form over the twinkling nightscape, billowing like cigarette smoke and creating a veil. Snow was forecast. Other than the light dusting on Christmas Day no more had fallen, although it had got bitterly cold. Ella stepped into the warmth of the restaurant and took a glass of champagne from a silver tray. *Three hours until midnight*, she told herself. *All you have to do is talk a little, eat a little, and smile a lot. As soon as the celebrations are over you can get back to bed and stop pretending your life didn't end six days ago.*

Ella spent most of the cocktail reception staring out of the window and listening to the jazz band. Occasionally someone would recognise her, even with her new hairstyle, but she found that if she kept her back to the party she was relatively safe.

'Oh, there you are.' Felicity took her hand and pulled her through the throng of sequins and furs. 'We're being seated for dinner, and I have a big surprise for you!'

Their table was at the front of the stage. Ella sat down and knocked back another glass of champagne, looking at her mother expectantly.

'What do you mean?'

Felicity smiled and turned to Richard. He gave a nod, and into his pocket he placed his mobile phone that moments earlier he had been speaking animatedly into.

'We're being joined by a very special young man, someone you have missed dreadfully, and who we know you'll be over the moon to see!' she chirped, looking at the entrance and waving.

Ella strained to see over the heads of the guests. A man in a dark tuxedo was walking toward them, but she couldn't see his face. Her chest tightened and her stomach churned. Had they found Zac? He told her he would never see her again, had something changed? Would she be starting the New Year with him in her arms?

Richard stepped out of her line of vision and the man sat down beside her. It wasn't Zac.

'Hiya, sis. Haven't seen you in such a long time!'

CHAPTER TWENTY

Ella froze.

'I told you she would be shocked to see you, Sebastian,' Felicity said, beaming at her daughter. 'Isn't it wonderful, darling? He flew all the way back from … where was it again? Oh yes, all the way back from *Cambodia* to be here.'

Sebastian smiled at his step-mother and turned to Ella. 'You're looking great, sis. Love your hair.' He leant in closer, his breath hot in her ear. 'Very sexy.'

'Oh no! What happened to your face, Sebastian?' Ella's eyes widened in mock horror. 'Looks like you got a pasting?'

Richard stood behind his son and squeezed his shoulders.

'A pasting? Of course not! He's a ruddy hero, more like!' he shouted over his head. 'He told me all about how the children's wing of the hospital he's been building caught fire and how he ran back in to save a little girl. Hospital *begged* him to stay but he said he wasn't going to miss New Year's Eve with his old man and family, rang us straight away. That's m'boy!'

Sebastian patted his father's hand and turned to Ella.

'So how are you?' His voice was quiet and sincere.

Her mother also gave her a sympathetic look.

'I'm sorry, Ella. I had to tell him about you and that

Jack – I mean Zac, boy. He was so worried to hear you had spent every day crying into your pillow, said he wished he'd been able to be there for you and give you a big hug. Aren't you lucky to have such a caring brother?'

Two other couples joined them at the table. Richard introduced them as the Mayor of London, a foreign ambassador from a country Ella had never heard of, and their uninteresting wives. Richard and Felicity busied themselves quizzing her step-brother about his travels while the other couples made polite small talk. Their food arrived and Ella was thankful for the excuse not to have to speak to anyone.

She couldn't believe the nerve of Sebastian. She could see him out of the corner of her eye glancing at her, his gaze occasionally falling to her cleavage. She'd thought the last time she had seen him – limping out of her patio door – would be the last. Whatever was on that phone was obviously worth the risk. She picked at her second course, a tiny sliver of salmon on a triangle plate surrounded by an exquisitely painted design of red and black sauces. Food had no taste since Zac had left – she hadn't eaten in days and this was certainly not going to convince her to start.

Felicity and Richard excused themselves and headed for the stage. They were presenting the Mayor with a cheque on behalf of Richard's hotel chain for some local charity or other. The press stood in front of their table with their cameras ready, occasionally turning to shoot Ella or Sebastian.

She glanced at her watch then looked outside. Only another thirty minutes until midnight, not long now. The promised snow had finally started to fall and the entire restaurant was cocooned in a white woollen mist as the blizzard howled outside. Ella's head was pounding, as if a giant hand were shaking the elaborate snow globe they were sat in. She couldn't help but smile at the thought of all the money these idiots had spent and they couldn't even look at the view.

'Pleased with yourself?'

Sebastian sat down beside her. His left eye was a deep purple and still so swollen he could hardly open it. He wore a small plaster over the bridge of his nose and his top lip was puffy and red.

'Why are you here, you creep?' she said. 'You heard what Zac said, don't mess with me or he'll kill you. You've already seen what happens when you fuck with him.'

Sebastian shrugged and looked around.

'I don't see your magical boyfriend anywhere. Looks like he loved you so much he dumped you as soon as he thought he had competition. Now, are you going to tell me what the hell happened?'

Ella smirked.

'You got your arse whipped, that's what, and then you cried like a pussy. You got what you deserved, now leave me alone.'

Sebastian gripped her knee tightly under the table.

'Don't play dumb with me, you little bitch. That freak walked through walls. He pinned me to the fucking ceiling with magic. What is he?'

'I don't know what you're talking about. I think he must have hit you harder than you thought.'

'What's this then?' Sebastian held up a small digital camera and pressed play. Ella saw her bathroom and herself in the shower, the camera focused clearly on her face. Her mouth was open wide in the throes of passion. She had one leg resting on the shower wall and was pushing her hands onto the back of someone's head, which bobbed between her legs as she bucked and writhed. Ella hit the camera out of his hands and picked it up from the ground, hitting it hard against the floor until it smashed. Sebastian laughed.

'You stupid girl. I've made plenty of copies. Did you think I would just walk away? I had my camera in my car. You really should shut your bathroom window, the entertainment was fascinating. Not only did he fuck you something rotten but he grew wings and disappeared. That should make for an interesting YouTube video.'

'You bastard,' she hissed, holding on to the table edge to steady herself. She could see her parents exiting the stage and heading back to the table.

'Give me back my phone and we'll call it evens,' he whispered, and gave her knee another painful squeeze beneath the table.

'OK, let me call someone.'

Ella walked to the back of the restaurant and scrolled down her list of contacts, her hand shaking as she held the phone to her ear. She could only see one way out of this mess then it would all be over. She made a short call then sat back down.

'It's done,' she said.

Sebastian smiled, his tiny teeth glowing in the half light. Felicity waved at them and tottered over, her cheeks rosy from the champagne. The band had started and she was trying to convince Richard to dance with her.

'Come on, darling, this is my favourite song. I know you like a bit of Marvin Gaye,' she giggled, her arms around his neck.

'Wait a minute, kitten, we haven't told Ella the good news!' he said as Felicity sat on his knee and adjusted his bow tie. Ella looked away. Her mother was practically bouncing on his lap, for God's sake. Ella looked at Sebastian who had a smug look on his face. She didn't know how much more she could take.

'Well, darling,' Felicity said, her words blurring at the edges as she tried not to slip off Richard's lap. 'We've been having a little chat with Sebastian and he was telling us how he is planning on renovating his Chelsea pad, so we invited him to come and live at the house for the next couple of months. Richard and I were so worried about leaving you alone while we oversee the Dubai project, but now you'll have company. Isn't that super!'

Bile rose in Ella's throat. This couldn't be happening. Sebastian was never going to leave her alone, and with no Zac to protect her she was completely alone. She stood up, her chair scraping across the tiled floor.

'No way!' she screamed, flinging her fur coat over her shoulders and sending wine glasses shattering to the floor. 'No fucking way! If he moves back in, I move out!'

Felicity glanced around. Most of the guests had heard and were looking, and some of the photographers had started to take photos.

'Will you keep your voice down, you are causing a scene,' she hissed.

'That's all you care about, what the *public* think. How about what *I* think? Does *that* matter? Are you not even a tiny bit curious *why* I feel like this?'

Richard stood up and walked calmly over to Ella. He adjusted her coat around her shoulders and spoke softly in her ear.

'Let's go and get some fresh air.'

He led Ella out of the dining area. She twisted around in time to see Sebastian smiling sweetly at Felicity as she leant over to speak to him. There was no way she was going to spend another second under the same roof as that monster. It was his fault she had never felt comfortable with her parents, his fault she had never had a decent relationship with a guy, and his fault Zac had left for good.

Richard led her to the balcony that ran around the edge of the restaurant and opened the door for her. Outside was deserted. The snow was falling fast and Ella's feet crunched and squeaked as she strode to the plastered brick wall that surrounded the roof garden. She leant over the edge but couldn't see a thing; the beautiful London skyline had disappeared along with the noise and stress of the city. She stood with her eyes closed, snowflakes settling on her lips and hair.

'Come in now, Ella. You'll die a death out here.'

Richard was at the patio door looking at her laughing and twirling around in the snow. He stumbled as Felicity shoved him out of the doorway and charged at her daughter. She pushed her to the corner of the patio, out of view of the diners inside, and slapped her across the face.

'Don't you ever humiliate me again, you ungrateful cow. How *dare* you speak to me like that!'

Ella knew this was the end. She had no energy left. They had won and she had lost. She'd lost everything. Zac said she'd slipped off her Path, that by stepping into her life he'd altered her life plan. So what was she putting herself through this for? Zac was the only person that truly understood her. He would have done anything for her and now he was gone for ever.

'I can't do this, Mum.'

Felicity was shaking. Ella wasn't sure if it was from the cold or the white hot rage she could see burning in her mother's eyes.

'You're one of the most envied girls in the country, Ella.' Felicity shouted. 'You don't know how lucky you are to have us as parents. What on earth do you have to be upset about?'

'Why don't you ask your precious step-son?'

Ella pointed at Sebastian, who was now standing beside his father. Richard pulled him outside and shut the door behind them.

'I don't know what this is about,' Richard said. 'But if you have something to say to us, Ella, I suggest you do so now.'

The biting wind whipped around their legs and whistled through Ella's diamond earrings. She could no longer feel her feet, now submerged in snow.

'I lost my virginity to Sebastian on your wedding day,' she said, looking at her mother. 'I shouldn't have let him kiss me but I did, but then he wanted more. I said no. I was crying, begging him to stop, but he didn't listen. And I didn't go skiing over Christmas, I was at home with Zac. Last week Sebastian came back from his trip early because he thought I was on my own. He tried to rape me again but Zac stopped him and that's how he got beaten up and why Zac left me.'

Sebastian glared at his step-sister. Richard and Felicity

didn't have to ask if it was true, it was written all over his face.

'The police will want to question him soon. I have his iPhone and it's full of photos and videos of ...' A tear trickled down her cheek and she blinked, letting it fall. 'What he's been doing in Asia with the young girls there ... it's awful, it's ... Zac told Sebastian if he ever went near me again we would take the photos to the police, so my friend picked it up from me a few days ago for safe keeping.' Ella looked at her step-brother. 'But you couldn't keep away, you disgusting bastard! I just called my friend and your phone is with the police.'

Nobody moved. The snow continued to fall, settling over Ella's words that lay scattered at their feet. The sound of the night's festivities were muffled by the sheer brilliance of white that enveloped them, blinding them from looking anywhere but at the broken girl before them.

'Does that answer your question, Mum?' Ella said quietly, her tears scalding her frozen face. 'Is that enough to be upset about?'

Felicity ran to her husband and sobbed into his chest, her delicate shoulders trembling as he held her tight, but Richard's eyes were on his daughter and they were full of remorse. Ella watched Sebastian over her parent's shoulder as he opened the door and stepped back into the restaurant. She let him go, it was over. Felicity's face was smeared with mascara and her hair was limp from the melted snow. She untangled herself from Richard and stroked her daughter's pink cheek.

'My darling, my poor, poor baby. Don't you dare breathe a word of this to anyone. This will ruin us. It can't ever go public.'

Ella began to laugh. At first, softly, so softly only she could hear it, then it erupted out of her chest until she was bent over, gasping for air. Her mother stared at her, looked to her husband for help, then turned back to her hysterical daughter.

'Richard, do something. She's totally lost it!'

He shook his head at his wife.

'No, Felicity, *you* have.'

He looked beside him for his son who was no longer there and shouted Sebastian's name. Inside the restaurant, a group of guests that had just disembarked the lift blocked Richard's way to the exit. The glass lift bubble was barely visible as it worked its way down the outside of the building with her step-brother inside it.

Ella and her mother stood face to face. One way or another, Ella was going to find peace, she was going to see Zac, and she was going to feel whole again. It was time to go. She walked to the wall and looked over at the swirling mist. There was nothing but white. There was no beginning and no end. Balancing on a large plant pot, she pulled herself up and sat on the ledge.

'What on earth are you doing, Ella? That's enough dramatics for one day. Get down!' her mother cried.

Ella raised one foot up then the other and tried to find her balance, wobbling as the wind picked up her coat and hair. She straightened her long dress and unhooked it from her heels. Felicity stared up helplessly as Ella clambered on to the ledge above, where Felicity could no longer reach her feet.

'Stop, Ella! You're going to rip your dress. Everyone is counting down to midnight inside, get down before they realise we're missing. If you come back inside, we can pretend none of this ever happened.'

Through the dense fog, Ella could hear the faint sparks and whizzes of fireworks. She had her back to her mother but she could only see one face.

'Zac!' she cried.

Then she jumped.

HAMPSHIRE, 1973

Margaret Montgomery-White disliked more than she liked.

She required three things in life; order, silence, and respect. Tall and willowy, she wore her hair in a candy-floss bun and adorned her swan-like neck in a multitude of jewelled necklaces, predominantly pearls and diamonds. She couldn't abide anything that wasn't real.

Her acquaintances – for her friends were few – often remarked to one another that Margaret's hardness was a result of her being childless.

'She should do more charity work,' they said, 'or get a dog.'

Margaret wasn't prepared to subject herself to the filth and neediness that either would entail.

'Of course love is bound to disappear if you have nothing to pour it into,' they would whisper over Afternoon Tea. 'Look at her, with nothing to love in her life she's nothing but an icy, soulless husk.'

Since the day Margaret had married Charles, he had tried in vain to produce a son and heir to his fortune, a successful tea empire that had been handed down through generations until it lay squarely on his shoulders. His work was his one and only true love – it excited him more than any woman had ever done.

'I can't let my business die alongside me, I need a

son,' he would remind her every morning. 'I'm nineteen years older than you, it won't be long until I retire. It is your duty to give me a son!'

And so night after night he heaved his bulk over his wife's slender frame, no longer making any attempts to kiss or touch her. His heavy breath would hiss in her ear with the exertion of his endless jabbing. Like a sharp knitting needle he poked and burst every last bubble of happiness left in her tiny heart which struggled to beat behind her crushed ribs. During those nights she would leave her body beneath his and let her mind wander, attempting to grasp any wispy strands of memory that floated like summer clouds around the room, as her husband incessantly plundered for the last remains of hope hidden inside her.

Her parents had decided she was to marry him before she had met him. She could no longer recall her first impressions of her husband or whether anyone had asked her opinion, but she did remember having felt hopeful. Not in love, but at least excited about what life had in store for her. How she wished she could return to those safe childhood days and feel hope again. Or feel anything at all.

When, in her early forties, Margaret discovered the first signs of the menopause, she privately rejoiced. She went to a Harley Street clinic and explained to the doctor that her cycles had diminished, that she had been feeling a little more unsettled than normal, and that she required a prescription for appetite suppressants as her new love of French pastries was causing her petite frame to bulge. Although her husband was taken with her new plump breasts and rounder bottom, she certainly was

286

not. Anything that further encouraged him utterly repulsed her.

She had expected to walk out of the doctor's office with a packet of pills and a list of menopausal guidelines, but instead was told she would have to wait a further week for the results of her blood and urine tests.

It was on the night of her and Charles' twentieth wedding anniversary, during a silent meal at home that had been prepared by their cook Agnes, that Margaret received the call from the doctor himself. He said the Lord was smiling upon them and that she had nothing to fear, she wasn't being stripped of her womanhood but in fact would be giving birth to her first child in just over four months' time.

She calmly replaced the receiver and returned to her meal. She would deal with the news in the way she dealt with every other aspect of her life – with poise, dignity, and copious amounts of gin.

Margaret loathed her daughter from the moment she expelled her from her body. The final push ripped through her with a searing heat that rendered her motionless. But Margaret was past caring about her own ashen remains; she was merely relieved that her body was no longer occupied.

As the midwife beamed and cut the cord, Margaret closed her eyes and turned her head, waiting for the screaming baby to be taken away. She instructed the midwife to bottle feed the infant, informing her she felt too dizzy to breastfeed. She wondered for how long she could make excuses before she would be forced to look at the mewing bundle that had been placed in the plastic cot beside her.

Once showered and dressed, she told the nurses she was ready to see her husband. He marched into her room and glared at her.

'It's not a son, Margaret. I can't possibly pass the business to a girl!' He ran a plump hand over his damp face. 'This won't work. We will have to ensure she marries well as soon as she is able; find her a suitable husband that can be trusted with the inheritance.'

Margaret pulled the thin, starched blanket over her shoulders.

'Do as you wish, Charles. I want nothing further to do with either of you.' Her voice was hollow, a distant echo. 'You will choose a name and a nursemaid and I will remain your wife legally, not in any other sense. You can take her home alone. I will be going away for a few days.'

Charles nodded mutely as Margaret turned her bony back to him and finally slept the sleep of a free woman.

Bewildered and nervous, Charles arrived at his empty house and stood at the threshold, staring into the hallway and wondering what he was going to do. He'd placed an advertisement in the local newspaper for a nanny but had secretly hoped she wouldn't be required, that Margaret would come to her senses and return home in a day or two.

His little girl began to whimper in his arms, her cries growing in ferocity until she was screaming in sharp fits, kicking out at his awkward embrace.

'Señor White, I can help?'

A young lady peered over his shoulder. Slight and dark, she was dressed in smart black trousers and sensible shoes, and in her hand was a bucket filled with rags and assorted bottles. He'd asked his secretary to send a cleaner to make the house presentable for Margaret's return and had forgotten. The young lady held out her arms for the baby and he gratefully handed over the bundle of fluffy blankets.

'There's formula in the nursery, girl,' Charles said stiffly. 'It's on the second floor, the yellow room.'

She found the kitchen and switched the kettle on.

'I am Juliana,' she said. 'And the baby? She has a name, Mr White?'

Charles waved his hand.

'Why don't you choose one, we're not really that fussed.'

As the olive-skinned girl found her way around the kitchen, he looked her up and down. She was rather fetching. She had thick, black hair to her waist, a lovely round bottom, and large blue eyes like a china doll – an arresting combination for a foreigner. Perhaps the baby had brought some perks with her after all.

Charles smiled and breathed a sigh of relief as he headed to his office for a well-deserved cigar. It was decided; he would hire the girl as a nanny, move her in, and things could go back to normal.

Juliana chose the baby's name as instructed, but Mr Montgomery-White wanted something prettier. 'Call her Lily for short,' he announced, and it suited her. She was a delicate child with porcelain skin and blonde hair.

Lily was a colicky baby, who in the absence of a mother and her milky scent, would contort herself into a twisted rope of hysteria after every bottle feed. Juliana, who within a few days of her new role loved the baby like her own, would fret every morning at the sight of the sleep-deprived Mr Montgomery-White. He would scowl as he scraped at his burnt toast and holler that no woman in his household could do a thing right.

'I don't ask for a lot!' he would shout. 'A decent meal, a clean house, and a quiet child. Is that too much to expect?'

Agnes and Juliana would bow their heads and attempt to soothe the baby, resorting to taking her out on long walks in her pram until she would collapse, exhausted, and fall into a fitful sleep. After an especially trying night, Juliana waited for her master to finish his breakfast then crept into the dining room.

'I'm sorry, Señor White, we don't know what to do. I think she wants her mama.'

Charles glanced up from his broadsheet, his bushy white eyebrows and pinprick eyes barely visible behind the giant newspaper.

'Speak up, woman, and I won't have any of that spic talk in my house. Queen's English only. I am *Mister* Montgomery-White.' He shook his newspaper. 'And as you very well know, her mother is not here. She is your responsibility until she is old enough for formal education, so I suggest you work it out. Quickly!'

Juliana scurried upstairs to her room, tears filling her clear blue eyes. Lily lay in her Moses basket, red, rigid, and screaming, her arms above her head in surrender to rage. Juliana had not come all the way to England to live on the coast as a nanny. She had been heading to London in search of her own mother, a beautiful blonde girl from the East End who Juliana had been told had loved her with all her heart before having to let her go during the war. Juliana was on her own adventure, and she was not going to settle for anything less than a happy life.

She unzipped her small suitcase. She owned very little, so it wouldn't take her long to pack her stuff and leave. As she lifted a pile of clothes out of her drawer, her hand closed around something smooth and cold and she smiled. The porcelain music box was the only thing she owned that had belonged to her real mother, and inside, now yellow with age and creases so sharp small tears had appeared, was the note her mother had written to her thirty-two years previously. Juliana thought about the Spanish woman she called Mother.

Juliana had been fifteen when her parents told her she was adopted. It came as a surprise to her; she had always felt part of their large family with her dark hair, although her blue eyes had been the talk of the village.

Her adopted parents had arrived at the East End Docks of London after fleeing from the Spanish Civil War and their quiet, sun-bleached village in the South of Spain, landing straight in the centre of The Blitz.

'You have to believe in angels, *hija*,' her Spanish mother used to tell her, 'because one brought you to our door in the middle of a war. In the dead of night a large, kind lady came to our home and made us parents, just like that, as if she knew that in her arms she carried the answer to all our prayers. We didn't tell a soul you weren't really ours, because in our hearts you always had been.'

Juliana had been handed over to the Spanish couple along with a bag containing some tired baby clothes, a feeding bottle, a tin of dried milk, and a small china music box with a note inside.

Juliana reached for the music box and read the note, the words of which she knew by heart.

Dear Juliana,

I don't want to say goodbye but I ain't got no choice. Your Pa is looking down from Heaven and will make sure you get a new mummy what will look after you better than what I can. See the world, little one. Never be scared to love and stay with the people what make you happy – there ain't really much more to life than that. I promise we will meet one day. Until then, I will always love you. I hope your new Ma plays you this tune and it makes you as happy as what it made me. Dolly x

Juliana looked down at the screaming infant and wondered, does life really give you second chances? She opened the lid of the small white box and Lily's screams dissolved to a whimper. The baby turned her head to the magical sound and struggled to focus on Juliana's face.

The child didn't know what it was to have a mother that loved her, but Juliana could change that. Maybe her search for her own mother had led her to her destiny, a different version. The two stared at each other, mother and daughter again, a bond that could never be broken.

One year later, Margaret Montgomery-White returned, took one look at Juliana and her charge, and made the servants' quarters in the attic her new home. And that's where she stayed, alone, never to venture downstairs again.

By the time Lily was eleven, she discovered that being

herself ultimately meant disappointing somebody, so she learnt to adapt. It proved to be an invaluable lesson that would serve her well.

For Juliana she was a happy, easy child who enjoyed the simple things in life, like watching wild ponies run through the nearby New Forest and listening to fireside stories about little white villages that God had scattered over the Andalusian mountains like snow. For her father she was obedient, polite, and studious. He asked for nothing more. For her mother she learnt to be invisible.

Montgomery Hall was her parents' rambling farmhouse on the outskirts of Lindhurst in the South of England. It was a small village and theirs was the largest house, which like Charles' business, had been passed down through generations of Montgomery-Whites. The eighteenth century stone building was surrounded by acres of green fields, one of which housed a large stable for Ebony, the black stallion Lily's mother had once been so fond of riding. Lily attended the local village school, which Juliana had fought tooth and nail to keep her in. Had Charles had his way she would have been sent to boarding school as soon as she could walk.

Lily's days were spent playing on the village green, running around the labyrinth of rooms and outhouses in her large home, and practising her Spanish with Juliana. It was a bone of contention with Mr Montgomery-White. He hated that his nanny and daughter communicated in a different language to him, but Juliana had explained that ladies in high society were expected to speak more than one language so he had agreed on the condition he would also hire a French tutor for the girl.

It was easy to forget it was four people that lived in Montgomery Hall, that high up on the forgotten landing was the Lady of the Manor. Since her unceremonious return just after Lily's first birthday, she had remained at the top of the house, a heavy presence that bore down on everyone below. Weeks would pass when Margaret didn't venture downstairs and days when they wouldn't hear a sound. At eight o'clock prompt every morning, Juliana would accompany Lily up the four flights of stairs and they would stand to attention outside Margaret's door until they were summoned.

Lily had never seen her mother look anything but impeccable, her hair as high and stiff as the rest of her, her flowery perfume mingling with the sweet tang of her breath. Her vast attic room overlooked green fields and the stables. Against the long back wall of her bedroom leant dozens of dark canvases covered with inky black and blue strokes of oil paint, which filled the room with dizzying fumes. Open windows were forbidden in her mother's presence.

'Shut the door, child.'

'Good morning, Mother,' said Lily that morning. 'I hope you are well.'

Margaret didn't reply, but instead passed a critical eye over her uniformed daughter.

'Who did your hair like that?'

'Agnes, Mother.'

Lily looked down and spotted a new scuff on her patent shoe. She tucked it behind her other ankle, praying her glance would not bring it to the attention of her mother.

'Get the nanny to redo it. That cook's hands are only

fit for pummelling pastry.'

Long silences would often pass between mother and daughter. Lily would use the time to see what had changed in the room from the previous day. Sometimes a new painting would appear among the others by the door, a bookshelf may have been re-organised, or a new empty bottle added to the row that stood by the door, their labels facing the wall like errant children that had disappointed their mother. Each and every one having failed to satisfy Margaret's expectations, the next promising to be better than the last.

'That's all for today, go and learn something,' her mother said.

With a wave of a hand, Lily was dismissed and she walked quickly to the door and into the waiting arms of Juliana.

'It wasn't so bad this time,' she whispered as they made their way downstairs. 'She didn't even look at my shoes.'

They both took long breaths, the air getting lighter the further down the house they got. Lily thought of the charade as nothing more than an everyday exercise, like brushing her teeth or saying her prayers. It was the only contact she had with the Mistress of the house, and Lily struggled to believe the old ghost was really her mother.

At night she would lie in her bed, her eyes as wide as saucers as Juliana would read her tales of Cinderella and Rapunzel. There were other girls living in castles and towers with uncaring mothers – all she needed to do was be a good girl and one day the perfect man would save her. It was always the good girls that got to escape, the pretty and well-behaved ones that did as they were told. She clung on to that thought, never imagining it would serve her so well in the future.

Lily sat at the kitchen table practising her long multiplication. She was in the last year of primary school and had to work hard if she wanted to go to the local secondary school where the most popular girls in her class were going. She was excited; Juliana had promised she would be allowed to ride her bicycle to school on her own like the big girls did.

'Your father is home from business tonight,' Juliana told her. 'Agnes and I need to get some groceries, let Mrs Dupont in for your French lesson in twenty minutes, OK? We won't be long.'

Lily nodded and gave her nanny a peck on both cheeks. She loved the way she was treated like a grown up now and was trusted to be home by herself. The summer holidays had seemed daunting at first; she'd feared the impossible task of filling such a yawning stretch of time, but she had nearly made it through to the other side. She had been allowed to play on the village green if the local children needed fielders for their game of rounders, but no one came back to her house. They called her Loopy Lil. They knew about the mad mother locked in the attic and they would egg each other on to hide in the field and see if they could throw a pebble at the window, although none dared get close enough to succeed.

Lily followed her nanny to the front gate, picking a fallen apple off the ground and heading for Ebony, who had spotted her and trotted over to the fence. The horse was older than her and she felt sorry for him. He no longer liked to be ridden and Father had forbidden further lessons, he said the animal was too cantankerous and unpredictable. Lily had her own theory; she thought the sight of her on the horse reminded him too much of her mother when she was a young rider. He had mentioned it once when he caught her flicking through old photo albums. People that remembered Margaret when she had first arrived at the village had remarked to Lily how much she resembled her mother. She knew they were right as her father looked at her strangely, as if she was growing up on purpose and stealing her mother's vigour. The older and prettier she got, the madder her mother got.

Lily glanced up at her mother's attic window and thought she saw movement from behind the curtain. It was rare for them to be open before midday. She looked again. This time the window was opening a fraction, stiffly from lack of use, but wide enough for her mother's arm to fit through. A bony white hand, stark against the ivy-clad wall, was beckoning her. Lily could just make out the silhouette of her mother through the window pane. Had she been watching? Was she in trouble for feeding the horse? Lily had already been up to her that morning and everything had appeared normal – if normal were the correct word.

She made her way back to the house, careful not to tread on the damp earth and mark her shoes. She checked her appearance in the hall mirror and straightened her skirt before climbing the stairs, the sound of each footstep resonating in time to her thumping heart. The sweet scent of juniper berries and white spirit seeped through the crack beneath the bedroom door. Lily hesitated.

'Come in, child.'

Her mother was still standing by the window, which was now firmly closed. Her eyes, which were normally quick and alert, were glassy. She turned her back and looked out over the field and stable.

'I've failed you.'

Lily didn't reply. She noticed three new paintings had appeared. This time the dark swirls of paint had taken form. They looked like grotesque faces, clawed wings, and hands. Except for one, which – although dark like the others – had a pair of bright blue eyes that stood out from its shadowy face. Lily stared at it, imagining they were her mother's eyes.

'I never wanted to be a mother,' Margaret said. 'Even after I saw you, I didn't want you. Isn't that the most awful thing a woman can say? Come here.'

Lily moved closer to the window and stood beside her, as physically close as the two had ever been. As they looked at the garden and over at the endless sea of green she pictured herself out there beneath the cool canopy of trees. She imagined the scent of bright green leaves shooting through the dry barks of ancient trees, the perfume of bluebells and sunshine on damp earth instead of the nauseating smell of freshly applied paint and the two empty bottles of gin at her feet. Those bottles hadn't been there that morning; they were new to her mother's collection of glass soldiers.

'Ebony was my horse,' Margaret said. 'I loved riding him. I bought him the year before I was pregnant with you; he was going to make me feel young again. But, of course, you stopped me riding him. Doctor's orders.'

'I'm sorry,' Lily whispered.

Her mother turned to face her and laughed, a sound

that crackled like dry newspaper. Sharp at the edges, it tore its way through the heady fog in Lily's head. If she had been permitted to cover her ears she would have.

'You're sorry? *You*! Whatever for?' her mother cried. 'For having the audacity to exist, you poor, wretched child? It is *me* who should be sorry. I've been absent from your life from the moment you entered this pathetic world. I've been absent from my own for many years.'

She turned her face away and directed her words to the horse in the distance.

'Your father is leaving me. He has a doctor coming this afternoon to assess my health, maybe even take me away. He always knew I was unhappy but did nothing, the arrogant beast!' Margaret's eyes had come back to life and they drilled straight through her daughter's, willing her to answer. 'He fears me. I've always been the one thing he couldn't control, the only person that hasn't bowed to him. Well, I tell you what, young lady, neither will you! If I can do one good thing, one last thing, I will make sure you do not become me. Do you promise?'

Lily didn't move. She had been holding her breath for so long, tiny specks of light danced and darted before her. She blinked and nodded.

'You think I don't know what love is, don't you?' she said. 'Why would you? I've never shown you any. I had it once, long before I met your father, but I followed duty, money, and success instead. I did what was expected and I failed at it. But you!'

Lily jumped at her mother's raised voice, the thick air cloying in her throat.

'You were my salvation and I pushed you away. See these?' She swept her bony arm in the direction of the

299

canvases propped against her wall. 'These are the faces that come to me in the night, the voices that talk to me. Ten years they have kept me company. I'm not listening to them any more. I'm old and I'm tired. Come.'

Margaret lay on her bed on top of the bright white sheets that were perfectly folded, hospital corners at right angles.

'I'm going to take a nap, and you will stay with me. You are the one good thing to come out of so much misery and I need to be reminded of that. Don't go anywhere, please.'

Lily did as she was told and lay beside her mother, holding her cold hand that trembled like the fragile skeleton of a winter leaf.

'I should have loved you,' her mother said. 'Because I do.'

A tear trickled down Margaret's dusty cheek but she didn't brush it away. She closed her eyes and held her daughter's hand tighter. Lily didn't move except to turn her head to her right, finding herself face to face with the portrait of the blue eyes. She lost herself in them; they were telling her she would be fine. Her mother's grip softened and the room grew silent, but still Lily remained. She drifted in and out of sleep, the paint fumes making her head heavy and thick. She thought she heard the distant sound of a doorbell then fell back to sleep, resurfacing to eager calls of her name and the sound of feet on the stairs. The sun had disappeared and the light in the room was now cold and grey, but the eyes in the painting continued to shine as the voices got closer.

The bedroom door crashed against the wall, sending

gin bottles tumbling and smashing beneath thunderous feet.

'Good God, what the hell is going on!' her father's voice boomed.

Juliana was at Lily's side, shaking her, her voice tight and wavering. '*Ai dios, mi hija*,' she sobbed, her thick hair in Lily's face. 'What did she do to you? *La bruja*.'

Lily didn't have time to answer before a strangled cry filled the room. Her father's large frame towered over her, filling up her vision.

'She's dead, you stupid, *stupid* child! Why did you just lie there, why didn't you get help?' Flecks of saliva rained down on her as her father shouted in her face. 'Your mother's taken enough pills to kill a horse and you let her, you did nothing! I will never forgive you for this.'

They were the last words she heard her father say that summer before she left for a different school, a boarding school in the North of England where nobody knew her or would call her Loopy Lil. She would reinvent herself; she could be that girl with the big house in the country, with a mummy and daddy that loved her, and a stable full of horses. The girl she nearly was. She would study hard, she would do well, and then she would escape. Her mother had taught her the only lesson she would ever need in life.

Be what people need you to be, that way you'll always be safe.

PART FOUR

Hear my soul speak:
The very instant that I saw you, did
my heart fly to your service.

Shakespeare, *The Tempest*

CHAPTER TWENTY-ONE

Ella was floating on a cloud.

The silence was deafening. She felt nothing, and saw nothing but white light above her, below her, in her mind, and pouring through every part of her. She was finally free.

She tilted her head, and through the clearing mist spotted the Thames pushing its way through the city, along with the yellow pinprick lights of the tiny cars and the patchwork of roof tops.

Look at that, she thought. *Life hasn't stopped for me.*

She could hear a soft, rhythmic beat. Was it her heartbeat? Did she still *have* a heart? Her eyelids dropped and she returned to nothing.

Felicity's screams sliced through the icy air. Within seconds, she was surrounded by a mass of dark dinner jackets, urgent voices, and camera flashes. Pure horror coursed through her veins. She couldn't think, she couldn't see, she couldn't feel, she screamed and screamed, as if expelling every last breath from her lungs would rid her of the image of her daughter plummeting to her death.

Upon hearing her screams, Richard forgot all thoughts of catching the next lift after his son and followed her howls to the restaurant balcony, where he stood helplessly as the urgent hands of strangers pulled and ripped at his wife's white gown. Felicity was horizontal in the air, kicking out at their heads, while a portly waiter prised her fingers one by one from the balcony wall. Richard watched as she was finally dragged away from the edge. Her nails were torn from their nailbeds and deep crimson smears ran along the newly plastered wall following her desperate attempts to pull herself to the ledge.

He pushed his way through the throng and reached his wife. Her hair was dripping wet and matted and a single snowflake hung from her fake black lashes. She looked right through him, her eyes wide with terror and her mouth distorted in a Munch silent scream.

'What happened?' he shouted. 'What's going on? Where's Ella?'

Silence descended, peppered only by the sound of Felicity's rasping breaths. Nobody answered. Nobody but his trembling wife knew.

Sebastian scurried through the hotel lobby, glancing over his shoulder. He was alone, thank God. He couldn't believe the fucking bitch told them! What a prick-tease, ripping his life away from him in one breath. She was probably still up there, exaggerating about what he had done, making him out to be some kind of monster. He wasn't going to let her get away with it. And what about his bloody iPhone! Why hadn't he deleted those pictures! Little bitch had double-crossed him. He had to get as far away as he could. He'd shown her the best part of the recording – after that the footage had become distorted. He'd seen the whole freaky scene for himself but it wasn't on film. It was just meant to be something to blackmail her with, but it had backfired.

Wrapping his thick black scarf around his neck and over the bottom half of his face, he stepped into the darkness, the snow falling so fast it disorientated him. The piercing wail of a siren stopped him in his tracks and he threw himself flat to the wall. How could the police have got there so quickly? He looked around but he couldn't see where to hide. Then he heard it again. It wasn't a siren, but a woman's scream, so naked and primal it was like sharp slivers of ice piercing his veins. Oh God. He ran as fast as he could, at once enveloped by the white night.

Ella stirred and opened her eyes. Zac's beautiful face was looking at her as he cradled her in his arms.

She smiled, 'It worked. I found you.'

Her eyes adjusted to the bright white around her.

'Is this Heaven?'

Zac stood up, and she fell with a thud to the ground, pain shooting up her thigh as her hip hit the ground. She was still wearing her fur coat, which looked and smelt like a damp dog, and her heavy dress clung tightly to her, soaking wet to her knees. One of her shoes was missing and the heel on the other was at a strange angle.

Zac stood before her in jeans, trainers, and nothing else. His majestic wings were tucked behind him but still visible around his rippling shoulders. He glared at her.

'Heaven? Are you fucking out of your mind, Ella! This isn't *Heaven*, this is as close to Hell as you could have taken us!'

His voice boomed through the cluster of trees surrounding them, sending a flock of fat pigeons shooting out of the branches and clumps of snow falling at his feet. She recoiled as he loomed over her, his wings growing along with his voice.

'This isn't Heaven, you idiot, this is Hampstead Heath. Did you think if you died we would be reunited in eternal bliss? Did your stupid romantic fantasies think that throwing yourself off Europe's tallest building – on New Year's Eve no less – in front of your family and the press, was the best way of ensuring we met again?'

Ella's face crumpled. She was freezing cold but his eyes burnt with such ferocity she could feel her skin scorching with shame. She wrapped her arms around herself trying to contain her wracking sobs.

'I watched the whole thing, Ella. I was begging you not to do it. I thought you were just trying to get your mother's attention. What was I meant to do? I've told you a *million* times you have a destiny worth waiting for; *you* chose this life. It's not a computer game you can just re-start when it gets too tough.'

She looked up, her tears leaving dark tracks across her ghostly face. His voice softened.

'Ella, I never lied when I said I would love you for ever. But tonight I flew with you in my arms across half of London. Your mother watched you kill yourself. Your step-brother is on the run from the police, who are right now wondering if your hysterical mum needs to be sectioned because they can't find your body!' He ran his hand through his hair. 'You created this mess and I don't know what we are going …'

His voice trailed off as he swung around, there was a rustling in one of the bushes.

'Man, on my life I swear I just saw a huge duck with a

woman in its beak.'

'Whatever,' said the second voice. 'I fink you been taking too many lugs of that spliff. I don't see no flying ducks.'

'On my life, I did. Actually, maybe it was a swan, but a really big one, yeah. It landed behind that bush. Come on.'

The voices were getting closer. Zac grabbed Ella's wrists, fell to the ground, and pulled her on top of him. Burying his wings into the fresh snow, he pushed her head down to his and kissed her passionately, her soaked glittery dress riding up her parted thighs.

A teenage boy in a woollen hat and heavy black boots reached the clearing and stopped. The moonlight bounced off the snow, highlighting his pockmarked skin. He squinted at the figures embracing on the ground and the corner of his mouth twitched into a small smile.

They were really going for it. Maybe if he stood still they wouldn't notice him. This shit was hot – *she* was hot. He couldn't see her face, but he could hear them panting and her faint moans. Her tight body was rubbing against the bloke's crotch, her legs on either side of him, and his hands were up her dress. Her round arse and black thong were showing as the guy pushed her body harder into his. The boy adjusted his jeans.

'What you staring at, man?' His friends had caught up with him and stopped when they saw the couple on the ground. The three friends didn't move until Ella looked up, saw they were staring, then pulled her dress down over her thighs.

'Uh, sorry, thought we saw something,' muttered the

tallest boy, dropping the remains of a joint into the snow.

Zac lay still. He couldn't risk raising his head for fear of dislodging the snow around his shoulders. The first boy stepped forward and pointed at the dark grey sky.

'Mate, don't suppose you saw a big white bird fly over here? Like a heron, or a really big ...'

The boy's friend smacked him around the head and they both smiled apologetically while the third kid snorted into his gloved hands. They finally turned around and trudged back through the clearing in the trees.

'Man, that was embarrassing,' their voices floated through the undergrowth. 'Why the fuck were they shagging in the snow? That's some kinky shit! And I thought *we* were sad spending New Year's getting stoned on the Heath.'

Ella waited until she could no longer hear them and went to stand, but Zac pulled her back down and kissed her again, his hands sliding up her freezing legs.

'Hey, forgot to say your haircut's really sexy. Suits you.'

She sat astride him and pulled him up so her coat was around them both. He got to his feet without letting her go, her legs wrapped around his waist. She ran her hands along his broad back where his wings had been, amazed there were no indentations or bumps. She tried not to think about it too much – it still freaked her out.

'Quick, get in here in case we get more visitors,' he said, nodding at a large holly bush beside them.

'So this is your big plan?' Ella said, as he lowered her down onto dry land beneath the boughs. 'We just hide in the woods for ever?'

He shook his head and placed his hands on her hips,

walking forward until her back touched the trunk.

'We need to get moving shortly, but there's something I need to do first.'

He pulled off her coat and slid the straps of her dress down, her nipples hardening as the cold air brushed against them. She could feel him stiff against the fabric of her dress. Spiky twigs were catching in her hair and holly leaves lightly scratched the backs of her knees as he kissed her neck.

'Ella, I only have to look at you and you get me like this.' His hands held on to her behind as he pushed himself against her. 'I've never seen you look more beautiful than when you threw yourself off that building.'

'That's a really weird thing to say, Zac.'

He stopped, his eyes were black with desire.

'Maybe, but it was the happiest I have seen you look.'

'That's because I was thinking of you. I'm always thinking of you.'

'Ella,' he groaned, kissing her collarbone. 'I didn't think I would get to touch you again. You don't understand – I've always been able to control myself, but with you I feel wild. Right now I just want to get inside you. I want to fuck you in the freezing snow until you can't take any more. I think I've been in this body too long, it's taking me over.'

He pushed her dress further down her shoulders until it hung off her waist, and then he pulled her hands above her head, running his hot tongue over her hard nipples. Her head shot back, her hair snagging on a branch.

'That's because you're becoming more man than angel,' she said, panting. 'Not that I'm complaining. Does that mean you aren't angry any more?'

'Oh, I'm *really* angry,' he said, lifting up her dress and hooking his finger through her thong. 'I'm furious, in fact. Enough chat, turn around.'

'So now what?' Ella asked, pulling on her coat.

'We get you home.'

'As in my house? You're crazy! My parents will have a fit.'

Zac did up her last coat button and planted a kiss on her forehead.

'You think they've gone home for a cup of tea and an early night? Your mother was hysterical. She's probably talking to the police right now, plus the press will be all over them. It's been less than two hours since you jumped. We have time, come on.'

Ella clambered out from under the boughs of holly. The glare from the snow made visibility easier – seeing that the park was empty, she beckoned Zac. She couldn't find her broken shoe so stepped through the snow barefoot, watching the icy particles shine between her toes.

'What are you doing?' she squealed as Zac grabbed her around the waist and lifted her high off the ground. 'Put me down!'

'No way, it's dark,' he laughed. 'You might cut your feet or get pneumonia or step in dog shit.'

'Well, you can't hold me like a naughty child all the way home.'

He smacked her bottom and she giggled.

'Go on, get on my back and I'll carry you,' he said.

'OK, but only if I can put my disgusting animal skin coat around us both. At least it's warm, even if some poor creature had to die for it.'

The streets were deserted – should anyone see them, they would look like another drunken couple on New Year's Eve. She wondered if she would have time for a hot shower before … what? She didn't have a clue what the next step was. She wrapped her arms around Zac's neck and rested her chin on his head.

'What are you thinking about?' he asked.

'How I wish we'd met in spring instead of autumn. Why it is every time I'm with you I end up soaking wet?'

'What can I say,' he said, reaching round and stroking up her leg. 'You're always wet because I'm utterly irresistible.'

She giggled and kicked at his chest with her bare feet.

'Maybe we should go back and look for my shoe. They were really expensive, my mum's going to kill me!'

Zac stopped walking and strained his neck to look at her. 'Ella, your mum thinks you are *already* dead. Life is never going to be the same. We have a long road ahead of us, you better get your head around that.' They walked the rest of the way home in silence.

CHAPTER TWENTY-TWO

'Let me get this straight, Mrs Fantz. You are saying you definitely saw your daughter, Ella, is it? You *definitely* saw her jump off this ledge?'

Richard's dinner jacket was draped over his wife's shoulders and she leant against the wall of the restaurant, grasping a glass of water in her trembling hands. She nodded, staring through the window at the patio outside.

'We've gone over this a hundred times!' Richard said. 'I told you that when you arrived.'

The policeman glanced at his notepad again.

'Yes, Mr Fantz. The only problem is, as you are more than aware, the story doesn't exactly add up. We are on the, what, 97th floor?'

'99th' replied Richard.

'Right, and the building is a glass drop. It has no architectural features that would interfere with a falling object, or in this case, person. So, in theory, one would expect to find, one,' the police man held out a finger, 'a body at the base of the building, and two,' he held up a second finger, 'witnesses that saw someone jump, fall, or land. We've been on the scene for over an hour now and we have neither.'

Felicity remained still, holding on to her drink as if it were a life raft.

'Are you calling my wife a liar, officer? Look at the

state of her! Why would anyone make this up?'

The policeman suppressed a yawn and rolled his shoulders.

'We have witnesses saying a lot of alcohol has been consumed this evening. They saw your wife and daughter arguing shortly before stepping outside. They also saw your son, err ...' he looked at his pad again, 'Sebastian, leave the terrace and enter the restaurant with you running behind him a few minutes before midnight.'

Richard nodded impatiently. 'Yes, yes, that is correct. So what is the issue? Why aren't you on the street looking for Ella's body?'

The policeman's radio crackled to life and he sighed, walking to the back of the restaurant to answer it. When he returned, his harried expression was replaced with one of confusion.

'I'm afraid we're going to have to take you both to the station for further questioning. The facts are that your wife here has not uttered a single word since we arrived, and we have no witnesses that can tell us whether they saw Ella stand on the ledge or walk back into the restaurant. You say it happened at midnight, when conveniently all other guests had gathered on the dance floor, away from the scene. As if that is not cause enough for concern I've just been informed that a personal item of your son has been handed into the Soho police station. Perhaps you can help us shed some light on that, too?'

Felicity grasped Richard's arm, the broken nails that remained piercing through his shirt sleeve.

'They think I'm like my mother, don't they? Don't let them lock me away, Richard, please. I'm not seeing things!' she screamed. 'I'm not crazy!'

The gravel bit into Ella's numb feet as she walked down her garden path like a ghost revisiting her past. She reached for Zac's hand as she unlocked her bedroom door and they stepped into the warm room. Her skin tingled as feeling flooded to her fingers and toes, her wet dress trailing behind her and leaving brown smudges on the carpet.

The adrenaline had worn off, and Ella ached all over. Peeling off her sodden dress she climbed into bed and curled herself up as tightly as she could, naked and shivering. After the anguish of the last five days she didn't think she had any tears left, but she cried so violently her chest felt bruised. She mourned her old self; the girl who back in September had started university and was nervous about making new friends, fitting in, and getting a boyfriend. The girl whose biggest worry was her annoying, overbearing mother.

Mum, what have I done!

Ella sobbed into her pillow, crying for Zac and the sacrifice he had made to save her. He had been forbidden to return but he had, and she had no idea what it meant for their future. Not that they'd ever had a future – they'd been doomed from the start. He had always known that and had tried to distance himself from her since the beginning but it had been *her* who had pushed and pushed.

She could hear Zac opening and closing drawers and cupboards but she didn't care. Everything was her fault. If he had never told her the truth they could have been in her bed, watching Christmas television and laughing. She wished she had never met him, but then how could she have gone her whole life without having felt what she had those two magical days when he was just a boy she loved?

Her covers flew up, sending a cold blast of air over her damp body. Zac was standing over her wearing a thick jumper and clean jeans.

'Come on, we have work to do.'

She tried to pull the duvet back but he threw it on the floor.

'You got us into this mess,' he said. 'Get out of bed and pull yourself together.'

Reluctantly she sat up and caught sight of herself in her mirrored wardrobe doors. Her damp hair was tangled with leaves and twigs, her face smeared with mud and make-up, and her eyes puffy – she looked like she had been in a fight. Ignoring his protests she stomped past him to the bathroom and stepped into the shower, closing her eyes and letting the force wash over her sore limbs. She didn't take long but when she emerged he had already packed a canvas bag and was standing impatiently at the bathroom door.

'What's this?' she asked, pointing at the hold-all.

'We have to leave. Do you still have the money I left here in October?'

She nodded. She also had over three thousand pounds in cash in her bedside table. Her parents were fond of handing over wads of money to her every time they left the country, which was often.

'Good. When you changed your surname, you got a British passport. right? Does that mean you still have a Spanish one in your old name?'

Again she nodded and he smiled.

'I need you to leave all non-essentials behind. Your

bank and credit cards, your UK passport, your mobile, and your laptop. We need time and we don't want to be traced. OK?'

'No, I'm *not* OK! What's going on? I'm really tired and can't take this in.'

Zac handed her some fresh clothes but didn't answer.

'Where are we going?' she repeated.

'Home.'

They were in the taxi heading for Stansted airport with one bag between them. When the cab had pulled up at the house, Ella had recognised the driver as the one that had taken them to her house after the Tube incident. The cabby had given them a cheery wave when he saw them and chatted animatedly about how he had dropped some guests off at Richard's hotel earlier that evening. He wondered aloud why they weren't there and made a cheeky comment about them eloping together, but he had sensed the tension after a few minutes and stopped talking.

'There's a flight that leaves for Malaga in just over an hour,' Zac said after a long silence.

Ella looked at her watch: 3.48 a.m.

'Are we staying at my old house? Juliana's brother and his family live there now. Mum was so distraught when she died that she said her family could keep the house. But I can't just turn up with no notice.'

Ella slammed shut the glass partition between them and the driver and turned to Zac.

'Are you going to explain what your grand plan is? I've done everything you've asked and you have hardly looked at me since we arrived at my house. I know I was an idiot, and I will be eternally thankful for you saving my life, but will you stop punishing me!'

He continued to stare out the window into nothingness.

'Zac!' She pulled his arm and he turned to her, but she wasn't expecting to see his eyes swimming with tears.

'You'll get on the plane, Ella, and you'll rest. I'll meet you at Malaga arrivals hall. Needless to say, I have other forms of travel.'

His pale face shone intermittently, lit by the orange motorway lights. Ella's lips were dry and her eyes were itchy with exhaustion. She shivered. She had dressed in a woollen jumper, jeans, and her warm parka but was freezing cold. He pulled her to him and stroked her hair.

'Put this on, please.'

He handed her a fine gold necklace with a cluster of lilac stones hanging from it, which she recognised immediately as her mother's.

'Where did you get that? Why ... I don't understand.'

'Amethyst. It will keep you safe. I will explain when we get to Spain. Rest a bit, we will be at the airport soon.'

CHAPTER TWENTY-THREE

Ella managed no more than an hour of broken sleep on the plane. She was thankful it had been a near-empty flight and a dark cabin; nobody had taken any notice of her. No doubt they didn't want to be on a flight at the crack of dawn on New Year's Day either.

She spotted Zac immediately at the arrivals hall, his still solemn stance singling him out from the groups of people waving name cards and hugging relatives. Wordlessly, he took her bag and led her to the car hire desk where she insisted on the most expensive model, a red two-seater that reminded her of her car in London. Finally she would have the chance to put her foot down on a road that wasn't bumper to bumper with irate commuters. A few minutes later, as they joined the motorway on the outskirts of Malaga, she began to regret her choice. Zac wouldn't tell her where they were heading and he didn't want her to drive.

'You're going too fast, Ella.'

'Leave me alone, it's you who insisted we skip the country so at least let me enjoy myself.'

'This isn't *Thelma and Louise*, we're not on some crazy road trip. Slow down.'

'Shut up.'

What was it with him? He saved her life and was now acting like bloody God. Pompous twat! When did he get so bossy? She preferred him when he was an awkward homeless guy she hardly knew.

She pushed her foot down further, the engine's flare vibrating beneath her seat and giving her a mischievous sense of satisfaction as she watched the speed dial climb from 130 to 150.

'That's enough, Ella.'

'Piss off.'

'You'll have an accident, there's a tunnel coming up.'

'Will I? Is this the way I die?' she asked.

Zac shook his head.

'Then I'm sure my guardian angel won't let anything happen to me.'

She undertook the lorry in front and pushed her foot down as they raced through the tunnel. The newly risen sun momentarily blinded her as she came out the other side. Her head banged against the window and the car skidded to a halt, the lorry speeding past them, blaring his horn.

Ella blinked, then realised she was in the passenger seat with Zac now behind the wheel.

She ran her finger along the delicate bump on the back of her head.

'What the fuck, Zac! You can't just magically swap seats with someone when they're driving!'

'I told you to slow down.'

'We're horizontal across two lanes. Move!'

Zac smiled, the first one she had seen since she had left him at Stansted airport.

'Don't worry, the next car is one minute, thirty-eight seconds away.'

Ella rolled her eyes and crossed her arms. Not only

was he a self-righteous prick but he was enjoying himself. She stared out of the window as he restarted the engine; she had forgotten how stunning the Andalusian landscape was in winter. The turquoise waters of the Mediterranean glimmered invitingly on her left, dotted with white triangles of sailing boats. To her right, mountains rolled into the misty distance. It was much greener than she remembered, but then her memories were of summer and this was January, the start of heavy grey clouds and tropical rainstorms. As if the skies had been listening, thick raindrops began to clunk on the windscreen. She rested her forehead against the cold window, careful not to let it touch her sore head, and allowed her eyes to close to the sounds of the pattering rain and rhythmic swipes of the windscreen wipers.

When she opened them again, the rain had stopped and she could see the signs for Marbella. She sat up and squinted through the glass.

'You need to take the next junction,' she told him. 'Double up over the bridge and head away from the sea. Do you need me to direct you?'

Zac looked at her as if he had forgotten she was there.

'Where do you think we are going?'

'My old house? Or we could go to Richard's a bit further on, the gatekeeper will let us in.'

'No, we aren't going to either.'

Ella gave a dramatic sigh and threw her arms up in the air.

'Do you know how annoying it is to have you as a boyfriend, or whatever the hell you are? I am never going to be right. Mr 'sent from heaven above' knows all. I'll never be able to compete with you. You speak every language that's ever existed, you can be anywhere at any time, you probably know the date of my death, and who I'll be in the next life. It's so debilitating, what the hell do you want from me? What can I ever do for you?'

Zac lay his hand on her knee and gave it a gentle squeeze. His face softened and he blinked slowly.

'You have shown me what it means to live and what it means to feel. I never knew the extent of what love meant until I felt it in every cell of my body. You are in my heart, on my mind, your name is always on my lips, my fingertips ache from the last time I touched you, not to mention what you do to other areas.'

Ella laughed. He sounded like a Mills and Boon character – from anyone else it would have been cheesy and weird but she loved the way he spilled his heart out without an ounce of embarrassment. She placed her hand over his, thinking back to the day she had given him the phone and they had sat just as they were now.

'I know you think I'm a know-it-all, but it's you who has pulled the strings from the very beginning. Plus there are two things you can do that I never will be able to.'

'Oh, come off it! What?'

'For a start you look great in photos and I don't.'

'Leave off, Zac, you're gorgeous. What do you mean?'

She thought back to the blurry images she'd tried to capture of him in the back of the taxi. What had he said? *'You'll never get a decent picture of me'*.

'Angels don't appear in photos or film,' he explained. 'Good job, really, or our cover would have been blown by now. Imagine all the YouTube footage of us that could have been made. Our atomic make-up works at a much higher frequency than yours. Human eyes have become accustomed over millions of years to see us but machines haven't.'

'Oh,' Ella said, thinking about Sebastian and his video. Had he been bluffing? She doubted he would upload it now he was wanted by the police, but if Zac wasn't visible in it then it wasn't nearly as awful as she had feared. 'Wait! So I'll never own a photo of you? After everything we've been through I'll never have anything to remember you by?'

A lump was forming in her throat. She was tired and it was making her emotional.

'Hey, don't be sad, there are a few paintings of me around if you're that desperate.'

'You what?'

Zac laughed. 'Mainly fifteenth to seventeenth century artists. I'm even on the ceiling of the Sistine Chapel. Michelangelo was a great man but he was a bit of a perv, used to insist on running his hands over my chest to help him with the contours of his sculptures.'

Ella snorted. She no longer questioned the things he told her. She doubted there was anything left to say that could surprise her.

'So what's the second thing? What other weakness does the great Zadkiel possess?'

'Electricity, which like cameras has only become an issue recently.'

'What about it?'

'I can't use it. It's the high atomic frequency thing again, angels can't get it to work.'

Ella's giggle bubbled over into roaring laughter. The tears that had been threatening to spill all morning finally had permission to flow, and they rolled down her cheeks which ached from her wide grin.

'Oh God, this is too much. You can throw a man in the air without touching him and walk through walls but you can't switch the lights on?'

'That's correct.'

His lips twitched and the base of his neck turned a light pink. His discomfort only made her laugh harder.

'I'm glad I amuse you,' he said. 'Truce? Perhaps you'll stop sulking now?'

Ella nodded and tried her hardest to stop smiling. They were slowing down and turning off the motorway at a town called Estepona. She had never heard of it – her mother wouldn't venture west of Marbella for some reason. The road headed over a couple of roundabouts and beneath an underpass then tapered into a narrow road that snaked its way up the mountain. They were the only moving object for miles save for a few goats in the road that forced them to slow down intermittently.

'I hate goats, they're evil,' Ella said.

Zac laughed again. 'You've always said that. The first time we met, in our first life together, you said they had devilish eyes and strange mouths.'

'It's true! Where are we going, by the way?'

'Don't you want to hear more about our first life together?'

He'd been evading her questions since London and this time she wasn't going to be dissuaded.

'Of course I do, but first tell me what the hell we're doing out here in the sticks. We head into the hills and hide out for a bit until the police lose interest, is that the plan? I'm still not sure what we're running from. I mean, no one will believe I jumped if there was no splattered body on the pavement, and it's obvious I came home after and packed my stuff. I'm nearly twenty years old. I'm no missing kid or in danger. What exactly am I in trouble for? Who's looking for us?'

Zac's face hardened, He was clenching his back teeth again and the muscles in his jaw jumped nervously.

'Mikhael.'

'Your boss?'

'Yes. Archangel Michael, otherwise known as the Winged Warrior, Angel of Death, Prince of Heaven ... and the leader of our realm. He was the one that dragged me back.'

'Will he not drag you back again, now you have disobeyed him?'

'No, he's even angrier now.'

'So what does he want?'

'To kill us.'

'What? Stop the car!'

Ella wrenched the door open and scrambled out, her arm catching in the tangled seatbelt. With one boot in the foot well, she fell to the ground and grasped at the dry earth, bunching the razorblades of wild grass tightly in her fist. She took a gulp of mountain air, drinking it in and quenching the cloying dryness that the car's heaters had been pumping into their lungs since the airport. Zac's old trainers were inches from her face as he stood over her, the drone of the car's engine the only sound. Swallowing sharply, she looked up.

'Why?'

'Because we broke the rules, *his* rules. Your path was set and I changed it. You chose your life and you chose to end it and I had no right to intervene. I returned when I had been forbidden, potentially revealed myself to more people, and interfered with your fate. I've run out of chances, Ella. He won't call me back now, he'll end it for both of us on earth. He's on his way.'

She extracted herself fully from the car and sat back on her knees. The sun peeked over the crest of the mountain, spreading a soft, golden sheen across the landscape and bathing its rocky edges in a veil of silence. All was still. Even Mother Nature was holding her breath.

'Oh God,' Ella muttered, lifting her face to the heavens.

'You're wasting your time. Mikhael is more powerful than your fictitious God.'

Ella was exhausted, too tired of running and thinking and wishing she could go back and do everything differently.

'So what can we do? Is there anyone that can help us?'

'Perhaps. There is only one man that can help, and that's who we're on our way to see.'

'Who is he?'

Their eyes met and she held her breath. She knew the next words he uttered would change her life.

'Your father.'

CHAPTER TWENTY-FOUR

Felicity sat on the floor of the wine cellar oblivious to the cold stone tiles beneath her. She used to go down to the basement when she needed peace and quiet, but this time the thunder inside of her was relentless, throwing itself around the lining of her mind like an emaciated tiger in a too-small cage. Patches of white dust smeared the seat of her trouser suit and speckles of wine patterned her white blouse like blood.

She plunged the corkscrew further into the dusty bottle, pulling it out prematurely and ripping the cork in half. She pushed her finger into the bottle, vaguely aware that her nails were still torn and bloodied, and watched the broken cork bob about in its inky waters. She didn't bother with the glass at her feet but drank directly from the bottle. It tasted of nothing.

The cellar door creaked and light spilt down the steps. Strands of her hair caught and tore on the wall as she turned to face the advancing footsteps.

'Felicity, darling, there you are. I've looked all over the house ...' Richard crouched by her side. 'What on earth are you doing on the floor, sweetheart? Have you not slept? Come on, up you get. Give me that.'

He took the bottle out of her hand and frowned at the label.

'Darling, that's a 1995 Chateau Margaux. These aren't for drinking.'

He pulled her to her feet and walked her to the cushioned seating area that had been created out of an alcove in the wall. Richard occasionally invited his friends for cheese and wine tasting and his wife had suggested the booth and candles for ambience. He didn't know she liked to visit the labyrinthine cellars and walk among the grey bottles. There was something about its musty smell and being underground that comforted her. Sometimes it did more than that. On one occasion, when she had been down there with Richard choosing a bottle to take to a dinner party, she'd wondered what it would be like to make love there, to breath in its stale air and feel the grittiness of the hard floor against her back. She imagined the old walls soaking up the sounds of their love-making. She'd kissed Richard hard and pushed him into the alcove where they were now sat, but he'd simply smiled indulgently and reminded her they were running late. She'd never tried again.

There was the tinkling sound of glass beneath his feet and Richard stumbled as he sat Felicity down. An empty wine bottle skittered across the flagstone floor and he picked it up.

'1998 Petrus Pomerol? Goodness, Felicity, at least stick to the same grape. How long have you been hiding down here?'

'I don't know. What time is it?'

She was surprised she wasn't slurring; perhaps she had drunk herself sober.

'Eight o'clock.'

'In the morning?'

'The evening. God, have you been down here all day?'

She'd had no contact with anyone since they had returned home from the hotel. Her phone had run out of battery and was still in her handbag upstairs. She hadn't considered that Richard may have been looking for her, or anyone else, for that matter. The only person she wanted to hear from was Ella, but she was dead.

'I lost my daughter last night, Richard. She jumped off *your* hotel, after accusing *your* son of raping her. Remember? Or maybe I'm crazy, or a liar, or a mad, attention-seeking liar!'

She tried to stand but her head was too heavy and threatened to drop off her shoulders. She held it in her hands instead, looking up at him through her fingers.

'Do you believe me, Richard?'

He nodded, avoiding her stare, his eyes settling on the smashed wine glasses beneath their shelf and her beige stilettos tossed like a broken toy beside them.

'The police are doing all they can,' he said. 'They said they couldn't treat it as a missing persons enquiry as she's an adult and you saw for yourself that she's been back home. It was a horrid argument you had, that's all, she just needs some space and will be back soon. As for Sebastian, well, they're going through his phone ... and ... we'll see what they say.'

Felicity shook her head slowly and emitted a low, guttural sound, a cry of anguish and despair so primal that Richard visibly shuddered. He laid a hand on her hunched shoulder.

'I think you need to see the doctor again. He can give you something for your nerves, help you get things into perspective.'

She shook her head as vigorously as she could. Richard cleared his throat and took her hand.

'Well, I have something to show you that may put a smile on your face.' He dipped his hand inside his jacket. 'They found it at the East London site where the head office is being built.'

'You've been at work? How can you work when all this is going on!' she cried.

'No, darling. The foreman had it delivered. I've been with the police all day as well as our PR and legal teams to try and keep this unsavoury business out of the press for a bit. The police wanted to talk to you about the photos on Sebastian's phone but I told them you were asleep. Had I known you were down here drinking away my fortune ...' He attempted a laugh but it died on his lips.

'What did they find?'

'The police won't go into detail over the phone. Photos of some kind.'

'No, the builders, what did they find?'

Felicity wasn't interested in Richard's work but she wanted to talk about something, anything, that would take away the image of her daughter throwing herself off the roof.

'Right, yes, of course.' He held out his fist, turned it over, and slowly opened it to reveal a golden ring resting on his palm. 'I cleaned it up, it was a miracle they found it among the rubble but the site used to be a row of shops in the 1940s, apparently, and was bombed during World War Two. I had to have experts on the scene in case they found bones or something. Sorry,' he mumbled, recognising his faux pas too late.

Felicity stared at the unusual ring, its three lilac stones placed haphazardly along its edge.

'That's mine,' she said.

'Well, it is if you want it, dear, of course. In fact, it reminded me of your necklace.'

Felicity reached up to her empty neck, her eyes widening with fear.

'My necklace! Where is it?'

'You took it off last night, you wore the diamonds instead.'

She moved her wedding and engagement rings from her left hand to her right and replaced them with the old thin ring. It was a perfect fit. She felt elated but couldn't understand why. The ring, the cellar's low ceiling, the dim lights, and stale air were all familiar, it was all correct except for Richard – he was the wrong man. She thought back to her necklace. It had been given to her by Ella's father, who said it would protect her until the day she took it off. The day she had lost her daughter. It finally made sense.

'She's alive. I know where she is. I know where to find Ella.' She staggered to her feet, pushing her husband out of the way. 'Ella has my necklace and she's with Zac. I get it now; I know where they've gone.'

She laughed, tears streaming down her face.

'Felicity! Wait a minute, slow down. I don't think you're very well, my love. Perhaps you should have a lie down, a bath at least, get some clarity.'

She stopped at the steps of the cellar and turned to him. She was electric, untouchable, more alive than she had been since before Ella was born.

'I have to go. I'll get the first flight I can in the

morning. I can see it clearly now. Last night was just a small part of a big whole.'

She passed her hand over her husband's sunken cheek. She hated leaving him but he wasn't part of her story any more. Perhaps their chapter was over.

'You aren't the man that can help me with this. Tell me you understand.'

He placed his hand over hers and leant into her caress. 'No, I don't, but I trust you and I love you very much. Where are you going?'

'To the past,' she answered, kissing his thin lips and running up the stairs two at a time.

CHAPTER TWENTY-FIVE

'Where the shagging hell are we?'

Zac rolled his eyes and slowed down.

'For an intelligent girl, you really do have a limited vocabulary,' he said. 'See that village with the bell tower over there? That's Las Alas.'

'So?'

'*So,* this is where your father lives.'

Zac stopped the car and Ella looked around. There was nothing but green fields and wire fences. The clouds had clung like thick smoke to the mountaintop as they had driven to its peak, but the sun was burning its way through the mist and the car was heating up. Ella ran her fingers through her damp hair and pulled her shirt away from her chest, fanning it to cool down. Her stomach clenched. She was finally going to meet her dad. Did he know about her? What if he didn't want anything to do with her and turned them away?

'No wonder my mum never spoke about him. What is he, some backwards country hick?'

They pulled into a small lane that led to a tiny cottage, not much more than a shepherd's hut. It didn't look like anyone was home. A rusty bicycle was propped against an old wine barrel planted with herbs, chickens pecked at the damp earth, and sheep bleated in the distance. There's no way her mother would have wanted any of this – she must have got drunk one night and shagged a farmer's son and been stuck with the consequences. Christ, Ella had lived an hour away from her father all along and never knew.

Zac parked the car at the side of the house and Ella stepped out, straightening her coat and smoothing the creases out of her jeans.

'What are you going to say to him, Zac?'

He leant back in the car seat with his hands behind his head and closed his eyes.

'I'm not going in, you are.'

'You have to be shitting me! What am I going to say? *"Hi, I'm your long-lost daughter, on the run because I jumped off a building but my angel lover saved me?"* For fuck's sake, Zac! I'm not doing this, let's go to Marbella and get drunk.'

'No.'

'But I don't know what –'

'Ella, it's time. I'll stay here and I won't leave you, I promise.'

She picked at her thumbnail and chewed what was left. Fine, what was the worst that could happen? She took a deep breath and knocked on the door. There was no answer and she looked back at Zac, but he had his head back and his eyes closed.

She banged louder and heard a chair scraping, then shuffling footsteps getting closer. The door creaked open slowly and it wasn't her father who answered, but a middle-aged priest.

'Hola, is Señor Santiago de los Rios here?' she asked in Spanish.

The priest wasn't listening; he was staring at her

mother's necklace around her neck.

'Er, sorry, I must have the wrong house,' she continued, peering over his shoulder into the dark, cramped interior. 'I'm looking for a man called Santiago del los Rios. I don't know his first name.'

The man frowned and stroked her new golden hair, his chocolate eyes staring into hers.

She had seen those eyes somewhere, other than in the mirror.

'Ella?' he said. '*Mi niña*, you are here!'

He pulled her to him and held her tight. Ella stood motionless. Who on earth was this priest?

'I have waited nineteen years for this day,' he said. 'Is Lily with you, is your mother here?'

Ella pulled away from him.

'Who are you?'

'I am Leonardo Santiago de los Rios. Your father.'

This was her father? She leant a hand against the peeling door frame to steady herself. Perhaps he was mistaking her for someone else.

'My mother is called Felicity,' she said.

Leonardo waved his hands in the air. 'Of course, of course, she uses her full name now. Is she with you?'

Ella shook her head.

'Come in, come in. Are you hungry? I have some soup on the stove. You must call me Leo, no one uses my full name except my mother. I can't believe you are here. You have Lily's necklace. I gave it to her in this very house. She's OK, isn't she?'

Ella nodded and followed him into the living room, a bowl of soup on the table and a cat curled on a cushion by the open fire. Leonardo walked to the back of the cottage to a tiny makeshift kitchen – there was no fridge or washing machine, just a gas stove, a worktop, and a pantry. He ladled soup into a bowl and offered it to her, and then seeing how her hands shook he changed his mind and took it to the table.

'You're a priest,' she said.

'That's right.'

'So my mother had … I mean, Mum and you? Is that allowed?'

'No, but technically I wasn't a priest then. We knew each other for very little time but we had known each other for ever, if you understand what I mean.'

She did. She knew exactly what he meant.

'You haven't asked why I'm here,' she said.

'I'm sure you have your reasons and will tell me when you're ready. Eat, come on, you are skinny like Lily was. How did you know where to find me?'

Ella shook her head and took a sip of the soup. It tasted of water and grass. She put her spoon down and looked at the door.

'I came with my boyfriend.'

'Your boyfriend? My goodness, all I ever wanted to do was meet my baby girl and she's already a woman! Is he from here, your boyfriend?'

'No, he's definitely not from around here,' she said. 'He's outside, actually, in the car.'

Leonardo jumped up. 'Invite him in, you can't leave him out there. He must be a good man to wait so patiently.'

'Yeah,' she muttered, 'he's a saint.'

She looked out the window and watched Zac leaning against the car. His shoulders were hunched against the wind and he was staring at the clouds that were rolling in and growing darker. She beckoned him in and he opened the door.

'Lord Zadkiel,' Leonardo cried, throwing himself to the ground like a Muslim at prayer, his forehead touching the floor and his arms stretched out on either side of him.

'Leo,' Ella whispered. 'It's OK, get up.'

The priest stayed crouched on the ground.

'Leonardo. *Papa!*' Ella hissed. 'Bloody hell, this is awkward. Leo, he's with me.'

Her father looked at her from his kneeling position, his eyes searching hers.

'Don't worry,' she said. 'I know who Zac is and I know *what* he is. I take it you do too.'

'And your boyfriend?' Leonardo asked, his head turning to Zac then to her and back at him.

'You're looking at him.'

Zac helped him up and placed a hand on his shoulder.

'*Padre*, I think you should sit down. There is a lot we need to explain.'

This should be good, Ella thought.

The three of them drank musty red wine, then they ate the soup and bread, more bread than soup, and drank more wine. There was no point holding back – there was something in the way the priest looked at Ella that made her want to tell him everything. He wasn't going to judge her, she knew that, and he may even understand.

By the time the sun had set behind the mountains, Leonardo was up to date with everything Ella and her mother had done since she'd been born. She realised she couldn't tell him anything about Felicity that she couldn't remember herself because she'd never asked about what her life had been like before she was born. What a selfish daughter she'd been. Juliana would have known Felicity's past, but it was too late to ask her. She would sometimes tell Ella to be kinder to her mum and hint at the tough childhood she'd had, but Ella had only fixated on her own lack of a father and how her life was different to everyone else's.

'That is quite a story, *hija*,' the priest said, pouring them another glass of wine. He smiled but his eyes were sad. He looked at Zac then at the ground.

'I know this is difficult for you, *Padre*,' Zac said. 'But you need to understand, I have always loved your daughter. I've allowed myself to fall for her. I want to be with her for ever and we need your help to make that possible before it is too late.'

Ella had never heard him say that to anyone else. It made everything that had happened disappear, it made everything feel worthwhile. She got up from her chair and stood behind Zac, wrapping her arms around his neck. He turned and kissed her, stroking her cheek.

'I'm not like the other angels, *Padre*. This isn't a matter of curiosity. You know only too well how everyone is created to be with their true other half, that person that makes you feel whole. If you are lucky, you find them straight away. Most don't. I have had the torture of watching Ella in every one of her lives. I have been at her births and at her deaths but we have never been together. What we have now is what I have waited so long for, it's what we had at the very beginning. Remember how you felt when you first met Lily?'

Leonardo looked up at them and wiped his eye with

the back of his hand.

'Yes of course,' he replied, looking at his daughter. 'Ella, I have followed your and your mother's life every day since you became famous. You have no idea what it feels like to type her name into a computer and see her beautiful face on the arm of a millionaire. I buy British magazines every week in the hope of seeing you in them. She seems happy. Is she?'

The cottage was getting gloomy now the sun had set, but Ella couldn't see a lamp or any light switches. She shrugged.

'I didn't recognise you with your hair like that,' Leonardo continued. 'But you have my eyes and your mother's smile. I have loved you as much as any father can love his little girl. You don't know how much I hate myself for letting Lily and you slip through my fingers. I put my stupid egotistical delusions first and I have lived the rest of my life regretting it.'

Ella was confused. Felicity had insinuated that Ella's father was a waiter and a drunken one-night stand. She'd made every effort to paint the ugliest picture of him possible to make her daughter despise him so much she would never look for him. Why would she do that? The man was heartbroken.

'How did you and Mum meet?' she asked. 'I mean, what went wrong?'

Leonardo left the room, returning with a pile of thin, tattered papers.

'I'm probably not the best person to ask, let your mother tell you herself.' He handed Ella the pages. 'She wrote to me after you were born. That is why I have never left this house. It's my only link to her and I have always

341

prayed that one day you or she would return.'

Ella looked at the dog-eared bundle on her lap and untied the ribbon holding the letters together. She peeled off the first faded page and began to read.

CHAPTER TWENTY-SIX

Dear Leo,

I started this letter over a year ago. Actually, it wasn't meant to be a letter, it was a collection of diary entries and the garbled notes of a bereft insomniac. They were my necessity, a way of transferring you from my thoughts and making you real again, moulding you out of paper and ink.

As soon as I close my eyes, a film of our life together runs before them on fast forward. I get no rest. I see you and I feel you in everything I do. You don't just come to me in pictures, but in sounds and tastes and smells. Since when has the aroma of baked bread made anyone cry? But it does, it drags me straight back into your arms, entangles me in your cool, white sheets, and wipes away my pain for just a millisecond until I remember we will never be together again.

I am wringing my heart out onto these pages hoping you will make sense of the messy puddles. I will always love you, Leo, I want you to know that, but there is something else I need to tell you, the main reason it has taken me so long to find the courage to write to you.

The morning I arrived in Tarifa, I was lost. I didn't know where I was or where I was going, I was also very confused.

The morning before, I had walked out of my family home with no intention of ever going back. I had lied to my father and agreed to go to a Swiss finishing school in order to be eligible for my inheritance – I never told you I am a very rich woman, did I? He paid me the week before I was due to leave and I escaped to Spain instead. I ran away to the only place that still held magic for me, Tarifa – the pretty sea-side village my childhood nanny had talked about every night as I drifted off to sleep. I had burnt all my bridges and was wondering whether there was still a path left for me to take.

I'd been sitting beside a large rock on the beach for nearly an hour with my feet buried in the grainy sand. The wind was relentless and it whipped my hair into my eyes and mouth but I didn't think of moving. A lone dog walker hurried past in the distance and gave me a quick glance, wondering what the English girl was doing sitting alone so early in the morning. I couldn't be anything but English, could I? Long hair the colour of melted butter, brand new backpack, white feet in flimsy flip flops when the locals had only just put away their furs.

I thought I was alone, hunched against that rock willing the sound of the waves and howling wind to blow away the bitter shards of guilt and disappointment that were embedded in my thin skin. Then I saw you run out of the sea with your surfboard.

I think you were the first one to speak. It was 'Hola' or 'Que tal', I can't remember. You were just being polite, so I said nothing. Your bundle of clothes were behind the big rock I was sitting beside. Had I not chosen to sit there, we may never have met. Imagine that.

You were facing away as you got changed. I watched,

transfixed, as you reached behind your back and pulled down the long chord attached to the zip of your wetsuit. The new sun shone off your dewy, tanned skin and I was amazed that you were wet beneath the suit, silly, but I thought wetsuits were meant to keep you dry. You rolled your shoulders, sending the muscles beneath your skin rippling like the waves you had just been riding, and then you pulled down your sleeves and the rest of the suit until it hung firmly around your waist.

I managed to tear my eyes away just in time as you turned around and smiled, bending down low beside me to grab your bag and struggle into your damp T-shirt. Your face was so close to mine I could see tiny specs of sea salt drying on your stubbly jaw and the white creases around your eyes from where you had squinted up at the sun. Maybe I imagined it, but I thought I could smell the water evaporate off your warm skin. You smelt of freedom.

'Hola,' you tried again. 'Buenos dias', and this time I smiled back. I thought I'd feel shy staring into your brown eyes with those thick lashes – completely wasted on a man, by the way – but I didn't. They shone with kindness and acceptance.

'Estas de vacaciones?' you asked, the ends of your words dropping into the sand. I had never heard the Andalusian accent on a man before, just Juliana. She made it sound rough and, dare I say it, a little common. But on you it was gravely and gentle, your voice only just above a whisper.

'Yes, I'm on holiday. Kind of,' I answered, hoping my Spanish sounded as fluent as my teachers had told me it was. 'I've only just arrived. You're a surfer?'

'I am a beginner, and I'm here on holiday too. I'm

actually from Ronda, up in the mountains, but I don't get a lot of surfing practice there,' you laughed.

I can't tell you how wonderful it was to sit beside you, the sun gearing itself up for a hot morning, and simply stare out to sea in silence. I was so comfortable I nearly shuffled closer and rested my head upon your shoulder. Instead I matched your smile with my own.

'I'm Felicity,' I said. 'But everybody calls me Lily.' 'Like the beautiful flower. I'm Leonardo.'

I fiddled with the zip on my backpack, trying to think of something to say.

'Do you know any good hotels around here?'

I hadn't planned what I would do when I got to Tarifa, but it was dawning on me that I had all the time and money in the world to do whatever the hell I liked, and with whomever I liked, and it was exhilarating.

'Come,' you said. 'I will show you the best place in town.'

You stood up. The sand had stuck to the legs of your damp wetsuit and you slipped on your white Havaianas. You held out your hand and helped me up.

'I am staying at a great hostel with a few friends,' you continued. 'It's clean and, most importantly, cheap.'

I never did meet those friends. I still wonder if they exist. From that day on there was only enough room in the universe for the two of us. You had your bag over one shoulder and your surfboard under the other arm, but you still picked up my huge rucksack as if it weighed nothing.

We headed away from the sea in silence, our flip-flops the only noise on the quiet, sandy street, then you turned left into a maze of narrow white-washed houses so close together I could have stretched out and touched the houses on either side. Bars were opening their doors and young girls in aprons wiped down tables and scrawled illegible dishes on the blackboards outside.

'Are you hungry, Lily? They do great churros con chocolate here.'

My new favourite breakfast! Remember how often we would sit in that little street and dunk crispy doughnuts into hot chocolate. How if no one was looking I would lick it off your chin and make you laugh.

My stomach rumbled but I shook my head. All I could think about was showering and sleep. I had left my house early so my father would think I was getting on the Swiss flight his secretary had booked, and I had spent most of the afternoon and night at the airport waiting for my late flight to Spain.

You slowed down and leant against a crumbling wall. Above your head was an old tile set in plaster bearing the name 'Plaza del Angel'. It was a tiny square with a simple church that had been squeezed and moulded between two crooked houses. Ivy and bougainvillea climbed its sandstone walls and a black cat stretched and curled in a puddle of sunlight.

I thought of my father and what I had done, how I had walked straight out of his life with no intention of ever returning. He had been a man that was difficult to like, but I had let him down in so many ways. I looked back at the old church and wanted to throw myself at the feet of the Virgin Mary. Juliana had always said She watched over all her children and forgave them of their every sin.

'Do you work?' I asked you.

I don't know why I said that, probably just to fill the silence; I hadn't yet learnt how to enjoy the stillness.

347

'No, not yet. I've just finished studying, I'm twenty-five and still a student. This is my first holiday, some time to think things through.'

We were both in limbo.

'This is it.' You pointed at an orange sign swinging outside a whitewashed house in front of the church. 'Hostel De Silva. It is new but very reasonably priced. The owners are Portuguese. Apparently their son is a famous film director and he bought it for them a few years ago. Come.'

The entrance was typically Andalusian, with a studded wooden door that opened into a dark reception and an interior square with a fountain in the centre. I used to love stepping into that shady doorway and feeling the heat slide off my shoulders. A flight of stairs led to the bedrooms running along an internal balcony, each step decorated in tiles of bright, Moorish design.

It didn't have a bar or restaurant, yet there were always wonderful cooking smells lingering at the entrance. That day it was fried chorizo, and my stomach complained again.

An impossibly beautiful woman with sandy-coloured hair and large almond eyes stood behind the desk nursing a newborn. I peeked into the bundle in her arms. She said his name was Joshua and that she was staying with her in-laws while her husband was away. She had an American accent and explained that the receptionist would be back shortly, before disappearing out the back through a beaded curtain. In all the time we were there, I never saw that woman smile.

You leant against the wall as if you had all the time in the world while I drummed my fingers on the reception desk. Your arm was still wrapped protectively around your surfboard and my bag hanging off the crook of your elbow. I didn't understand what you were still doing there, in your uncomfortable wetsuit, getting sand over their clean floor.

I took my purse and passport out of my rucksack and you gave me a strange look as if you were trying to work something out. Do you realise there is a stillness about you that is both unnerving and comforting?

'Why have you been studying for so long, Leonardo? Are you going into law or medicine?' I asked, glancing at your long fingers and wondering what miracles they could perform, then immediately blushing at my own innuendo.

'No, unfortunately I don't save lives, just the odd lost soul.' You laughed but I didn't get the joke. 'My calling is a lot more spiritual.'

Then you told me, just like that, as if it were something people spoke of every day. Looking back, I wonder whether it was then that you knew you had it wrong. Was saying it out loud the turning point? You were a trainee priest! Thank God I'd been leaning against the reception desk or I would have stumbled. I doubt I am the only person who has said this to you – I'm certain I'm not the first woman to have thought it – but you are the embodiment of what a man should be. You are handsome, kind, funny, adventurous, and protective. I'm sorry, I don't mean to embarrass you. I can see you frowning as you read this, but it's true. I couldn't possibly understand (I still can't) how anyone like you could choose a life like that. The world is lacking in good men, Leo, and you had extracted yourself from the pickings. It wasn't fair. Perhaps I even said it out loud.

'Why?' I asked.

I had a million thoughts running through my mind but that simple word summed them all up.

'It's difficult to explain. Since I was fourteen I have known I was born to serve God.'

And then you told me everything. It's a sad tale but I still don't think it explains such a drastic decision. You told me how your father was ill so you turned to God because the local priest offered you answers you couldn't find anywhere else. You explained how your father's death resulted in your mother falling into a deep depression and how you promised God you would serve him if he set her back on the road to recovery. I understand how all of that would make you a verdant Catholic. But a priest? A celibate man of the cloth? You must have seen the look on my face because you tried your hardest to lighten the mood.

'Everyone was shocked, especially my family. They thought I was gay when I told them, said it was the nineties and that I didn't have to go to such lengths to hide it..'

'So you aren't?' I asked. 'You like, I mean liked, women?'

'Yes, I still like women. I like women very much, Lily.'

You said that with a hint of a smile and that was when I knew I loved you. That very second, honest to God, I felt it like a wave crashing over me. It wasn't just the news that you were suddenly unobtainable that made you more alluring, there was something about you, something familiar.

A short, dark man with a gruff voice appeared behind the desk and grunted at us. I wanted to continue talking to you but the receptionist was staring at my chest (he had no choice, do you remember how tiny he was?) and gave me a form to fill in, asking me a string of questions until he was finally happy and handed over my key.

'Room twelve!' you said, peering over my shoulder. 'We are neighbours. Follow me.'

The receptionist frowned at your enthusiasm to do his job. There was no lift and our rooms were the last two on the top floor, beyond the internal corridor and up in the eaves. I peered through the landing window and smiled at the view of the sea beyond a cluster of tiled rooftops. I wanted to jump up and down and scream out loud at my freedom.

'How about we go for breakfast, Padre Leonardo? Let me get changed and you can show me the sights.'

You'd opened your door and I could see into a sunny, tidy room. It surprised me. I don't know why or what I was expecting, perhaps a large cross on the wall or a silver goblet beside the bed. You handed me my bag and I nudged you playfully.

'Are you really a priest? Or is this some elaborate chat-up line?'

I wish I hadn't said that. You looked at me with such sadness.

'I wouldn't lie, not to you.'

The air shifted then, did you feel it? It was as if someone had switched the light on. I practically heard the click.

'What do you mean? We don't even know each other,' I said.

'I'm not sure that's true.'

You took my hand and my breath caught. I was falling

and you were the only one that could catch me. I snatched it away and fumbled with my key, shoving the door open with my shoulder and throwing my bag inside. My head was foggy and I couldn't see properly – I blamed it on hunger.

'I'll see you in fifteen minutes?' I called. What you said next will haunt me for a lifetime. 'It will be my pleasure, my Señorita.'

I turned around but you were gone.

Standing under the lukewarm shower, I tried to gather my thoughts but it was impossible. Your face kept swimming in front of my eyes, much as it does now, and I kept hearing that word over again. Señorita. I knew what it meant, but coming from you it felt important.

I used to read lots of romantic novels as a child and I remember wondering whether this intense connection between us was just my over-active imagination. From a young age my father berated me for believing in what he called my 'make-believe world of happy endings'. He blamed Juliana for filling my head with stories of princesses that always found their prince and maidens that overcame impossible obstacles to be with the man of their dreams. Up until then, I'd had very little experience of men, dreamy or otherwise.

I stood in front of the mirror and slipped on my cotton dress and leather sandals, tying my wet hair into a loose bun. I didn't see myself in the reflection – I saw many different people. My life had been a series of chapters where in each one I had played a different part. I still do. I have my mother's neck and my father's blue eyes but the rest of me back then, inside and out, was a complete stranger. I hoped you would help me get to know her better.

My chest ached with an unknown sadness and loss that was linked to you in some way. I could see you leaving me, or at least a version of you, the image was hazy but the emotions so clear. Perhaps it was a premonition. I had to see you straight away, I couldn't wait. I yanked open the bedroom door just as you did the same.

You were dressed in khaki shorts and white flip flops. Your hair was still wet and a pair of Ray-Bans hung from the V of your navy T-shirt. I shut the door behind me and looked into your dark eyes. You were right, we already knew each other.

'I've missed you so much,' you said. 'I should never have left you.'

I ran to you, burying my face in your neck. I raked my fingers through your freshly washed hair and inhaled the scent of soap and sunshine and something more, something intoxicating.

'Ai mi amor,' you said. Your eyes searched mine and it was the first time anyone had looked at me properly. 'You are so beautiful, you look just like a doll. Has anyone ever told you that?'.

I shook my head but I wasn't sure, perhaps they had, a long, long time ago. Perhaps you had.

'Would it be too soon if I told you I loved you?' I whispered.

For a long time you didn't reply, then slowly you leant in and kissed me. Your stubble rubbed my jaw, making my face tingle along with the rest of my body. Your kiss was what I had been waiting for my whole life, longer than that. All the years of loneliness, of loss and emptiness, were filled by the touch of your lips. It was you that had been missing all along, just you, and by some kind of miracle we had finally found each other.

Your kisses deepened and I stumbled into your room, kicking the door behind us. We leant against it and your hands were now slowly running down my arms to my waist. As you kissed my neck the thin strap of my dress slipped down and exposed my lacy bra. I quickly pulled it up and pulled away, struggling to re-focus. Your look was serious but your eyes were hungry.

'Leo, what are we doing? You're a priest! Aren't we breaking a law or something?'

You took my hand in yours and I felt safe again. You have a way of knowing what people need; I suppose that's what makes you a good priest. You stroked the inside of my wrist with your thumb.

'Mi cariño, in three months' time I shall become a priest. I've always known there was something important out there waiting for me, something that I wanted to dedicate my life to.' I held my breath. 'I thought that something was God, but now I realise it was you.'

I kissed your hand and grinned at you.

'I planned to return to Madrid at the end of August,' you continued. 'Instead of sitting my final exam I shall tell the Bishop I won't be entering the priesthood. I can't imagine a life without you, Lily. Will you stay here with me?'

Anyone else would say we were crazy. We had only just met, what strangers spoke to each other like that? But we weren't strangers, were we? We had simply been apart for a lifetime. I wrapped my arms around your neck and clung tightly.

'Leo, I will never leave you,' I said.

Not a day goes by without thinking of those words. I remember every single one of them, as if they were etched on to my mind, permanent grooves in my heart. I told you I would never leave you, that was true. You said you couldn't imagine a life without me – that wasn't.

The sound of seagulls and crashing waves swept in through your open window, and sunshine bathed our bodies as we lay on your bed. We had been kissing and exploring each other for hours, your fingers stroking paths across my body as if retracing your way back home. The day wound and stretched into an eternity. I couldn't think of a single reason why I should move from your side. We had been waiting for each other for ever and there we finally were.

The sun climbed ever higher and the light breeze through the muslin curtains carried with it the noise of the cafés getting ready for lunch. I peered out, expecting to see the scene on pause, a town frozen in temporary animation; surely we were in our own universe? My arms rested on the warm windowsill and my chin on my crossed wrists. All I could see in the distance was endless blue, the sky and the sea merging into one. That was what I yearned for, that seamless union.

'Leonardo, I want you.' My voice sounded far away.

'You have me,' you whispered in my ear.

We were finally where we had always meant to be. We were together. We were home.

By mid-afternoon the smell of freshly baked bread was too delicious to ignore and you threw on your shorts and ran downstairs, returning with your arms full of glazed pastries and fruit. We laughed as we fed each other and you followed a trail of watermelon juice with your tongue as it trickled down my chest. I blew at the crumbs caught in your hair then you pulled me astride, your kisses tasting of cinnamon.

'I've never done this before,' I murmured sleepily into your shoulder as Tarifa settled for its siesta.

You kissed the top of my head. 'Neither have I,' you said. 'We will live our lives side by side, just you and me, with sand beneath our feet and the wind in our hair. I don't know what job I will get, if I ever manage to tear myself away from you long enough, but I promise you I will look after you and you will want for nothing.'

And I believed you, for a long time I had no reason not to. I lay in your arms, thinking of my bank accounts heavy with zeros and an endless life with you.

The next day, I checked out of the room I'd spent all of ten minutes in and moved into yours.

Remember the look on the receptionist's face? He was dying to know what was going on. He knew you were a trainee priest. How we laughed at how we'd become the hotel gossip.

Our hazy summer days were spent lying down; in bed, on the beach, or deep in the wild grass of the surrounding hills. We would stare at the wispy clouds and birds of prey that circled the yellow fields and go hours without saying a word, just exchanging glances and smiles. I wondered how I'd gone eighteen years without ever having felt such happiness.

Some days you would take me and your surfboard to

tiny secluded bays and laugh at my attempts to stay upright. I didn't once think about England, my exam results, or even whether my father had checked I had turned up at the Swiss academy. I had you, we had money, and beyond that I couldn't think of anything else I needed.

Occasionally I would overhear a local woman playing with her children and it made me think of my childhood and dear Juliana. She would have been outraged that I was living with a man out of wedlock, a trainee priest no less, but she would have been proud of me for having the courage to follow my dreams. I planned to call her after the summer and tell her about my One True Love. Of course, by the time I did call her it was to tell her something totally different.

The middle of August arrived and with it, an air thick with tourists. Our beach wasn't ours any more, it was now jammed with families. We'd walk along counting how many times someone would exclaim 'I didn't realise Tarifa was the most southerly point in Europe! Did you know it's where the Med meets the Pacific?' and they would stand on that strip of earth between the two oceans marvelling at the calmness of one and the ferocity of the other. Within a week I too would be standing on that strip, the tranquil waters of our time together turning to crashing waves with the power of one hastily scribbled letter.

'We can't stay here,' you said one morning as we lay tangled in a clammy embrace. We always held hands in bed, even as we slept. You were stroking the inside of my wrist, you did it without thinking and it turned me on so much. You thought it was hilarious when I told you, so you would do it all the time, the more public the better. It

was our little code. I must have looked nervous because you laughed.

'Tranquila, I just mean it's too hot on the coast. Let's go to the mountains and you can meet my mother.'

I changed four times the next morning. What does one wear to visit the mother of a soon-to-be priest that has changed his mind and decided to spend the rest of his life with you instead? If you noticed my nerves you didn't say anything. I settled on a simple white skirt, flowery top, and sandals. Perhaps I was trying to look innocent and virginal so she wouldn't think I was some man-eating tramp.

Your mother and I loved each other from the start.

You must have called her before we left, because as soon as we pulled into her narrow street she was running towards us, her apron still on but her lipstick freshly applied. It took you for ever to park and she stood beside the car bobbing up and down, trying to catch a glimpse of me. I smiled, the flowers I had bought her wilting in my lap. As soon as we got out, I was the first one she hugged, flowers forgotten and crushed at our feet, and she cried huge, gulping sobs on to my bare shoulder.

'Ai que niña mas preciosa, has salvado mi hijo' she kept saying. I hadn't uttered a word but she'd already decided I was your beautiful saviour. You poor thing, you just stood there not knowing whether to introduce us or take our bags out of the car. Was that a brief shadow of guilt I saw pass over your face? Perhaps, considering the outcome, it was more serious – was it doubt or regret?

You look nothing like her you know. You look a lot more like your father from the photos I saw that day.

She's tiny and dark, she couldn't look any more like a Spanish mama if she tried, but I was surprised by how young she was, in her mid-forties, you said. You forget my mother was the complete opposite; she was old when she had me, she was tall, thin, cold, and distant. Everything about your homecoming was warm and welcoming. She made me feel like more of a cherished daughter in those first five minutes than my own mother had done in her entire life.

'It's a pleasure to meet you, Mrs Santiago de los Rios,' I said, letting her plump my cushion before settling in the large velvet armchair. Her face lit up and she turned to you, exclaiming how well I spoke Spanish. She did that all day, do you remember? Every time she wanted to ask me something she addressed you like I didn't understand, then she would kiss me each time I answered back in Spanish, amazed and thrilled that the young 'rubia' spoke her language.

'Call me Imaculada,' she insisted, so I did.

We ate a huge meal and she didn't stop talking, she told us her friends and sisters were overjoyed you were getting married (that was news to me, did you tell her that? What were you planning?), and that no one except Father Pedro was disappointed. She said she was looking forward to meeting my family, then hugged me even tighter when I said I no longer had one (what else could I say?). She told me how happy she was that she would finally get to be a grandmother and that her biggest fear about you becoming a priest, and being her only child, had been dying without ever having held her grandchild.

I still cry about that. Look what we took away from her, Leo. She would have been a wonderful grandmother.

I could have chosen differently, I could have sent you this letter months ago, but it was your decision to leave.

That night you squeezed yourself onto the tired sofa and I slept in your childhood bedroom.

I couldn't sleep that night. Did you? I imagined I could hear you breathing through the thin walls. I missed your touch, it was our first night apart since we'd met.

'We have to get back to Tarifa,' you announced the next morning. I was as shocked as your mother.

'Pero hijo,' she cried. 'You just got here.'

'The sooner we leave, the sooner I can get back to Madrid and speak to the Bishop.'

She looked sceptical, she didn't want us out of her sight. She knows you better than I do.

Our arms filled with your mother's food parcels, we headed back to the coast. I love the way the light moves over the Andalusian mountains, how the thick clouds part to let the sun shine as if God himself is pointing a spotlight onto the little whitewashed villages saying 'Take a look at that, isn't it beautiful'.

I can still see them now, you know, I can see them out of my bedroom window but I have never headed back up them. Not in that direction, anyway. Yes, I am still in Spain. How could I go home when you were it?

After half an hour of giddy bends, we turned off down a rocky path hidden by overgrown brambles.

'I have something to show you,' you said.

I didn't see the little stone cottage at first, just a huge field peppered with ragged boulders and the odd stray goat and sheep. The house was old and crumbling and looked as if it had been built by hand using rocks from the very earth it sat upon. The wooden roof was covered in specks of yellow moss and the faded blue door hung on its hinges. You held it open for me and we ducked inside, the sun shining rods of light through the holes in the roof. There was dusty furniture and a magnificent stone hearth with a black pot in the centre.

'What is this place?' I asked.

My sandals left footprints in the dry earth that had blown under the door and small weeds grew through the cracks in the window pane.

'This is my house,' you said.

I was waiting for you to crack a joke, say you won it playing at cards or you had camped in it as a kid, but you didn't. Instead you wiped a chair clean and motioned for me to sit down.

'This house has been in my family for generations. My grandfather's grandfather built it for his wife; he was a shepherd in these hills. It has belonged to every son in my family and now stops with me.' You rubbed your face and looked at the ceiling. 'This is the first time I've been here since my father died. It was where we came hunting. My mother never came, she said it was a house for men.'

'It's lovely.'

'No it isn't, not any more, but it will be. This will be our family home, Lily, for the summer months, at least. There is no electricity or plumbing but I have big plans. Our children will breathe life into its old stone walls.'

Your enthusiasm was infectious as we ran around the tiny hut, you explaining supporting beams and extensions and I suggesting green curtains for the tiny windows and a mirror above the fireplace.

'Does this house even have an address?' I asked.

'Of course. Casa La Vaca, Las Alas. It may be well hidden but it has been here for ever.'

'Cow House? I thought your ancestors were shepherds?'

'They were, they also had a strange sense of humour.'

I have often wondered how I would have sent you this letter had I not asked you the name of the house. It seemed the most obvious place to send it to – I didn't want to bother your mother, the poor woman has no doubt suffered enough, and I have no clue where you work. In fact, I have no idea if this letter will be read or whether you ever returned to the hut in the hills. Perhaps I am now long dead and some village children far off into the future are poring over these pages wondering who the ill-fated Leonardo and Lily were. That thought saddens me, so I will continue to write as if you will be reading my words within days of me sending them, that way I can continue to talk to you without having to hear your voice or risk feeling your touch.

'What is Las Alas?' I asked.

The sun had disappeared behind the mountain and the rooms were flooded in shadow. You held my hand and led me to the bedroom. The window whined as you prised it open and leant out.

'See that village? That is Las Alas.'

The mountains were lilac now save for a splash of white over one side. Like fresh snow it glittered in the setting sun. A rocky mound with an ancient bell tower rose proudly over the sprawling village.

'What's that building in the middle?'

'That is the ancient chapel of La Madre Sagrada. It has been there since the Moors, it is my sanctuary. Many

362

times as a child I walked to the village and climbed that hill to gaze over God's land. It was where I first dreamed of becoming a priest, except now I dream of walking you down its aisle.'

The room was bare but for a magnificent mahogany bed that took up far too much space. It was too grand for such a simple home. I imagined us as parents lying in that bed and staring out of the window onto that magnificent view as our children ran through the wild grasses. We sat down on the mattress which let out a dusty sigh.

'Close your eyes, I have something for you,' you said.

You swept my hair away from my neck and I shivered. No matter how brief nor light your touch, I always wanted more. Something cold brushed my throat and it was a long, gold chain, its intricate pendant studded with gemstones the colour of our lilac mountains.

'It was my grandmother's,' you told me. 'She never had any daughters or granddaughters so it was left to me. It has been in my family since the Spanish Civil war, I was always told it was magical and would protect the person who wore it. I hope I'm right.'

You kissed me and it sealed our fate. I vowed that I would never take the necklace off, and I kept my word. Your grandmother's necklace has worked so far, Leo, and I know it will continue to do so.

That night in our hotel room, the day before your trip to Madrid, was the longest of my life. The streets of Tarifa were empty, bathed in the bright light from the heavy moon. The stars were so much bigger and brighter than in England, and you said it was because we were closer to heaven.

363

I lay down beside you as you slept soundly, a smile frozen on your lips. You had gone to bed happy, feeling like a man teetering on the edge of our new life together. You were so eager to make that leap into our for ever. I didn't see it that way – for me, tomorrow was a deep, dark hole sucking me in. I knew I had a matter of hours left with you, that once you left I wouldn't see you again. Don't ask me how I knew, I had felt it from the moment you kissed me.

The moon shone through our window as bright as daylight and I propped myself up on my elbows and ran my fingers over your three-day-old stubble, marvelling at how every tiny hair was a different shade of brown. Your long lashes cast feathery shadows over your cheekbones and your lips parted, letting out short, sweet sighs with every breath.

I stared at you for a long time, drinking in every detail, filing away an exact carbon copy of your beautiful face so it would last me in your absence. How I begged the moon to make that night last for ever. I thought if only I could keep awake the silvery light would not turn golden, but of course it did.

The next day arrived as unceremoniously as it always has and I waved you off until I could no longer see your car. That day and the next were filled with endless nothing until one evening I woke in a panic. I had fallen into a fitful sleep after lunch and didn't wake until past six in the afternoon. My body was aching and exhaustion settled in my bones like cement in the cracks of a wall. I could hardly move but I needed a chemist and an answer and I wasn't prepared to wait until the morning. I threw on some clothes and stumbled down the stairs two at a time.

'Miss Lily,' called the receptionist as I passed his desk.

He'd found an excuse to pester me every day since you'd left. His beady eyes would travel up my bare legs and find their resting place at my cleavage, a light sneer playing at his lips. Although I had always been polite, that evening I waved my hand dismissively and was saved by the ring of his phone. He listened intently to the caller and gave me a wolfish grin as I ran out the door.

When I came back, I was shaking. I had felt tired for days and jogging down those streets in such heavy heat had left me with a stitch. I was grateful for the coolness of the hotel and stood a moment, enjoying the light spray of the fountain on my arms.

'Miss Lily, I have something urgent for you.' The receptionist's oily voice was laced with a level of glee I had never heard before. He held out our room key along with a small white envelope. Any other day I would have looked at it properly, noticed the loops and swirls of your hand which had written my name upon it, and would have torn into it straight away. No one but you knew I was there, after all. But I had a small paper bag in my fist, the contents of which was the only thing on my mind. I stuffed the note in the back pocket of my jean shorts, much to the midget's annoyance, and ran up the stairs to the bathroom.

You are a smart man. I'm sure by now you have guessed the true reason for me writing this letter. I was pregnant. I stumbled out of the hotel in a daze, the test still in my hand. I was eighteen years old with no home, no mother, a family I had walked away from, and a boyfriend who was still technically a priest. It sounds catastrophic when you put it like that, but I didn't care, none of those things bothered me in the slightest. The only reason that tears streamed down my face was because when I saw the little line turn blue you were not beside me to share my joy.

I was so excited; I kept picturing how happy you would be when I told you. I dreamed of whether we would marry right away or tell your mother first. How delighted she would be.

My feet instinctively led me to the beach where we first met. I walked along the strip of land that separated the two seas and picked my way over the rocks at the end to a secluded patch of sand. The dusky sky was streaked with rainbow clouds and the beaches were emptying. Silence settled on the waves like glitter and the salty air was sweet and tangy. I sat on a rock and looked across the horizon. I was trying to get comfortable when I felt the crunch of paper in my back pocket and remembered the letter the receptionist had been so eager to give me.

Can you see it? Can you see the image of me sitting alone on a windswept beach with waves lapping at my toes and two possible futures? One hand held a plastic stick with a dot of dye that announced me a mother, and in the other a scrap of paper waiting to rip my life apart and tear out my soul.

My darling Lily, *your letter read,*

A miracle has happened. God Himself has come for me and I can no longer deny my destiny. I'm sorry I had to do this by letter. To see your beautiful face would have made it impossible for me to return to my path. Forgive me for my desertion but it is for the greater good. I know you will understand. My faith is too strong but my heart will forever belong to you.

I love you, and will love you for eternity.

Leo.

So many questions fought for breath in my mind. What miracle could have been so great to cast a shadow over our magic? Would it have been different had you known about the baby? How did your letter reach me? The envelope had my name on it but no stamp or address. The idea of you travelling all the way to deliver it without seeing me is too much to bear.

Again and again I went over your words, picking and dissecting them, reading between the lines, looking for an answer that was not the obvious one. I wouldn't allow myself to believe you were walking away from me, from us, from our child! Had you left me for another woman I would have fought. I would have beaten your mother's door down for you, sat in your crumbling shepherd hut for years until you returned. But God? Who am I to compete against Him? He always gets His own way.

I sat on that rock until darkness swallowed me and the chattering of the cicadas competed with the commotion of my mind. The moon was full and swollen and the wind had died down to a warm caress. I took one last look at your note and tore the corners off, letting them flutter to the pools of water at my feet. Bit by bit, I turned your words into confetti that speckled the black sea and rose and swelled on the low waves. They gathered around my icy ankles, your words refusing to leave.

The waves of the Atlantic behind me were getting

angrier and smashed against the walkway. I turned to them, preferring to gaze at the tumultuous frenzy of white foam and ragged coastline than the gentle swell of the Mediterranean.

In the distance, on the mainland, I could make out the eerie silhouette of Castillo Catalina, an eerie Gothic weather centre on the hill. Large rocks surrounded it but the house remained stoic, defiant, her empty turret windows staring blindly out to the same waves you had been riding the day we met. I wanted to join her gazing out to sea. I wondered if I could get up to the flat roof, if it was high enough to jump from, and whether the rocks below would be sharp enough to cut through my pain.

Then I thought to my own mother's end and history's unceasing twists and loops. Could I take a child to my deathbed? Could I surrender to darkness, her darkness, when inside me I held a burning light of hope?

A light breeze stroked my cheek and carried with it the sounds of a flamenco guitar. One or two faint notes to begin with, not unlike the tune the wind plays in the dry summer grasses. I held my breath and listened. The landscape was silver and still. The moon cast just enough light to see by. I followed the melody back to my secluded bay and its gentle waters where I saw the figure of a gypsy boy sat on the sand, his white shirt shining against the stone wall and his feet bare. Dark, wavy hair covered his face as he bent over his guitar, his fingers plucking at the taut strings and my soft heart. He didn't look up until I was beside him.

'Please, don't stop on my account,' I whispered in Spanish.

He gave me a lazy smile. His eyes were dark purple in

the moon light. He winked and went back to the guitar. I recognised those eyes immediately as the same ones that had looked at me from my mother's canvas the day she died; they were filled with the love of a millennia and had seen your words written all over my face. Leo, your miracle took you away from me, but mine saved my life.

I sat beside the boy and closed my eyes, letting the notes wash over me. The music stopped and I opened them. He was looking at me, his fingers brushing along the chain at my neck.

'That's an interesting necklace.'

'It's all I have left of him.'

'Not quite,' he said, nodding at my flat stomach.

He put down the guitar and took my hand. I let him.

'Potestatem Amethystus.'

'Pardon?'

'Your necklace, it's amethyst. It will protect you, and your unborn daughter, Arabella. She's special.'

He was telling me everything I wanted to hear; perhaps he was a ghost of the future or a travelling gypsy trying his luck. I didn't care, I wanted to believe him.

'I've lost him. I've lost everything,' I said, but my tears had all dried up. I never shed another for you after that day.

'No you haven't, you are tied to one another for eternity and will find each other in the next life. There is always a second chance to make the right decision.'

I didn't want to hear mystical platitudes. I wanted to know how I was going to survive.

'So I will be alone for the rest of my life? This life?' I asked him. I'm sorry Leo, I'm sure had you been visited by a being so profound and wise you would have quizzed *him about the cosmos and our place in it. Perhaps I should have done, but my life was over and I needed a reason to carry on living it.*

The boy smiled. He was beautiful, so perfect, not real at all.

'You will know who you are destined to marry when you see him. Don't look for him; he will be searching for you.'

'But how will I recognise him?'

'He will give you back your life, and you will be the woman who has filled his dreams.'

He picked up his guitar again and I walked away, floating on the hypnotic sounds of gypsy love and lost promises.

I checked out of the hotel at midnight. The beautiful American woman was behind reception, but without her baby.

'I'm Lily,' I said

'Serena.'

'Are you OK?' I finally asked. 'You always look so sad. Why?'

Her lip twitched as she attempted to smile. 'A man, what else? Men will always have their strength, Lily, but what they don't realise is that our valour is hidden beneath our beauty. If a woman can no longer fight, she must wear her armour well.'

Her words haunted me as I travelled to my new future and I think of them each morning as I apply my makeup, my armour, building the walls higher and higher around my soul where you reside.

Three hours later, I was in a hotel eighty kilometres

away. Juliana was on her way and I no longer called myself Lily.

Arabella Imaculada Santiago de los Rios was born last April. I call her Ella, it suits her better. She looks just like your mother but with your eyes. At least your long lashes have not been wasted. I have nothing to compare her to; I don't even have a photo of you. After sixteen months without you, I'm scared the wonderful man that swims before my eyes day and night is distorted, that he is someone I constructed out of fragments of dreams. Memory can be a vicious liar.

Your daughter and I have a good life and we are very happy. Her only family is me and my childhood nanny. Juliana, upon returning to me in Spain, told me my father passed away three weeks after I left. She'd had no way of letting me know, having only discovered I wasn't in Switzerland after his death.

My father was lucky, really. He managed to escape this life without having to swallow the bitter pill of disappointment that flowers from love. He never got to discover that the daughter he thought he knew so well was a mirage of his own making. I wish I knew what it was to not have swallowed that pill.

Still, I have a lot to thank you for.

I wear a reminder of you around my neck. I carried a piece of you inside me for nine months, your blood ran through mine, and hidden deep in my heart, where no one will ever find them, are the memories of the most magical days of my life.

I will write to you every year on Ella's birthday and will keep imagining that these letters are being read by you. That is all I can ever give you. She would have loved her father as much as I did. As much as I still do. It's a sad loss for us all.

I wish you well, Leo, and I pray your path leads you to happiness.

    Yours for eternity, Felicity x

CHAPTER TWENTY-SEVEN

Ella looked up from the letter at the men sitting before her, men that a few months ago she had known nothing about but were now a part of her. One her own blood, and the other her very soul.

'What the *fuck* is the matter with you both?'

She pointed at Zac, as if picking him out from a line-up.

'It was *you* that that convinced Leo to leave Mum, wasn't it? And it was *you* playing the guitar on the beach that night.'

Zac nodded indifferently.

'You meddling bastard!'

She thought of her mother's reaction the first time she had met Zac and he'd played the guitar at the table. The same tune, no doubt. She couldn't begin to imagine the fear and confusion her mother had suffered. She rubbed her eyes as she thought of the way she had treated her mother after the shameful scene. The way she had shouted and accused her of seeking attention.

'Calm down, Ella. That's enough,' her father said, attempting to put an arm around her. 'You forget you've only heard the story from Lily's point of view. There is a lot more to explain.'

Ella shrugged him off and got to her feet to face Leo.

'As for you, you spineless coward, why didn't you tell

her face to face? Would you have still chosen to serve your false God if you'd known about me?' Leonardo hung his head. 'What did she mean about her mum taking her child to her death bed? Did my grandmother kill herself in front of her? You knew, and you still walked away!'

Ella gulped as her words caught in her throat. How could she have been so cruel? Felicity had been with her mother when she'd killed herself and then Ella, her own daughter, had thrown herself off a building in front of her. Why hadn't Zac told her? She saw now how little she really knew about her mother – Lily, Felicity, Mrs Fantz, all those women she'd created in order to protect the scared little girl inside. Felicity had made Ella's life a safe sanctuary, protected her from the truth, and all this time Ella had hated her for it.

Leonardo handed his daughter a small glass filled to the brim with amber liquid.

'Drink this,' he said.

'Leave me alone.'

'Please, it will make you feel better.'

Zac was leaning against the bookshelf beside the fireplace where he had remained the entire time she'd been reading the letter. He watched the interaction between her and Leonardo as if they were a film, and not a very interesting one at that. His face was blank and unreadable.

'Speak! Don't you have anything to say?' she shouted, but he didn't move.

'I'm waiting for you to sit down and calm down, Ella. You won't understand what I have to say until you're willing to listen.'

She sat back down without looking at Zac and threw

the shot of liquid down her throat. It burnt, but after a few seconds her shoulders relaxed and her breathing returned to normal. A million questions pushed against the sides of her brain, making her temples ache with pressure. Although a million more answers presented themselves. She now realised her middle name had come from her father's mother. She understood why her mother never took off her necklace. And of course, she now knew why Felicity didn't trust Zac. Most importantly of all, Ella finally understood she had been wrong about being unloved – her mother had wanted her more than anything else in the world. Her mother loved her. Every decision Felicity had ever made had been for Ella.

'Go on, Zac, tell me how this is OK, seeing as you always have an explanation for everything,' she said.

Zac smiled at the priest and turned to Ella.

'Your mother and father struggled in their former life together to make the right decision,' he began. 'Ted was his name before this life. He chose the righteous path and Dolores accepted it against her better judgment. It killed him, and ultimately her. In this life, your parents wished to be given the same choice, to see if they could learn from their previous mistake and choose each other. They failed.'

Ella looked at her father – he had aged ten years in the last few minutes. He pushed his hands through his thick hair and closed his eyes.

'Ella, my precious child, Lord Zadkiel makes it sound very clear cut and simple, but it wasn't at all,' he said. 'Zadkiel has told me about my and Lily's former life together. I understand you were there too, that we have a habit of letting you down, but of course I have no recollection of it any more than you do. I can only explain my actions from *this* life.' He sat on the sofa beside her and took her hand. 'As far back as I can recall, I have heard voices. They would speak to me in the night, tell me I was their messenger, and that I was on this earth to serve a higher purpose. Imagine what that does to a young boy. I didn't tell a soul – people from my village were dragged to hospital for less. It made me think that perhaps the voices were not a curse but a sign. I spoke to my priest about the calling and reasoned that my vocation had been chosen for me. Of course everything was forgotten the moment I laid eyes on your mother. She was the very air I breathed. The voices stopped and I no longer cared if I was special or not. I *was* in her eyes and that was all that mattered.'

'So then what?' Ella said.

'So, I headed for Madrid, but the Bishop was not free to see me for a couple of days. The second night in the capital, Lord Zadkiel came to me in a blazing light. I imagine you have seen it; it's quite spectacular and very frightening. You can't blame him, *hija*, he uttered one sentence only. He simply said, 'I am Angel Zadkiel, you must make a choice and follow your heart.'

Leonardo looked at Zac, whose eyes were full of the love and forgiveness that the priest had been unable to grant himself.

'I let my ego rule my destiny again,' Leonardo continued. 'I misunderstood. I chose the option I thought made me special. I made the same mistake before. In 1941, I abandoned your mother for my country, this time I left her for my God. Both times, she was carrying my daughter.'

'So why didn't you tell Mum in person? She would have understood. Why were you so rash?'

'This happened in the early hours of the morning, and by a strange coincidence,' Leo chuckled and raised his eyebrows at Zac, 'which I now know don't really exist, my neighbour was going to Cádiz that lunchtime on business and was passing Tarifa. I wrote Lily a note, too tired and deliriously excited about my celestial visitor to think clearly. As soon as my friend's car turned the corner, I realised the extent of what I had done and regretted it immediately. Very few people had mobile phones in those days, not anyone I knew, anyway. I had no way of contacting my friend so I called the hostel straight away and asked for your mother.'

'Let me guess, the receptionist had the hots for her and fobbed you off?' Ella said.

'Exactly. By the fourth call, I sternly told him he was forbidden to hand over any letter that had arrived for Lily, that he was to tear it up and tell her I was on my way. He agreed, he promised me. What your mother didn't know was that with the necklace I had given her came a ring, a very old and precious ring that was part of a pair. I intended to propose to her.' He handed Ella a thin golden ring encrusted in small lilac stones. It was beautiful and matched her mother's necklace, still around Ella's neck. 'I drove through the setting sun and into the night with it in my pocket. I wasn't prepared to come that close to losing her again. I hadn't eaten all day, it was stiflingly hot for September, and an hour from Tarifa I was desperate for the bathroom, but I didn't stop. My car shook as I clamped my foot on the gas as hard as it would go.

'When I got to the hostel it was eleven thirty at night

and the receptionist jumped when he saw me. Straight away, I knew he had deceived me, I could see it in the way he squared his shoulders and raised his chin. He didn't bother to lie, he told me she was out and hadn't returned. Her key was still hanging on the hook behind him so I knew he was telling the truth. He said I was an insult to God to lead such an innocent girl astray and that whatever was in that letter had most probably been read by now because she'd been gone for hours. I didn't let him finish, I pulled him over the desk by his collar. I remember the tips of his trainers squeaked as they dragged along the shiny wooden surface. I threw him against the wall and I'm ashamed to say I hit him very hard. I cannot say how hard as I didn't stop until I was dragged off him.'

Ella stared at her father in wonder, regretting ever having called him a coward. If only her mother were there to hear what had happened, to see Leo's face and know how much he had loved her.

'So you missed each other by half an hour? If you had got there at midnight you would have seen her checking out?' she asked.

'So it seems. An old man pulled me off the receptionist. I presume it was the hotel owner, but he didn't know who I was. Nobody had seen me arrive, and the unconscious receptionist was the only one that knew my connection to your mother. The old man yelled at somebody in the back room to call the police and I ran. I wasn't scared of the law – all I feared was that I had lost Lily, that she had read my letter and would do something stupid. I ran until I couldn't breathe, my mind and heart racing so madly I no longer knew my way around the maze of winding streets. I stopped in a bar to use the bathroom and buy a bottle of water then headed for the beach. I ran from one end to the other but it was deserted. For two hours, I went into every bar we'd sat in, every restaurant we'd dined at; I even sat by the rock where we'd first met. Eventually I collapsed in the doorway of the church in the Plaza del Angel from where I could see the hostel entrance. I sat and watched the sky tear above me and a golden sliver of sunlight begin to pour through, and there I stayed until the sound of the baker opening his shop awoke me. I begged him to help, to ask for Lily in reception and he kindly agreed, only to return a minute later to say she had already left. He gave me a small bag which held the few belongings I'd left in the hotel room along with my surfboard. I told him he could keep the board, I no longer had any use for it. I turned around, pushed at the heavy church doors behind me, and wept at the feet of the Holy Mother.'

Ella wrapped her arms around her father's neck and cried the tears she knew her mother had never been able to shed.

'I'm sorry, Papa. I'm so sorry I've hated you all these years. I didn't know any of this, Mum didn't either. She couldn't have. We could have been a family.'

Leonardo held her tightly and patted her head.

'My darling girl, you don't know how many years I've prayed to hold you like this and hear those words. I didn't even find out about you until you were five years old,' he whispered into her hair. 'That morning I drove back to Madrid, I sat my final paper and resumed my career as if the summer had never happened. I was sent to a small parish in the North. I called my mother upon my arrival and told her the news, the whole sorry tale. She refused to speak to me until the following year. My aunt told me my mother's hair went completely white that very night, although she has a sense for the dramatic.'

'Is my grandmother still alive?' Ella asked.

Leonardo pulled away and looked at his daughter. 'Yes, she is in her seventies now. She will adore you, Ella, she has a copy of every letter your mother ever sent me. She is your biggest fan.' He sat beside her and held her hand. 'I struggled with my job as a priest. You see his Lordship over there,' he nodded at Zac who was now staring out of the window at the darkening skies, 'he visited regularly, as did some of his companions. Gabriel, Uriel, Rafael, and of course, Zadkiel told me everything there is to know about their Kingdom and the history of human kind. The *true* history, not what was written about or taught in school. We would sit up til the early hours discussing philosophy, astrology, nature, physics, you name it. Your mother was right, I did quiz Zadkiel about the cosmos and our place in it.' Ella smiled. 'My most pertinent question was about God, and for years I wouldn't believe the angels when they told me He didn't exist. *They* did, so how could *He* not, I reasoned. I knew I was blessed to have a connection with the celestial realm, and eventually realised that the voices from my childhood had been right – I was the messenger, the bridge between two worlds, and I had to tell everyone. I began writing letters and lobbying for a meeting with Bishops and Cardinals expressing my concerns, to the point I thought I would be thrown out of the Catholic Church for blasphemy. Then one day a letter arrived for me from the Vatican. Word of my rants within the establishment had got to the Pope. Whether it was fear, curiosity, or something more sinister I do not know, but they kept me in Rome for a year, where I answered all manner of questions until I had a private meeting with the Pope himself. He is very small, you know, and old, but he is not stupid. He told me I was correct – it was not news to them and there was a small circle of men at the highest level fully aware that the church was built on a lie. My new job was to be their go-between, continue as a priest but work for the Pope directly, keep talking to the angels and guard the Church's Godless secret.'

'So if you are such an invaluable asset to the Church what are you doing here, in this rundown cottage, instead of some golden palace in the Vatican?'

Leonardo smiled.

'There is a place for all religions in this world; people's belief in God has done more good than harm. My knowledge helped the Church but was also a huge risk for them and every other faith. There are groups on every side wishing to tear down religion, and I would be their key to do that. I told the Pope I wanted to get back to my own people, *mi pueblo*, and I chose to settle here in Las Alas. I wanted to feel grounded again, and what better way than to go back to my roots? So I returned under the pretence of being the local priest. I hadn't stepped foot in this house since I had brought your mother here six years earlier and I feared her ghost. In fact, I prayed to the angels to accompany me, but they wouldn't. When I pushed open the rusty door and heard rustling I thought it was leaves and debris from the hole in the old roof, but it was your mother's letters. Six of them, the one you've just read and one for every year of your life. From that day on

I made this my home. She never stopped the letters; even after she married Richard she still shared with me her hopes and fears for you, and her desires. I've stayed here the entire time just in case she would one day return or you would come searching for me. Which you did.' He gave her hand a squeeze. 'Plus the angels like it here; the lack of electricity increases their power, not to mention that if anyone ever attempts to hunt down the "guardian of the secret", this quiet priest in his stone cottage in the middle of nowhere will be the last person they'll suspect.'

'Padre Leonardo is the world's leading expert on angels.' Ella and the priest turned to Zac who was now leaning against the wall beside her. 'That's why I brought you here, Ella, he knows my kind better than anyone and I hoped that together we might find a loophole to get us out of this mess.'

Leonardo sighed, settling back on the sofa and crossing his legs.

'Ah, now we arrive at the reason for why my two favourite people have come to visit unannounced,' he said. 'Come, my Lord. Take a seat and let us talk. As much as I feel blessed to meet my long-lost daughter's new, shall we say, boyfriend, I am more than aware this situation is not likely to end well.'

Zac patted the priest's shoulder and nodded, perching on the armrest beside Ella.

'The situation is not ideal. I believe it is the first time it has happened. I've been in love with your daughter for over two thousand years. I have watched her births and her deaths a hundred times. Sometimes I have been a part of her life, guiding her or comforting her in her last hours, but most of the time I have watched from afar. Until this time.' Leonardo reached for the bottle of whisky on the table beside them, grabbed it by the neck, and took a long swig. 'As you are aware relationships between angels and humans are rare,' Zac continued, 'but not unknown. If it had ended at that, we may have made it through unscathed. I've been earth-bound since early September ...'

'Wait, wait. My Lord, September was nearly four months ago. It isn't possible, how have you remained here that long?'

'*Padre*, I know it's strange. But my extended time on earth with your daughter has affected me. I have become aggressive, possessive, and irrational – more and more human – until I accidentally revealed my true self to her step-brother, and that's when I was dragged back by my Master.'

Leonardo sighed and rubbed his neck. Ella knew what was coming and looked down at her muddy trainers; this was not how she'd imagined her first meeting with her father.

'Last night, on New Year's Eve, Ella attempted to kill herself, and jumped from the ninety-ninth floor of her step-father's hotel in the belief it would bring us back together in Heaven.'

Leonardo swung round and glared at his daughter.

'You did *what*? And your mother, I presume, saw it happen?' Leonardo took another swig from the whisky bottle. 'Does she know you're OK? You must call her at once. Wait ... Zadkiel rescued you?' He turned to the angel. 'But, my Lord, you interfered in her Path! My goodness, of course I thank you but I fear you have something a lot worse than death coming for you.'

Zac looked to Ella and caught her eye.

'Yes, Father, and we have brought it to your door. I'm sorry, but you were our only hope.'

'Nonsense, I'm glad you're here. So, we have the great Mikhael on his way? Well, it has been some time since I last saw him. Never a pleasant experience. So how can I help?'

'At first I wanted to know if there was any way Ella and I could be together as earth-bound lovers, living and dying with each other for eternity. Now, of course, I would just be grateful if we could find a way to make it past tomorrow.'

The priest nodded and headed for the kitchen.

'You have both been stupid and reckless, but who am I to talk of the power of love? You've succeeded where I have failed; you followed your hearts and remained true to one another. Now come, it's already night and you must be very tired. I still have some soup on the stove and some bread and cheese. Let's eat and tomorrow I shall start my work. I may have some theories. But first we all need our rest.'

While Leonardo was in the kitchen, Ella walked over to Zac and fell into his open arms.

'I'm sorry I shouted at you and called you all those names,' she mumbled into his chest.

He held her tight, stroking her hair and kissing the top of her head.

'You think I don't know you by now? That I don't realise your words are a carriage for your fear? I have been waiting two thousand years to hear you say my name, Ella. A few curt words will never stop my love for you.'

She smiled and held him closer. His love for her was a heavy blanket around her trembling shoulders.

'Am I going to die tomorrow?'

'I've looked after you so far, haven't I?'

The cottage was drafty and the rotting window frame in the bedroom whistled with every gust of wind. With no power in the stone hut, Ella was struggling to keep warm. She had been lying on the lumpy mattress for over two hours. Her neck ached and although her body was limp with tiredness, her mind was racing.

She pulled the scratchy blanket up to her chin and shuffled closer to Zac, wrapping her arm around his waist and feeling his warmth radiate through her chest. She toyed with the idea of asking him to bring out his wings so she could sleep beneath them.

He stirred and turned to face her.

'He's gaining on us.'

Zac hadn't mentioned Mikhael since that evening's conversation, but her father had explained a great deal. He'd told her that Zac was ordained to follow Mikhael at all times. In the case of Fallen angels, Zac, along with at least four others from the Order of Shinanim, would be dispatched to bring the perpetrators Home and pass The Judgement, although that hadn't happened for hundreds of years. What Zac had done was a lot more serious, though. Leonardo feared this time the Archangel would come armed and it would be the end of her too if the priest couldn't think of a way out.

'Are you scared?' Ella asked.

Zac didn't answer. His breathing was slow and shallow but she knew he was awake. She sat up and felt along the edge of the bedside table for the camping lantern her father had left them. She had forgotten how silent and dark it was in the mountains at night. In the gloomy yellow light she watched Zac take off his thick, cable-knit jumper.

'Hot?' she asked.

'No, you're cold,' he said, handing it to her.

It was too large but it was comforting. It smelt of lemons and wet grass like her father's garden. Zac had packed very little that morning and she was dressed in his tracksuit bottoms, a T-shirt, and thick hiking socks. He pulled her down beside him and snuggled up to her back, his arms around her waist and his breath hot on the back of her neck.

'Won't you get cold?' she mumbled into the flat, hard pillow.

'You weren't worried about that last night when you had me on my back in the snow.'

She giggled as she remembered the look on the faces of the three boys finding them half naked on the heath.

'Was that only last night? No wonder I'm so tired. Less than twenty-four hours ago I wanted to die and thought I would never see you again, now we're in bed together in a Spanish farmhouse. My father, a priest, is in the next room and we are running for our lives from the King of Angels. Oh, and this might be our last night on earth together. No wonder I can't sleep.'

He moved in closer and tightened his arms around her waist, kissing her neck lightly.

'You asked me if I was scared. I am, but only because I don't want you to suffer any more. Everything that's gone wrong in your life has been because of me. I only ever wanted to be with you, but all I've done is complicate things. I should never have got off the bus with you.'

He was pressed against her and she knew he was thinking of their first kiss, the first time he had told her he had *fallen* for her. Now she understood what he'd meant; it was more than just love he was talking about – he'd sacrificed himself that night, he'd thrown away everything he'd ever done for her, and for what? Sex? Love? To have her know who he truly was?

She turned her face toward him and found his lips. Their kiss deepened and she gave a small sigh as she felt him stir.

'It's not fair, Zac. I want to be able to do this with you every night.' He groaned playfully. 'Seriously, I mean, I want to have the *choice* to do this when we want without running scared. We've done nothing wrong. We love each other, doesn't that mean anything?'

'Apparently not.'

'But you said all you need is love.'

'No,' he laughed. 'You're mistaking me for The Beatles. I said all there *is* is love, and sometimes even that isn't enough. Anyway,' his hands glided to her hips, under the hem of her jumper, and over her taught stomach, 'we may never get another chance to do this again, and I don't want to waste time having a theological debate.'

Ella squirmed under his touch. His fingers slowly travelled to her chest and brushed over her breasts. Her nipples hardened under his fingertips as he continued to gently stroke around them. She was aching, rubbing her legs together until she could feel herself getting damp. She pushed back against him.

'Ella, I can't get enough of you,' he breathed, making her shiver. 'I need to get as close to you as possible. I want to look at you, every inch of you, touch every part of you, smell you, taste you. I need to be inside you. If I could make us one person, I would.'

He lowered the waistband of her tracksuit bottoms and she looked at the door. 'What about …'

'Don't worry, he's fast asleep,' he said. 'Leo has the enviably tranquil mind of a man with faith.'

His hand stroked the inside of her thigh, his skin hardly touching hers. She bucked against him, both hands above her head pulling at his hair, pushing his kisses deeper into her neck.

'Please,' she breathed, 'please.'

Slowly, he moved further down her thigh, feeling her heat on the palm of his hand. As he cupped her, she raised her pelvis to meet him. His thumb moved over her in slow, rhythmic strokes and was rewarded with a groan as his fingers slid inside her. She was standing on the very tip of the abyss, the sensation building tighter and higher until the sharp hit of pleasure spread from her core and rose to her chest, slowly paralysing every muscle. Her breath stopped, her mind stopped, and she was nowhere but in the very now. His fingers continued to move inside her, his thumb rubbing in slow circles until finally she snapped. Arching her back, she buried her head in the pillow and cried out. Her body shook in delicious waves, every inch of her electric and her aching centre throbbing to the beat of her heart.

Her fringe was damp and sticking to her forehead. She was on her back and he was kissing her hard, his hair in her mouth, their hands entwined above her head.

'Get inside me. Please.'

'Not yet,' he said, his voice hoarse. 'I told you I wanted to experience every inch of you.'

He knelt between her legs and looked at her. He was so beautiful she wanted to cry. How could he be so manly yet not a man at all? His eyes burnt a deep mauve, more vibrant than ever.

'Zac, I may never see you again. Show your true self to me. Please, just once more.'

He smiled, a mischievous glint in his eye. He understood. He bent forward and kissed her, then worked his way from her lips to her navel, his whispering kisses traveling down her thighs and parting them until her heels touched the edge of the mattress. He stood at the foot of the bed, his face motionless.

The camp light let off little light, yet it was as if Zac was standing in front of the sun. His body glowed from the bright white light behind him, tinged in deep lilac that merged into purple and indigo. Ella stared at his magnificent frame.

Wrapping his hands around her slender ankles, he pulled her toward him until her knees were on either side of his chest, her toes nearly touching the ground. She tightened with each feathery kiss that climbed higher up her thighs, clutching at the bed's blanket in her fist. As he ran his tongue inside her, she looked up and she saw what she'd been waiting for. Behind his head his wings were beginning to unfurl, their stark whiteness illuminating the walls, growing wider and higher. The tip of his tongue flicked faster and faster and her pleasure mounted as his wings stretched and filled the room. Zac shifted his shoulders to accommodate them and moaned softly as

Ella looked to the heavens and let go. His wings dipped forward and stroked her chest with their soft tips. Zac held down her legs as she thrashed and bucked, desperately trying to keep herself from screaming out.

He stood at her feet once more, his jaw set and his eyes black with desire, and watched her return. Like a limp ragdoll, Ella smiled and let her head fall back on the bed. She was his in every way. He flipped her on to her front and pulled her by the waist, pushing himself inside her. She cried out at the sweet shot of delicious pain that soared through her.

'Arabella, Airn, Cristabel, Erika, Ava, Molly, Evie ...' With each thrust he called out, his breathing growing deeper and his hands tightening around her hips as he moved faster. 'Every one of them was you, Ella. It has always been you and it always will be. As long as there is life, there will be us.'

Finally he cried out her name, and she felt his head rest on her back as he slumped forward, their bodies trembling and his wings creating a soft canopy above them.

CHAPTER TWENTY-EIGHT

Zac unravelled himself from Ella's embrace and began to get dressed.

'Where are you going?' It was an effort to open her eyes; she felt like she'd hardly slept.

'What time is it?'

She turned on the small lantern beside her. It was dark and silent outside.

'I don't know. I'm going to wake your father up. We need to go.'

Ella sat up and rubbed her eyes, her limbs like liquid. She smiled at the memory of last night and gathered up her old clothes. There were muffled voices coming from next door. She still hadn't got used to the fact that the kind and gentle priest in the other room was her father, the man she had blamed for everything she had hated about her life. And she was pretty sure he was still coming to terms with the fact his precious daughter had spent the night with his angelic apparition. Her life was seriously fucked up.

She pulled her boots on over her thick socks and tied her hair in a ponytail. As she neared the bedroom door, she could pick out fragments of Zac and the priest's conversation.

'... I looked at every book I own last night, I can't find any reference ...'

'... please hide her, Father. I'll deal with him alone, it will be safer ...'

'... when the office opens I will speak to the Vatican, I have a theory ...'

Ella walked in and they stopped. The priest spread out his arms and took her into a bear hug.

'*Mi hija*, how did you sleep? I hope you were both warm enough.'

Ella looked over his shoulder at Zac and felt her face heating up. She tried to conceal her grin, but if her father noticed he didn't show it.

'I'll make coffee. I think you're both going to need some sustenance today.' Leonardo walked to the kitchen and placed an old tin pot on the gas stove. 'Perhaps a shot of brandy to wake you up, Spanish style?'

Ella walked over to Zac and draped her arms around his neck.

'Last night was ...' He cut her off with a kiss. 'Where we off to, Romeo?'

'We need to speak to your Father. Mikhael is getting closer and we have to prepare ourselves before we face him.'

Leonardo returned from the kitchen, ruffled his daughter's hair, and passed her a small glass of coffee. It was piping hot and smelled dark and alcoholic. She sat down quickly and placed it on the tiled floor. He then handed her a chopping board with a piece of bread, olive oil, and a knife on top. She put it beside her on a small table.

'In some cultures it's frowned upon to give your teenage daughter brandy for breakfast,' she said.

He laughed. 'Yes, well, most people's daughters aren't

on the run with a renegade angel. Have something to eat, *niña.'*

Zac joined them on the sofa but refused breakfast.

'We have until nightfall,' he said, 'if we're lucky. I can feel him getting closer. There has to be a way to avoid his retribution. There has to be a way I can stay here with Ella.' He spoke quietly, more to himself than anyone in the room. Ella looked at her father, who was staring at the chopping board.

'My Lord, I believe the answer lies in the length of time you've resided with us. I've been thinking.' Leonardo picked up the small bread knife and walked toward Zac. 'Nephilim angels, like you, can't stay more than a few days – which is normally the length of their missions on earth.'

Zac nodded.

'But you, Zadkiel, have been here over four months. The only beings that have that ability are the seven Archangels – Gabriel, Raphael, Uriel, Raguel, Selaphiel, Barachiel and, of course, Mikhael.'

Zac frowned. 'I know,' he said. 'But haven't I been able to stay here because I love Ella?'

'No. Love isn't enough to keep you here, Zadkiel. It has to be something stronger. It's been playing on my mind all night – you should be weak by now and losing your powers. But from what I can see, you are only getting stronger. I've never seen that before, but I may have the answer.' Leonardo knelt at the angel's feet. 'You say you were born to a woman, and fathered by an unknown angel?' Zac nodded. 'Who told you that?'

'Mikhael.'

'And did he say why you couldn't come back to earth

and live your future lives in a human form, as any other Nephilim has the choice to do?

Zac shrugged and looked down.

'If Mikhael was telling the truth about your parentage then you would have been able to reincarnate and join Ella in her previous lives. You would also be able to hurt like a human but have the ability to heal quickly.' He took Zac's hand and ran the bread knife along the palm of his hand. Ella gasped but Zac didn't flinch. 'Look.'

A large gash appeared in the angel's hand as the priest plunged the knife and pulled down along his flesh. There was no blood. By the time Leonardo had pulled the knife away, the cut had disappeared.

'I don't understand,' Zac said quietly, looking from Ella to Leo. It was the first time Ella had seen him look anything but in control. 'Why do I not bleed? What has this got to do with Ella and me being together?'

Leonardo stood back up and put the knife down. 'Because, my Lord, I believe you were *not* born to a human woman. I believe you were born to two celestial beings during their time on earth, and as only Archangels can spend longer than a few days on this earth, I believe you are, in fact, a true Archangel. The only one of its kind. And if you *are* the son of two such beings, then you are the most powerful of the seven Archangels remaining. *That* is why Mikhael wants to keep you with him, and why you were never able to come back after your first life with Ella.'

The three sat in silence, Zac staring down at his healed hand. Did it mean that all along Zac could have done as he pleased? Did it mean he was stronger than the one being he feared?

Zac rubbed his face and looked up. 'Leonardo, your theory doesn't add up.'

'Go on.'

'Well, one would presume I would take on the physical human attributes of my parents. My hair colour, eyes, skin tone? Because you know as well as I do that once an angel adopts a human façade it doesn't waver. They are blond or dark-haired, male or female. That's why angels have been depicted the same through centuries, because we don't change what we look like.'

Leonardo nodded.

'I always presumed my father was one of millions of lesser angels and my mother a dark-haired woman,' Zac said. 'But if I look like this because of what my parents look like – and my mother had to be an Archangel so she could stay on earth for at least nine months – it doesn't make sense. Because there are only two female Archangels, and neither of them have olive skin or blue eyes. In fact, quite the opposite. Selaphiel has African features and Remiel looks Asian. Each one of us reflects the multitude of different beauty on earth, it makes it easier to fit in when we need to. So, neither of the Archangels are my mother.'

Leonardo frowned. 'Unless ...'

Ella and Zac looked up at him expectantly but Leonardo was on his feet, gathering things into a bag.

'Come, we have to go right away,' he said, clearing away their undrunk coffee. 'We have a lot of research to do. We can grab something for breakfast in Las Alas. I need to get online and make some calls. Zadkiel, your mother may well have been the eighth Archangel – the one no one will speak of. I need to check my notes.'

Leonardo was mumbling excitedly as he rushed around the cottage, clearing up and picking up piles of papers. He threw their coats at them.

'*Venga*! We must go. Now!'

Zac was still staring at his feet. Ella looked from him to her father.

'Where exactly are we going?'

'My work apartment in the village. I don't like it as much as my cottage, but I can't work from here with no electricity or internet.'

Ella jumped up and put her coat on.

'Are you telling me we've been staying in this isolated, cold, derelict hut for two days when you have an apartment in the village? For fuck's sake!'

CHAPTER TWENTY-NINE

Felicity couldn't give the taxi driver an exact address, but he didn't seem to mind. She asked him to head for Las Alas and hoped she would remember the rest of the way.

She was glad he wasn't as fast as the other cars on the motorway because once they passed Marbella, she needed to concentrate. She doubted the landscape had changed much in twenty years, but it was already late afternoon and it would be getting dark soon.

They travelled in silence, the slight jerks of the driver's greasy head the only indication that he hadn't gone back to sleep. After an hour they turned off the motorway and headed to the mountain, the bends and potholed roads making her nauseous. In fact, the entire situation was making her giddy.

What was she thinking? That Leonardo would be miraculously awaiting her arrival and welcome her with open arms? He could be living on the other side of the world for all she knew, or no longer a priest and shacked up in the tiny cottage with his seven children. He may even be dead. She had sent him twenty letters since Ella had been born, but she had no idea if he had even received them. Maybe all this time someone else living in that cottage had been reading them. Maybe she would arrive to find them scattered among the dead leaves beneath the door.

The sun cast a morning shadow over the jutting peak of the mountains, and in the distance stood their tiny chapel hunched like an eagle on the edge of a precarious ledge. Its bell tower loomed over the tiny white houses of Las Alas, as if the church were ready to spread its wings over the villagers below. She couldn't be far from the cottage now, and if luck was on her side she wasn't far from Leonardo, her daughter, and the answer to the question that had haunted her since she met that beautiful gypsy boy with the piercing blue eyes. Who was Zac?

'Turn right here, please,' she told the driver, squinting at the road ahead and struggling to find the gap in the trees where the house was. The driver turned around in a daze. It was the first time she had spoken since they left the airport.

'*Aqui*? But it's a dirt track. Are you sure?'

'Yes, slow down, the entrance is quite hidden.'

The driver cursed under his breath and manoeuvred the car carefully through the brambles and overgrown hedges. They crawled along, both of them straining to see in the bitty light of the dawn, until the trees thinned and a large wooden gate appeared. Painted in neat, deliberate writing it read 'Casa La Vaca' and beside it, in bright white and yellow, was a painting of a lily. Felicity smiled. It was probably a coincidence – the gate was new and had probably been painted by someone else. She wondered what else had changed and who, if anyone, would be waiting for her.

The path was longer than she remembered and cut through fields full of sheep. A lone donkey looked over the wooden fence at her. In the near distance, the warming sun spilling a dusky glow over its aged-spotted roof, she could see the cottage. Her and Leo's cottage; a warmer and homelier version of the same place she had visited all those years ago. She paid the driver but remained in her seat, blinking back tears at the green curtains in the window and another image of lilies on the bottom corner of the wooden door. Had he been waiting for her?

The driver was worried about leaving her in a field in the middle of the mountains, but she assured him she had a phone and would call his number if she needed another ride. She waited until the taxi was out of the gate before turning her attention to the front door. Her raps bounced off the valley walls and the donkey brayed in response. It felt sacrilegious to disturb such peace, so after three attempts of knocking, she stopped. There was no answer or movement inside.

She cupped her hands against the window and peered through the curtains but all was still and dark, just her ghostly reflection and hallowed eyes staring back at her. She couldn't remember the last time she had stepped out of her house without worrying what she looked like. She had little make up on, flat shoes, and her hair tied back. All she had been able to think about was finding her daughter, but now her head was filling up with memories of clammy Tarifa nights with the only man that had ever known her. The *real* her.

She reached for the door handle and turned it, surprised to find the house unlocked, and stepped over the threshold into the cold, grey air of her past. The embers from a recently lit fire threw little light. She fumbled along the walls for a light switch and her hand knocked over a pile of papers. She picked them up and took them to the fireplace for a better look; they were her letters. He had got them after all.

Returning to the side table, she saw Ella's Spanish passport. Relief flooded through her – her baby was safe. Beside it was a thin golden ring, which she picked up and turned over in her hand. It was identical to the ring Richard had given her, its lilac stones scattered along the edge. She slid it onto her wedding finger and pushed it against the other one. It was a perfect fit. As the two merged, they formed a cluster of stones that matched her lost necklace. What did it mean? A ring found in the remains of a World War Two bombed shop which had given her a peculiar feeling of déjà vu, and a second ring belonging to the person that had given her its matching necklace. The necklace that Leo and the gypsy boy had told her would protect her. The necklace she hoped was now protecting her daughter. But from what?

Felicity threw herself onto the old sofa and allowed herself finally to cry the tears of relief and regret that, until now, she hadn't known had been burning a hole in her heart for the last twenty years. Where were Ella and Leo? And what did Zac have to do with all of this?

CHAPTER THIRTY

Leonardo's apartment in the tranquil village of Las Alas was above the church bookshop. The quiet, cobbled street was lined with squat, whitewashed houses adorned with red flowers in terracotta pots. It was early morning, but the village was asleep save for the distant echo of a farmer's pony climbing up the steep road.

'Before we do anything, I really need a bath. Do you mind?' Ella asked as they entered Leonardo's large apartment. It was sparsely furnished except for two long walls lined with books. Ella peeked into a number of rooms until she found the bathroom. 'Do you have a spare toothbrush? Then we can have those churros and chocolate for breakfast. I know you two have a lot of research to do, but I'm too filthy and hungry to think straight.'

Zac and the priest glanced at each other.

'Take your time, *hija*,' the priest replied. 'Zac and I have enough to work on.'

Zac wasn't sure exactly what they were meant to be looking for, but the emotions coursing through him were unfamiliar and they scared him. He wasn't who he thought he was. For over two thousand years, he had thought he was a Nephilim, one of thousands; when in fact he was an Archangel made from the union of two others. A son of secrets. Ones he and Leonardo had just a few hours to discover. The Judgement was always conducted at dusk, they didn't have long before Mikhael and the other Archangels descended to kill him and Ella. How could they possibly find all the answers before nightfall?

Zac knew what happened to The Fallen: this wasn't the first time an angel had descended from grace and broken the rules. Others had killed on earth, revealed themselves when it wasn't part of the plan, or changed a person's Path. But none had refused to return for the love of a woman, and none had been the son of two angels. What was to become of him?

'Who is my mother, Leonardo?'

The priest joined Zac at the large dining table and placed a pile of books before the angel.

'I have no idea,' Leonardo said. 'This is everything I have on the history of Archangels. There is no record of there ever having been more than eight, and these records go back further than you do. There's no mention of a dark-haired female angel. The only Archangel to have been murdered by Mikhael was Satan and ... well ... if you take into account the absence of God, all records of that judgement are somewhat distorted. We have no accurate record of what the original fallen angel even looked like on earth.'

'Do you think my past is the secret to my salvation, *Padre*'

'Isn't it always?'

Leonardo and Zac spent the next hour in silence, the priest researching the history of The Fallen through the Vatican online records and Zac flicking through the pile of ancient books. The images of his choir, his own kind, were always the same – Mikhael as the long-haired blond soldier was the only accurate one. The others were either depicted as variations of the Jesus model or sexless blonde female angels. Zac smiled, these ridiculous old paintings did nothing but assist them in staying hidden and able to do their job among the people.

'Who's this?' Ella was in the doorway, her wet hair in a towel, holding a small canvas. 'Sorry, Leo,' she said. 'I was having a bit of a nose around your apartment. You have some really cool things. Then I saw this.'

She handed the canvas to Zac and sat in front of the computer.

'I'm going to check the internet, see if my disappearance has made the news.'

Zac wasn't listening – he was staring at the small oil painting of a beautiful woman wearing an intricate gold and amethyst necklace. Her hands were in the prayer position and on her fingers were two matching rings. Zac's heart quickened. He knew exactly who she was.

'That was Contessa Lucia, the wife of a notorious Italian villain from the 17th century,' Leonardo said.

Ella looked up. '17th century? But she has Mum's necklace. I thought it was a painting of your grandmother or something.'

'No, I know nothing more about the woman. I found the canvas in the Vatican vaults, I have no idea what it was doing in there but when I saw her necklace I explained I needed it for research. There was no note attached to it, they didn't see it as being of any value so they let me keep it here. I'd forgotten about it.'

403

Zac turned it over; there was nothing written on the back.

'Leonardo, what was the story your grandmother told you about the necklace?' he asked.

'You know what family legends are like, I doubt it's a very reliable story. She told me the necklace and rings were given to her by her father after the Spanish Civil War. He was fighting in a village in the Pyrenees and his comrades were talking about an angelic apparition, a beautiful woman who had appeared to them and made love to every one of them over the course of three days.' Leonardo looked at his daughter, but Ella was looking at the laptop in concentration. 'Well,' he continued, lowering his voice. 'My grandmother was old when she told me, so I don't know how much is accurate, but the men talked of a naked angel who would follow them wearing nothing but this necklace and the matching rings. There was an attack on the village one day. Those that had made love with the mysterious woman never died and said it was thanks to their angel. News of this woman spread, and every man searched for her. One day my great-grandfather came across a man bleeding in the street, moments from death, but told him he had found the mesmerising woman and taken her jewellery. He handed him the necklace and rings and told him to look after them, that they were powerful.'

'What happened to the second ring?' Zac asked.

'Apparently it was given to friends of my family who escaped the war to London. They had no money, and my family insisted they sell the ring on arrival in England.'

Zac frowned. The Italian painting was four-hundred-years-old, and the soldiers talked of a beautiful woman wearing the same necklace in the 1930s, yet he would recognise that face anywhere. It had haunted his dreams for two thousand years.

'Shitting hell, look at this!' Ella cried.

Leonardo and Zac rushed to her side, where a copy of an old American newspaper was on the screen. The front page was a grainy black and white image of a beautiful young woman with the same thick dark hair. Her face wasn't that clear but around her neck was the necklace. *Lucinda Bright, Sentenced To Death For Her Part In Town Massacre* the headline read. It was dated 1908.

'I was searching for "mysterious woman with amethyst necklace" and got this. Isn't that the same woman from the painting?' Ella asked. 'How can that be?'

It was her. All three women were the same, in three countries, four hundred years apart. Zac touched the woman's face on the screen and the computer went blank.

'Zac! For God's sake!'

Leonardo unplugged it from the wall and switched it on again, but the screen remained blank.

'It's his energy, *hija*, it happens. This is my third laptop in two years.'

'But I wanted to read about who she was. What was that you were saying about family legend? About a naked angel and that dead man? This is really weird, don't you think, Zac? Zac! You OK?'

He was sitting on the sofa, his head in his hands. It had been two thousand years since he had last seen her, but nobody who ever set eyes on her could forget her face.

Ella walked to him and pulled his head into her chest. She stroked his hair as he let himself fall into her. He had to stay strong, for all of them – there had to be an answer and there wasn't much time.

'You know her, don't you?' Ella said to him. Zac nodded.

Leonardo joined them at the sofa and passed Zac a glass of water.

'She's my mother,' he said. 'But I don't understand. If she's been on earth for hundreds of years, and she'd been an Archangel, how could she have had a photo taken of her? She would have to have been human. It doesn't make sense. I remember her, she wasn't an angel.'

'When did you last see her?' Ella asked.

'In Fiesole, Italy. I was six when she disappeared. She had sent me to collect firewood and when I returned home, she was no longer there. I was taken in by a shepherd and raised alongside his other farmhands. Mikhael told me she had been no one important, just the village whore, and that she had abandoned me. I don't remember much about her except her beauty, the smell of her hair, and how much she loved me.'

Leonardo was still staring at the oil painting, tracing his hands over the woman's neck.

'But if this is your mother, then she *must* be the Archangel we are looking for. But who was she? Why was she in human form for so long?'

'And why does she have my mum's necklace on in all the pictures?' Ella asked.

Leonardo frowned. 'Ella, come here,' he said. 'Pass me the pendant.'

He turned it over in his hands, held it up to the light, and stroked it. There had to be something special about the jewellery. Then he saw it – three tiny marks on the back of the mounted stones. He recognised them as angelic symbols.

'What is it?' Ella asked.

Leonardo passed the necklace to the angel, who squinted, trying to decipher the markings. 'It says something.'

Leonardo ran to the back of the room and returned with a large magnifying glass.

'Try this,' he said. 'My goodness, it never occurred to me to look at the back. After I acquired the painting, Lily already had the necklace and –'

'Shhhh, *Papa*, let's see what it says.'

Zac smiled. Leonardo was right – the owner of the necklace was an angel. A fallen angel. And the message could well be the key to him staying on earth.

'We need to get back, *Padre*. I think the rest of the message is on the rings.'

'But I only have one,' he said. 'Who knows where the other may be.'

Zac shrugged. 'It will still help. Let's go.'

CHAPTER THIRTY-ONE

'This ridiculous car was your daughter's choice,' Zac said, moving Ella's elbow away from his chin as she wriggled into position on his lap. Three people in a two-seater sports car on a bumpy mountain road, they must have looked ridiculous. The journey to the village had been uncomfortable enough, but now they were returning to the cottage with extra sheep feed and hay, it was farcical.

'You don't need to travel in cars, Zac,' Ella said. 'Why couldn't we meet you there?'

'I told you, I'm not leaving your side.'

She turned to her father. 'Remind me again why we are going back to that cold shepherd's hut when there's a TV and a microwave in your apartment?'

Zac took a deep breath and looked out of the window. Leonardo smiled.

'Zac needs the ring and I have to tend to the animals.'

They had eaten a small lunch in the village, but they'd all lost their appetite. Zac had hardly said a word since the apartment. They clambered out of the car and Leonardo headed for the barn.

'I'll start feeding the chickens. It looks like it's going to rain.'

'Let us do that, *Padre*,' Zac smiled. 'You go back to the cottage.'

409

Zac raised his eyebrows and Leonardo nodded, turning back to the house.

'Why did you say that, Zac? It's freezing out here, and starting to drizzle.'

'Ella, you can be bloody tiresome sometimes. I wanted us to be alone.' He cupped her face with his hands, his eyes gazing into hers. 'This is it.'

'What do you mean?'

'Mikhael is nearly here, and there are things I need to say before it's too late. When I check the markings on that ring, I will know for certain if there truly is a way for us to be together, I will no longer have to fear Mikhael and I will also be one step closer to finding my mother. But whatever happens, you need to promise me one thing.'

'Anything.'

'Get back on your Path, Ella. Life will slowly bring you everything you need to continue in the right direction, you just need to recognise the signs. And have faith – because the day I do come back, whether in this life or the next – it will be for ever.'

'Don't say that. We might still be OK!'

He pulled her into his embrace.

'Whatever happens to me, to us, I will never stop loving you.'

'Why does it feel like you're saying goodbye?'

'Because I am.'

The fire in the cottage had burnt to a dull glow. Leonardo placed another log on the pile and felt his way to the kitchen to fetch the gas lamps. He hoped Ella and Zac didn't stay too long out there, it was getting cold and he knew with every passing hour that Mikhael's arrival was imminent. He lit the lamps and placed them around the room, the branches of the trees outside scratching the window pane as he fiddled with the dial of the transistor radio. Listening to flamenco calmed his nerves.

'I remember this tune.'

Leo looked with a start over at the sofa, where the silhouette of a woman sat. When she stood, the flames from the fire dusted her long neck in gold.

'You came back,' he said.

She nodded. Neither of them moved.

Leonardo had seen many photos of Felicity, in the newspapers and on websites, and couldn't believe how easily she had transformed herself into a millionaire's wife. But right now, she was his Lily, looking like she had just stepped off the beach in Tarifa.

'Our baby is fine,' he said, walking to her and pulling her into his arms. Her hands clasped his back and her body went limp with relief. This was what he should have done all those years ago

'I'm sorry,' he said, his lips brushing against her collarbone as he spoke. 'I'm so sorry, Lily. I came back for you, I did, but I was too late.'

Her fingers clung to him and he held her until her shaky breaths returned to normal.

'Where is she?' she asked, pulling away, her eyes roaming around the room. Leonardo pointed out the window at two dark figures in the distance.

'They'll be back shortly,' he said, taking her hand. 'She will be so glad to see you. It was a terrible thing what she did, she knows that. She finally knows our story.'

Felicity looked at him and he wondered what she saw.

411

Was he still the young man she'd fallen in love with? She glanced at his hand holding hers and he realised he was stroking the inside of her wrist. He stopped, feeling his face prickle, then lifted her hand to the light.

'I see you found my ring.' He peered closer at her hand. 'How did you get the other one?'

'You gave it to me, when we were a different couple in love,' she said with a frown. 'It was you, wasn't it? It's always been you.'

He nodded.

'I have a lot to tell you,' he said. 'About us, about our daughter, and Zadkiel.'

'Zadkiel?' she said, sitting on the sofa slowly. 'Zac, her boyfriend?'

'He's a lot more than that.'

They sat together, her body curling into his and her head resting on his shoulder. She listened as he told her about an empty heaven, a world full of angels, and their many failed lives together.

CHAPTER THIRTY-TWO

Ella pushed open the door to the cottage and stopped in the doorway, in front of her was something she didn't think she would ever see. Her mother and father were sitting on the sofa, hand in hand, smiling. Felicity turned at the sound of the door and jumped to her feet.

'Mum!' Ella ran at her mother. 'I'm sorry. I'm so sorry!'

'No, *I'm* sorry, my darling. Leo has told me everything, I was such a fool. I should have known your father would never have left us, I should have been there for you.' Felicity hugged her daughter then looked up at Zac beside them. She blushed, unable to meet his eye.

'It was you, wasn't it? The gypsy boy?'

Zac nodded and Felicity gently laid a hand on the angel's cheek.

'Thank you, Lord Zadkiel. You saved mine and Ella's life on that beach, and you did it again on New Year's Eve. I am forever indebted to you.'

'No, you aren't. I've tried to help but all I've ever done is fail your daughter.'

'Not at all! I did,' Felicity replied. 'You've always been there in my place. Where I went wrong you have made it right. Evie, Ella ... I let them down but you never have. You tested Leo and you tested me and *we* failed. I understand that, because this is who I am. This has always been my family and *this* is where I am meant to be. No matter what happens, a mother's love is the strongest force of all.'

Ella saw a fleeting shadow pass over Zac's face at the mention of the word 'mother'. She'd been apart from her mother for a couple of days, but what did two thousand years feel like? Ella hugged Felicity again, tighter this time.

'This is yours, Mum,' she said, unclipping the necklace from around her neck.

'I think Zac needs it now,' Felicity said, 'and these.' She slipped the two rings off her finger and handed them to the angel along with the chain.

Zac looked at the jewellery in his hands and peered inside the rings. He smiled and looked at Ella with hope in his eyes.

'I was right, there might be a way.' He turned the rings to the firelight so she could see the markings on the inside.

'What does it say?'

'*The fallen shall rise again.*'

'I don't understand,' Leo said.

'You will,' Zac replied, looking out of the window. His knuckles turned white as he gripped the window pane. 'They're here.'

The light outside was dimming as the storm clouds rolled over the top of the mountain, the raging wind flattening the high grasses. A man was crossing the field toward them, flanked by three people on either side.

Zac put the jewels in his pocket and ran to the door. 'Ella, get back. This is something I have to do alone.'

414

'No! Zac, He wants me too.'

'He can't have you. Leo, keep her away.'

Seven figures now stood motionless in front of the house. Two women and five men. The tall, blond man leading held a wooden staff in his hand, which he lifted and pointed at the house. Ella felt herself being dragged forward. She held onto her father but his hold wasn't tight enough. She flew past Zac and out into the cold rain where a silver-haired man caught her. He looked like a Viking with his furrowed brow and square jaw. His thick fingers held onto the top of her arm.

'Let her go,' Zac cried as the cottage door swung shut, trapping Leonardo and Felicity inside. Their cries were drowned out by the howling wind.

'Zadkiel, we are gathered here today to pass your Judgement. Kneel.' The blond man's voice bounced off the hills.

'Please, Lord Mikhael! Have mercy.'

Zac knelt at his master's feet and removed his shirt, his magnificent wings unfurling behind him. The muscles in the angel's shoulders rippled under the strain of his pose, and his back arched as his wings fought against the wind like a galleon's sails in a storm. He bowed, placed his hands in the prayer position, and rested his head upon them.

This is Archangel Michael? Ella thought. She was expecting fire and brimstone, a glowing mane at least. This man in farmer's clothing looked neither scary nor powerful. The harps and halos had clearly been left behind with the Bible. Mikhael looked at her expectantly, raising his eyebrows and tilting his head.

'Ella?' Zac whispered. 'Kneel. Please.'

'No! Fuck you, Mikhael. I'm not falling at the feet of any man, least of all yours,' she said, looking the Archangel in the eye.

Zac's muffled groan was barely audible.

'Zadkiel, you may stand,' commanded Mikhael, raising the palms of his hand as if giving a sermon. 'So, this is what you've fought against us for?' He pointed at Ella. '*That*?'

The Viking angel returned behind his master and Zac instinctively rushed to Ella's side and took her hand. Although now closed, Zac's wings stroked her bare arm, giving her flashbacks of their last night together and sending shivers down her spine. Mikhael mistook her shudder for trepidation.

'You are right to fear me, girl. Our worlds were not created to be merged. Our laws were not made to be broken.'

'You're wrong,' she spat. 'You don't scare me. I know love is the strongest power there is and that's what Zac and I have. Nothing can stop that, not your laws, not death, and not you.'

Mikhael remained still; his icy blue eyes boring into hers and daring her to look away. His hand gripped his wooden staff, pushing it deeper into the damp grass at their feet. The wind was blowing a lot stronger and the trees bowed at its force, as if they too were being commanded by the ethereal being. The clouds above them darkened and light rain began to fall. A faint rumble sounded in the distance, joined by the familiar sound of rustling paper. Wings. Ella sensed it before she looked up, but she was not expecting the sight that greeted her.

Archangel Mikhael towered above them. His hair,

which had previously been tied back, flowed freely around his shoulders in long blond strands. His cap and clothes had been replaced by a silver breast plate adorned in an intricate golden pattern. He wore a bright red cape that blew behind him, and in place of his wooden staff he held a magnificent sword. The weapon was as tall as Ella and glinted in the single beam of sunlight that had broken its way through the storm clouds. His creamy wings were magnificent, large and angular, with tips a vibrant crimson and feathers longer and slimmer than Zac's. Like razor blades dripping with blood, his wings were so wide they obscured the six Archangels behind him, who also displayed their own feathered auras.

'You will *not* defy me, child,' his voice rumbled, reverberating through her chest. He pointed at two angels beside him. 'Barachiel, Selaphiel, take her.'

Zac tightened his hold on her as the two female angels stepped forward. Ella recognised the tall, dark-skinned woman as the beautiful manager at Indigo. She still wore her bright blue suede heels, but this time a pair of slim golden wings fanned around her. Beside her stood a petite Asian girl with short blonde hair. She too had wings, which were smaller with flecks of silver.

'Please don't do this,' Zac said, moving Ella out of their grasp.

They each took one of Ella's wrists and pulled her away from Zac. She screamed his name until the angels placed a hand over her mouth and her voice disappeared, her mouth opening and shutting soundlessly.

'Zadkiel.' Mikhael motioned for the angel to stand before him.

He hesitated and looked at Ella. The manager placed a

hand at Ella's throat and raised an eyebrow at Zac. He tensed his jaw and stepped forward.

'Yes, my Lord.'

'You know why we are here. We must pass Judgment on you both. You violated the most sacred of laws – you disclosed your true self, you fell for a human, you altered her life Path and that of those who shared in it, and most heinous of all you intervened when she made the decision to end her life.'

'Master, forgive me.'

'No. That cannot be done.' He held up his sword. 'She must face Death Eternal. As long as this girl exists in this world of theirs, you are useless to us. Today, she will die and never return'

Zac's indigo eyes widened and he shook his head in tiny motions.

'No, please, I beg you!'

Mikhael took a step forward and held his sword over Ella.

'Don't worry,' the Archangel said to her. 'It is too sharp to hurt. I'll be quick.' He raised the weapon higher. 'Your soul must decease. This is the word of the Lord.'

There was a cry from the cottage as Leo jumped through the open window and ran at the Archangel, Felicity stumbling behind him.

'My Lord, there must be another way!' her father shouted.

The tip of the Archangel's sword was inches from the crown of Ella's head, and she took a long, ragged breath as she attempted to still her beating heart. She wanted to say goodbye, tell her parents and Zac that she loved them, but she still had no voice. Instead, she looked on in horror as two angels ran at Leonardo, knocking him to the ground. Ella recognised Gabriel at once as the handsome barman from Indigo, the one with the *Vogue*-like cheekbones. So the Archangels had been there all along, from the very beginning, watching her and reporting back to their master. She and Zac had never stood a chance.

Her father thrashed out at the men. 'Rafael, Gabriel, let go! You *know* me. You can't do this to my daughter. I've only just been reunited with her.' Gabriel looked away from Leonardo and Zac, unable to meet the eye of either.

'Where is your humanity?' Leonardo cried.

Mikhael turned to the priest. 'Leonardo, we have no humanity. That is where Zadkiel has always failed – he thought your kind were superior to us. He has always been this way. His mother was the same.'

Zac jumped up at the sound of her name.

'My mother?' he cried. 'What did you do to her?'

'What I should have done to you a long time ago.'

The Archangel put down his sword and turned to Zac, placing his hands on the angel's shoulders. 'She was bad, Zadkiel. She had to go. She wouldn't come Home, insisted on staying and experiencing what she called the truest of love, carrying her own child. As soon as you were old enough to survive alone we passed Judgment on her. We removed her wings and killed her.' He lifted a curl from the angel's hair and sighed. 'You look just like her, you know. When you died in your first life you wanted to come back, look for your girl again, but I couldn't let you. You belong with *us*, not the kind that lured your mother away. Not that any of that matters any more, because without Ella you won't have a reason to leave again.'

Mikhael turned to Ella but Zac pushed him out of the way.

'You're a liar, Mikhael! You have no power over me and you won't touch her.'

The Archangel rounded on him.

'Who are you to question your Master?'

Mikhael had guarded his dreadful secret for two thousand years, but the force behind his outburst had confirmed to Zac what he had suspected since the moment Mikhael had descended on them. It was all lies. Zac was no Nephilim – he was a purer, more powerful Archangel than any of them, and Mikhael had just given away the last part of the puzzle.

'You are *not* my Master, Mikhael. You are my father.'

The two female angels gasped, and Rafael and Gabriel, on either side of Leo, looked at each other. The two remaining angels behind Mikhael stepped forward but he pushed them back.

'Enough, Zadkiel! You are nobody.'

'You're wrong. I am Archangel Zadkiel, son of secrets and the one true angel. I was born to two Archangels. I am the only one of my kind and I have the power to choose my own destiny. I choose Ella.'

Mikhael threw himself at Zadkiel as his son rolled to the floor, picking up the Archangel's sword.

'You loved my mother, Mikhael. Admit it! You feared the force of your feelings, which is why you fear *my* love for Ella. That ends today. Today I will be free.'

Zadkiel lifted the sword above his head, his dark blue eyes staring into his father's icy blue ones. Mikhael looked around at the other Archangels, who had now let go of Ella and Leonardo and were stepping back from Zac.

'Gabriel? Rafael?'

They looked at the ground.

'You lied to us, my Lord,' Gabriel said, looking at Zac with something close to sorrow.

'Archangels are not allowed to unite among one another, that is the biggest of sins. *You* taught us that,' Rafael cried. 'You fathered a child with one of our own and murdered her when you were as culpable.'

Zadkiel drew the sword higher.

'Mikhael, kneel.'

The Archangel's face was as cold and still as his bright eyes but a fear danced behind them. He crouched at Zac's feet, his wings spread out so far on either side that they covered the feet of his Choir. The Archangels began to retreat and Ella felt her voice returning. But she had no intention of making a sound; she wanted to see Zac finish this once and for all.

'You may not know the meaning of love, Father,' Zac said, 'but you *will* understand the feeling of loss.'

Lowering the sword behind his own back, Zac swiped it from one side to the other, the blade slicing through his own wings. He collapsed to the ground, his shoulders a gaping wound and his wings a bundle of muddy feathers beside him.

'No!' Mikhael cried.

Ella ran to Zac's side, the other angels parting to let her through.

'Zac! What have you done?' she screamed. 'Zac! Don't leave me. You can't do this, you can't go.'

He looked up and stroked her cheek with his fingertip.

'Do you trust me, Ella?'

'With my life.'

'Then have faith. Follow your Path and I will find you. The fallen will rise again, remember. This is the only way. Goodbye, Rivers. I'll always love you.'

Leonardo pulled his daughter away as the six Archangels gathered around their Master and his son on the ground and held hands. Their wings formed a bright shield around them as they knelt on the ground and bowed their heads low. Then they were gone.

The rain began to fall, large, heavy drops that drenched Ella's face and merged with her tears. The wind whipped her hair and stung her eyes, the landscape around them an empty green blur. A single white feather floated past her, a white speck against a deathly black sky. She caught it and held it to her lips.

She knew mistakes didn't happen in Zac's world, but miracles did. He'd promised that he would return, all she had to do was wait. Just as he had always waited for her.

THE END

#ThePathKeeper

Follow the hashtag on Twitter, Instagram and Facebook to keep up to date with my latest news on the series, share your thoughts and enter competitions. I love hearing from my readers and will do my best to get back to you all, especially those that leave a review on Goodreads and Amazon. You can also visit **njsimmonds.com** for the latest info.

Want to know what happens next and whether Ella can live without Zac? Turn the page to read the first chapter of 'Son of Secrets'...

N J Simmonds

Son of Secrets

Chapter One

He had completed her once, but now she was empty; staring down into a deep dark chasm of her own making. Every night she fell asleep fearing that the next day would be the day that she would finally fall into the terrifying abyss and never see light again.

Ella didn't know why she had let it get this far, but it was becoming a habit. A distraction. Like a quick stop in a fast food drive-through she would slow down, take what she wanted and devour it, desperate to feel full and whole again. Then she'd be sick to her stomach. Sick with what though? Guilt? Loss? Misery? Anger? Or maybe it was nothing. Just deep black nothing.

'You're beautiful,' he said, his lips brushing against her ear lobe. She didn't like it when he did that, but she let him. 'You are like a peach. So juicy.'

His dark hair reached his tanned shoulders and his brown eyes were black in the half light of her room. Every guy was beginning to look the same. She turned away from him and let him caress her breasts, wincing at the roughness of his fingertips against her soft skin. He entered her from behind, quickly, like it didn't even matter. She didn't care; she preferred it that way anyway. It was better when she couldn't see their face and she could replace it with the face of another.

Bringing them home always seemed like a good idea at the time. Then, just as quickly, it didn't. This one was nice enough and if she closed her eyes and thought back to the big old bed in the tiny shepherd's hut, hidden deep within that rain-soaked Spanish mountain, she'd be fine. If she thought of blue eyes and white feathers and last words she would climax. After all, that was the only reason why she let it get this far...to remember him and to forget him.

'Are you okay, Ella?' the man asked, their bodies now nothing but a sweaty tangled mess of limbs. He brushed her hair off her shoulder and planting a kiss in its place. 'We make love and you're happy,' he pronounced his aitches like he was clearing his throat. 'But now you look sad, like you want to be somewhere not here.'

She didn't answer.

'Maybe I go, yes?'

Ella turned around and looked at the man, more of a boy really, and realised he was far too young to understand.

'Sorry, it's not you Pablo.'

'My name is Paulo.'

She turned away from him and sighed. He slid out of her bed and put on his shirt and trousers, stuffing his underwear and tie into his pocket. It was still dark outside, but through the window she could just make out a thin sliver of gold on the horizon.

'I go. It's fine. You don't have to explain.'

Ella couldn't be bothered to walk him to her front door. She could already feel self-disgust drip drip dripping into her veins. Just like the last time with the last man. These boys helped for a small moment in time, but as soon as it was over their presence multiplied her pain.

'Ella, one more thing,' Paulo called over his shoulder. 'Did I get the job?'

She turned around. She had no idea what he was referring to.

'The interview yesterday. You needed a chef? I got it, yes?'

Ella got out of bed and walked naked to her front door, opening it for him wordlessly. Paulo looked down, his eyes following his own footsteps out of her apartment and along the hotel corridor. She slammed the door and let out a low moan as she flung herself back on the bed still warm from their bodies. Her pillow muffled her scream.

'Where are you, Zac? Look what I have become!'

Book Club Questions for
The Path Keeper

1. The Path Keeper isn't your usual 'girl meets boy' love story. What do you think it was about?

2. One of the themes of The Path Keeper is how a person's past defines their future. Zac asks Father Leonardo, 'do you think my past is the secret to my salvation?' and the priest answers 'Isn't it always?' Do you agree?

3. What did you think of the protagonist Ella? Was she likeable? Was she worthy of Zac's undying love? Did her character change as the book progressed?

4. Why do you think Ella continues to chase after Zac, even after he has repeatedly pushed her away? What does her desperate desire to rescue him say about her as a character?

5. The author paints a very modern picture of angels living among us and presents a plausible explanation for the absence of God. How do you think that fits with the book's concept of reincarnation?

6. Felicity's childhood plays a huge part in how she sees herself and how she develops as a parent. Which is most responsible for our evolution to adulthood – nature, nurture or fate?

7. Names are very important in The Path Keeper; Ella hates her adopted surname and was christened a totally different name but Zac calls her Rivers, and Felicity used to go by the name of Lily. Do you think names define us? Can we hide behind a name?

8. Lily learns to adapt her personality to each person she meets in order to survive, do you think this helped her? She is told that 'if a woman can no longer fight, she must wear her armour well' – what do you think that means?

9. Josh is the one that Ella has chosen to be her true love in this life, but Zac is her soul mate from her very first life. Is it possible to be in love with two people at once? Do we ultimately have power over our own Path?

10. How does the weather in the book mirror the storyline? Would the story have been the same had it been set in the summer?

11. What is the significance of the Dolly, Ted and Evie's storyline, and how does the past lives of Felicity, Leo and Ella affect their current lives? Do you think that Juliana was conscious of having found her mother in the soul of the baby she was caring for?

12. Ella tells Archangel Mikhael that love is the strongest force there is and it can override everything. Do you agree?

13. At the end of the book Zac discovers that his mother was a fallen Archangel and that she was banished by his father Archangel Mikhael...who do you think she may be? Do you think we will meet her in the sequel 'Son of Secrets'? How do you think being parted from her son for thousands of years will have affected her?

14. The book focuses on love in all its guises – from first loves and friendships to the bonds between family and soul mates. Did the book make you rethink your relationship with the people you love?

15. Do you think Zac and Ella will ultimately get together, or are they destined to be star crossed lovers for all of eternity?

About the Author

Natali Drake is an accredited member of The Society of Authors and writes as N. J. Simmonds. She is a freelance brand consultant and writer and has had her work published in various UK newspapers, websites and publications including *The Mother Book*. In 2015 she co-founded *The Glass House Girls,* an online magazine for women who need to be heard. Originally from North London, Natali now divides her time between her two homes in the South of Spain and The Netherlands where she lives with her husband and two daughters. *The Path Keeper* is her first novel from the series, her second book *Son Of Secrets* will be available from late 2017. Follow her writing adventures at njsimmonds.com.

With Special Thanks to

The Accent YA Editor Squad

Aishu Reddy

Alice Brancale

Amani Kabeer-Ali

Anisa Hussain

Barooj Maqsood

Ellie McVay

Grace Morcous

Katie Treharne

Miriam Roberts

Rebecca Freese

Sadie Howorth

Sanaa Morley

Sonali Shetty

With Special Thanks to

The Accent YA Blog Squad

Agnes Lempa

Aislinn O'Connell

Alix Long

Anisah Hussein

Anna Ingall

Annie Starkey

Becky Freese

Becky Morris

Bella Pearce

Beth O'Brien

Caroline Morrison

Charlotte Jones

Charnell Vevers

Claire Gorman

Daniel Wadey

Darren Owens

Emma Hoult

Fi Clark

Heather Lawson

James Briggs

James Williams

Jayana Jain

Jemima Osborne

Joshua A.P

Karen Bultiauw

Katie Lumsden

Katie Treharn

Kieran Lowley

Kirsty Oconner

Laura Metcalfe

Lois Acari

Maisie Allen

Mariam Khan

Philippa Lloyd

Rachel Abbie

Rebecca Parkinson

Savannah Mullings-Johnson

Sofia Matias

Sophie Hawthorn

Toni Davis

Yolande Branch

For more great books, and information
about N. J. Simmonds, go to:
www.AccentYA.com